CHAIN OF EVIDENCE

Ridley Pearson

CHAIN OF EVIDENCE

WHEELER
PUBLISHING, INC.
ROCKLAND, MA

★ AN AMERICAN COMPANY ★

Published in Large Print by arrangement with
Hyperion in the United States and Canada.

Wheeler Large Print Book Series.

This is a work of fiction. All characters are works of
the author's imagination; no similarity to persons
living or dead is intended. Any factual mistakes or
liberties taken are the author's responsibility—I
offer my apologies, up front, for any such errors.

Set in 16 pt. Plantin.

Library of Congress Cataloging-in-Publication Data

Pearson, Ridley.
    Chain of evidence / Ridley Pearson.
        p.   cm.
    ISBN 1-56895-268-6 (Hardcover)
    1. Police—Fiction.   2. Large type books.   I. Title.
[PS3566.E234C48   1995b]
813'.54—dc20

95-42765
CIP

When your world turns upside down, you find out who your friends are. This book is dedicated to my best friend (whose idea sparked this story)—Bradbury D. Pearson.
Thanks, Bro.

Thanks to:
Brian Defiore, editor; Al Zuckerman, literary
agent and editor

Sheriff Walt Femling, Hailey, Idaho; Gary
Mazone, Vernon Police; Asst. Chief Ward,
Hartford Police Department

Mary Peterson, Nancy Luff, manuscript
preparation

Special mention to: Jeramie Dreyfuss, Emily, Ben
and Harry—for being there

PROLOGUE

He heard her coming before she reached the top of the stairs. Wild and angry like someone possessed, the rage welling up within her from an addiction so powerful that two weeks earlier he had discovered her passed out with a bottle of rubbing alcohol still clutched in her spotted hand.

She roared at him as she dared to negotiate the stairs, suddenly a two-hundred-pound ballerina, one hand counseling the banister, one eye held shut to stop the dizzies. "You bring it to me, Boy!"

That was her name for him: Boy—the only name she had ever called him. They both knew what "it" was. The Boy got it from the neighborhood liquor store every day—or the days that she had the money to buy it. The old man with the white stubble beard handed him the brown bag out back in the alley, and the Boy carried it home dutifully. To him it was poison. To her, heaven.

She hadn't had the money today, but she would have forgotten that by now, and she would have convinced herself that he was holding out on her, and when she became convinced of that then the world became a frightful place for the Boy. She possessed big, powerful hands, like paddles, and the stern will of a self-appointed tyrant. She knew nothing of forgiveness.

1

He lied about the bruises in school. Made things up. The school nurse had given up asking questions, hearing his inventive tales. People knew about his mother: This town, nestled in the Connecticut countryside, was a tolerant place.

He heard her swollen feet ticking off the eleven stairs. How many times had he counted down along with her descent? He shuddered. Would his reminders, his arguments, be enough today? And why did his feet always fail to run when she approached? Why did he stand there facing her, awaiting her, as if some magnet drew them together? He knew that his survival depended on her not seeing him, not getting that hold on him. He knew that he had to hide.

He stood frozen in place. He could tell what she was wearing just by the swooshing sound of the fabric: the Hawaiian colored housedress, worn like a giant zippered tent about her puffy white skin with its bright red blotches and unexplained black-and-blue marks. *Whoosh*, she descended. She cleared the bottom step and, faced with the choice of two directions to go, somehow attached to his scent and headed toward him—she, a person who couldn't smell burnt toast placed before her.

That was all she had eaten for the past three months: one slice of toast that he left by her bedside in the morning before he headed to school. She awakened closer to noon, and then drank well past midnight, her television turned up too loudly, her glassy eyes fixed to it like the eyes on some of the Boy's stuffed animals. Dead eyes, even when she was trying to slur through her words at him. Dead for years. But not dead enough, he thought, as she charged through the kitchen door, flinging it open with a bone crunching effort.

He passed through the laundry room door, backing up—always backing up, he couldn't seem to run *forward* when she pursued him; he allowed her to control him. The cry of the hinges gave him away. A trickle of sweat slid coldly down his ribs and his throat went dry: When he ran from her she hit him harder.

Out through the laundry room window, the sun's fading rays, muted by a stranglehold of clouds, washed the horizon charcoal gray. A pair of geese, their necks stretched like arrows, cut north over the hardwood forest where the Boy had a clumsy fort built high into a tree. In the summer he could hide in the fort, but this was not summer and he was running out of places to hide—she knew them all.

And here he was in the laundry room. A dead end. Worse: a huge pile of dirty clothes erupted from the plastic laundry basket, and despite the fact that he was in the midst of doing the laundry—as if she didn't already have enough to be mad about—sight of this dirty pile was likely to add to the punishment.

He reached for the bleach because it occurred to him he might throw it into her face and blind her, though he didn't have the heart to do so, and besides, he discovered the Clorox bottle was bone dry empty. He stared down into the neck wishing that by some miracle it would suddenly fill and save him from her wrath.

He glanced around at a room that offered only a back door into the cold. And if he went out there, she would lock him out; and if she locked him out and anyone found out, then they would take her away from him—this had been threatened more than once. And that, in turn, would mean living with his uncle, and if the Boy had it right, the uncle was a drug dealer and small time hood—Italian and proud of it. He went to *church* twice a week. The Boy wanted none of that.

On the other side of the door, he heard his mother's footsteps crunch across crumbs on the kitchen floor as she drew closer. Sometimes she forgot all about him a few minutes into the pursuit. *Not today*, he realized.

The bell to the dryer sounded—*ding!*—and it called magically to him. The dryer! *Why not?* he wondered. Without a second thought, he popped open the door and, with her foot-falls approaching, frantically gathered the clean clothes and stuffed them into the blue plastic basket with the purple four-leaf clovers. He slid one leg inside the machine but burned his hand on touching the tumbler's gray-speckled rim. He debated taking whatever it was she had in store for him, deciding instantly that *any* burn was better than *that*. He pulled himself into a ball, his knees tucked into his chest in a fetal position, his lungs beginning to sear from the dry, metallic heat. He hooked his fingers onto the filter's gray plastic tab mounted into the door and eased it quietly shut. *Click.* He winced. Even in a fit of rage, she had the ears of a mountain lion.

He had inherited those same ears, or perhaps

it was something that he had developed, but whatever the case, he heard her push the laundry room's springed door open, heard it flap shut again behind her like the wing of a huge bird.

He could picture her then, as clearly as if he were standing in the room with her. Her soft, spongy body slouched and immobile, her dazed head swiveling like an owl's, scanning the room dully, attempting to reason but too drunk to do so. His disappearance would confuse her—*piss her off*. If he was lucky, she would begin to doubt herself. She would forget how it was that she had found her way into the laundry room, like a sleepwalker coming out of a trance. *Whoosh*: the sound of her as she patrolled past the dryer, her movements heavy and exaggerated. His heart drummed painfully in his chest. His lungs stung from the heat. *Whoosh*, her dress passed by again. He grabbed hold of the door in an effort to keep it shut should she try to open it. If he frustrated her, she might give up.

A tickle developed in his lungs, stinging and itching at the same time. It grew inside his chest, scratching the insides of his lungs and gnawing a hole into the back of his throat.

"Where are you, Boy?" she called out hoarsely, the phlegm bubbling up from the caldron.

He swallowed the scratching away—attempting to gulp on a throat bare with searing heat—refusing himself to cough and reveal his hiding place. His chest flamed and his nostrils flared, and he thought he might explode his lungs if he didn't cough.

"Boy?" she thundered, only a few precarious feet away from him.

Tears ran down his cheek. He exhaled in a long, controlled effort that denied his body any right to a cough. And when he drew air in again it attacked his throat as if he had swallowed burning oil.

But this pain was so small compared to what she might inflict that he gladly accepted it, even allowing a self-satisfied smile to overcome him in the darkness. He was indeed the "clever devil" that she often accused him of being. And as he heard her storm back out of the room, off to another area of the house where she would threaten her terror until blacking out in a chair, or on the sofa, or even on the floor, he debated where and how he might steal some money in order to placate her, and buy himself another night of survival.

CHAPTER
1

Another one? he wondered, the sense of dread as great as anything he had ever experienced.

On his way back from his only trip to the beach all summer, Detective Joe Dartelli heard the call come over the radio and sat through the better part of a green light before someone had the good sense to honk and awaken him from his moment of dread.

The code was for a suicide—not that the codes did any good, the local press monitored these frequencies like sucker fish clinging to the belly of the shark, and they knew every code, could interpret even the slightest inflection—but it was the added word, *"flier,"* that caught Dartelli's attention. A jumper.

Another one.

By the time he reached the front of the downtown Hartford Granada, the patrol personnel had already run the familiar tape around the crime scene, holding a few morbid curious at bay, and two impatient news crews. They were lucky: At eleven-thirty at night the downtown core was virtually deserted; the insurance executive set stayed out of the city at night unless there was a function. Better, the late news had already ended, making this tomorrow's news. Dartelli spotted an unmarked Ford Taurus cruiser clumsily parked near the front, and a black step van that Dartelli recognized immediately as Teddy Bragg's evidence collection van. Stenciled across its back doors were the words: HARTFORD POLICE DEPART-MENT FORENSIC SCIENCES DIVISION. Calling Bragg's detail a division was a bit of a stretch, given that it consisted of only two people. But maybe that made the public feel better about their tax dollars.

Dartelli double-parked the eight-year-old red Volvo 245 wagon and left the emergency flashers going, and flipped around the visor with the paperwork that identified the car as one belonging to an HPD detective, so that it wouldn't be cited or towed. He climbed out of the air-conditioned comfort into a soup of nearly unbearable heat and wicked humidity.

He wore a pair of blue madras Bermuda shorts, loafers with no socks and a white golf shirt from Scotty's Landing, a fish and chips joint in Coconut Grove, Florida, the souvenir of a vacation long in the past. The patrolman at the door didn't recognize him and tried to shoo him away before Dartelli's police ID gained him passage.

"Good evening, sir," the patrolman said, apologetically.

Joe Dartelli nodded, though there was nothing good about it at all. An African-American spread out on the sidewalk, the media closing in. He clipped his ID to the collar of the shirt.

"Who's on it?" Dartelli asked.

"Kowalski," the patrolman answered.

The detective nodded again. *Figures,* he

thought. When shit went bad it rarely hesitated to go all the way.

"Fifth floor," the patrolman informed him.

He heard an ambulance's approaching siren climbing in the distance, rising in both volume and pitch, as if it might arrive in time to save the cooling remains that filled the cheap suit spread out bloodied and disfigured on the sidewalk. A body bag and the coroner's wagon was more like it, and even then a shovel and hose were going to be needed.

August in New England: He had never seen any tourist brochures bragging about it.

He approached the elevator with a sour stomach that had nothing to do with the hot dog and mustard that he had called lunch. His stomach was instead the result of a toxic combination of fear and guilt: *Another one.* He felt an unyielding pressure at his temples delivering an unrelenting splinter of pain that felt as if it pierced the texture of his brain.

He recalled the last suicide that he had attended, three years ago, and the resulting investigation, and he felt dizzy enough that when the elevator car moved he reached out for the railing to steady himself.

I did my job, he reminded himself, recalling the death that the paper had quickly dubbed the Ice Man. It had been a disgusting winter of seventeen ice and snow storms, two blizzards, and a ten-day period when the mercury never crossed five above zero. In March, a melting snowbank revealed a frozen John Doe—the Ice Man.

I followed procedure, he told himself. But he

9

knew the truth: For the sake of a friendship he had looked the other way. He had investigated, written-up and filed some potentially damaging evidence, the facts of which, when linked one to the next, seemingly related to the Ice Man case—though indirectly, and circumstantially—electing not to bring the evidence to the attention of the lead investigator, Detective Roman Kowalski. For the past two years he had internally debated that decision—now, he questioned it.

I did not break the law. This, ultimately, carried the most weight with Dartelli. He had stretched the law, perhaps to its limit, but remained within its bounds. To be found out might cost him a reassignment or transfer, but it was a job filled with difficult judgment calls, and he had made his, like it or not. The discovery of this second such suicide, however, added a burden to that earlier decision. Had he misread that evidence? Had his decision to ignore the evidence now allowed a second killing?

Despite the air-conditioning, he began to sweat again and he coughed dryly and his lungs hurt. He blamed the Granada Inn. It was a decent enough chain, but this particular hotel was a piece of shit. Its nickname was the *De Nada*—"of nothing," in Spanish.

There were two uniformed patrolmen guarding the fifth floor, and Dartelli attributed his Bermuda shorts for his being stopped for a second time. Kowalski, who thought the world revolved around him, sized up Dartelli's garb and said in his heavy Bronx accent, "The only known witness is a stoned Jordon across the street. You want to do something, you could take a statement."

Detective Roman Kowalski had too much hair—bushy, black, curly hair escaping his shirt-sleeves and collar; his eyebrows cantilevered out over his tight-set dark eyes like a pair of shelves. Kowalski had five o'clock shadow before noon. He was too vain for a beard, but it would have saved him a lot of time and effort.

Kowalski chewed on the end of his trademark wooden match. A pack of Camel non-filters showed through the breast pocket of his polyester shirt. He carried the bitter odor of a chain-smoker. The man reveled in the image of the renegade cop. Dart had no use for him. When he cleared a case it was only because he got lucky or beat up a snitch. He had a horrible clearance record. He bent every rule there was and got away with all of it, the darling of the upper brass.

"I'm off duty," Dartelli announced.

"So fuck me," Kowalski said irritably. "You want to nose around, take the statement. You want to be off duty, go home and be off duty. What the fuck do I care?"

"I saw Bragg's van."

"He's working the scene now," Kowalski said, indicating the motel room. "Listen, you don't want to help out on your day off, I got no problem with that. But then make yourself scarce, okay? I got no mood this time of night for no show-and-tell."

"Across the street?" Dartelli asked. He wanted a look inside that room, and a chat with Teddy

11

Bragg. He had to know what they had so far. He headed back toward the elevators.

"Nice shorts, Dart," Kowalski called out down the hall, using his nickname. "You look like you're ready for recess."

Joe Dartelli, his back to the man, lifted his right hand and flipped the man his middle finger. He heard Kowalski chuckling to himself.

It was good—they were getting along tonight.

The witness wore his New York Knicks hat backward, the plastic strap across his forehead. His dark green, absurdly oversized shorts came down to the middle of his black calves. Dart displayed his shield to the patrolman keeping the kid under wraps and the boy's face screwed up into a knot, and he shifted uneasily from foot to foot like a member of a marching band. Rap music whined loudly from a pair of fuzzy black earpieces stuffed into his ears. The smell of marijuana intensified the closer Dart drew to the kid. Dart indicated for the kid to lose the tunes. He introduced himself formally as Detective Joseph Dartelli, Crimes Against Persons Division of the Hartford Police Department. He did so within earshot of the uniform, and he noted the uniform's name in the spiral pad alongside the date and time. He took down the kid's name and drew a line beneath all the information, annoyed by what the courts put a person through.

"You don't look like no cop," the kid said.

"You don't look like a reliable witness," Dartelli countered. "You looked stoned out of

12

your gourd. You want this patrolman and me to search your person?"

The kid shifted nervously. "Just making conversation, Jack," he said.

It was true, of course, Dartelli looked more like a Disneyland visitor than a robbery/homicide cop, but it was important not to let his witness gain a sense of superiority or confidence. Walter Zeller, Dartelli's mentor and former sergeant, had once schooled him to quickly judge the witness—right or wrong. A cocky witness was to be kept off guard, a reluctant witness nurtured and comforted.

Dartelli had the nervous habit of thrusting his tongue into the small scar that he carried on his lower lip where a tooth had once punctured through. The accepted explanation for this scar was that an out-of-control toboggan had met a birch tree when Dart had been a twelve-year-old with too much nerve and too little sense. The truth was closer to home. The old lady's swollen claw had caught him across the jaw in the midst of one of her delirium-induced tantrums and had sent him to the emergency room for four stitches and some creative explaining.

Dartelli wore his curly head of sandy hair cut short, especially over his forehead, where the front line was in full retreat. He had gray eyes and sharp bones and fair Northern Italian skin that most women envied. In the right light, Joe Dartelli looked mean, which came in handy for a cop. The artificial street lamp light produced just such an effect, fracturing his features into a cubist, impressionistic image of himself, masking his otherwise gentle features. "Tell me what you saw," Dart complained, irritated by the heat. He barked up another cough, his lungs dry despite the humidity. It was something he had come to live with.

"Like I'm parking that Buick over there, Jack, you know? And the suit has left his sunroof open, right? So I'm making it shut, okay?—looking right up through it—when that boy done dives out the damn window and smears his ass all over the fucking sidewalk. Blood everywhere."

"Dives?" Dartelli questioned, doubting the statement immediately. There was no such thing as a reliable witness. No such thing.

"Right out the window, Jack: I'm telling you." He arched his big hand with its long fingers and pink skin under the nails, and imitated a dive as he whistled down a Doppler scale to indicate the fall. "Bam!" he said when the hand reached the imaginary pavement. "Fucked himself bad."

Dart was thinking about bed. About how it had been a long day, and that he had been stupid to stop and involve himself. A piece of shit witness. Some sorry piece of dead meat oozing from a suit across the street. *Who cares?* he asked himself, trying to convince himself to give it up.

But he knew that he couldn't walk away. "Did he jump, or did he dive?" Dart attempted to correct for the second time.

Inside his painful head came that unwanted voice: *I did my job.*

"I'm telling you that the motherfucker dove."

"Head first?"

"Damn straight. Just like the fucking Olym-

14

pics." He raised his hand for the reenactment, complete with the sound track. He was definitely stoned out of his gourd. *Shitty witness*, Dart thought again.

But then there was the Ice Man, whose injuries also indicated a headfirst dive, though the body had been struck by at least one snowplow and moved several blocks before lodging in a snowbank for anywhere between four days and two weeks, making any positive conclusions about his sustained injuries a matter of conjecture. But he had taken a dive; and this guy had taken a dive. Coincidence? *Shit*!

What Dart had seen stuck to the sidewalk seemed to support this witness: The jumper's head was caved in, most of his face gone, his upper body a broken mess. What had once been his left shoulder and arm were now folded and crushed underneath him. Doc Ray and Ted Bragg would have more to say about the exact angle of impact, though neither was likely to spend much time with the case. Suicides cleared quickly.

But Dartelli knew: Jumpers didn't dive, they jumped—even off of bridges, where water presents the illusion of a soft landing. There were exceptions to everything, of course, he just didn't want to have to explain them. He felt like tearing up the sheet of notepaper and burying this sordid detail right there and then. *You did it once, you can do it again*, the unwelcome voice inside of him claimed, punishing him, forcing him to do anything but.

Dartelli instructed the patrolman to take the

kid down to Jennings Road and wait for either him or Kowalski in order to make the statement count.

"I can't leave my crib," the kid complained.

Dartelli told the patrolman, "He gives you any shit, search him and bust him and let him sort it out."

"I can cut me some time," the kid offered quickly.

Dartelli eyed him disapprovingly. *Piece of shit witness*, he thought. *Piece of shit case.*

Dartelli returned to the *De Nada*, passing his sergeant, John Haite, who was currently holding court with the smattering of media. Haite did not like the night shift—the two Crimes Against Persons squads rotated into the slot, and for those weeks, Haite was worthy of avoiding. Dartelli did just that.

By the time the detective reached the room, Teddy Bragg, the civilian director of the Forensic Sciences Division, was standing in the doorway smoking a cigarette and looking impatient. "Working with a girl can be a nightmare."

"Woman," Dartelli corrected. Samantha Richardson, the other half of Bragg's team, was no girl.

"Whatever. She's like my wife—always telling me what to do. Bossing me around. I mean who needs it? I get enough of that at home."

"She's in there?" Dartelli asked rhetorically, hearing the vacuum running on the other side of the door.

"Running the aardvark, treating this thing like

we got the Simpson case or something. The guy decided to kiss the cement—so what's to vacuum? What's the big deal?"

Bragg was mid-fifties, short and lean with penetrating brown eyes and a top row of fake teeth. He had the disposition of a high school science teacher. His skin was overly pale and he looked tired. Dartelli knew that the man wasn't feeling well, because Bragg was usually the first to demand thorough evidence collection.

"Some Jordon offs himself," Bragg continued, smoke escaping his lips. "Who really gives a shit?"

Race, the detective realized. Half the department referred to blacks as "Jordons," and although they left the Italians alone, they called the Latinos "Panics." Four gangs controlled the north and south ends. There had been fifty-eight homicides over the last twelve months, in a city that five years earlier had seen fifteen. The gangs and their violence, divided along ethnic lines, had stereotyped their races in the minds of most cops; there were very few police operating without some form of prejudice. To make matters worse, the gang problem had become so severe that Hartford—prior to the task force crackdown—had been singled out on *20/20*, a network prime-time news magazine, as being one of the worst cities in New England. Now the department had its own dedicated gang squad—although the territory wars continued, and the body count mounted weekly.

"You give a shit," Dartelli replied. "I know you better than that, Teddy."

"I don't know, Ivy. I'm not so sure I do anymore." He sucked on the cigarette, and the action drew the skin down from his eyes, and he looked half dead. "You been in those neighborhoods—the projects. I tell ya, maybe they're better off dead." He finished the smoke and looked around for something to do with it. "You could always take over for me."

"No chance." The only HPD detective with a master's in criminalistics, Dartelli had long since established a professional rapport with Bragg. The detective took some heat from his colleagues for his educational background—most of the dicks had come up through the ranks, and some resented Dartelli's fast track. Having taken his degree from New Haven University, he was mistakenly associated with Yale, and therefore lived with the nickname Ivy. But he had also won some attention and respect from other detectives for his longtime association with the retired Walter Zeller and the detail he afforded his crime scenes. His homicide clearance rate reflected his thoroughness—Dartelli regularly topped his squad's clearance board.

Bragg rechecked his watch and said, "I am *not* going to spend all night at the stinking *De Nada*, damn her."

At that same moment the room door opened and a tall, lanky woman sporting a pageboy haircut and flushed cheeks said, "Ready, boss." She set down the aardvark, a canister vacuum cleaner, specially-fitted with a removable filter for hairs-and-fibers collection.

Kowalski appeared down the hall with an

attractive hotel manager at his side—he was a skirt chaser of the worst order. He caught up to Dartelli and reported, "No sheet on the guy. His name is Stapleton—David Stapleton."

No criminal record: The news came as a welcome relief to the detective. It was one less thing to connect him to the Ice Man "suicide."

The four of them entered the room together, Kowalski leading the way followed by Bragg and Dartelli, with Richardson taking up the rear, camera gear slung around her neck. The female manager stood outside the room, watching them.

Sam Richardson had marked with Day-Glo police tape the lanes where she had vacuumed for evidence; these were the areas in which the men were permitted to move about. She monitored their movement closely. The room was not large enough for all of them, the result somewhat comic.

"The bed is unmade and appears to have been slept in," Bragg recorded impatiently into a hand-held tape recorder.

"Fucked-in is more like it," Kowalski contributed in his usual display of tact.

Bragg reported his findings, dictating as he went along. Studying the bedsheets, and the area immediately around the bed, he said, "Red pubic hairs. Empty condom wrapper—a *vaginal* condom wrapper. Strands of red hair on the pillow. Evidence of sexual discharge."

Richardson took photographs of the bed and then stripped the bedding and bagged it and marked the bag.

Kowalski, glancing out the open window, said, "Is any of this really necessary for a fucking flier?"

"Your call," Bragg informed him, obviously hoping to be sent home.

Kowalski met eyes with Dartelli, who had been openly critical of Kowalski's lax attitude at crime scenes. "What the fuck?" Kowalski said. "We'll give it the five-dollar tour."

The woman shot pictures of the bathroom, following closely on Bragg's heels as the man's voice rang out. "We've got some additional red pubic hairs on the toilet rim and also in the shower stall."

Dartelli moved to the bathroom door. Bragg, down on his hands and knees, continued, "Seat to the toilet is down. Flecks of cosmetics rim the sink—mascara, maybe some base.

"We've got a damp towel in a pile on the bathroom floor, and a damp bar of pink hotel soap in the higher of the shower stall's two soap holders, indicating someone took a shower, not a bath.

"The shower cap has been used, now crumpled into a ball on the shower's surround. So the person taking the shower goes firmly into the Jane Doe column." Stabbing a wad of tissue in the plastic trash can, Bragg announced, "One discarded vaginal condom." He prepared a plastic evidence bag and picked the condom out of the wad with his gloved hands and studied it by holding it up to the light. He dropped it into the bag and labeled it.

"Semen?" Dart asked.

"We'll test for fluids."

Kowalski stated, "So the guy hires a hooker,

has a little trouble getting it up and does a Louganis out the window. What's the big deal?"

"Hooker?" Richardson questioned indignantly. "Why, because she practices safe sex? Do only the hookers that you run with wear vaginal condoms, Detective?"

Kowalski, openly verbal against women detectives, was not loved by the females on the force. He stuttered but didn't get out a full sentence.

Bragg offered his opinion of what the evidence told them. "They do the business. She showers, maybe with him, maybe alone, and she leaves. Then for his own reasons our boy does a swan dive out the window. Nothing here indicating a struggle. No sign of foul play." All this, he recorded into the tape recorder for the sake of his report. Dartelli welcomed this explanation as much as anyone, but that voice inside of him was unrelenting. He argued internally that there was nothing here linking this in any way to the Ice Man. *And yet . . . And yet . . .* He couldn't let go of his own guilt; just the similarity of the jumps troubled him.

He suggested, "I'd like to have a talk with his visitor."

"Yeah," Kowalski agreed, "but it will probably cost you just for the conversation. The trim is probably twenty and goes for fifty a night. Maybe the boys downstairs got a list of redheads," he said, referring to the Vice/Narcotics Division.

Richardson exhaled audibly in disgust.

"Natural color or a dye job?" Dartelli asked Bragg.

"We can test for that," Bragg conceded, taking

21

it as a request, clearly unhappy with the direction the investigation was taking.

Dartelli had a thin line to walk: He needed to rule out any connection to the Ice Man, to discourage anyone pulling those files or that evidence for comparison, while at the same time satisfying himself that there *was* no connection, for to make such a connection placed the blame for the death partially on him.

Bragg offered, "We can try to develop latent prints off the door hardware, the window and frame, armchairs, bathroom fixtures. We get something useful we run the prints through ALPS. Anything else?" He wanted out of here.

Richardson had gone on a photo safari in the main room. She called out, "Did any of you guys see that the doodad has been taken off the window?"

Kowalski, alone with the two men in the tiny bathroom made a face consisting of one part boredom, two parts disgust.

Dartelli joined her in the other room.

The dirty glass window was a slide frame, and opened left to right. The "doodad" she referred to was a preventer—a piece of aluminum that screwed into the frame to prevent the window from sliding open more than four inches. City code—a means to prevent children from practicing their Peter Pans. The room's only other window had its preventer in place, and approaching it, Dartelli noticed that the screw head took a special tool, like the hardware in public toilets. He slid the open window shut and studied the screw hole where the preventer had been removed. The threads shined brightly. *Recent*, he thought.

Wearing plastic gloves in this kind of heat was oppressive. His fingers were waterlogged and the skin shriveled. Using his fingertip, he explored the hole. "Let's shoot it," he requested.

She fixed both cameras with macro adapters and fired off a round of closeups—two from the color-transparency Nikon and two from the Canon black-and-white. As she did so, Dartelli searched for the preventer and screw that had been removed. Richardson picked up on this, and without a word, joined him in his search. They checked under the beds, the bare drawers of the clothes chest, rimmed with black cigarette burns.

"Not here," she announced.

"No," Dartelli agreed, meeting eyes with her. "Roman," he called out to Kowalski, who had gone back to flirting with the manager in the hallway and seemed bothered by the interruption.

Dartelli stated, "You checked the guy's record."

"So?"

"Off of ID found on the body, or his registered name?"

"Registered name," the other detective replied.

Stupid shit, Dartelli thought. He inquired irritably, "You did or did *not* check the body for identification?"

"Coroner will do that when he inventories the personal effects. You want to go sponging around in that mess, be my guest."

23

Dartelli headed straight out of the room, passing the detective and the manager.

Kowalski called out to him, his voice like that of a child who was missing the point. "What the fuck are you doing, Dart?"

Dartelli didn't answer.

He enlisted the help of the two large men from the coroner's body wagon to help him roll Stapleton. Samantha Richardson, showing a great deal of internal strength, photographed the grotesque body, including closeups, and then together the three men heaved the body over, two patrolmen shielding the body from the media and gawkers with a hotel bedsheet used as a curtain.

Dartelli found the searching of the man's warm blood-soaked pockets both tedious and trying, though blood and guts no longer bothered him. He had become numb to such things. Richardson documented the entire process on film, including the contents of each pocket: a small black comb in the back jeans pocket; a thin wallet in the front left—confirming the man's identity as David Stapleton; and in the front right pocket, some quarters and dimes, a stick of gum, a packaged condom, and the special screwdriver required to remove the window's preventer.

Encouraged by discovery of the screwdriver, Dartelli searched each pocket three times, growing a little more disgusted and a good degree more frantic with each attempt. The missing preventer was just the kind of annoying detail that would haunt him and increase his suspicions, and thereby, his sense of guilt.

24

Richardson, changing rolls of film, suggested the dead man's watch pocket.

The detective had not noticed this pocket, sewn below the belt line, but above the right pocket; he could hear the voice of Walter Zeller chiding him for the oversight. Zeller had a low tolerance for such mistakes.

Distant lightning flashed in the clouds, electrifying the sky. A moment later, thunder rumbled and rolled down the Connecticut River, sounding like rocks spilling down a hill, echoing in the caverns created by the downtown high-rises. It was a night that Dartelli would have liked to climb to the roof of his apartment building and drink a beer while awaiting the rain—enjoying the light show, or to drive a ways out of town and take his dog Mac for a walk in the woods. Instead, he had his hand in a dead man's bloody pocket, and a chest knotted in fear.

He shoved his gloved index finger into the tiny pocket and withdrew the small tab of aluminum and the screw used to fix it to the window frame.

A few huge drops of rain slammed onto the sidewalk like small bombs.

Richardson glanced up into the sky. "I love the summer rains," she said, shaking her short hair side to side.

Relief swept through Dartelli at having found this piece of evidence. Even so, the suicide continued to bother him, and though he willed it to go away the feeling persisted. He looked into the mashed face of the victim—he could just make out where the nose had been. An hour earlier this man had been alive, and the warmth

25

of the body, the immediacy of the death, had an unusual and profound effect on the detective: He *cared* about the victim. Rookies cared. Family members cared. Eleven-year veterans could not afford such indulgence.

The rain fell harder and a light breeze picked up and moved some of the hot dry air, and the night opened like a curtain. The rain washed the red blood off his hand and the aluminum preventer and screw that he held there. Rivulets of blood dripped to the sidewalk, diluted and pink.

"It's like God's answer to the heat," she said, her face still trained toward the heavens, her blouse wet and translucent.

"Yeah," Dartelli said. "I know what you mean." He wanted to talk to the redhead. He wanted to talk to Stapleton's girlfriend—if she could be found—regardless of her hair color. He wanted this thing closed up tight, his secret protected, but he feared it wouldn't be. The faceless head seemed to be looking up at him. "What?" he asked the face suddenly, sharply. Angry.

The rain fell more strongly. The coroners approached with the body bag. They wanted the body. Now. They wanted out of the rain.

"Joe," Richardson said, her voice revealing her concern over his outburst, "let's get out of the rain."

Dartelli couldn't take his eyes off the face. It wanted something from him.

"Joe . . .," she said, stepping closer, noticeably upset.

Dartelli stood and walked past her, off into the rain toward the Volvo with its flashing lights. Another clap of thunder tumbled from the sky, shaking the windows of a nearby building as it landed. He didn't feel like talking to anybody. Not even her.

He regretted his own past actions, and he wished to God that he had a second chance; he prayed to God that David Stapleton was a fluke coincidence. *People do jump out of windows*, his reasonable voice argued.

But in his heart, he knew better.

CHAPTER
2

Teddy Bragg looked like a candidate for bypass surgery. Dartelli worried about him. His skin was the color of watery cottage cheese and he lacked the nervous energy that had given him the long-time nickname Buzz. His eyes were bloodshot and his breath bad, and he had buttoned his shirt incorrectly, making him into an old man, but Dartelli didn't have the heart to point out the buttoning error because Teddy Bragg took such things extremely personally, and when his mood went sour, everyone around him suffered.

"I got a total staff of two, don't forget," he said, apologizing first, which troubled Dart. "And I gotta run this by Kowalski—I'm perfectly aware of that—but you're the one who asked about the apartment, so you're the one I called."

The lab ceiling was water-stained acoustic tile, the floor, paint-stained cement. Too much stuff had been taped and removed from the walls, leaving dark holes in the cream-colored paint. What remained of the evidentiary lab communicated by an open door with the pantry-size area in which a behemoth photo developer churned out crime scene photographs and mug shots, lending an inescapable toxic odor to both areas that gave Dartelli a quick headache, and Teddy Bragg his rheumy eyes.

"I can wait if I have to, Buzz, it's only a suicide." *Lies*. One begot the next.

"That wasn't your attitude on Monday."

"It's Thursday. I have other fish to fry." Dartelli tried this out on the man, despite the churning in his stomach and the tightness in his chest. For four days he had slept poorly, haunted by the image of Stapleton's crushed face, and the suspicion that the past had surfaced like Ahab's whale. He wanted whatever Bragg had, wanted it badly, but felt more like his alcoholic mother when she tried to hide her bottle. *No one must know*, he reminded himself.

"I gave it to Sam," he said, meaning Samantha Richardson, the other half of Bragg's department. Richardson handled all of the photography and most of the evidence collection, while Bragg dealt with the scientific analysis that wasn't shipped out to the State Police, administration, and most of the court testimony. "I sent her with a uniform

28

as an escort because I was hoping to get her back alive."

"Stapleton's apartment," Dartelli clarified, itching for whatever information Bragg could supply and trying to appear nonchalant about it. The area north of the city where Stapleton had lived was not safe for a Caucasian out of uniform, even in the daytime.

"We didn't lift any red pubic hairs or head hairs, for that matter. And though the neighbors knew there was a girlfriend involved—a lot of shouting, evidently—she, Sam, didn't get a name from them."

Dartelli had wanted to handle these interviews himself but had decided that on a north end suicide it might attract unnecessary attention within the department for him to express such interest. Leaving it to Bragg and Richardson had been difficult. Dart liked to maintain control, but he had complete faith in Bragg—at least when the man was healthy.

"No name?" Dartelli asked, frustrated by the thought he might have lost his chance to connect Stapleton to whoever had been in that room with him.

Lots of unanswered questions remained: Why had Stapleton traveled downtown to the *De Nada*, if his intention had been to commit suicide? And if his intention had not been to commit suicide, then why did he come prepared with the special screwdriver? And if his sole intention had been to have a whore on the night of his suicide, then why had Vice/Narcotics failed to produce the missing redhead? Given the two-hundred-dollar finder's fee offered for information leading to the woman's identity, it seemed inconceivable to Dartelli that they still had no solid leads. This was not a big town.

"I didn't say that," Bragg corrected, "just that the neighbors were worthless as usual."

"You *did* get a name!" Dartelli said, seizing on the fact and belying his external calm. *Give me the fucking name!* he felt like shouting.

"Sheesh, think you won the lottery or something," Bragg said suspiciously. Knowing he had the man, Bragg was withholding the vital information. "No sign whatsoever of this woman currently residing in the apartment with Stapleton, except for an empty closet and a couple of empty drawers in the bathroom. Maybe she moved out, or something. And as I said: no red hairs—all black. Sam said the place was trashed up pretty bad; guy lived like a slob."

"Her name?" Dartelli asked, as calmly as possible.

"And she didn't find a note, or anything even close to explaining why he might have took the dive." Studying Dart's reaction, he said, "I didn't think you'd like that."

"I need the woman's name, Buzz. That's where I start."

Attempting to sound definitive, Bragg stated, "You're *not* going to ask us to compare fibers." Adding quickly, "Not on a north end jumper, for Chrissakes. Put it to bed."

Dartelli hesitated and said, "Not for a north end jumper, no."

Bragg looked bothered. Dartelli couldn't be

sure if he was reading the man right, or if Bragg was indeed physically ill, but he was acting oddly, as if he might be concealing something. "Buzz?" Dartelli inquired, reminding himself at that moment of Ginny Rice because she always used Dart's name as an interrogative, and it bothered him.

"Priscilla Cole," Bragg volunteered, heading off Dart's inquiry. "Sam found phone and electric bills in the name of Priscilla Cole. Got to be the girlfriend."

Making note of it, Dartelli thanked the man.

"What's bugging you, anyway?" Bragg asked.

Dartelli tried his best to wash the concern off his face. "Nothing."

"About this jump, I mean," the lab man said. "I felt it from the get-go."

"I'll be happier once I've talked to this redhead," Dartelli explained. "Loose ends, you know."

"Zeller," Bragg said.

Dart's throat constricted and he felt choked. *Does Teddy know?* he wondered.

"He turned you into a worrier, just like him," Bragg stated.

The explanation flooded Dartelli with relief. "I'll take that as a compliment," Dartelli managed to say, though his throat remained tight, causing him to sound emotional.

Bragg nodded. "You could do worse than remind me of Walter Zeller," Bragg complimented him.

"Priscilla Cole," Dartelli repeated, hoping to

end the conversation. He didn't want to be talking about Zeller.

Escorting Dartelli past the smelly photo machine and to the door, Bragg said, "Stay tuned."

Dartelli left with a nagging bubble in his throat: "Stay tuned" was Teddy Bragg's warning for something unexpected. Dartelli didn't want any surprises in this investigation. *The man jumped,* he reminded himself.

He headed upstairs feeling ill at ease and nauseated. Perhaps whatever illness Teddy Bragg had succumbed to was contagious.

Bud Gorman looked like an underpaid, middle-aged accountant who had elected to allow his hair to fall out and couldn't be bothered to disguise this with a rug. He had thick glasses, a gap between his front teeth, and a red nose with flanking Irish cheeks. Standing at five foot five inches, he wore a size forty-six-short sport coat, and had an eighteen-inch neck that made his neckties hang funny. There was enough glare coming off the top of his head to prompt Dartelli to want a pair of sunglasses. When he spoke, it sounded as if someone were choking him: He chain-smoked non-filters.

"I don't have shit on this girl Cole, Joe. My guess is this guy took damn good care of her, because she doesn't have *any* kind of credit history. I mean *nothing*."

"Nothing," Dartelli repeated, disgusted. Dead ends—they would etch it on his gravestone someday. Bud Gorman worked for GBT Credit

Services, and as such had access to every credit database in the country. Any credit rating, bank account, or credit card account was his. He had access to the records of ninety percent of all major retail firms issuing personal credit, including all department stores, major oil companies, hotel chains, travel agencies, major airlines, and phone companies. If a person spent anything but cash, Bud Gorman could track it. Usually this was done for the purpose of protecting companies or tracking demographics, but for Joe Dartelli it was done as a public service, quietly, and for free. Bud Gorman liked sport cars—thanks to Dart, he had not paid a speeding ticket in over five years. If James Bond had a license to kill, Bud Gorman had a license to drive.

"And I tried to find you something, Joe. You gotta know that's right—because I could hear it in your voice, and I can see it in your face now. And I feel like shit that I can't help you, but that's the way it is with some people." He studied Dart's disappointment. "If I had access to government entitlement programs, I have a hunch that's where your Ms. Cole would be. And I *do* have some contacts over at IRS, though as you know, my gut take on this is that she's not filing income anyway, so why use up our welcome over something like this? But it's you call, I want you to know."

"No credit history?" Dartelli was incredulous.

"That address is damn near in the projects, Joe. It's not that surprising. Not really."

"I've lost her?"

"Maybe, maybe not," Gorman said, dragging

33

a stout hand nervously over his shiny head. "Maybe not," he repeated.

"Help me out here, Bud."

"Insurance," the man said, speaking clearly. "Maybe she's covered, maybe not, but if she is then she'll be in the database, and her address will be current."

"Health insurance?" Dartelli questioned.

"Fair odds that she's covered, Joe."

"Lousy odds," Dartelli argued. "The David Stapletons of this world are the exact demographic that go without health insurance."

"Shit, this is an insurance town, Joe. *Everybody's* got some kind of coverage."

Dartelli knew it was true: Hartford people carried inordinate amounts of insurance, the same as Rochesterians used only Kodak film. But what this meant to Dartelli—what Gorman was suggesting—carried a personal agenda for the detective. The last thing that Dartelli wanted was to go hat in hand to Ginny Rice asking for favors. And she was the only insurance person that he could think of. *I won't do it,* Dartelli promised himself.

A promise broken with his next phone call.

CHAPTER
3

By five o'clock on a hot August day, the Jennings Street booking room held an air of confusion:

voices shouting; detainees complaining; attorneys arguing; parents protesting; police officers of every rank, dress, and both sexes attempting to manage the chaos. The special task force on gang violence had brought in twenty-three Hispanic teens for booking and questioning. Dartelli and others had been enlisted for the raid.

The air-conditioning had failed two hours earlier. The air hung heavy with the tangy odor of perspiration and the deafening roar of constant cursing and swearing. The room, like the building, combined cream-colored cinder block walls with vinyl tiled floors in a urine white. The acoustic ceiling tiles were stained from the leaks that had been ongoing throughout the building for the past three years. The place reminded Dartelli of a cross between a post office and a prison. At the moment, it felt more like a high school principal's office.

Dartelli was consulting with a fellow detective on how to book one of the kids found in possession of a nine-inch switchblade. The two were speaking in normal voices despite the cacophony. He glanced up as a red file folder squirted between a pair of bodies, and he registered that this folder was directed at him. It shook, inviting him to take hold. And then he saw attached to the folder a graceful, feminine hand, and attached to this hand, an elegantly muscled and tan forearm covered in fine, sun-bleached hairs. Before he saw her face, he identified the voice of Abby Lang.

"Joe? This is for you," spoke that voice. The folder shook again. "We should talk."

He had never really looked at her arms before; he didn't spend a lot of time looking at a person's arms. But she had a nice pair.

Lieutenant Abigail Lang worked the Sex Crimes detail alone. Two years earlier she had managed to sheer the detail off of Crimes Against Persons—CAPers, as the dicks referred to it— but not without resentment, both of her rank and the power her separated detail afforded her. Dart had admired the move, one that had required a great deal of political savvy to accomplish, but he'd never had any interaction with Lang. Until the moment this file was shoved at him.

She wore her straight blond hair turned in at the shoulder, and had the kind of Nordic looks that might have stopped traffic ten years earlier. In her mid-forties, she was a handsome woman with bright, interested eyes, a coy smile, and a small, slightly upturned nose. On television, she might have played an attorney or a nurse.

Dartelli accepted the folder and felt obliged to thank her, but she was squeezed by two sides of a competing verbal exchange, and all but her perfume disappeared, leaving Dartelli drinking in a deep inhale.

"Nice," the other dick said, looking in her direction.

"Agreed," answered Dartelli, who didn't have time to think about Abby Lang, although he furtively searched for a second glimpse of her. If he had taken a moment, he might have realized that he had sat alone in his apartment for too many months since his break up with Ginny, had awakened to a television screen filled with

36

electronic lint far too many times, trapped in the darkness and solitude of a beer-induced coma. Had retreated too far into himself.

Control was his issue. His mother; Zeller; the women in his life—he always granted control to others, surrendering himself to their whims, desires, and emotions. During his worst depressions, he allowed himself to believe that he had been a puppet for most of his adult life, never navigating his own way, but dancing along with the strings that dictated his actions from high overhead. This feeling of being at the will of others could nearly paralyze him at times. Secretly he wanted to believe that he stood behind the wheel of his own ship.

As he glanced at the folder, it was not the name GERALD OBRIGHT LAWRENCE that caught his attention but instead, the two letters that preceded the booking number, SC—Sex Crimes. Had Dart not ignored the evidence gleaned late in the Ice Man investigation, evidence that confirmed the Ice Man was in fact the serial rapist dubbed the Asian Strangler by the media—for his Asian victims—then that file too would begin with these same two letters.

But he had chosen to ignore the evidence for the sake of a precious friendship. Sergeant Walter Zeller's wife had been viciously raped and murdered by the elusive Asian Strangler, and the evidence discovered by Dart irrefutably identified the Ice Man as the Asian Strangler. With the very real possibility that Zeller had cleverly avenged his wife's brutal killing, but with absolutely no concrete evidence supporting this, his partner and protégé had chosen to let the evidence slide, electing not to put Zeller through an ordeal that ultimately could not be proven anyway.

And now, like the great white whale resurfacing, this folder brought the Ice Man back.

Dartelli, file in hand, navigated his way out of booking and down the hall to CAPers. He examined the opening pages of the report.

Gerald Lawrence had been detained seven times on suspicion of sexual molestation of minors; he had been arrested and convicted only once, late the previous year. Having served five months of a four-year sentence, he had been released and paroled on probation eleven weeks earlier.

Lawrence had hanged himself four weeks later.

Dartelli stared at the file. *A suicide. A sex offender.* His best ideas rarely came to him in flashes of brilliance, instead seeping into him as a trickle, a faint voice that suddenly, for reasons unknown, gained in both volume and clarity. As he sat before this file, he asked himself, *Coincidence?* His chest tightening, he sensed someone behind him and spun around in his chair.

Abby Lang stood about five foot seven. She had square shoulders, a delicate neck, soft eyes and full, high breasts. She wore ordinary clothing, but it didn't look ordinary on her. "Am I interrupting?" she asked, stealing a peek over his shoulder.

He told her no, she was not interrupting.

She handed him a second file, this one from CAPers, his own division. It too was marked with Lawrence's name. "It was Kowalski's case," she informed him. "Lawrence's suicide. But I keep the Sex Crimes files locked up, and I thought you might want to see it."

"Why?" he asked, the guilt seeping into him. *Did she know about the Ice Man?* he wondered. *Had she connected the Ice Man to the Asian Strangler investigation?*

"That jumper last week. Everyone's talking about how hot and bothered you were by it."

"Everyone?"

"Sam Richardson. She said you took it pretty hard."

Dartelli knew the truth. Roman Kowalski, the hairy-chest-and-gold-chain detective who drove a red Miata and bench-pressed two-ten, was loathed by nearly every woman on the force. Abby Lang was leaving it for Dart to see the connection between the two suicides: the investigating officer.

Turning back to the file, he offered for her to pull up a chair, which she did.

Lang saved him the trouble of reading. "Gerald Lawrence was known in his neighborhood as Gerry Law. He hanged himself from a ceiling light fixture using a length of lamp cord. He left a note that read quite simply, 'I can't live with my crimes. Forgive me.' There was no booze found in his blood workup, and though half an ounce of pot was discovered in the apartment, there was no THC in his blood at the time of death, and no indication of foul play. Place was locked from the inside. Kowalski closed the case with little more than writing up the necessary reports, although it took him a couple of days to do so." She sounded a little annoyed by this.

Dartelli allowed as how any CAPers detective would have acted in pretty much the same way; suicides cleared quickly.

"Listen," she confessed openly, "this is the kind of thing I celebrate. A known piece of shit takes himself out. Saves me time and energy. Five months on a five-year sentence? That's justice?" she asked angrily. "But it was a suicide, and it was investigated by Kowalski."

"Meaning?" If she had evidence to support that Kowalski had somehow mishandled the investigation, then it was a case for Internal Affairs, not CAPers, not him.

She didn't answer his question directly. "Gerry Law worked the young girls in the neighborhood. Befriended them. Got them to trust him. Obtained a promise of secrecy. And then the horrors began. He took his time with them to make sure he could count on their secrecy— broke them in slowly. Kept some of them for several years. Took photos and videos. Sold some of them, used the photographs to blackmail the older ones: 'You wouldn't want your mother to see this.' Pure slime. Discarded those over fourteen. We had some mothers who suspected someone in the neighborhood, but couldn't find a witness. He had them all too well trained."

"You knew but couldn't do anything?" Dartelli asked incredulously.

"Suspected," she corrected. "This kind of abuse is often first noticed in the bathtub at home or at the doctor's office. It's insidious because it's not always that obvious, depending on the act. A doctor has to know what to look for. Parents— mothers in particular—are often the worst: They don't want to believe what they see. Happens all the time."

"But you busted him," Dartelli recalled. He leafed through the CAPers file, studying the photographs of the hanging. Lawrence's body hung by the neck from a length of wire fixed to a ceiling light fixture that was itself pulled out of the Sheetrock.

"Sure. We got lucky, but only once. Seven arrests, one conviction—you know the drill."

Dartelli also knew the frustrations that went along with such work.

As he reached Bragg's forensics report, she asked him, "Why use a strand of lamp wire? Does that sound right?" He flipped forward to the detailed report of the apartment's contents.

"What are you saying?" he asked. But he understood the question perfectly well: She doubted the suicide.

She said, "If you're Lawrence and you're planning to do something like this, why not get a piece of rope?"

Dartelli hurried through Bragg's crime scene report. It lacked detail, indicating a hasty job typical of both a suicide investigation and Kowalski's lax approach—the usual cotton and synthetic fibers expected in any home, some copper filings from the lamp cord found on the floor under the body, nothing special.

"How did you finally get him?" Dart asked,

trying to keep her away from questioning the suicide.

She answered, "An eighteen-year-old girl came forward. She had seen some *Oprah* program that dealt with sexual abuse, and realized what had been done to her and how she had blocked it out. We put her on the stand and she identified him, but she fell apart on cross and that cost us. He gets five years, commuted to one—out in six months; five, as it turned out, because of prison over-crowding. I mean, here's a piece of shit that had done over a *dozen* young girls by some counts, and he gets virtually nothing."

Dartelli pulled out the medical examiner's report.

Abby reached over his shoulder and flipped past to a photocopy of Lawrence's suicide note. "Let me ask you this," she said. "You're Gerry Law, slime ball pervert, and here is your last comment to the world. Two sentences, the grammar correct, the message simple. 'I can't live with my crimes. Forgive me.'"

Dart studied the photocopy. The lettering was jerky, indicating stress—understandable, he thought, given that the man was about to kill himself. Nonetheless, the wording was curious, though he was loath to admit it. *What is she after?*

"The choice of words is what intrigues me," she said. "The word *crimes* for instance. Is that how a guy like this thinks? *Crimes*? I've inter-viewed *dozens* of these men, Joe. It doesn't ring right with me." He could see in her doubting expression that he faced trouble. "Does that sound right to you? Some down-and-out slime ball living on the edge of Bellevue Square?" She answered herself, "It sounds more like a prosecuting attorney than Gerry Law."

Or a detective, he kept to himself, thinking of Walter Zeller.

"What if Gerry Law was into drugs?" she asked. "What if he has a Narco record as well?"

Roman Kowalski had worked Narcotics before coming over to CAPers; Dartelli finally saw what she was after—she suspected Kowalski. *Not Zeller.*

She had nearly flawless skin, belying her age. She nibbled at her lower lip as she concentrated and said, "The Narco files are kept separate, same as mine. Without access to those files, we'd never know if there was a connection between an investigator and these suicides or not."

"Listen," Dartelli said, feeling heat spike up his spine, "this is interesting, Abby, but I doubt there's any great cover-up going on here." There had been a shake-up in the department a year earlier. Two Narco detectives had been sent packing. She was still sniffing these same bushes.

"You're CAPers, Joe. You could take another look at the Lawrence case—maybe it's connected to Stapleton."

Maybe it is, but not in the way you think. It occurred to him how convenient it would be for him if it could be connected to Kowalski. Realizing that she had handed him the Lawrence file not for his sake, but because of her own curiosity, Dartelli wondered how to shake her interest. "What is it you want from me, Lieutenant?"

"It's *Abby*, Joe. Please! And you know how it

is with me and CAPers. How far would I get with any of this?"

It was true, her rank and privilege were coveted and the source of much envy and resentment in CAPers. Sexism was rarely discussed, but it existed. "Any of *what*, Abby?"

She offered him a look of annoyance and disappointment that reminded him of his mother. He felt a pang of guilt and he wanted to shout: *Leave me alone!*

She reminded, "Two *suicides*, both investigated by the same detective—one, with a questionably worded note. You were at the Stapleton scene, Joe. All I'm wondering . . . what I'm asking . . . was there anything there to suggest any kind of—"

"No," he cut her off. "Nothing." *Leave it alone*, he mentally encouraged. *Drop it.*

The interruption infuriated her. "You, Joe? You're not one of *them*?" She meant the clique at CAPers, the old boys' club. No, he wasn't one of *them*; he was Ivy, the outcast with the education—only Zeller had included him. "Don't tell me that. I don't believe that for a minute. We're not so different, you and me. And *don't* tell me to go running to Internal Affairs, because you know damn well that would be the beginning and end of it. Kowalski is far too well connected."

Roman Kowalski was loved by all. Perhaps the worst cop on the force, the biggest fuck-off, and the detective with the best connections to the top, the most friends and allies. "You want me to stir up trouble? Is that what you're asking?"

"Just forget it," she said, standing up, glaring down at him, and then storming off.

He wanted to call out to her—to stop her and tell her that yes, he too was curious. But he sat in his chair watching her go, hurting, knowing somehow that things were different now, and that with Abby's involvement he would have to beat her to the truth.

He looked at the open file in his lap. She was good; she was thinking; she was trouble.

Damn her, he thought.

CHAPTER
4

"You look tired," Dartelli told the man, feeling both curious and nervous about this impromptu meeting. He hadn't lost any sleep over Bragg's "stay tuned" comment of a few days earlier, but he hadn't forgotten about it either.

Bragg looked worse than tired, sick maybe, the kind of sick that steals color from the cheeks and reddens the eyes and paints an inescapable sadness over a person's demeanor to the point that it's hard to look without asking questions or offering advice. Dartelli didn't know where to start; Bragg's condition seemed irretrievable. Looking at him was like looking at a sad old dog. Dartelli felt sorry for him.

"I am tired," Bragg confirmed needlessly.

"And I haven't got good news, I'm afraid." He waved a finger at Dart, leading the detective out of his small office and across the hall to the pantry-size partial lab on the other side of the photo processor. Some computer equipment was gathered cheek by jowl in the far corner alongside some plastic milk crates stacked and used as shelving. That same finger directed Dartelli to a worn office chair. Three of the four wheels had survived its years; Dartelli tilted left and slightly back, feeling as if he might tip over any second. Bragg took the newer chair, the one immediately in front of the keyboard and oversize monitor. He placed his hands on the keyboard; his skin was shriveled and looked old—*too many chemicals*, Dartelli thought. *Too many hours in laboratories*. There were reasons they offered retirement at twenty years; Dartelli could spot those who had passed the date.

Bragg said, "We can go over hairs and fibers until the cows come home. It's all neat and sweet. Buttoned up nice. Woman there—a hooker maybe, on account of finding both the vaginal condom and the one in his pocket—seems like overkill for a real relationship, doesn't it? She likes to dye herself red. We confirmed that. So what? He likes redheads. What do we care?

"They were in bed together; I can prove that," he continued. "She took a shower. She used the toilet. I'm good on both of those. Sometime later our Mr. Stapleton decides to test the effects of gravity. Nothing real new. In terms of trace evidence, nothing out of the ordinary, nothing

46

sending up red flags. That's what we got on the one hand.''

The computer came next, and not as any surprise to Dart, who was waiting anxiously for whatever had tightened Bragg's throat to the point he had to squeeze out his words. He was excited about something. When he was really gassed about one of his discoveries, he went instantly hoarse.

"One big difference between the laws we both deal with. Yours are made by man and they vary all the time according to courts and juries. Mine are laws of nature, and they don't vary an iota. I can't *make* them vary, even should I want to—and sometimes I want to real bad.'' He slapped the space bar dramatically, and the screen came alive with color. It took Dartelli a moment to see that he was looking from above, down the face of a building at a sidewalk. It was done in computer graphics, and though realistic, it did not look like anything Dartelli had seen: not quite a photograph, not quite a drawing.

"I know this place,'' Dartelli said.

"The *De Nada*,'' Bragg informed him. "The particular laws I'm referring to are the laws of physics. They dictate the rate at which an object will fall. You can't screw with that, no matter what. This is a three-D modeled visualization program—computer animation but governed by the laws of physics. How fast and at what angle of trajectory an object falls determines where it lands—pretty simple. In this case, vice versa—we know where Stapleton landed. We measured it. We photographed it. We documented it every

47

way available to us—and that's considerable. Doc Ray's pathology report tells us that wounds on Stapleton indicate that he struck that giant cement pot *before* he landed—one of those pots designed to keep trucks from driving into the lobby, although at the Granada Inn I think that might be an improvement."

Dartelli felt obliged to chuckle, though he felt a little tense for this reaction.

Bragg went on. "That pot is a fair piece of change away from the wall, which is what got me interested in the first place." He glanced at Dartelli—he had mischief in his eyes. "Enough of my flapping," he said. "I'll let my fingers do the talking."

The screen changed to a color photograph. Bragg told him, "This is from inside Stapleton's hotel room." He hit some more keys and the photograph faded away, replaced by an exact replica in computer three-dimensional graphics.

"Nice," Dartelli said.

"Slick piece of software," Bragg agreed. "But notice the restrictions. Place is a sardine can. Foot of the bed practically hits the dresser; you can't even open the bottom drawer all the way—I tried that, remember?" he asked curiously. Dartelli didn't remember. "Enter David Stapleton." He touched a few keys and a three-dimensional stick figure appeared in the room, looking like an undressed mannequin. "The animation lets us interact with Stapleton's possible trajectories in a *scientifically accurate* model," he emphasized for Dart's sake. Bragg revered science the way theologians talked of God.

He worked the keyboard again, returning Dartelli and the screen to the outside, this time from the sidewalk perspective where a crime-scene photograph showed a bloodied Stapleton folded on the sidewalk. He once again manipulated the system into performing a metamorphism between the photographic image and one that was the result of computerization. Stapleton transformed into that same white mannequin.

"We work backward." He controlled the software so that the mannequin slowly unfolded itself, lifted off the sidewalk, connected with the rim of the enormous cement pot, and then floated up into the air, feet first, head pointed down toward earth. Dartelli recalled the black kid's description of Stapleton diving out the window, the kid whistling as he waved his large hand in the air indicating the dive.

Bragg said, "The specific trajectory allows us to compute velocity necessary to launch Stapleton out the window in order for him to travel the distance he actually traveled. Any other velocity, and he lands in a different spot, connects with that pot differently, or misses it altogether.

"Then," Bragg added, "we look at three different scenarios: stepping off the windowsill, running at the window and diving, or . . . being thrown."

Dart's breath caught and heat spiked up his spine. The chair wavered and nearly went over backward; he caught his balance at the last possible second.

"We ask for new chairs," Bragg said, "but we

never get them." He worked the keyboard. "Check this out." The screen split into two halves: on the left, a side perspective of the interior of the room; to the right, a frontal image of the hotel and a graphical chalk mark where Stapleton had hit. The computerized colors were unnatural, the image eerie.

The mannequin walked to the window, climbed to the sill and awkwardly squeezed through the small opening and disappeared. On the adjacent screen the computerized body appeared and fell through space. It landed feet first near the building's brick wall, far from the chalk mark.

"He didn't simply jump," Bragg said. "So did he dive?"

The mannequin reappeared inside the hotel room. Feet on the floor, the head exited the open window and the body disappeared. In the communicating window, the body fell slowly and struck, headfirst, well away from the cement tub and the chalk mark.

"No," Bragg answered. "He did not dive."

Dartelli noticed that he had tuned out all else; he felt as if he were inside the computer screen.

"We have his weight programmed into it, his height. If he had an extraordinary build I might tweak things to make him appear stronger to the software. But he's basically a normal build, and I'll tell you something—he needs a hell of a lot more velocity," the scientist explained. "So, let's make him run for that window." The software showed the mannequin attempt to run through the room for the window. The tight quarters required an awkward sidestepping. "You should have seen us trying to convince the thing to do that dance," Bragg said. The mannequin struck the window, and fake pieces of glass went out with him. "We tried ten different times to get him out that opening with the speed necessary. He went through the glass every time. Turns out he would have had to start the dive back by the bed to make it out that opening with the necessary speed. That computes to traveling three feet, perfectly level through the air—Superman, maybe, not David Stapleton."

Dartelli said, "And that leaves—"

Interrupted by Bragg. "A little help from my friends."

A second mannequin appeared in the room, appropriately, dark gray, almost black. It picked up the Stapleton mannequin by the neck and waist, took two running steps toward the window and ejected the body. In the adjacent screen the body appeared and floated downward. It fell short of the cement tub, but drew much closer to the chalk outline than the other attempts.

"We got it right on the second try," Bragg announced. "He would be a big guy, or one hell of a strong woman or smaller man, to accomplish this."

The gray mannequin was noticeably larger this time. Two steps and the body was thrown from the room.

It came out the window parallel to the ground, arced, rolled, and the left shoulder impaled itself on the cement tub. The body lurched back, the head snapping sharply, and the mannequin smacked to the sidewalk in a crumpled heap.

Bragg worked the keyboard. The crime scene photograph reappeared, perfectly replacing the computer graphics. An exact match.

"Wow," Dartelli said, rocking forward tentatively in the chair. *A big guy*, he was thinking. He had a couple of candidates in mind.

"My sentiments exactly." Ignoring the screen and the photograph of Stapleton's bloodied heap, Bragg faced him. "The unfortunate part is that it's not proof, Joe. It can certainly be used to sway a jury or a judge—I'm not saying that it's worthless—but we have no other evidence to support someone spear-chucked Stapleton from that room, and the evidence that we do have contradicts it fairly strongly, given that it would have taken an Amazon woman—an easy six feet, one-eighty, one-ninety. If she's under six feet, then she's built like Schwarzenegger."

Dart's attention remained on the screen. "So it *suggests* homicide but doesn't confirm it."

"Precisely."

Dartelli wormed his hands together, and fidgeted in the chair. Its springs creaked under his weight. A dozen thoughts flooded him, but one quickly rose to the surface.

Bragg seemed stuck with his own thoughts. A heavy silence settled between them. The screen showed the photograph of Stapleton's ungainly corpse, twisted and awkward—painful, even to look at.

It has started, Dart realized.

He felt a surge of panic as Bragg said, "I don't

want to make a big deal of this, but I'm going to try the software out on the Nesbit jump—the Ice Man."

Dart was thinking that both Zeller and Kowalski closely matched the physical requirements that Bragg had put forth. Zeller was right around six feet, barrel-chested, built like a pickup truck, not a sedan. He had lost a considerable amount of weight after Lucky's murder—*but not his strength*, Dartelli thought.

"Why bother?" Dart asked, thinking: *He knows!*

"It would be an interesting test of the software, wouldn't it?" Bragg asked rhetorically.

"I suppose," Dartelli answered, trying to sound bored.

"That one never cleared," Bragg reminded.

"True." Dart was wishing the man would leave it alone, and yet he, too, wondered what the software would reveal. "I'd be interested in the results."

The lab man typed instructions into the keyboard and the white mannequin representing David Stapleton once again came out of the window in a dive. He floated, twisted, and he fell, connecting sharply with the cement tub before being thrown to the sidewalk. Dartelli felt the collision in his bones. "The software is on trial with us. I need to test the modeling," Bragg said. "This could work well for me."

"I wouldn't make a big deal out of it," Dartelli cautioned the man. "Rankin would not exactly welcome pulling that particular case back out of the uncleareds."

"Agreed," Bragg said, knowing the political sensitivity of the case, and no doubt recalling the battering the department had taken from the press. "But it could be done quietly—strictly to test the software."

Dartelli felt sick. *What if the software suggested that the Ice Man had not jumped?* he wondered.

"I'll give it a try," Bragg said.

Dartelli said carefully, "And for now, maybe we keep it our little secret."

Teddy Bragg nodded, and as his fingers danced, the animated David Stapleton was thrown from the window once again, catapulted to his contorted death five stories below.

CHAPTER
5

Abby Lang's Sex Crimes office was as dismal as the rest of Jennings Road. It was hard to improve upon linoleum and acoustical tile, although she had given it her best. She had hung a few pieces of artwork on the cinder block walls, had a vase of dried flowers on her desk, and there was classical music playing softly from the boom box. An adagio for strings. She, like Dart, had a personal computer on her desk; there were only a few detectives who went to this expense.

"Sit," she said as he entered. "And shut the door."

Dart obeyed. It was in his blood.

"Check that out," she said, indicating the Gerald Lawrence file. Dart had worried that this might be about Lawrence; he had come armed with a number of arguments, but he suddenly forgot most of them. She said, "Page numbers of Kowalski's log." She added, "The thing is, he didn't need to include his log, but he was trying to save himself the paperwork. You ask me: He put his foot in it. There are pages missing."

Dart spotted what she was talking about. Kowalski had merely admitted photocopies of his field notes as some of his case material. On the actual report it read: *See attached.*

"But it's typed up," Dart pointed out to her, finding himself in the awkward position of defending Roman Kowalski. "What's the point of typing up your field notes instead of just typing up the report?"

"It's OCR—optical character recognition," she reminded. "Everyone's using it to cheat on their reports."

Dart was familiar with the scanning software that could turn handwriting into printed text, but this was the first that he heard of this particular application. "A shortcut," he said.

"Exactly. It's not why the department invested in OCR, but it's probably the most popular use at the moment."

It made a world of sense to Dart: keep legible field notes, scan them into the computer, edit them on the word processor, and submit them as your report—thus avoiding the tedious duplication that writing up a report typically required. It made him question his own practices.

Following her suggestion, Dart checked the page numbers of the typewritten field notes and discovered a gap between pages three and five. "Four is missing," he observed. Abby said nothing, continuing to type on her terminal. Dart checked through the rest of the report in case page four had merely been placed out of chronological order. Page four did not exist.

Dart said, "So he didn't have any use for whatever was on page four. That's hardly significant." Dart rarely used even a third of his own notes.

"Oh, yeah? Take a look at this," she suggested, scooting her chair back from the screen. "To use the OCR software, you have to scan the material first, right? And the only scanner we have is in Records—and that's a PC, it's not one of the networked terminals."

"Meaning?"

"The scanner takes the handwritten notes and turns them into a graphic. The graphic is read by the OCR software and turned into text that can be read by a word processor." Dart didn't need an education on OCR. Abby clearly sensed this. She said, "It creates the files in its *own* directory. What Kowalski does is go down there, create the file, and print it up. He doesn't *move* the file; he doesn't erase it."

"You're saying that you lifted his original file?" Dart inquired, impressed.

"*Voila!*" she said, pointing to the screen. "Kowalski's scanned Gerald Lawrence notes."

She had copied the file to disk and had moved

it to her own PC. *Industrious of her*, he thought, realizing he would have to watch out for her.

Dart read the screen. Recognizing the kind of notes that had been taken, he realized immediately that Kowalski had interviewed a witness to the Gerald Lawrence suicide. Quotation marks peppered the page.

Dart's first instinct was to believe the witness had proven a washout, as so many did. It would explain perfectly why Kowalski had not bothered to include the text of the questioning. Dart snagged the file—Kowalski's official investigative report—from Abby's desk. Procedure required the investigating officer to list the name, or names, of each and every witness to the crime, including those deemed useless. Dart could find no reference to any witness.

"Her name is Lewellan Page," Abby announced.

Dart read quickly down the screen. He didn't like being behind Abby on this. Reading, he protested, "She's twelve years old, Abby!" greatly relieved. "No wonder he didn't bother listing her."

"But he *interviewed* her, Joe," she reminded. "He's required to list her." She hesitated and asked, "So why did he leave her out? What did she see?"

"Abby," he cautioned, "it's speculation." But for the second time the hopeful thought nagged at him: *Is Kowalski involved in this?*

She advanced the screen to the bottom of the page. Her finger pointed out a sentence. Dart read:

"*I seen a white man. A big white man. He gone on upstairs and . . .*"

"The next page is missing," she informed him.

Dart reread the material several times. *Ohmygod*, he thought. A *white man*.

"I want to talk to her, Joe. I want to know what it is—who it is—that she saw."

"Can you find her?"

"I don't know," she said."But if I do, I want you there."

CHAPTER
6

Jackson Browne's music played in the background. He sounded lonely. So was Dart. Ginny wouldn't agree to meet him at his apartment, and he had no desire to chance an encounter with some boyfriend of hers. So it was to be neutral ground—Smitty's Bar, a place neither of them haunted, not that Dart haunted any bar. He was more a library man, though loath to admit it.

It was a yuppie bar, with dark wood furniture, white linen, and an island bar that dominated the entrance. It catered to an insurance clientele, white men and women in their thirties wearing dark suits, drinking light beer, and making conversation in the most animated voices they could muster.

Aside from the core downtown, with its

gleaming sky-scrapers, the only place a bar like this could exist was West Hartford and the valley. Whites, a minority in this city, had to pick their watering holes carefully.

Jackson Browne sang that he would do anything, from flying airplanes to walking on the wings. Dart had felt like that once with her. And maybe, just maybe, she had felt that way with him. But it had failed. Dissolved like a figure walking into a thick fog. He had watched it recede, had reached for it, called out to it, and cried when it had vanished, for such things can never come back—at least that was what she had said.

Ginny Rice turned a couple of heads when she entered, not so much for her looks as her presence—she commanded attention. He thought of her affectionately, though he hoped she wouldn't sense this, and he feared that she might because for her he was an easy read. She wore blue jeans, a brown bomber jacket zipped halfway to counter the air-conditioning, a teal blue stone-washed silk shirt and the diamond and gold heart necklace that he had given her on an insignificant anniversary. This outfit alone set her apart from the nearly uniform crowd, just as Dartelli's khakis and blue blazer had differentiated him. She had cut her dark brown hair short, well off her shoulders. She had a perfect nose, small lips and eyes the color of the shirt. A matching pair of gold studs occupied her left ear—nothing in her right. That was Ginny: always something just a tad different. Tomboy. Fantastic athlete. Yet dignified and graceful when she wanted to be. She was somebody else's now—he had heard the rumors. He swallowed dryly, attempting to clear his voice, wondering once again why he had allowed it to happen.

"Hey, Dart," she said, pulling the chair out for herself. If he had stood, if he had helped her with the chair she would have been angry at him, so he fought the urge and just sat there. Use of his abbreviated last name was not a formality; she had always called him this. He thought of himself as Joe Dart most of the time, thanks to her. She unzipped the bomber jacket. A couple of the guys were still looking—Ginny knew this, but she was accustomed to it and accepted it as flattery. She wiggled a smile onto her face, like an actor practicing in a mirror. His heart banged in his chest. *Let go*, he told himself.

He had been told that time heals all wounds, but if that were the case, then time was moving awfully slowly and the wounds still felt raw. And seeing her—the freshness, the comfort with which she carried herself, her apparent happiness—was salt in those wounds. Dart was still back on the time line somewhere. He felt adrift. He had lost Zeller and Ginny in the same two-month period. He had not yet recovered.

Jackson Browne was plaintive—he had messed up a relationship. *You and me both, pal*, Dart thought.

"You look good," she lied. She ordered a Dewar's on the rocks with a twist from a woman who had looked good to Dart a few minutes earlier.

He thanked her and returned the compliment,

and she managed that same fake smile again, and his heart stung. She didn't want to be here; she had better things to do. He could have died at that moment.

Shut up, Jackson, Dart thought. He didn't want to hear about someone else's pain, he had enough of his own. *Bad idea, coming here*, he realized. He looked around and his eye found the door.

"I saw you on television," she said. "I thought you'd regained some of the weight, but I guess it's true what they say about the camera adding ten pounds."

"I'm okay," he said, but they both knew.

"Good." The Dewars arrived and she insisted on paying. She had to stretch to reach into her front pocket and Dart realized her every little movement thrilled him, and he hated himself all the more.

"How's Mac?" she asked.

"Great." Together they had recovered the Labrador from the animal shelter the weekend before they had broken up. He and Ginny used to visit the pound every Saturday morning. One of the rituals of the relationship. Twelve years old, arthritic, mostly deaf, the dog had been found hiding under a porch, stabbed eighteen times with a knife. No longer had a voice box— when he tried to bark he sounded either like a balloon losing air, or gears grinding, depending on his message. He owned a serious limp, very few teeth, and the sweetest disposition on God's green earth. The attendant at the pound had named him Mac the Knife, and it seemed appropriate enough, and Dart had kept the name and the dog. Ginny loved Mac too, though she tried not to show it; she was private with her pain, Private with her pleasure too. Dart called out and ordered a vodka—he needed something stronger than the beer that was now empty in front of him.

The waitress didn't like being yelled at from across the room. Ginny didn't like it either. Dart felt like shit.

"So?" she asked, her patience wearing thin, the conversation running out of easy topics.

"I feel a little foolish asking this," he admitted.

A patronizing grin.

He wished there were a way to start all over. This conversation, this relationship—everything.

"I need your help," he told her.

This seemed a great relief to her. Perhaps she had feared another reconciliation attempt, the tears, the pain, the impossibility. She sampled the Scotch, smacked her lips, and set down the glass carefully onto the coaster.

"Professional?" She gloated. Her work had, in large part, been responsible for the demise of their relationship, and here was Dart on bended knee asking for her talents. The irony was not lost on either of them.

He nodded. Where was that vodka? "Yes. Information," he said.

She waited him out. He didn't like that.

"Insurance records. Medical insurance," he said softly. "Do you have access to that?"

"You know better than that, Dartelli."

Her job, which lacked a specific title but fell vaguely under computer programming, gave her access to everything to do with the major insurance companies, and what she didn't have legally, she had anyway—at her probation hearing the judge had called her "a wizard." The paper had called her "a hacker." Dart had called her "Babe," but usually only after making love, and certainly never around friends. Had she not repeatedly broken the law, he realized that they still might be together. *Or was it that she was caught at it?* Dart wondered. The department forbade an officer from consorting with a convicted felon, although they had once discussed how there were ways around such restrictions. He knew that even now she spent her evenings behind that screen invading networks, accessing files to which she had no legal right. With her it was an addiction—it rated right up there with sex. She was good at both.

She was the only person he knew that had been offered more jobs, more money, *after* being busted and placed on probation. The calls had flooded in. It was as if, by being caught, she had earned her degree. The FBI had been quoted saying, "She knows more about computers than Bill Gates." It had ended up an endorsement of sorts. She was earning three or four times Dart's paycheck. Fine with him if she paid. She got four weeks' vacation and an expense account. He had heard that she was driving a Lexus. He wondered what the judge would think of that.

She asked, "What specifically do you need?"

"I wish I knew."

"Well, that clarifies it." One of her complaints with him had been what she perceived as his reluctance to state his position—she had called him wishy-washy, slippery, and dishonest. It brought back bad memories.

Bad idea, he thought for the second time.

"I've lost track of a possible witness—the girlfriend of our suicide, our jumper. She lived with him, we think. But we can't pick up a paper trail—an address, a phone number. Insurance records were suggested as a way of tracking her down." He paused, studying her. "And while you're at it . . .," he added, awaiting a grin from her, "I thought I might try the suicide too—see if he was facing a fatal disease, or something like that, some reason to explain the jump."

"The almighty Bud Gorman let you down?" she sniped. Over the course of their relationship, Ginny had repeatedly offered to supply the financial information that Gorman provided Dart, but the detective had steadfastly refused because technically it fell under criminal activity. His willingness to break the law using Gorman but not her had been a perpetual sore spot.

He shrugged. "The guy's name is David Stapleton. If we've got it right, his woman is called Priscilla Cole." He passed her the names on a blank piece of notepaper.

She didn't so much as glance at the names; her eyes were locked onto his. She held the gaze for an interminable amount of time. Without looking, she reached out, found the Scotch, and drained it. He refused to break eye contact; he could be as obstinate as she. He had spent years lost in those eyes. He felt a little drunk.

"I miss you," she said softly. Was she making it up?

"Yeah," he answered.

"It's not serious . . . What I'm in now . . . It's a filler, something to take up the time, warm up the nights, give the weekends meaning." She reached for the drink again but realized it was empty. He felt like offering her his. "You could use someone," she encouraged.

"That's the thing," Dart offered. "It would be using, I think."

"That's okay, as long as it's clear."

"No. Not for me it isn't."

Her eyes grew sad, but she never broke their eye contact.

"Want another?" she asked. He wasn't sure what she meant—another *chance*, another *drink*? He nodded.

She raised her hand, flexed her wrist, and pointed at the table. She never took her eyes off him. Never confirmed that the order had been received. But the drinks arrived minutes later, and Dart thought how typical this was of her. *In control*. In command. He started feeling angry with her; he wasn't sure where that came from.

He touched the notepaper again, breaking eye contact.

She scooped up the names, neatly folded the piece of paper, and slipped it into her shirt pocket, impatient with him.

"It's true about missing you," she told him.

"I don't want you breaking any laws." He wasn't sure what to say, so he said this, and then wondered why. Of course he wanted her breaking laws.

"Heaven forbid," she mocked. "It might reflect on you."

More salt.

She picked up her glass—it seemed a familiar movement to her—and she said, "Let's see how far I get."

"Yeah . . . okay," Dart said, not entirely sure if she were talking about insurance records, or their relationship. As much as he felt drawn to her, torn by their breakup, he understood that his tendency was to be attracted to women who needed him to save them. His relationship with his mother had established this, and he had continued it through several relationships and into the romance with Ginny. He had repeatedly rescued her when she had been busted for her computer hacking—there were times he felt it was his only purpose in the relationship. He knew he needed to break that cycle. If he were to go back with her, no matter how tempting, he'd simply start it all again—he felt clear on this. Even so, the heartstrings tugged.

When she swallowed, her throat moved sensuously. His visceral attraction pulled at him, despite his reasoning. But his reasoning won out, and not long after, she stood and left.

So, why, he wondered, drinking alone once again, did it hurt so deeply to see her go?

CHAPTER
7

Four days later, Dart found himself standing out on the sidewalk in front of the Jennings Road headquarters alongside a restless Ted Bragg. He could hear the sound of boat traffic out on the Connecticut River. The late August air was like a cocoon, smothering every living creature that ventured outside. Dart would have preferred to have remained inside with the less than exceptional air-conditioning, but Bragg had insisted they meet out here so that he could smoke. Dart toed the sidewalk restlessly, waiting for Bragg to say something. Patrol cars came and went.

"I ran the Ice Man stats into the animation software, like I said."

"You said a week or two, Buzz," Dart reminded, surprised at how quickly the man was getting back to him.

"I'm motivated," Bragg said irritably. "This software is on trial. I gotta decide whether or not to buy it, and it ain't cheap!"

Dart felt a worming sense of worry twist his gut, and tried to hide it. He felt slightly schizophrenic, the constant din of his internal voice nagging and chattering away, reminding him of his oversight during the Ice Man investigation and the repercussions now resurfacing.

"Came up with the same results," Bragg announced wearily, clearly disappointed.

Dart felt his words catch in his throat. *The same results*! He wanted to question this immediately, to cast doubt on the findings, but the burning intensity in Bragg's eyes silenced him. "You're saying that the Ice Man did not jump?" *The Asian Strangler*, he thought to himself. *The man who killed Zeller's wife.* "The Ice Man was *thrown* from that window?" Dart's mind was reeling. "You can prove that?" He worried that Bragg's finding might reopen the case; and then, a moment later, what a horror that might bring Zeller. *There is no secret that remains a secret forever.*

He had to focus to hear what Bragg was saying—his mind was running through damage control. A dozen internal voices competing for his attention. Was he in part to blame for Stapleton's death by not speaking up three years earlier? Was he wrong in assuming Zeller had been involved? *There was no proof*, he reminded himself.

Bragg said, "That's what the software suggests, yeah. Though I gotta tell ya that it makes me question its validity. I'm not so sure about this. I mean: I run it on two cases, and two for two it comes out that the guy was tossed. You kidding me?" he questioned. "Seems more like a glitch to me. I'm gonna call the company and have a little chat. I wouldn't get too worked up about it just yet, Ivy. Let me do a little research. Maybe there's a glitch in the code—something like that. As you pointed out, the Ice Man investigation was an embarrassment to this entire department—hell if I'm gonna be the one reopens that one. Rankin would burn me at the stake."

"True enough," Dart said encouragingly, his heart beginning to beat again. But the worry burned inside him.

"Let's you and I remember," Bragg explained in a concerned and patronizing tone of voice, "that I checked this out *on my own*. My idea! So let's leave it at that. I was fooling around is all—testing the software. There's no paperwork on this. Just me experimenting with some new software. So unless you're in a god-awful hurry to bring the wrath of god down on the both of us, I'd just as soon keep this under wraps for now. Early versions of software like this are always glitching. Always! Ten to one the stuff is fucked up somehow. Trust me."

The issue *was* trust, Dart realized, but it had little to do with Teddy Bragg. It was about the public's trust in Dartelli to investigate fully; it was the faith the department vested in its detectives; it was Dart's respect for Walter Zeller—his mentor and former partner—and his refusal to bring the man down for nothing more than suspicion. "A software problem," Dart repeated, his throat dry. He coughed.

"Exactly." Bragg met eyes with him, silently conveying the message, *Don't question this.*

Dart felt the need to spill his guts, to let *someone* in on it. The Ice Man was the Asian Strangler—a fact no one but Dart knew; the Asian Strangler case remained uncleared—and Walter Zeller had possessed the most personal reason for wanting the Asian Strangler dead. Three years ago that had been the end of it. *But now?*

"Are we clear on this?" Bragg asked.

Dart nodded, his voice too tight to answer.

"Just so we're clear on this." Bragg took a long pull on the cigarette, blew the smoke high into the air, and added, "I'll send you up a copy of Doc Ray's prelim on Stapleton. Blood toxicology shows no street drugs, no nothing that would suggest narcotics of any sort. Aside from a lot of crushed bones, the only things of interest are a couple of needle marks on the inside of the man's left elbow."

"A junkie?"

"No, that's the point," he said impatiently. "Nothing in the blood tox to suggest that. Blood donor maybe. Plasma center? Who knows? Maybe low on fluids—people have trouble this time of year, this kind of heat."

"Blood alcohol?" Dart asked.

"Insignificant." After a moment, Bragg asked, "What, Ivy? Why that look?"

"No drugs, no alcohol? In a jumper? How often do we see that?"

He shrugged. "How often do we see a jumper?" he asked, irritably. "Listen, I'm taking it as *good* news. You want to make trouble with it, you talk to the Doc yourself."

"Stapleton didn't jump, Buzz. You said that yourself."

"That was when I was trusting this software," the man reminded. "Other than that damn software, we've got no evidence of foul play—everything we've got supports a clean jump." He

70

waited, as if he expected an objection from Dart. "Don't make trouble out of this, Ivy. Give me a chance to check this stuff out."

"Sure," Dart said. But inside, he was dying. The Ice Man had been murdered; the proof he had been lacking was now staring him in the face. He remained outside long after Teddy Bragg had left him. *There will be more killings,* he thought.

A car honked behind him. He turned around to see Abby Lang behind the wheel. She was waving at him to join her.

CHAPTER
8

When Abby Lang signaled Dart over to her car window, he immediately sensed that she was bringing new trouble, and began plotting to avoid whatever it was that she wanted of him. And yet, at the same time, he felt a need to monitor her. He didn't want her wandering too far afield.

She told him, "Kowalski's witness has agreed to talk to me." She handed him the address. Perhaps it was the combination of her blond hair and blue eyes, or her flawless skin that took a decade off her age, but she emanated an eager, youthful enthusiasm that rumbled from within her like a pot boiling. To others it might have come across as a naiveté, but to Dart it felt more like a concentration of energy—as if she were a

71

battery of sorts, and that battery partially discharged when he met eyes with it.

Autumn was not far off, and the first signs of it frosted the edges of some of the leaves with color, and the air smelled of it, and the sun's rays felt different—things no longer shined, they glowed. He wondered why he had noticed none of this until now.

"It's just north of Bellevue Square projects," she cautioned. *A bad neighborhood*, he thought.

"This is not the best time of day for that area."

The projects were safest from sunrise until eleven in the morning, because the gangs were late-night phenomena and the kids slept late— drugged, hung over, exhausted.

Abby responded, "Tell me about it. But she's willing to talk, so I'm going."

"One block north of Bellevue Square? A white woman? Alone? Are you kidding?"

"Is that a sexist, racist, comment, Detective?"

"*I* wouldn't go in there alone," he stated honestly.

"Well, then, I'll keep you company," she declared with a wry grin, leaning away from him and popping open the passenger door.

"No, no, no," Dart protested, standing his ground.

"Get in," she said, glancing beyond him at the gathering of patrolmen standing by the headquarter's front door, "or I'll make a scene."

They met eyes, and he sensed that she meant it.

He found himself walking in front of the car

and climbing in alongside of her. "This is a bad idea," he warned her.

"Live a little," said Abby Lang.

Lang's blond hair whipped in the wind of the open window. He caught the silhouette of her tiny nose in profile and the elegant, even graceful line to her chin. "Do you have kids?" Dart asked. *Where had that come from?* he wondered.

"Three."

"How is it? The family life?"

She glanced over at him and glared. Her blouse ruffled and billowed. "It's the best thing and the worst thing that ever happened to me. One part joy, one part chaos. Highly recommended." He sensed little or no sarcasm in her.

"Married?"

"Once upon a time. Only it didn't work out that way—like the fairy tales, I mean."

The palms of his hands went damp; he felt nervous.

"Are you flirting with me, Dartelli?" She looked over and grinned.

"What?" he asked incredulously. "No," he answered lamely.

She shrugged her shoulders. "Oh, well."

They turned right and drove into the heart of the north end. They rolled up their windows and Abby turned on the air, and Dart checked to make sure all the doors were locked. White people rarely entered the north or south end—not without a blue uniform—and the residents of the projects rarely ventured into the downtown core. If the gangs crossed north to south, there was bloodshed. Three separate cities co-existed poorly, side by side. The police refereed.

"Do you like ice cream?" she asked him.

This question was so far from his thoughts, Dartelli took a moment to answer. "Who doesn't like ice cream?"

"What flavor?" She added, "And don't say vanilla."

"Vanilla."

"Damn it all."

"I can be a major disappointment," he apologized.

"Yeah? And you think you're alone in that?"

"Meaning?"

She smiled that self-contented smile of hers and angled her head toward the air-conditioning vent, enjoying the cold breeze. She addressed the windshield. "Chocolate frozen yogurt with raspberry sauce."

"Maybe I am flirting," he announced honestly.

"We're only talking about ice cream. Rest easy." A few blocks later, she asked, "What was Ginny's flavor?"

"Mint chip."

"I *hate* mint chip," she proclaimed.

"Yeah, me too," he said, grinning.

"I kinda figured that," she said. "Just by the way you said it."

Passing the Bellevue Square projects it occurred to Dartelli that these kinds of living conditions did not belong in a city in central Connecticut, in the United States of America. It seemed unimaginable that this kind of barren wasteland

74

of urban decay could be but a scant few minutes from the city's revitalized downtown. Bellevue Square looked so much like a prison that it wasn't too surprising that many of its teen residents ended up in one. Decrepit, shell-shocked buildings; storefronts boarded up with graffiti encrusted plywood; sidewalk curbs ankle deep in litter. And not an aluminum can in sight.

Blacks and Hispanics attempted to stay cool on front stoops, curbs, and perched in open windows. A wasteland, like something from a futuristic novel. Dart took this all personally. The system had failed miserably. To drive through the projects was to experience total despair. He felt it in the pit of his stomach.

"Park it where we can keep an eye on it," Dart suggested as they neared the address.

"Point taken."

If the car were identified as belonging to two white people, it had a life expectancy of about ten minutes. Only the stenciled announcement POLICE, which Abby placed on the dash, offered them any hope of returning to the vehicle and finding it driveable. And that was no guarantee.

Abigail Lang and Joe Dart climbed a cement staircase under the glare of a bare sixty-watt bulb, along a plaster wall scarred from an endless stream of furniture being moved up and down these flights.

Entering the apartment, Dartelli pulled off his jacket and unfastened his collar button and reached for his handkerchief to mop his forehead.

Lewellan Page was a twelve-year-old black girl, wiry thin and bug-eyed, with small budding breasts stabbing at her tight T-shirt. Dart met eyes with her, smiled at her, but faced with a cold, expressionless stare, immediately saw her not as a child but as a victim. Abby clearly saw this too.

On the drive over, having never met her, never seen her in person, a very savvy Abigail Lang had described Lewellan Page down to her long, sinewy legs and high cheekbones—this because she fit so perfectly the description of Gerry Law's former victims. Realizing that there were at least another dozen Lewellan Pages in and around this same neighborhood filled Dart with a sadness that manifested itself inside of him as a painful silence. No longer a child. Not yet a woman. Lewellan Page blinked up at him with something like terror in her eyes: Perhaps to her all men were Gerald Lawrence.

The girl took a chair at a black enamel kitchen table. Her mother was still at work, which was awkward for Dart, because they couldn't use anything the girl said without her mother's advance permission to interview her. She said she did not have a father, which hurt Dart: She did not know the difference between having and knowing. Her brother was out on the streets somewhere. The one-bedroom apartment was immaculately clean, though spare of furnishings. The small green couch and gray overstuffed chair in the claustrophobic sitting room were trained on a television. The pillow and folded blanket indicated that someone slept on the couch— probably the brother, who no doubt came and went. The apartment door had four heavy-duty locks on it and a police bar. The kitchen window near the fire escape had been boarded up and three pieces of wide metal strapping bolted to the inside.

One look at her living conditions, this young girl home alone, and it was not difficult to imagine the befriending tactics of a Gerald Lawrence. As the three of them began to skirt the inquiry, Lang expertly creating a rapport with the girl, Dart was struck by the girl's maturity, and it occurred to him that Kowalski was wrong to distrust her statement because of age.

Prompted for what she had seen, Lewellan was forthright, showing Abby and Dart how, from her kitchen window, a person could see down into both the dirt parking area behind Lawrence's Battles Street tenement, and a pair of windows that she claimed belonged to the dead man's apartment.

"Did you know Gerry Law, Lewellan?" Abby asked.

The girl looked down at the chipped linoleum floor and nodded. "Yes, ma'am," she said, "I did."

"And did you like him?"

The girl shrugged, but she was clearly uncomfortable, even frightened.

"Did he like you?" Abby asked, accustomed to such questioning, though Dart felt squeamish.

"Sort of," the girl answered.

Dart did not want to be here for this. He wondered why he had bothered to come here at all, why Abby had dragged him into this, and he thought that maybe it was emotional punishment, a way to insure that he would not take a way out, not drop the suicides the way he felt tempted to. A few weeks and both David Stapleton and Gerald Lawrence would be little more than a pair of files collecting dust in the records room.

Abby's eyes flashed darkly at Dart. She seemed to read his thoughts, and she did not approve. *You're not going anywhere*, they said. *Help me out here!*

"Tell us what you saw," Dart requested gently. He did not want any more of her case history. He did not want confirmation that this small girl had been locked up with Gerald Lawrence for even an afternoon. Dart reached for his collar and realized he had already unbuttoned it; he sucked for air, suddenly claustrophobic.

The girl's large brown eyes begged at Dart, and yet she was scared of him. "It was some old car. Blue, maybe. Gray." She shrugged. She was bone thin. Much too pretty. Too real for Joe Dart at the moment. He wanted out of there. "Old, you know. Come around back here and park. Big man get out. White man, you know. He go up the back stairs there," she said, pointing in the direction of the outside.

Dart moved to the window. He didn't want to hear this. He said, "It was late. It would have been dark."

"No, not dark. The light come out of them windows down there. It's plenty bright enough." She studied Dart. "You think I be lying, same as that other man," she said, referring to Kowalski.

Abby glanced up at Dart condescendingly and then said to the girl, "You saw a white man get out of his car—a blue car—and climb those back stairs?"

"Big man. Yes, ma'am. Gray maybe—the car."

"And what did you do then, Lewellan?" Dart asked, hoping to discover some inconsistency that might invalidate her as a witness and at the same time explain why Kowalski had left out her statement. Hope built inside him that Abby's instincts were right: perhaps the connection was Kowalski, not Zeller. What a pleasure it would be to bring down Roman Kowalski.

"I watched," the girl answered. "The Man come sneaking around our alley late at night, and I figure somebody gonna get arrested, maybe kilt." She nodded at Dart, and he felt a chill down to his feet. Bellevue Square entertainment— arrests and shootings. Said with excitement, as if this window were just another television screen.

Dart considered the possibilities. Gerald Lawrence could have been a dealer, his white visitor a customer. Kowalski could know something about that, having been Narco once. *The buyer could have been a cop*, Dart realized, looking for Kowalski's motivation. A cop buying drugs near Bellevue Square, or performing a shakedown was just the kind of information that Kowalski would attempt to keep quiet. If he handled it on his own, if he hushed it up, he could protect a fellow officer and pick up some chits to barter later in his career.

"The white man was upstairs about five minutes," Abby repeated.

"Yeah, and no shooting." She told Dart, "My

79

mama tell me when there a shooting to get under a table. Head down and under a table."

Five minutes was enough time to make a buy and get back down to the car, Dart thought. It didn't seem to him near enough time to fake a suicide. He experienced another wave of relief—he had jumped to conclusions by considering Zeller. *Guilt,* he thought, *is a form of illness.*

He looked at Abby and saw sadness. Someone so young, her eyes said to him. Someone innocent. *And innocence,* he thought, *is like a balloon— once punctured, it's gone. There is no making it whole again. No making it well.* His mother had stolen a different innocence from him; he felt empathy for this young girl.

"What time of night was this, Lewellan?" Abby asked.

"Between eleven and eleven-thirty."

"You were up that late?" Dart asked. He wondered if this was a possible crack in her story.

"I don't sleep so good. My mama reads to me after the news is over, then maybe I sleep for a little while."

"Why don't you sleep well?" Abby asked.

"Bad dreams."

By the name of Gerald Lawrence, Dart thought. He glanced at Abby. How could a person volunteer to work Sex Crimes? How could she live with this day after day?

Abby asked the inevitable question, and as it registered, Dart looked away. "Did Gerry Law ever ask you over to his place?"

"I don't know."

"We won't tell your mother," Abby promised.

She knows exactly what to say, Dart thought.

He looked back as Lewellan Page shrugged and focused her attention on the cracked linoleum again. She nodded sheepishly. "He had bunnies," she said. "White bunnies."

Dart felt a stinging in his eyes, and caught himself with fists clenched. *Why bother asking this?* he wondered. He didn't want to hear any of this. But then he realized how important a question it was—perhaps enough animosity and hatred toward Lawrence had built so that a neighbor had killed the man and made it look like a hanging. Maybe there was no white man involved at all. Maybe Kowalski had discovered the hint of a murder and decided a scum like Lawrence wasn't worth the taxpayer's money.

Abby's face held an expression of infinite patience and compassion. Dart admired her; his own face probably held a look of horror. He could see in the young girl's fear and hesitation that she had indeed been in Lawrence's lair, had petted those bunnies. *A victim.*

Attempting to fend off her confirmation—not wanting to hear it—he said impatiently, "Well, you've certainly been a big help." God help him, he would *not* bring this girl downtown. He no longer cared about Kowalski's missing pages. *Let it go.*

But for Abby this was simply another investigation, another case; she had seen dozens of girls like Lewellan Page. She would not allow Dart to close the questioning. "Are they nice bunnies? Cute bunnies?" she asked.

The girl nodded. "Yes, ma'am."

81

"Lewellan, did you visit Gerry Law that night?"

"At night? No way. Only when Mama's at work. Mama don't like Gerry none. Mama don't want me seeing the bunnies." She asked Dart, "You know what happened to them bunnies now that Gerry is dead?"

Dart spun around and left the room, his throat constricted, his vision blurred.

Kill all the Gerry Laws you can find, and there would still be more, he thought. He wanted to change this girl's life, to turn back the clock.

"Abby," he called out, hoping to end this.

But he heard her voice from the other room as she asked softly, "Do you think you might recognize this white man if you saw him again?"

Dart didn't hear an answer. He could picture those thin shoulders lifting into that shrug, the eyes expressive with fear. There was a picture of Jesus Christ on the wall and another of the pope by the door to the bathroom. There was a picture in Dart's head of Gerald Lawrence hanging at the end of a lamp cord. Cut him down with a pair of wire cutters. Zip him up inside the ME's black body bag and forget about it. Who cares about him? Why bother to investigate? Kowalski was right: good riddance.

"Abby," he called again.

"Come in here a minute," she answered.

Reluctantly, Dart reentered the kitchen.

"Tell him what you just told me," Abby said, glancing at Dart, and punishing him for his desertion.

"I saw the white man pull the chair out from under him."

Dart stood there, slack-jawed. For a moment it felt as if his heart had stopped. The rationale that he had formulated in his head—the drug deal, Kowalski chalking up a favor—evaporated.

Several thoughts coursed through him, from how lousy a witness she was: a twelve-year-old victim of sexual abuse; to Kowalski's missing pages.

The chair. He recalled the photograph: the chair lying on its side, spilled over as if kicked away.

Standing up and glancing out the kitchen window, Abby asked, "Were the shades up or down?"

Dart recognized that tone of voice: Abby didn't believe the girl. *Thank God!* he thought.

"The shade was down. Gerry always had the shades down. Said the bunnies didn't like the sun." She turned to face Dart and explained, "But it was hot that night, and there was a wind, you know, and the shade blowing back and forth, and it moved once, and I saw that white man pull the chair, and I saw Gerry's feet . . . you know?" She glanced over at Abby, and paddled her hands out in front of herself. "Like he was running, you know? Running real fast."

Dart felt paralyzed. Lewellan Page had witnessed a murder.

To Abby the girl said, "Fritz ran away. That's my dog. Mama'll let me have bunnies now that Fritz is gone. Said no bunnies as long as we have Fritz, but Fritz is gone now, gone for good." She nodded enthusiastically.

Fifteen minutes later Dart and Abby Lang were back in the department-issue Taurus soaking in the air-conditioning. Abby stated strongly, "She killed the dog, or let him go, or gave him away."

"You think?"

"She wants those rabbits."

He had a witness now that in many ways he did not want, and yet felt grateful to have. Someone had murdered Lawrence—*the same person who killed the Ice Man?* he wondered—and no matter who this person turned out to be— even if Walter Zeller—he had to be stopped, and right away. He couldn't help but think that he might have stopped this killing if back then had he spoken up. He felt cold all of a sudden.

"Why would Kowalski leave her out of his report?" she fired at him.

Kowalski was a big white man; Dart understood what Abby was saying. He objected, "She could be lying about the guy's color. About any of it."

Abby kept her attention on the road and slowed for a red light. "I don't think she's lying," she said.

"No," he said, though he wanted to bury the whole thing. He thought he understood Kowalski now more than ever.

Mistakes compound other mistakes, Dart reminded himself. You overlook something three years ago, and it comes back to haunt you. *I did my job*, he reminded himself, wondering if a board of inquiry would see it that way, wondering if his career was on the line. He felt like a fuck-up. A fool. He considered a transfer—someplace in the

South, away from the winters. People might attribute it to his breakup with Ginny. It was a good time to try.

But the better part of him knew that he could not outrun the truth. *Better to stay and fight.*

Abby asked, "What exactly is going on with us, Joe?"

Dart felt his face and spine go hot. How could she disconnect from Lewellan Page so quickly? Was that what Sex Crimes did to you, numb you, the way Homicide turned you into a comedian?

She wanted an answer; she didn't want to repeat herself.

"Let's forget the ice cream," he said.

"I'm not talking about ice cream." Abby found a stray button on her blouse and closed it. She steered clear of a slow-moving truck, turned at the jai alai fronton and crossed over the tracks. She parked in the back of the Jennings Road building, and just before they climbed out of the car, announced, "I know what I know. I know what I'm feeling from you. For you. It's scaring me a little."

"You're good company, Abby."

"Okay," she said, accepting this.

But Dart didn't accept his own explanation. He wanted to say something. She was more than good company; he was interested—the couple of years that separated them didn't bother him a bit. She was a fighter; a comer. She spoke her mind, and when she met eyes with him he felt it inside.

Whereas she seemed to have faced all of this, to have reconciled herself to the obvious, he could not. Not verbally. And so he said nothing: Another deliberate omission on his part. Would he pay for this one as well?

CHAPTER
9

After weeks of routine work in which it was easy to lose himself, Dart still retained a folder on his desk containing five mug shots that little Lewellan Page had identified as likenesses of Lawrence's killer. To her credit, the faces appeared similar— renewing Dart's faith in her as a witness. He stumbled onto the folder on a Wednesday after-noon in early October and decided to do something about the worry that he had been living with since the interview. The only step that he could clearly see was to steal a look at some files that he did not have authority to access. The risk had kept him away from them, but on this particular Wednesday he snapped. He had to do something before another "suicide" turned up.

Dart walked down the hall to Abby's office, shut her door quietly, and asked her out for an ice cream.

"An ice cream?" she asked, viewing him curi-ously—as much for the way in which he had shut the door, as his question. "It's *October.*"

"Someplace away from Jennings Road is all," he informed her.

They met eyes and he sensed that perhaps she understood. They agreed to meet in the parking lot a few minutes later.

The Oasis Diner was across town on Farmington Avenue, on the way to the Mark Twain house and West Hartford. The first triple-wide diner in the country, the Oasis retained its art deco interior, which included a total surround of stamped stainless steel and movie stills of Brando, Monroe, and James Dean. Dart had vanilla, Abby raspberry with chocolate sauce.

"So?" she asked. The drive over had been in complete silence.

Dart said, "Kowalski was Narco before Homicide. Doc Ray's preliminary of Stapleton turned up some injection marks. They may be nothing, but it's possible that Stapleton—maybe Stapleton *and* Lawrence—were dealers. The point is, we'll never know because Narco records are shut away, and after what they've been through, if we go asking questions, we're likely to open up a hornets' nest and have Haite asking a lot of questions that neither of us wants to answer until *we* have some answers. Are you with me?"

"All the way," she said, rolling her tongue over the chocolate sauce. She made no attempt to disguise her enjoyment and then licked her lips. "Lawrence was a cover-up?"

"It depends if we believe Lewellan Page or not," he said.

"She wouldn't survive on the witness stand, if that's what you're asking. No. She'd be torn apart by the psychologists, who would discover her abuse and create all sorts of reasons she would want to invent someone killing Gerry Law. That's my professional opinion. Personally, I believe her, and I think that you do too, or we wouldn't be sitting here, and you wouldn't look so tired and bothered."

"If we apply through Internal Affairs for Lawrence's Narco file, it will take a ream of paperwork and six weeks. Plus countless interviews and reports, and at some point we'll have to put everything out on the table."

"In the meantime, we aren't sleeping well," she said, sampling the ice cream again. She drew it into her mouth on the end of a white plastic spoon and skimmed the surface softly with her lips stealing a little bit of the prize at a time, until what was on the spoon disappeared and she went after more. He sensed no intention on her part in making this overly sensual—it seemed more her way of eating her ice cream, but Dart had a difficult time with it. What would it feel like to be kissed by her?

"I'd like to get inside the Narco file room," he confessed.

The spoon stopped inside her mouth. She returned it to the paper cup and put a napkin to her lips. "You *what*?"

"We need to know, one way or the other, if either Stapleton or Lawrence was ever investigated by Narcotics. It's our only hope of connecting Kowalski to Lawrence."

She set the spoon down, noticeably more pale. She looked around, as if he might have been overheard. "You must really trust me," she said, staring at him. "Does the word *suspension* mean anything to you? Or how about the words, *suspension without pay*? How about an IA investigation with *you* as its target?" She pushed the ice cream away. "If you're using me as a sounding board, Joe, then take this advice: Forget it. They'll suspend you, maybe toss you. They'll make an example of you—that's how it works." She cocked her head at him. "What is *that* look?"

"Narco is empty by one in the morning. They're all out working the streets or eating doughnuts or killing time at strip joints. By three, they go home. CAPers is up and running, but it's down the hall. Thursday through Sunday the cleaners start at midnight. The rest of the week, they go eight to eleven."

"What they say about you and your research is true, isn't it?"

"I can't watch the hallway and go for the files at the same time."

"No way." She didn't hesitate a nanosecond.

"It can't be done?"

"No, it can't," she confirmed.

"Not without help," he pressed.

"Message received. Now hear this: No way!"

"Your office has a clean view of the hallway. With the door left open, you could see down that hall, could warn me. Sometimes there's a late bust. Predicting traffic flow in and out of that division is never a sure bet."

"It would make me an accomplice."

"We carry pagers. They can be set to vibrate instead of beep, did you know that? If you were to program your phone to dial my pager number, then it would take only seconds to warn me. It takes exactly nine seconds to walk down the hallway and reach Narcotics once you've rounded that corner."

She shook her head, looking amazed that he had already timed it. "And whoever it was would recognize you."

"I'm dressed as a housecleaner. I wear a ball cap, glasses, and a press-on 'stache. I keep my head down. No one ever looks at the wombats. Not at one in the morning. I push my cart out the door, and I'm gone. Besides," he offered, "that's *my* risk, not yours. If I'm caught, I acted alone. You've done nothing more than pull an all-nighter. How unusual is that?" He spoke *sotto voce*. His heart was beating fast, and he was sweating. The vanilla was melting in front of him, untouched.

She reached out, snagged the spoon, and guided it back between her lips. "I suppose you already know the order that housecleaning cleans in. Which offices are done first?"

"I can do this alone," he reminded, "but I thought I'd ask you first. I'm pressuring you, Abby, and I'm sorry. Let's drop it."

She removed the spoon and pursed her lips. She looked at him quizzically, skeptically, squinting in a way that felt as if she were measuring him. Testing him. "You're right about IA. Putting the request through them would probably take several weeks. But break into Narco's files based on the testimony of a victimized twelve-year-old girl? Does that strike you as odd?"

"Don't look at me like that." He toyed with the ice cream, but wasn't hungry.

"You're really pissing me off here, damn it."

"Good."

A tension had settled between them, uncomfortable and gnawing. "I think I've lost my appetite," she declared.

At 3:00 A. M., Dart, wearing a fake mustache, blue jeans, and a dark blue ball cap, entered the department's basement housecleaning closet, where he located both a cart and a navy blue smock that the service people wore. There were four workers assigned to clean the two-story building. Dart, heading upstairs exactly at 1:00 A. M., estimated that he had a over an hour for a job he thought would only take a few minutes.

He had rarely found use for the speed key given him by Walter Zeller some four years earlier. Zeller had claimed that no investigating officer could get by without one, despite their illegality. The speed key was shaped something like a small flat pistol. It magically picked most locks with the squeeze of a trigger and was the preferred tool of car thieves because of its simplicity—insert the tongue into the lock, squeeze and hold the trigger, rotate, and the lock was open. Dart hid it under a stack of green cotton rags on the cleaner's cart.

The mustache itched. The glue had dried, shrinking his upper lip in the process. If he sneezed he might send the thing across the room.

He used his cellular phone to call Narcotics'

second-floor office. He allowed it to ring eight times, thrilled that no one answered.

He pushed the cart out into the hall, headed quickly to the building's sole elevator, and rode up, his heart rate increasing with every yard. This exploit reminded him of trying to rob money from his mother's wallet atop her dresser bureau—he would steal the money, not for himself but so that when she checked the wallet to send him out for a bottle, she would lack money.

The elevator doors slid open, and at a distance of thirty feet, down the long ugly tile corridor, he caught eyes with Abby Lang. He felt stunned. Elated. She sat behind a desk inside her Sex Crimes office, looking both tired and concerned. Instinctively, Dart felt down for his pager and switched the beeper off so that if it were called it would vibrate, not sound. She was clearly there to help him. Nothing else could explain her presence at this hour.

As he rolled the cart toward Narco, Abby picked up her phone and touched a single button. Less than five seconds later, the pager clipped to Dart's belt began vibrating. He reached down and cleared it—like silencing an alarm clock. She did not look up at him but kept her head aimed down at her desk and the paperwork that seemed to absorb her.

Dart had a lookout—an accomplice. An angel on his shoulder.

The listing cart's front right wheel chirped. Dart awkwardly navigated it to a position in front of Narco. He knocked, waited, and then knocked again. With no reply, he slipped his hand beneath the stack of green rags and removed the speed key. The fact that he was violating regulations distrubed him. If caught, he would have some tough explaining to do. He was the cop turned criminal, and for a moment he couldn't bring himself to do this. But the hope that Kowalski, not Zeller, was responsible for the murder/suicide of Lawrence, and the possibility of connecting Lawrence to Stapleton drove him on—anything to quiet his guilt.

With the speed key the door opened effortlessly. It was illegal in all fifty states to own such a device, and Dart suddenly understood why.

As in hotels, the housecleaners at Jennings Road blocked open office doors as they worked. Dart did just that, though only partially screening the room inside so that the closet used as a vault to contain files remained obscured from the hallway.

He switched on the interior light, emptied a trash can into the hopper on his cart, and placed a beat-up feather duster on the desk top closest. His watch face read 1:03. The cleaners would be arriving any minute and would start on the first floor. He had plenty of time.

The file room closet was locked, but the speed key made quick work of it. The light switch was mounted on the wall outside. Dart studied his situation, planning, predicting every movement required should his pager alert him to a visitor. He had to keep all actions to a minimum, and so rather than venture inside the room, he stood there figuring how to avoid being caught. He relocked the file room door, so that once shut it would be locked and not require him to fiddle with it. He used a green rag to block it open, and tested that by kicking the rag free, the door would close on its own. Then, with the light on, he stepped inside and looked to judge the line of sight: If someone showed up unexpectedly, this person would quickly have a clear sight of the open file room.

The light switch on the wall was on the far side of the hinges, meaning that Dart would have to kick the rag out of the way, get himself around the door, helping it close as he went, and then hit the light switch. But this light going off would be picked up even sooner by someone entering because the office door to Narcotics had an institutional smoked-glass panel, and a change in background light would be noticeable. He reviewed the situation; deciding he had things in the right order, rehearsed them once while counting in his head. *Four to five seconds*, he guessed. When combined with the five or so seconds that Abby needed to alert him, it would be too long.

He grabbed the mop and headed directly to the hallway's broom closet, filled the rolling bucket from the soapstone sink, wetted the mop and, carrying a yellow plastic sandwich board warning of a WET FLOOR, hurried to the end of the hall near the stairs and the elevator. He mopped the floor furiously, making it as wet as possible, then placed the sandwich board in the center of the hall. With all this water he hopefully had bought himself some extra time while also slowing down any approach.

Back inside Narco, Dart unlocked the file room for the second time, blocked the door open with the rag, and switched on the light.

The room was crowded with gray metal utility shelving along all walls and a pair of opposing stacks in the center. All the shelves were crammed with folders.

Dart checked his watch. This could take a while.

A rolling stepstool allowed him access to the top shelves, which was where he found the L's. Dart was surprised by the number of files, each representing a Narco investigation, an arrest, or a snitch. The city's drug problem was huge. He fingered the spines: *L . . . A . . . W . . .* and came up with five files carrying the last name LAWRENCE. Splitting his attention between the files and the open door, Dart nervously inspected the spines of each of these five files. Charles "Buster" Lawrence, Eldridge Lawrence, Philip Lawrence, Maynard Franklin Lawrence, Lawrence Taylor Lawrence. No Gerald. Dart hadn't thought to memorize the dead man's social security number, or driver's license number for comparison, and people like Lawrence used enough aliases that it seemed plausible that any one of these five could be his. Dart took the time to go through the folders again opening each to a mug shot or crime scene photo. One by one he eliminated them; no Gerald Lawrence to be found. If Lawrence had been investigated by Narcotics, it hadn't been in the recent past.

Disappointment depressed him.

He didn't need the stool for Stapleton. The *S*'s were in the center aisle with *S* . . . *T* . . . *A* at eye height. Again, he thumbed through the spines, all marked with color-coded stickers.

A phone rang, not ten feet from him. Dart's heart skipped and his chest froze, and for a second his head swam. The phone in the outer room rang again, seemingly louder, and a third time. Hurrying, he overcame his anxiety and started pulling files stickered *S* . . . *T* . . . *A*.

Stacker; Stadler; Stafford . . . He had to pull each file out a ways in order to read the name on the spine. He looked down the line of similarly colored stickers, realizing there were dozens of *S-T-A*s to go. He jumped forward by a group of ten: Stands . . . Standzleff . . . Staples . . . Stapleton. Three of them: Clifford, David R., Edgar. He tugged David R. from the shelf, but felt distracted by the possibility of someone walking in on him.

He pulled open the file. There, looking back at him, was the mug shot of a younger version of the jumper. He pulled the paper clip and flipped through the pages to the write-up. *Possession and distribution of a controlled substance.* David Stapleton had been busted fourteen months earlier for dealing speed. Dart's finger raced down the sheet to the name of the lead detective: *Roman Kowalski.*

His pager vibrated at his side. "Careful, it's wet!" he heard a slightly hysterical Abby call out loudly.

Dart flicked off the pager, shoved the Stapleton

folder back into the stack, and turned for the file room door.

It took four strides to reach the green cotton rag bracing the door. Dart kicked the rag out of the way and rounded the edge of the closing door in a smooth motion, his right hand seeking out and locating the light switch. As the file room door thumped shut, the light went off simultaneously. Dart picked up the feather duster and beat the desktop violently, the result of too much adrenaline.

He heard a male voice in the hallway call out, "Someone done already clean up here?" A moment of silence lapsed. "Hey, lady, someone already done this floor?" Dart could hear the man's footsteps and the rattle of the man's cart as he drew closer. Ironically, this was worse than being discovered by a Narcotics detective who would pay little or no attention to the lowest of the low: a janitor. But one cleaner erroneously covering another's territory was certain to raise some Irish.

Answer him, Dart mentally encouraged her. He pushed his cart, but only a few inches because the bad wheel cried out, and then ensuing silence engulfed him. There was no way to hide the cart without drawing attention. Dart stood inside the Narco offices feeling completely exposed.

"Somebody *done* mopped the hall," Abby answered. "What do *you* think—that they did it for *fun*?"

The cart stopped rattling, signaling that the man pushing it had come to a halt.

Dart turned and slipped the speed gun into the

file room door, prepared to use this as his hideout. The cleaner wouldn't have a pass key. The unexplained cart would present a problem, but at this hour would anyone make a fuss?

The silence dragged out. Had the cleaner spotted the open door to Narcotics, or had Abby's tone merely humiliated him into thinking this through?

"You could always clean it a second time," she offered sarcastically, regaining her composure. "You people never do a very good job the first time anyway."

"Ain't you a peach," the man replied. "No wonder your sorry ass is working late," the man replied angrily. "Who the hell would want to be with you?"

"Fuck off!"

"Bitch."

"What's your name?"

The cart began to rattle again, and this time more quickly. The cleaner was beating a hasty retreat. She had pushed this into the realm of a personal argument, and as a police officer—as a client—she carried the stronger hand.

Dart waited through the agonizing minutes for the elevator to arrive. He then edged his squeaking cart out into the hall and closed the door. When he glanced at Abby, she was shaking her head at him in disappointment. Dart fingered the brim of his hat in thanks and raced to the elevator, stopping only to snag the WET FLOOR sign and stash it on his cart. He had to return the cart to the first-floor storage room as quickly as possible. He didn't want the cleaning company raising any questions and if he could pull this off, then when the cleaner reported the conflict, Abby would be gone, the floor would be dry, the sign gone, and there would no evidence that any cleaning had taken place. The result would be an impression that the cleaner was trying to shirk some of his duties.

Dart rode the elevator nervously, his finger resting on the CLOSE DOOR button, ready to push.

As the elevator doors slid open, he smelled cigarette smoke and heard a man and a woman in conversation. At this hour, he assumed them to be cleaners. He needed to return the cart and then get out, both without being seen.

The hallway was clear. The voices appeared to be coming from down toward the Property Room, where a door led to the parking lot. *Grabbing a smoke*, he realized.

"Johansen! Get over here!" a voice called out from Dart's left as he was stepping into the hall.

"Coming," the male smoker hollered back.

Johansen, the smoker, would have to pass the elevator to reach that other voice.

The detective stepped back into the car and punched the CLOSE DOOR button. Nothing! He punched it a second time and the doors finally responded, though to Dart they seemed to close more slowly than any pair of elevator doors he had ever encountered. The footsteps of the two smokers approached quickly, and it sounded to him that they would reach the elevator before the doors shut fully.

He tugged the cart parallel to the elevator car's

side wall and squeezed himself with his back against the panel.

But the elevator interior was done in mirror, he realized too late, and as the two smokers passed by, the woman glanced into the car and saw Dart's reflection in the mirror.

Had he managed to appear calm, he might have pulled it off, but as it was, with his face screwed up into a knot and his eyes locked in terror, he gave himself, and his false identity, away. This woman worked with only three other people, and Joe Dartelli was not one of them.

The elevator doors thumped shut, and the car groaned as it lifted.

Dart had not pushed the second-floor button; someone had called the elevator.

Had the desk sergeant been alerted? Were they already looking for an imposter.

Dart tore off the mustache and shed the green work apron, preferring to be discovered as detective Joe Dartelli than a cop inexplicably impersonating a cleaner. As the elevator crawled upward, he prepared himself immediately to voice a complaint about the cleaning cart being left in the elevator.

The elevator bounced to a stop and the doors slid open.

Abby Lang stood facing him. Dart stepped out into the hall feeling vulnerable.

For a brief second, Dart felt caught off guard—his complaint waiting on his lips. He told her triumphantly, "Kowalski investigated Stapleton in a meth case."

When she spoke, tension strangled her words.

"A patrolman came by the office. They know there's an extra cleaner in the building. He headed down the stairs. Told me they would work room by room, both floors. He's young. New to the force. Bored, probably. Taking it *very* seriously," she said. "Did you sign in?" she asked anxiously. During the night shift, all officers, regardless of rank, had to sign in and sign out; the desk sergeant tracked who was there.

"I used the back door," he informed her. "And I didn't call down." He added, "There are worse offenses." There would be no official record of his having entered the building. To him it was a minor offense, but the more he thought about it, one that might be associated with the imposter cleaner and end up a nightmare. The more he considered it, the worse it looked.

"Not good," he admitted.

"We can try the stairs," she suggested wearily, knowing it was a bust.

"The first thing we do is distance you from me," he announced. "You use the stairs. I'll figure something out."

"No," she objected. "I'm part of this."

"You're not."

"I am."

The elevator doors closed, indicating that it had been called.

Dart tried to think of any way out other than the elevator or stairs. It was a fairly large building, though only two stories. And in a room-to-room search he'd be trapped

He thought about walking down the hall, around the corner, and into CAPers, but there would be a skeleton crew there who knew that this wasn't ~~this~~ shift.

"What about the crib?" she asked.

Windowless, a glorified closet used for poker games and quick naps, the crib had been converted from unused storage space. If empty at the moment, Dart realized that he might be able to feign sleep there without raising too much suspicion—although questions would still be asked.

"I'm official," Abby reminded. She had signed in properly. "I have every right to be in this building. Stay here." Dart watched her as she hurried down the hall, passed Narco, and threw open the door to the crib. She reached in and turned on the light.

"Clear," she hissed down the hall at him.

Dart ran to catch up, and as he did a thought occurred to him—a way to avoid the questions—though the likelihood of her going along with it was slim.

They stepped inside and he shut the door and locked it. They were both breathing hard.

"Now what?" she asked. "A game of cards, I suppose?" she asked sarcastically, "At one-thirty in the morning? Oh Christ!"

"Take off your clothes," Dart advised her, already working down his own shirt buttons.

"Yeah, right," she snapped.

"Now!" he said strongly as he continued undressing. He glanced over at the sad excuse of a couch, and Abby Lang blushed, understanding him.

"Oh, shit," she said.

102

"It'll work," he told her.

"Oh, shit," she repeated.

He threw his shirt onto the back of a chair and unfastened his belt and unzipped his pants, adding, "But only with both of us."

She hesitated, looking once to Dart, and then again at the sagging couch. Her fingers reluctantly found the buttons to her blouse and she began to undress herself. As her blouse hung open she suddenly moved more quickly. "I have to tell you," she said apologetically, "that I'm not real comfortable with my body." She mumbled something about having had children and being forty-six, and it was the first time that Dart knew her age.

"I would have guessed mid-to-late thirties," Dart reported honestly, sitting down to pull off his socks.

"No, no, no," she sat straight, clearly uncomfortable with which piece of clothing to remove first. Her blouse hung open and her jeans were unbuttoned and unzipped. "How about the lights?" she asked, sitting down on the edge of the couch and waiting.

Dart tossed her one of the two blankets folded on the shelf. She caught it. He turned off the light and banged a shin coming over toward the sound of her jeans rubbing her skin as she slipped out of them.

A young patrolman would not pursue identifying two detectives sexually engaged in the crib. He would switch on the light, apologize, shut the door, and go tell stories. *It might just work*, he thought. It also occurred to him that it might get them *both* suspended, and he felt awful about that.

Sitting down on the couch, his shin throbbing, Dart felt embarrassed.

He heard the unmistakable snap of her bra coming off, and she whispered, "Underwear?"

"Let's leave it on." His skin prickled with heat.

"Agreed!" she replied.

"Sorry about this," he said, groping in the dark for her.

They hugged awkwardly, clumsily, and lay down together. She pulled the blanket over them. "How weird," she said. But then she wrapped her arms around him strongly and held to him tightly, and said, "This is *not* a pass, Joe. I'm frightened."

"You didn't need to—"

"Sh!" She held him more tightly. "A little late at this point."

As if to punish himself, Dart suddenly became aroused. He wanted to say something, to make some excuse, to apologize, but he said nothing, attempting to move away from her instead but finding the couch too narrow.

Abby said, "This definitely goes into the books as the strangest first date." She chuckled; Dart laughed, and then they shushed each other, which only served to make them laugh all the harder. Their chests bounced together with the nervous laughter and it fed on itself until it was uncontrollable. Trying to suppress it only made it worse.

Rubbing herself against his erection, still laughing, she said, "Maybe someday we can make the most of that."

"I've got one for you," she added, the both of them tight with laughter. "What if they give up the search?"

Dart buried his face into her shoulder and muffled his laughter. "We could be here all night," he said. He felt her nodding along with him.

When she placed her open hand on his head and held him to her skin, their laughter stopped, running down like a windup clock. The mood changed in this instant. Dart felt his arousal even more substantial. She stroked his back.

"Abby?" he said.

"I know," she answered in a whisper, while her hands kept petting him. "No harm in hugging, is there?"

And so they hugged each other intimately, warmly, affectionately—the kind of hug that can take the place of breathing, he thought. *It can take the place of food, and confuse time, and stop all thought.*

"Maybe they won't come," she said, kissing his cheek and moving toward his lips. All humor associated with that thought had passed.

He kissed her, tentatively at first, and then with the passion that consumed him. She returned the kiss, parting her lips and opening her mouth to him.

When the door opened a few minutes later, Dart failed to look up. He had planned to say *Get the fuck out of here*, because he enjoyed the irony of the statement. But he just kept kissing her instead, oblivious to the intrusion.

The voice of the young cop said hastily, "Sorry, sir," and the door bumped shut.

Abby Lang began to laugh. She held Dart close and whispered, "I'd forgotten all about that."

"Yeah, me too," said Joe Dart.

CHAPTER
10

Knowing what had to be done, and doing it, were two different things, especially given the consequences: death. Contemplating another man's death was a power all its own. As much as this man wanted to believe otherwise, to ignore the palpable high coursing in his veins was nearly impossible. Tonight, his was the power of God, there was no denying it. He felt drawn toward intoxication, but he resisted this. He felt like humming, and so he did, though out of tune— he had never held a tune in his life.

He stood on a Hefty garbage bag just inside the back door and stripped naked, revealing his uncomfortably thin body. Carefully stepping off the garbage bag, he turned it inside out, capturing the clothing, and slung the bag over his shoulder like Santa Claus, and carried it through the sitting room, up the narrow stairs and into the bedroom, where he set it down into the closet.

He entered the bathroom still humming, his gaunt frame a stranger to him—he still thought of himself as the muscular beefmeister he had once been. Wearing the latex gloves that he had donned prior to entry, he opened the medicine cabinet. A small wire showed in the metal seam of the cabinet, and as he pulled on this the entire cabinet came free of the wall, and he set it aside, revealing a clear glass vial, a box of disposable syringes, and a box of needles. He removed the vial and a single syringe and a needle and returned the medicine cabinet to the wall so that he could see himself in the mirror.

He hated this part: the needles, the pain.

Standing before the mirror he studied his face, wiped the alcohol-soaked cotton ball across the sun-hardened, aged skin, lifted the syringe, and pricked the needle into his top lip, wincing with the puncture, and drawing a drop of blood. The injected fluid stung and itched at the same time—histamines—and the lip swelled and enlarged almost immediately, turning a bright red, as if an insect had bitten him. The lower lip was next, and again he winced. He worked his lips, as would someone standing too long in the cold, and attempted to speak. "Good evening," he said to the mirror, working his puffy lips painfully until they formed the words more clearly. "Good evening, Mr. Payne."

Another injection, just below the mandible joints, produced swollen jowls and distorted his face magnificently. But it was the two shots, one below each eye, that altered him to the point of establishing a new identity. He was, at once, a squinty, puffy-faced bulldog with gray hair showing around the edge of the Yankees baseball cap—synthetic wig hair sewn to the edges of the cap, not his at all.

The image in the mirror was no longer that of the man who stood before it, but instead one Wallace Sparco—the name on the bills, the apartment lease, and even on the credit cards that had bought the clothes hanging in the upstairs closet. An invented identity. The man did not feel himself as Sparco—he wouldn't allow himself to go that far, to allow that dangerous switch to be thrown in his head. He knew damn well who he was and what was going on here—he was going to kill a man. A worthless piece of shit. He was going to fix things. He was more than willing to make the sacrifice necessary. Prepared. But he would not allow himself to enjoy it—despite the occasional rush—try as part of him did to do just that—and he would not allow any part of himself to fool any other part: It was wrong to kill, regardless of the justification; he knew this in his heart, his soul, in the quiet depths of his being. He was doing a job, that's all. Charity work.

He kept humming as he drew the cosmetic pencil through his thin eyebrows, darkening them. He envied Pavarotti that enormous talent, that gift. He thought of Mozart as a freak—some step beyond genius. Einstein belonged there with him. Michelangelo. Cuban cigars. Mexican beer. The stuff of life.

And in this mirror, another man, a man of his invention—there were many ways to play God.

You do what you have to do, he reminded himself.

The face that had started in this mirror before

the charade of the injected histamines was one this man hardly recognized as his own: gaunt and drawn, pale, with jaundiced eyes. He thought of himself as handsome, but the face he saw there was not.

He drove an old beat-up Mazda two-door, registered to Mr. Wallace Sparco, dressed in Mr. Sparco's clothing, and wore Mr. Sparco's old brown shoes, Timex watch, leather belt, and carried his nylon wallet. He slouched as the fictitious Mr. Sparco slouched and yet he hummed as only the driver hummed.

He drove up the hill toward Trinity College, the view to his right a spectacular display of the sparkling lights of the valley, and slowed before turning left as the street became chaotic with costumed college-aged trick-or-treaters out for an evening of self-abuse. The costumes were products of educated imaginations, and the willowy, womanly legs, clad in black tights, were those of eighteen-year-old WASPs, wobbly from beer and steadied, no doubt, by concern and giddy anticipation. Mr. Wallace Sparco drove slowly through the teeming students, reminded of Mardi Gras. He beeped his horn lightly and turned left, not understanding exactly why he bothered to drive up the hill but deciding each life, even that of Wallace Sparco, was entitled to the occasional distraction. Back on course, he made his way to Farmington Avenue and headed for the affluence of West Hartford only a short ten-minute drive away, where the dismal poverty of the south end ghetto gave way to the manicured comfort of the Caucasian enclave, where black gave way to white, and project housing to suburbia. The AMEX cards were quiet tonight, the downtown deserted. Parents were home supervising another Halloween. A few minutes past the retail core, Wallace Sparco turned right and, a few minutes after that, on into the nestled canopy of darkness and the colonial-style homes that hid here from the fear of the inner city only a few short miles to the east.

Wallace Sparco turned left onto Westmont and up the winding hill, then right onto Wendy Lane, driving to the very end of the cul-de-sac, where he pulled into and drove down the long driveway of the Tudor house marked with the Twentieth Century Real Estate sign, switched off his headlights, and parked. He waited five minutes in absolute silence. The area in front of the garage could be seen from only one aspect of one other house, a neighbor a hundred yards away through thick woods. The Tudor was shown occasionally, and when it was, it was often at night to accommodate a working couple. But it wouldn't be shown tonight because Wallace Sparco, introducing himself as Alfred Gluck, had booked a showing with the agent who carried the listing— the rendezvous planned at the agent's office, six miles away and scheduled for an hour earlier. By this hour, a no-show. Now, all his.

The back wall of 37 Orchard Street, covered in the gray, strangling veins of dormant ivy vines, could be seen through the two acres of barren autumn woods. Payne's young and attractive wife was said to be at her regular Wednesday dinner with friends, where she would remain until dropped off at 10:00 P.M. She was, in fact, fucking wildly with the man who headed the local community theater group, a man ten years her junior who paid an uncanny resemblance to Dustin Hoffman but possessing little talent. *At least acting talent*, he thought. She had never once, in the three weeks that he had kept her under surveillance, made it home before ten, leaving her husband, Harold, on this night, to become a victim. A statistic. A suicide.

Reviewing his carefully orchestrated plan, Wallace Sparco checked his Timex watch and saw that he had a full fifty minutes to accomplish what had to be done.

Plenty of time in which to play God.

CHAPTER
11

Colt Park occupied nearly twenty city blocks of open grounds, with copses of trees—maples, oaks, pines—a jungle gym and a parking lot. Like any of Hartford's city parks, after sunset it was not a particularly safe place. Dart kept his eyes open for movement and his ears alert. He felt on edge.

The occasional ghost or goblin appeared on the sidewalk, far in the distance, for this was the night of tricks or treats, a night any cop dreaded, a night as unpredictable as New Year's Eve or the Fourth of July. By midnight, the gangs would be out in full force. By one o'clock in the morning a teenager would be dead of a bullet wound; on Halloween, that was virtually guaranteed.

Dart waited for her in the early evening dusk that arrives in October like an unwanted cousin, waited beneath a yellow cone of an overhead street lamp, waited nervously for a woman he had loved too recently to forget but had loved too strongly to allow himself to fully remember, waited as a few early-fallen oak leaves tumbled across the grass sounding like spilled seashells, waited and felt hurt. The heat of Indian summer had surrendered to the insistent cool of autumn, the sky seemed a gloomier color, and the air had lost its fragrance. For the last two weeks, Dart had gone about his regular job of domestic assaults and gang-related homicides. But it was the string of suicides that occupied his mind. He had reviewed reports, studied photographs, and kept a keen eye on Roman Kowalski. He had not spoken to Abby Lang. Their night in the crib had not gone past kissing, and yet they passed each other in the halls with only a furtive glance, as if by sharing too much too soon, by breaking all kinds of rules together, personal and professional, they had erected a wall between them.

Ginny wore a dark overcoat that covered her to her ankles. A scarf curled loosely around her neck. She had parked out on the street and crossed the corner of the park at a brisk pace, properly concerned about her choice of location for the rendezvous.

Dart moved out from under the parking lot lamp, cloaked by the gray dusk, to where the two of them, observed from a distance, would appear as two indistinguishable forms in a quickly thickening mist.

"Hi," she said softly, unbuttoning her coat and removing an envelope that she then handed him.

"What's this?"

"Priscilla Cole, as you asked. Her med insurance records."

He had lived with Ginny long enough to interpret her expressions. The eight months that they had been apart seemed only a matter of days at times like this. "What about them?"

"One of the very seamy sides of the insurance world is the attempt on the part of the insurers to—as they put it: protect themselves from unforeseen losses. Unexpected losses. If you live in Los Angeles or San Francisco they may deny or limit earthquake coverage. If you're a known drunk they may refuse to insure your auto. The same practice carries over into medical coverage. Smokers may be restricted to certain qualified coverage, excluding or limiting what will be paid out for emphysema or asthma, lung cancer or other pulmonary disorders."

"I follow you."

"There is software in place in every major underwriter to flag possible 'high-risk' cases. It's insidious, but there you are."

"And you're involved."

"I police the software, right? I keep the code healthy and running. All kinds of software, including this screening variety. It locates and flags questionable accounts that are then reviewed in-house. If necessary, the coverage is reduced or even canceled. I'm part of it, Dart, just so you understand. Not proud of it, but part of it."

Dart felt restless and nervous, both a product of their surroundings and Ginny's blatant anxiety. He wanted to hurry her along, but knew better. She went at her own speed—in *everything*.

"David Stapleton's claims were not flagged, but his girlfriend's were—this Priscilla Cole."

"Flagged for what?" He'd hoped that Teddy Bragg's 3-D software was indeed glitched, but Bragg had gotten back to him complaining that the company claimed the software was error-free. For his own sake, he hoped that she might report that Priscilla Cole had been diagnosed with HIV, and that Stapleton had taken his own life to avoid its horrors.

"Battered-wife syndrome," she replied, her eyes fixed onto him.

This was not what Dart had expected. He had trouble forming his thoughts, much less thinking of something pertinent to say. His thoughts were stuck on the Ice Man and Gerald Lawrence—on sex offense. He'd been relieved that Stapleton had not had any such charges filed against him—only a Narco record, and that did not connect well with either of the other suicides. *And now this*, he thought.

She explained, "Priscilla Cole was repeatedly admitted to emergency rooms with unexplained contusions and fractures, vaginal tearing, bite marks—you name it. The software is written to identify such injuries and flag the account. Victims of domestic violence are denied coverage by all major insurers but one. There are laws being proposed to change that, but at the moment that's how it stands. She had two policies canceled, and was on the verge of losing all coverage because we're in the process, right now, of linking all major health databases. Once that is complete, everyone will know everyone else's secrets. There will be no switching companies in an effort to outrun your past."

"Or present," he said.

"Exactly."

"Stapleton beat her," he stated. He could hardly get the words out. *Sex offense*, he thought.

"We don't know it was Stapleton, no. There's no mention of him."

"But the addresses! What about the addresses?"

She nodded. "The second policy to be canceled had the Battles Street address that you gave me."

"Shit." Of the three suicides, Stapleton, Lawrence, and the Ice Man, all were—in one way or another—guilty of violence against women. And if someone were targeting these violent men to become victims themselves, there were now two clear ways that Dart saw to spot them: men convicted of sex crimes and men involved with battered women. It was a connection that ran tension into his neck and made his fingers cold. *Zeller?* he wondered again. He asked Ginny, "Can you get me a list of other women?"

"Abused women?"

115

"Yes."

"I can try."

"I don't want you getting yourself in trouble."

"It's not *legal*, if that's what you're saying."

"I could subpoena it."

"If you have a few years, you could, yes. My guess is that they'd deny the existence of any such list—it amounts to a form of discrimination, after all. Their claim is that the woman has the choice of leaving the man who is doing this to her—that to stay is a voluntary act. It's the old 'she wants it' argument. They ignore the psychological factors, the existence of children and families—it's barbaric, is what it is."

"If you could get it for me, then at least I'd have it while I go through the subpoena process. But I don't want you taking any chances, Gin. It's important to me that you understand that." He knew this was the type of challenge she lived for—to raid a computer system and lift information, but she'd been arrested and convicted once already—a second offense would be far more serious.

"I want to help, Dart. Don't ask me why, because I don't know exactly. Maybe I feel guilty about the breakup. Maybe I'd like to see us back together. I don't really want to think about all that. I just want to help."

"It feels awkward to me, your helping."

"You *asked* me to look into it for you."

Did he want to be in debt to her? It felt as if that were where they were heading, and it didn't feel good.

She said, "You're worried about me. How sweet."

He couldn't tell if she was being sarcastic or straight with him, and he wondered when it was that he had lost track of such nuances. *People get so close that they grow apart*, he thought, wondering if every relationship was doomed before it began and feeling an ache deep within him.

CHAPTER
12

Joe Dart headed home to spend the rest of his Halloween alone. He channel-surfed, finding nothing but stupid sitcoms with everyone in costume, and black-and-white monster movies with sinister sound tracks.

Two beers later, he conjured up the nerve to call Abby Lang. She answered on the third ring, and he asked if she was busy, and she said not terribly and asked what he had in mind. "Have you ever been a costume judge?" he asked her.

Together, they drove in and around Trinity College searching out the best costume. Dart was the designated driver. Abby sampled from a thermos of scorpions, her mood becoming lighter with each passing mile. An hour into it, she slid over next to him so that they were like two teen-agers cruising Main. When either of them spotted an award-winning costume, Abby would hop out of the car and snap a Polaroid, using Dart's crime scene camera. She then stood the photos on the dash, lined up like mug shots, until she accidentally bumped the defrost switch and sent them flying.

They rated a phosphorescent glow-in-the-dark skeleton highly; a monster with green hair and an enormous wart-encrusted nose won a place in their top five, as did a giant turtle. But the blue ribbon went to a group of seven students, each dressed as a spear of green asparagus, the lot of them bound together around the middle with a blue sash as if contained in a rubber band. Deciding that seven walking spears of asparagus could not be topped, the two headed to Abby's downtown loft, so that Dart could partake of the scorpions.

The loft was near the train tracks in a no-man's-land across the Bulkeley Bridge, an area of town unfamiliar to him. It was a second-story loft, accessed by a clunky old freight elevator that smelled of sawdust and burning electrical motors, and gave Dart the impression of entering an abandoned building. But on the other side of the steel door to the apartment was a world all Abby's. She had sanded the wood plank floors back to blond, and had hung seven white and green silk parachutes as her ceiling with the fixtures on the other side of the fabric so that the vast open space glowed in a soft, flattering light. White sheetrock walls defined the kitchen, to the right, and a bath, some partitioned bedrooms, an office, and closet to the left. Directly ahead, a pot-bellied wood stove served as the focal point of lawn furniture with green striped cushions, including two chaise lounges and a quirky chess set that she used as a side table.

"Do you play?" he asked her as he built a fire at her request.

"Is that a come-on?" she answered.

"Chess."

"Yes. And bridge and tennis and softball. And volleyball if it's a sand court. I can't play indoors anymore."

"Where are the kids?"

"I dumped them off with a friend," she answered. Then she added, "For the night." And Dart felt her answer clear down to his toes.

"That's where I'm lucky," she continued. "Being a one-person division, I can pretty much make my own hours."

He heard her mixing the drinks. He felt that he had somehow invited himself to stay with her, and that wasn't his intention—*or was it?* he wondered. The bottom line was that he felt awkward, stretched out on a chaise lounge beneath a parachute, a fire crackling in front of him and a woman, four or five years older than he, mixing drinks in a kitchen half a block away.

"You're going to love this batch," she announced.

She had pulled off her sweater and unbuttoned the top two buttons of her shirt. She had kicked off her shoes so that he could see her toes wiggle nervously as she took the chaise lounge next to him and placed a tray bearing a pitcher of scorpions and their two filled cocktail glasses. The paper napkins had Gary Larson cartoons on them, and the swizzle sticks read: Cactus Pete's Casino, Jackpot, Nevada. Dart felt outgunned.

She jumped up and put on a CD—south-of-the-border guitar instrumentals. He sipped the drink—mixed to kill—and felt himself relax.

"That was nice what you did for Lewellan," she said, her eyes on the fire. "Arranging with the mother to allow the girl the rabbits. A homicide dick with a heart—now there's a concept."

He felt his face flush hot. "It just seemed to make sense, that's all."

"You don't have to apologize. I'm not going to rat on you. I think it's sweet."

Trying to steer the topic away from himself, he said, "She's so . . . young? I don't know how you do it."

"Innocent?" she asked.

"That's what I wanted to say, yes. But she isn't, is she?"

"No. Not thanks to Gerry Law."

"I couldn't do your job."

"We each find our calling."

He wanted to ask her how she had ended up in sex crimes and sex offenses, and then he realized that he didn't want to know. He admired her. He felt a little intimidated. Could he date a lieutenant? "Packs a punch," he said of the drink.

"You can handle it," she replied, drinking down a liberal amount and wiggling her toes again.

The music took over, punctuated by sparks from the fire. She topped off his drink. He was well on his way to drunk. "The turtle was pretty good," she said, recalling the costumes.

"Um," Dart answered. "But the asparagus was genius."

"Yeah. Incredible. You went kind of weird after our night in the crib," she said honestly, the booze getting to her. "Was that so bad?" She added, "I thought it was fun."

He looked over at her, but she kept her attention on the fire, letting him look. He finally admitted, "I enjoyed it. I guess I felt awkward. I don't know."

"You've been treating me like I don't exist."

"I felt like I forced you into that."

"Into kissing you?" she asked. "Are you kidding?" She enjoyed some more of the drink. "Into taking my clothes off, maybe." She laughed. "It certainly was an interesting first date." She rocked her head and looked directly at him. Her eyes were smiling. Glassy. Her lips were a deep red and moist from the drink, and if their chaise lounges had been closer together he would have tried to kiss her. "What are you thinking?" she asked slyly.

"Nervous," he confessed.

"Good."

"Why is that good?" he questioned.

"I have my reasons." Abby got up and moved the table with the drinks and pushed her chaise lounge closer to his. She teased, "If this bothers you, keep it to yourself. I'm feeling particularly good at the moment, and I can be dangerous when I feel this good."

"I like danger," he answered, reaching out for her hand and taking hers. "Is this all right?" he asked.

121

"This is perfect," she answered, holding a knowing smile on her face. Dart felt suddenly at risk, under her spell—*her control*, he feared—and it made him uneasy.

"You're not going to freak out, are you?" she asked.

You know me already, he thought.

She explained, "I like your company. Especially tonight. I make no claim to ownership. I ask nothing more of you than to relax and enjoy yourself. We're both adults. We're allowed this now and then." She squeezed his hand in hers as a signal. "Okay with you?"

"I needed to hear that."

"Good. I needed to say it."

"It doesn't make me any less nervous," he told her and they both laughed—she confidently; he as a form of release.

She handed him her drink then, and with his both his hands occupied, she leaned over, her shirt falling away from her, and she kissed him wetly on the lips. She took his breath away, and she bit his lower lip and he felt it to his toes. He returned the kiss, awkwardly juggling the two drinks, and her hand found its way inside his shirt and over his chest and he was immediately aroused. "One thing nice about middle age," she whispered into his ear in a way that gave him chills, "is that you know what you like..what makes you feel good . . ."—she stroked his chest—"what turns you on. And even better," she added, "you aren't afraid to enjoy yourself." She helped him set down the drinks, and she climbed over the arms of the chaise lounges and straddled Dart and met eyes with him. "You know?" she inquired.

"It's been a long time," he told her, by way of apology.

"I'm a very patient woman," she said, pulling him forward so that he sat up, and tricking the chair into a full recline. Then she eased him back and lay down atop him, and a heat grew where they touched.

He wrapped his arms around her strongly and held her, and she nuzzled her chin into the crook of his neck, kissed him once lightly, and hummed affectionately. "There's nothing quite so amazing in this world as a good hug," she said. "Sex is over before you know it, but the right kind of hug lasts forever."

"Is this the right kind?" he asked.

"You bet," she answered.

Thirty minutes later, when a distant city clock chimed midnight, she took Dart's hand and pulled him out of the chaise lounge and led him around a Japanese paper screen to a small bedroom that contained a pine chest, two long rows of hanging clothes, and, on the floor, a futon with a down comforter. She turned and faced him and pulled the shirt over her head. Her bra was translucent, her nipples hard. She undid her jeans and stepped out of them, and Dart was reminded of their night in the crib. She said, "Do me a favor and at least take off your shoes."

She slipped under the covers, her back to him. Dart undressed fully and climbed in beside her, pressing to her back like spoons. He reached around her and cupped her breasts and hugged her, and she hummed. The air trapped in the covers smelled of her arousal and penetrated Dart to his core. They remained this way for several long minutes, Dart stroking her breasts lightly, Abby, head bent, kissing his arms and hands. It felt to him that they had been lovers for a very long time and that they knew each other's secrets and pleasures. His fingers explored her, and she slipped out of her underpants and bra, and she found a condom in a bedside box and said something about safe sex and rolled him over and put it on him. She kissed him then, and rolled them over together so that Dart lay atop her. "Gentle at first," she requested, taking hold of him and rubbing him against her in a way that offered her pleasure and made her shudder. "Rough at the end." She helped him to enter her, holding his hips to limit his penetration, and together they found a complementing rhythm. "Deeper," she advised, reaching around to his buttocks and thrusting him inside her.

He drew his tongue across her firm nipple and felt a ripple of energy crawl through her as she cried out and pulled him harder and faster, orchestrating him within her as she arched her back, driving her breast into his waiting mouth and opening herself to him fully so that as he cupped her buttocks and lifted her to him she encouraged him—"Do it! Give it to me!"—and shouted as Dart swelled inside her.

She came first, and Dart a second later, lifting her off the mattress and driving her head toward the wall, which she pushed against to force him even further inside her, and she cried out again, her eyes wide open in delight, spasms of pleasure milking his release, until they collapsed in a sweaty embrace, out of breath and spent with exhaustion.

She kissed his neck lightly and ran her fingers down his back and giggled approvingly. "I knew it," she said happily, the only words she offered. She held him tightly and wouldn't let him off of her, even after they slipped apart, lingering in the glow of the moment.

"Will you stay with me?" she asked.

"Uh-huh," he answered, kissing behind her ear, working down her neck, and finding her breast and kissing her there too.

"Maybe hugging comes in second," she said a while later, and Dart dozed off with a smile on his face.

A beeping sound, emanating from Dart's clothing, awakened them just after ten-thirty that same night.

He slipped out of bed.

"I protest!" she complained. "You traded out," she reminded him.

He carried the pager into the light of the other room and read the CAPers phone number off its LCD display. He called in to Jennings Road, speaking with Sergeant Haite. He hung up immediately, sneaked into the room, and collected his things. "Gotta go," he told her in a whisper, grateful that she, unlike Ginny, would understand such things.

"Will you come back?" she offered. "Please."

"I'll try. It's over in West Hartford. I'll be a couple hours at least."

"Why bother with something in West Hartford?" she asked, coming more fully awake. West Hartford was out of their jurisdiction. She answered herself immediately, confirming that even half-asleep she could think faster than most detectives. "Another suicide," she said.

"Right." He clipped the pager to his belt and checked his sidearm and holster. "Another suicide," he confirmed. "West Hartford asked for our help." Many of the neighboring towns had little more than patrol squads, using either HPD or the State Police for the bigger investigations.

"Any record?" she asked, flicking on the bedside light, with no inclination toward modesty. She had long since passed the age of pinup girl, but she had nothing to hide.

He hesitated, and she asked him a second time.

"A pornography conviction," he said.

"I'm coming with you," she announced, throwing the covers off.

Dart knew better than to argue.

Orchard Road climbed high up a hill, offering a spectacular view of the distant city. This was the high-rent district: half a million dollars and up for a three-bedroom on an acre. Woods. Ponds. Views. Beamers. Rolexes. Divorces. And silicon implants.

Dart pulled the Volvo into the curving drive and parked alongside an HPD patrol car in front of the brick-and-stone two-story house. Abby yanked the rearview mirror toward her and ran a brush through her hair. They both hung their badges around their necks and entered by the front door.

"Tuna's got the wife upstairs," announced patrolman Benny Webster. Tanya Fische, an HPD patrol officer, referred to as Tuna, was clearly Webster's patrol partner. "The wife popped a bunch of Valium and is in la-la land. No use to us until morning. We ain't touched nothing in the study. But it's a messy one," he said, eyeing Abby Lang as if she might have trouble stomaching it. "Single shot up through the roof of the mouth. Nine millimeter."

"Who's on it?" Dart asked.

"Kowalski and—" he answered.

Dart and Abby met eyes, interrupting the uniformed man.

"Something wrong?" Webster asked, seeing this.

"Everything's just ducky," Abby answered.

Webster continued, "And their assistant chief."

"West Hartford's?" Dart clarified. "Nolan?" he said, adding the name.

"That's him. Yeah. Only he ain't here. Showed up, talked to the K," he said, meaning Kowalski, "and took off. It being a suicide and all, he didn't seem too bothered."

"Wanted to brief his chief and prepare a statement," came the voice of Roman Kowalski. He looked tired; the buttons on his shirt indicated he had dressed hastily. "What brings *you* here?" he asked Dart.

"Sergeant Haite."

"And you?" he asked Abby.

She didn't want to explain her having been with Dartelli. She said for Kowalski's benefit, "'And you, *Lieutenant.*' Is that what you meant to say, Detective?"

Kowalski glared at her. "The wife was out with friends 'til about an hour ago. Comes home, finds the hubby spread all over the study. Calls nine-eleven." Kowalski eyed Abby again, and Dart realized that maybe he was busy with his arithmetic.

The entrance foyer had a low ceiling with hand-hewn dark timbers and plaster that had pieces of yellow hay stuck into it. To Dart's left, a gray-carpeted stairway ascended to the second floor. He passed a small stone column supporting a wicker basket filled with trick-or-treat candy and fresh fruit. He thought that on this of all nights, Halloween, there would have been, should have been, potential witnesses around and about.

"Did she find the house locked or open?" he asked Kowalski.

"If you want to sit in the fucking bleachers and watch, I got no problem," Kowalski said. "But if you want to play Twenty Questions, fucking take it somewhere else."

"You know what's amazing about you," Abby told Kowalski, stepping past him and moving toward the open study door, "is how delicately you handle the language."

He opened his mouth to reply, but she cut him off, raising a finger at him, "And be careful what you say to your *superiors*, Detective." With extra venom she added," 'Cause I'll bust you down to traffic, given half the chance."

Dart smiled at Kowalski and raised his eyebrows, taunting him.

Stepping up to Dartelli, Kowalski said earnestly, "I'm waiting on Buzz before I go in there. Don't touch a fucking thing." He pulled a pack of Marlboros from his coat pocket and stuck one in his mouth. "I'll be outside."

The study was the size of Dart's studio kitchen and sitting area combined. Oriental rugs, dark antiques, a stone-and-brick fireplace with two gargoyles supporting the four-inch thick, burl walnut mantel. A substantial puddle of blood on the rug below the deceased. Splatter pattern on the ceiling consistent with the top of a human head coming off. An oil portrait of a man with a bulbous red nose, who lived back when the river trade kept Hartford prosperous, ruled from above the mantel. Leather-bound books crammed the shelves, looking both untouched and unread. Window dressing. Dart noticed a few spaces between the volumes, like missing teeth.

The body was a mess, draped over a walnut chair with a needlepoint cushion. What remained of the head was angled back away from the blast and discharge of the weapon. The top half of the man's clothes was brown with drying blood— buckets of it.

"Harold C. Payne," Abby Lang read, fingering a mailing label on a copy of *Arts and Antiques* left on a cherry side table in the hall. "I didn't recognize him without his face."

"You remember him?"

"Cyber-porn. Fuck shots and D-cup starlets over the Internet. Mail-order photo-CD-ROM. Digitized pornography. The Feds brought him down, but I was consulted. Yeah, I remember him."

"Sounds like a real sweetheart," Dart said.

"Piece of work, this one. Hired himself four attorneys and got himself acquitted on all but the mail-order charge, if I'm remembering right."

Dart wasn't about to question her memory.

She said, "The whole area of pornography over the Internet remains a little fuzzy—you'll pardon the expression. It's still being sorted out."

"Is there a file on him in Sex Crimes?" Dart questioned.

She met eyes with him, understanding what he was asking. "No," she answered simply but delivering the message that she did not appreciate the implications of his question. Her eyes said, *No one gets in my files without me knowing about it.*

Attempting to change subjects, Dart pointed out the snifter of cognac on the partner's desk, a spilled ashtray at the foot of the deceased's chair, and the butt of a cigar on the rug. It appeared that Payne had poured himself a drink, had a smoke, and then ate a barrel.

A walnut armoire was wedged into the corner immediately to the left. The rest of that wall was floor-to-ceiling book-shelves. Four leaded windows occupied most of the wall behind the desk where a computer was set up on a custom-built return.

Before Bragg and the others arrived, while he still had a moment of peace, Dart studied the crime scene. A husband left alone while the wife went to a party, a glass of cognac, a cigar, and a bullet through the roof of his mouth. *The perfect suicide*, he thought, believing to his very core that Payne had been murdered. On the edge of the desk he spotted what appeared to be a gun-cleaning kit and what was clearly a box of shells. No suicide note that he could see, but the wife might have found one. The gun hung awkwardly from the dead man's right thumb; Dart could predict that paraffin tests would confirm that the same hand had fired the weapon, and he wondered how that could have been accomplished.

Unlike the other suicides, he viewed this one as the audience views a magic show: looking for the tricks. He tried to reconstruct how a Zeller or a Kowalski could paint so clear a picture. A speed key or other lock-picking device could get a killer inside—no trick there. But then what? Overpower Payne—knock him unconscious, careful to tap him on that part of his head that would later shatter when the bullet entered. *You would have to know about the gun*, he thought. Some advance work would have to be done. But guns were registered, and most home weapons were kept in bedside drawers or on the top shelves of closets.

What ate at him was the absence of physical evidence. At the Stapleton jump, the trace evidence—crucial to any investigation—gave no indication of the presence of a mystery visitor.

The Lawrence hanging evidence had come in the same way: Teddy Bragg's report indicated finding some copper filings on the body—these from the lamp cord used for the hanging, the anticipated random cotton and synthetic fibers typical to any floor, and head and body hairs, but only from the victim. No evidence to suggest foul play. The scenario before him placed out the same way—it appeared a straight-ahead suicide. Having been trained in criminalistics, this is where Dart put his faith—the transference of evidence was virtually impossible to avoid; hairs and fibers were in a constant state of exchange: the person entering a room deposited such evidence; the person leaving a room carried such evidence with him. Every variety of organic matter from leaves to pollen, car-floor carpeting, clothing, food, seeds, hairs, dirt, and dust. It seemed inconceivable that the suicides had been staged without any such evidence being shed— and Dart knew that this was *exactly* what the prosecuting attorney would say: "No evidence, no case."

Webster wandered over to check on them, and Abby asked him, "Did the wife enter the study?"

"Says she did, yeah. Said she felt for his pulse—his left hand." He chuckled. "Can you imagine thinking that the *thing* in that chair might have a pulse. You talk about dreaming."

"How long was she in the room?" Dart asked him.

"Don't know. Didn't say."

Dart, his mind on fiber evidence, dropped to one knee and brought his head nearly to the floor, looking into the room. To Webster Dart said, "She was wearing slippers: blue fuzzy slippers. Is that right?" He glanced up at the patrolman, who appeared not to remember.

"I . . . ah . . . ."

"Find out."

"Yes, sir." Webster took off a brisk pace, and Dart could hear him charging up the stairs.

"What?" Abby asked, kneeling.

"Get down low." Dart demonstrated, nearly touching his ear to the floor.

Abby teased, "I love it when you talk dirty," and then duplicated his actions.

"See them? The fibers?" he asked. "Play with your focus," he instructed.

"Got 'em!" she exclaimed excitedly. "Blue fibers!"

"Yup. And do you see where they lead?"

"To the armoire. Not to the body."

"Yup. And?"

She rocked her head, and they were nearly kissing, both of them with their ears to the hardwood floor. "There's a dark swath cut down the rug between here and the deceased."

"You're good," Dart told her. Her bottom was sticking high in the air, and for a moment he wasn't thinking about fiber evidence.

"And there's a lighter swath between the armoire and the desk."

"The nap is worn down."

"That's a hell of a lot of trips to the armoire," she pointed out.

"I agree."

"And the darker swath?" she asked.

"The nap is *raised*," he pointed out. "It's going a different direction from the rest of the nap."

"Why?" she asked.

"Exactly." With the pieces coming together in his head, Dart wanted into the room, and was tired of waiting for Teddy Bragg. He told Abby, "Wait here. Don't let anyone inside."

"Joe?"

He hurried off. In the foyer, he ran into Webster just coming down the stairs. The patrolman confirmed, "Blue fuzzy slippers, Detective. She's still wearing them."

Kowalski was admiring the view, working on his second cigarette. As Dart passed him, Kowalski asked, "Are you fucking her, Dartelli?" Dart kept walking. "The reason I ask is she has that look, you know? All rosy around the chest and neck. A little more smiley than normal for her. And because on account of I'm only seeing your car out here, so I'm thinking the two of you rode together, and it's kinda late for that." Dart reached his car. "She any good, Dartelli? You know, if what they say about how a woman's lips are the same in both places, I'd say you scored big."

"Shut up, Kowalski," Dart said, fishing two pairs of shoe covers and latex gloves out of the back of the Volvo where Dart kept a first-aid kit, a flak vest, and an evidence collection kit.

"Real nice mouth on her," Kowalski said.

Dart shut the back of the wagon and heard a vehicle approaching. *Probably Teddy*, he realized, deciding to hurry. He passed Kowalski but then stopped. He said, "You know, I used to think that you're as dumb as everyone says you are, as dumb as you act." The big man's head pivoted, and he looked into Dart's eyes. Dart continued, "If you've fucked with these crime scenes in any way, I'm going to have your ass." Smoke flowed out of Kowalski's nose, and he squinted at Dart with such loathing that the detective thought he might take a swing at him. "Tell Teddy that I went in without him."

"You can't do that!" Kowalski protested.

Dart held up the paper shoe covers. "So stop me." He turned and went inside.

At the study door, with Bragg's step van just pulling up outside, Dart and Abby slipped the paper shoe covers over their shoes and donned latex gloves.

Dart told her, "I want you to guide me. Keep me away from the blue fibers wherever possible, and off that raised nap."

Dart kept close to the near wall and reached the armoire without requiring any directions from Abby.

"Exactly what are you looking for?" she asked.

He opened the armoire, revealing a large television and an assortment of stereo equipment. He ran his gloved hand blindly along the interior of the piece of furniture.

"What's up, Joe?" she asked.

Dart's fingers bumped a stout piece of metal concealed beneath the first shelf. He hooked it, pushed it, pulled it. *Pop*! The edge of the armoire jumped away from the wall. Dart slid his fingers into the crack and pulled it open like a door.

"Jesus . . .," she gasped.

"Stay close to the wall," he advised.

Abby joined him. Dart pulled the armoire all the way open and found the interior light switch.

They heard the front door open and the voices of Kowalski and Teddy Bragg.

"Don't touch anything," Dart said as he led the way into the hidden room.

The room had no windows. The area closest to the hidden door was laid out like a computer/ video laboratory, the remainder dedicated to library stacks crowded with books of every shape and size, cloth and leather-bound. On closer examination, the books appeared worn and quite old. One of the stacks held several long rows of video tapes.

"Ten to one," Abby said, "this is the evidence that the Feds never found."

The electronic equipment included two computers, a white table, several lights on tripods, two video cameras, a scanner, a color laser printer, and a multiline telephone.

"Nice gear," Dart said.

"Major money," she said.

A VCR and twenty-seven-inch television occupied a separate table.

Kowalski entered behind them. Dart looked first at his shoes, furious the man had not worn shoe covers—in theory, any hairs-and-fibers evidence was now contaminated. This kind of behavior was so typical of the man, that Dart realized mentioning it was useless. Kowalski was useless.

Kowalski stepped over and opened one of the leather-bound books.

"Gloves!" Dart chastised. But the man had already touched the book.

Kowalski, ignoring Dart completely, flipped though the pages. "Geez! Enough to make even me blush." Abby peered over his shoulder, and Dart watched as her face reddened noticeably; she looked quickly away, stepped back and coughed, clearing her throat.

"I thought you was tough, Lang," Kowalski teased.

"Gloves, Kowalski!" Dart said irritably.

"Yeah, yeah."

"Gloves!" Dart repeated, stealing the book from the detective.

Dart glanced at it. The photograph in question depicted a naked woman suspended beneath a horse via a leather harness. In a challenge of proportions, she was engaged in intercourse with the stud, nothing left to the imagination. Dart slapped the book shut, revolted.

Kowalski had the tact to say, "You ever play horsey, Lang?" Wearing latex gloves now, he took the book from Dart, opened it and said, "Oh my god! This one's doing it with Flipper for crying in your beer! Fucking a porpoise, Dartelli. Get a load. Geez, what a pecker those things have!"

"Cool it," Dart reprimanded.

Kowalski held the book up in front of the woman. "What is that, Abigail, a porpoise or a dolphin?"

She averted her eyes, "No thanks."

Dart took the book away once again.

"Enough!" He added, "Act like a detective, just once."

"Easy, Fred," Kowalski said back to him as an obvious warning. He towered over Dart by a good three inches and outweighed him by sixty pounds. "Just having a little fun is all." He glanced at Abby and back to Dart. "She got no reason being here anyway."

Dart's mind froze.

Abby spoke up. "Smut like this, and you're wondering what Sex Crimes is doing here? Get a clue, Kowalski." She pulled a leather-clad book from the shelf, obviously incredibly old. She gently opened the volume. "Latin," she said, studying it. "Twelfth-century drawings." She turned the pages, shaking her head at what she saw. "It appears the Roman clergy enjoyed pornography."

Returning the bestiality book to the shelves, Dart told Kowalski about the federal charges against Payne and Abby's earlier involvement. Kowalski didn't seem to be listening. He seized upon the same book—a kid in a candy store—opened it and asked, "Hey, Dartelli, would you recognize a boa constrictor if you saw one?" He had the arrogance to laugh. "What about *half* of one?" He looked up at Abby Lang and said, "Talk about getting snaked!"

Once again Dart stepped over to Kowalski, but he was spared the confrontation by Ted Bragg, who entered and, in an angry voice, condemned them all for having entered the room before he had a chance to go over it. "This is a crime scene, not a convention!" he complained. "Get out!"

Dart said to Kowalski, "Go ahead, tell him about the rug."

Kowalski looked paralyzed.

"The rug," Dart repeated, cherishing the moment.

"What the fuck are you talking about?"

"Lieutenant?" Dart asked Abby.

She said to Bragg, "The wife claims to have entered and checked the body. Fiber evidence contradicts this—"

"What the fuck?" Kowalski blurted out.

She continued, "We have her crossing the room to the bookshelf, the desk, and here, to this room. Further evidence suggests a variance in the nap of the rug between the door and the deceased. Photos of that would be good to have before the place is walked all over."

"Nap?" Bragg inquired.

Dart answered. "Someone vacuumed that section of the rug, Buzz, long before we got here."

"Vacuumed?" Bragg asked.

"What the fuck?" Kowalski repeated.

Looking directly at Kowalski, Dart said, "Someone hoping to remove hairs-and-fibers evidence, in an effort to conceal what really went on here."

Bragg, his annoyance showing, said, "And what really went on here, Ivy?"

"It's a homicide, Buzz. I want it treated as a homicide."

"Who's lead on this?" Bragg inquired.

Kowalski, stunned and out of sorts, had yet to break eye contact with Dartelli. "I'm lead," he announced authoritatively, defiantly, "and until *you* tell *me* that we got evidence to the contrary, Teddy, we treat it the way we see it: a suicide. You got any reason to doubt that, then I'm willing to change horses, *if* and *when* we make sense of it." To Dart he said, "You have information I don't have?"

Dart just stared at the man. He was thinking that he'd gone too far, that it was time to close ranks.

CHAPTER
13

Not even the bathroom would work for his purposes. Dart needed someplace isolated, someplace there was no chance of being overheard, and preferably a location that wouldn't raise eyebrows. He ruled out either of the interrogation rooms because they would attract far too much attention. He ruled out the crib—too easily interrupted. A vehicle would work, he realized, though getting the two of them into the same car would take some logistics and, at this point, some negotiating.

And then he hit upon it: the elevator. Kowalski's use of the elevator, in what was only a two-story building, was the subject of much teasing within CAPers.

The opportunity arose a few minutes after the lunch hour, when both Dart and Kowalski were summoned to Teddy Bragg's office. Dart found Kowalski playing computer solitaire on a PC that belonged to another detective. Kowalski offered no apologies for using his time this way. Instead he said, "Just a minute, okay, Dartelli? I almost got this thing." Dart waited him out, his impatience mounting. Finally Kowalski lost the hand, closed the game off the screen, and spun around in his chair. "Piece of shit," he said.

"You played the jack of diamonds on the wrong pile," Dart informed him, not fully understanding why he began with confrontation.

"Bull-fucking-shit I did. I suppose you play the game more than me, huh? I don't think so. Mind your own fucking business."

"Bragg wants us downstairs. He has the initial workup on Payne."

"Sure. Why not?" As Kowalski stood out of the chair, Dart was reminded how large and how solid the man was. Suddenly the idea of a one-on-one confrontation in an elevator didn't seem like such a stroke of brilliance. But it was all he had, and he intended to follow through.

As they entered the hallway, Kowalski asked, "You taking the stairs?" Making it sound like a chore.

"No. Let's ride," he said, clearly surprising the man. He stabbed the CALL button, and a moment later they stepped into the empty elevator car. He felt his heart pounding, and the pulsing of a fatigue headache at his temples. This was a little bit like deciding to ride a wild bull, he realized. He pushed the button marked l, and the elevator doors slid shut. He tried to settle his nerves, knowing full well that Kowalski's reaction would be indignation. Dart counted to three and pulled the red STOP button. The car jerked to a halt.

"Hey, what the fuck?"

Dart faced the man. Kowalski had dark Mediterranean skin, haunting brown eyes and heavy, masculine features. If he had been fifteen years younger he would have been working Guess jeans ads. His center teeth were stained from smoking the non-filters, and his voice sounded like someone chipping ice.

Dart explained. "Lewellan Page."

"Who?"

"Lewellan Page—the girl who witnessed the Lawrence murder."

Kowalski made a move for the elevator control panel, but Dart blocked his effort. "Get this thing moving," he complained.

"I wanted to talk in private," Dart explained. "The point is not to embarrass you, but to understand your thinking. Your reasoning." An oxymoron if he ever heard one.

"Lawrence?"

Like talking to a bull elephant. "The suicide over on Battles," Dart reminded.

"The hanging?" the detective asked rhetorically, the case finally registering.

Dart couldn't tell if the man was acting or not; every detective had an actor inside.

"Oh, *her*." Kowalski said.

"Yea, *her*," Dart agreed.

"What's to tell?"

"You interviewed her. You wrote up that interview. And you kept it out of your report. Why?"

Kowalski looked confused—a child trying to connect the dots. He had to be wondering just how Dart had gained such knowledge, what else the detective knew, and how it all impacted him. He stuttered, "She's a *kid*, Ivy. What the fuck?" Attempting once again to reach past Dart, he said anxiously, "Get this thing moving—this is giving me the creeps in here."

It wasn't the elevator but the topic making him nervous, Dart realized. "She's a *witness*," he said emphatically.

"Bullshit. She's a bored nigger kid who sees whites as bad. The only whites she's ever seen are cops. They come and take people away. They make trouble. Get a clue, Dartelli. She gets me by the *cajones* and tries to invent some story about a guy doing Lawrence. I mean, give me a fucking break, will you? How do you operate this thing?" He stepped forward.

Dart maintained his position between Kowalski and the panel. "Not good enough," Dart warned. "She witnessed a Caucasian male pulling a chair out from underneath Lawrence. She described the man's flailing legs perfectly. I think she actually saw it. You're saying she invented it?"

"Probably saw it in a movie or something. How the fuck should I know? Did you bother with any of the rest of it? There was a note, I think. The place was locked up. No sign of a struggle. No evidence to suggest foul play. What's the fucking big deal?"

Dart felt confused. He believed Lewellan Page's story. Kowalski had investigated David

143

Stapleton while on Narco. Did Dart dare play that card as well?

"Was Lawrence involved in trafficking?" Dart asked, hoping to see a reaction in Kowalski that might tell him something.

"Drugs? How the hell would I know? Some pot found in the apartment, it seems to me. Nothing hard core that I heard about." Kowalski's expression revealed nothing—no surprise, no panic.

Don't trust it, Dart cautioned himself.

"Let me tell you something, Dartelli. I don't want no rogue cop prying into my cases, okay? You got problems with the way I'm doing things, you go through IA and we'll see what they say."

"Your buddies at IA, you mean," Dart said caustically.

"Fuck off. Are you listening to me?" He stepped forward, an intimidating presence. "What I'm saying is I don't appreciate your working my files without asking me, okay? Showing up at crime scenes uninvited. What is it with you? You go through channels from now on."

Here, Dart realized, was the ultimate in irony: a cop known for his misuse of the system telling Dart that he should play by the rules. The hypocrisy caused Dart to laugh and throw his head back. "You're too much," he said.

Then, in a whisper, as if he believed he might be overheard even on a stopped elevator, Kowalski leaned in closely to Dart and said in his coarse voice. "Listen to me, Dartelli, okay? Let's say that some white guy *did* do Lawrence that night—

144

hypothetically speaking. A big white guy on the edge of Bellevue Square at night. Let's think about this . . . Now how many candidates do we have for this person? Huh?" He held up his meaty hand and raised a single, chunky finger. "One: A junkie in need of a fix. That would mean Lawrence was a dealer, which we have no proof of. That would also probably mean a struggle of some kind. Okay? So where's the evidence? Two: What other damn fool would be ballsy enough to visit the square after dark? Who but a junkie goes into that area at night? Not even the fucking cabs, for Chrissakes. There's only one answer isn't there, okay?" He glared at Dart; neither man was going to say the word that teased their tongues. "I'm not real upset about some pervert like Lawrence ending up hanging from a wire. And I sure as hell am not going to use some twelve-year-old abused and abandoned nigger girl to rip open an investigation that could lead where we both know it could lead. Okay? What's the point? Let's just drop it."

Dart shook his head. "We can't drop it."

"Oh, for Chrissakes. Get off of your fucking white horse."

"We let it go because he's a sex offender? Is that it?"

"Fuck off."

"Or because it might involve one of us."

"I didn't say that," Kowalski protested.

"Sure you did."

The control panel buzzed as someone called the stopped elevator.

Kowalski said, "You think justice is just left to

145

us? That's bullshit. We're way the hell down on that food chain."

"Justice isn't up to us—it's up to the courts."

"Oh, *come on!*" Kowalski protested. "I mean *us*: human beings. There's other kinds of justice, you know. There's laws of the jungle. You stick your dick in a twelve-year-old and shit happens to you—car loses a wheel on the highway. Fucking radio falls into your bathtub. How the fuck do I know?"

"A cop fakes your suicide," Dart completed.

"Maybe. Yeah, just maybe. And who the fuck *cares*, Dartelli? Are you honestly *sorry* that this maggot ate shit and died? You are crying for this guy? Fuck him. Fuck anyone like him."

"David Stapleton, Harold Payne," Dart said. And then he realized, by Kowalski's expression, just how thick the man could be. By all appearances, Kowalski had not made the connection until that moment—one hell of a performance, if that's what it was.

"Fuck me," Kowalski said.

"They probably would have liked to," Dart answered. But in his heart of hearts, he ached. If Kowalski's surprise was legitimate, then Dart could remove him from suspicion, which left only one other. On some level he knew that the killer could be any one of hundreds—thousands—of people, but that did not register. One face, one name dominated his thoughts: *Walter Zeller*. He stepped out of the way of the panel.

Kowalski got the elevator moving again. The floor bounced. Kowalski cautioned, "You bring that girl into it, and you're in for some serious trouble. I'm telling ya."

Dart nodded. He saw Kowalski, and his possible involvement, in a different light, though he wasn't sure whether to trust it or not. "Wherever this leads," Dartelli cautioned, "then that's the way it is."

"You want to play Boy Scout, go join a troop." Being called a Boy Scout was among a handful of the most derogatory labels used among fellow officers. Kowalski added, "Lawrence got what he deserved." The car stopped moving and the doors opened. Kowalski took one step toward freedom, reconsidered, and turned to face Dartelli. "No that's not true. He got off *light*. If I'd done it," he said convincingly, "I'd have cut off his cock, shoved it down his throat, and let him choke to death."

Dart didn't move from the elevator car, thinking: *If you had done it, we would have caught you.*

Whoever *had* staged these suicides had done so brilliantly, and again, Dart could think of only one.

CHAPTER
14

As difficult as it was for him to face it, Dart realized that he had to locate Walter Zeller and question him. *Informally*, he convinced himself—*at least at first*. He would make it appear that he was seeking Zeller's advice, the protégé returning to the feet of the mentor. But he no longer had any doubt. It had to be done. At least three men were dead. Dart believed he knew why they had been selected. It was time to act before there were more.

For the last few months, the word around the department had been that after a brief stint with a security firm in Hartford, Zeller had been offered a better job in Seattle. Dart had believed all along that, better job or not, it was important for Zeller to move on, preferably as far away from his wife's murder as possible. Seattle certainly fit that bill.

But try as he did, Dart failed to raise a Seattle phone number for the former sergeant, either through the personnel office, directory information, or through any of the many friends Zeller had left behind. He was able to obtain a Seattle address for Zeller—a box number on First Avenue—and to determine that Zeller's pension checks were direct-deposited into a First Interstate Bank account, but beyond that, the trail ended: officials at the bank had the same box number, no residential address, no phone number.

None of this came as any great surprise to Dart, or put him off his effort. Most police officers, retired or not, protect themselves from possible revenge attacks by maintaining unpublished phone numbers and using post office boxes for mailing addresses. Zeller, whose desire for privacy was legendary and who had put away dozens of killers, could be expected to take such precautions.

While running an errand on a Tuesday in early November, Dart drove past Sam and Rob's Smoke Shop on Asylum Street and pulled over a block later. In direct violation of federal import restrictions, Sam and Rob's sold a variety of Cuban cigars out of their back room to preferred customers. During his twenty years of public service, Walter Zeller had been a regular customer and had developed a friendship with the owners.

The shop smelled of fresh pipe tobacco.

Rob, the older of the two proprietors, had died of lung cancer five years earlier. His brother Sam, in his late fifties, was bald with a brown mustache and red cheeks and high cheekbones. He wore a tattered green apron with the name of the shop embroidered in dull red thread. His shirt cuffs were threadbare, and a button had been replaced on one of them. He had a smoker's voice and a gambler's nervous eyes.

He did not seem to recognize Dart until the detective mentioned Zeller's name, at which point an association was made. For years, Dart had wandered the shelves of this outer room, while Zeller had negotiated for the Cubans in the back.

After the introductions were made, Dart told him that he had a difficult investigation on his hands, and that he had lost track of Zeller. "I thought that he might have had you send him some cigars—that you might have an address or a phone number."

149

"He went to Seattle," Sam informed him needlessly. "Vancouver gets all the Cuban brands—Canada, you know; no restrictions."

"So you haven't heard from him?"

"Heard from him?" Sam repeated. "He was *in* here not three weeks ago. Bought several boxes of—"

"Here? In the store?"

"I hadn't seen him in a couple years. Still too thin. He was complaining about a Dominican he'd been smoking and how they don't measure up. No question. His cigar has a hint of cocoa in the wrap. You can't find that in any of the Dominicans. There's only one cigar for each of us," he said, like a salesman. "Do you smoke a cigar?"

"No."

"Have you tried it?"

"No, thanks. Three weeks ago?"

"Three or four. Yes."

"And before that?"

Sam considered this a moment. "Hadn't seen him in years."

"When he came in here three weeks ago, how much did he buy?" Dart asked.

"Three or four boxes, I think it was."

"And how long will that last him?"

"The sergeant? A while, anyway." He thought a moment and said, "A month or more."

"And it's been about a month," Dart said.

"Yeah, that's right, isn't it? Sure, I see what you're saying. Maybe I can put him in touch with you."

Dart thought fast and spoke his mind. "Or

better yet," he said, "I could leave you my number, and if he came in, maybe you could stall him long enough for me to get over here and surprise him."

"Call you, ya mean."

"Right."

"I like that. Sure. I like putting people together. That's one thing about cigars," he advised. "They bring people together. After a good meal. A poker game. After a round of golf—it's a social activity, smoking is."

"Staying here, or visiting?" Dart inquired. "Did you get a feel for that?"

"Visiting, I think. He wasn't very talkative. Not the same man by any means. But who can blame him? I don't think any man could recover from losing his wife that way." Sam's face tightened, and Dart had the feeling that the loss of his own brother hung over him as well. "It's not easy," the man whispered, confirming Dart's suspicions.

A feeling of dread swarmed through Dart, like the first hint of the flu. It seemed implausible that Zeller would have visited the city and not looked up a single friend—Dart had touched base with everyone he could think of.

Dart handed the shopkeeper his business card. "Call me right away, would you please?"

"I love a good surprise," the man said.

"Yeah," Dart answered. "This will be a hell of a surprise."

Walter Zeller was not a rich man, having earned a policeman's salary for twenty-two years, and so it had confused even his closest friends when he left the city and refused to sell his house—the house where his wife had been raped and murdered. He owned the house free and clear, and it represented his single biggest asset, and yet he had refused to sell, giving no explanation. For Dartelli, no explanation was needed. Perhaps he was the only one of Zeller's friends to understand that part of the man, that specific quality, that would have made selling the house a further violation of his wife. Lucky Zeller had treasured the house—a rather common tract home in Vernon. The house was a brown ranch at the end of a cul-de-sac in a subdivision that hosted RVs, powerboats, and camper tops for pickup trucks. Dogwood Lane was oil stained from parked cars, its concrete gutters looking like chipped teeth. The limbs of the few mature trees, bare with winter's approach, reached for a sky of gray cloud and cold wind.

Dart parked in Zeller's driveway, wondering if he had quietly moved back from Seattle without telling anyone.

The building's brown siding was stained gray where water from lawn sprinklers had soaked it. Dart felt a pang of nostalgia, troubled by the sight of the unattended gardens, and he knew in that instant that Zeller was not living here. The sergeant, renowned for his green thumb, for the endless hours he lavished on his plants and gardens, would never have allowed his beds to go unattended. A four-foot apron of bare earth, choked by clumps of dead weeds, surrounded the house. A few of the flower islands that had been cut into the small lawn by Zeller's own hands had been covered over with gray gravel. *Buried, as Lucky had been,* Dart thought, knocking sharply on the front door. There was no answer, no sound of anyone inside. *No surprise,* he thought as he walked around the house and into the backyard, which flooded him with memories of barbecues, beer, and long discussions of the cases they had worked together.

He could recall Lucky's cooking and the sound of her high voice. Despite the passage of time, the image of her bound and gagged corpse called up effortlessly and struck Dart with a pain in the center of his chest and a stinging in his eyes.

The three years that it had remained vacant had taken its toll. The deck needed painting, as did the trim around the windows. He climbed onto the deck and knocked on the back door, and peered through filthy windows at a kitchen that he had, at one time, considered almost his own.

Memories continued to plague him, mixing with images of the suicide victims. His police half battled with his friendship half, his suspicions contradicting his faith and trust in Walter Zeller. The similarities between the suicide jumps of the Ice Man and David Stapleton were impossible to overlook: the lack of a suicide note, the computer simulation confirming the bodies had been thrown from the windows. And for the better part of three years, Dart had believed, without *knowing,* that Walter Zeller was to blame for the Ice Man.

He tried several windows, all locked. He wasn't

about to break in. By the look of the place, Zeller had never returned. Dart knew that the inside had been left exactly as it had been on the night of Lucky's murder. He had no great urge to visit that nightmare again.

He walked fully around the house and climbed into his Volvo, and sat parked in the drive for several long minutes contemplating Zeller's possible involvement. A chill ran through him, head to toe and back to the center of his chest. He loved Walter Zeller like a brother, like a father, in a way that others wouldn't understand. He didn't know if he possessed the strength required to do what had to be done. The mere *suggestion* of Zeller's culpability seemed itself a crime, certainly something that could not be raised with Sergeant Haite and the powers-that-be without a stack of evidence. Walter Zeller was the closest thing to a true hero that Jennings Road had ever produced. To arrest Walter Zeller on suspicion of murder would crush morale. The brass was certain to resist it without the smoking gun *glued* into Zeller's hand and twenty-five nuns as witnesses.

Dart could think of a dozen reasons too drop this investigation, and very few to continue with it.

But he backed the Volvo out of the drive, focused on finding Zeller and connecting him to the crimes, his trust and faith converted to anger and resentment.

CHAPTER
15

The following day Dart, Abby, and little Lewellan Page made the forty-five-minute drive to Sheffield through a cool but gorgeous afternoon. Mac the Knife patrolled the back of the Volvo, Lewellan offering her hand to lick. The spine of mountains bearing the northern stretch of the Appalachian trail were frosted with the first hints of winter. Lewellan, who had never been out of the Bellevue Square area of north Hartford, sat quietly in the backseat, eyes wide with awe, asking a nonstop stream of questions.

Tommy Templeton was well into his fifties. Since Dart had seen him last, his hair had gone completely gray. He was a big solid man, shaped like a barrel with legs. He had rough, hard hands that looked more like a carpenter's than an artist's. He had a deep voice, kind eyes, and a small scar below his lip.

Greeting the three of them at the front door of his hilltop home, he shook hands with Abby and Lewellan and admonished Dart. "Six years I've been up here, and you've never visited. You've called, what, once?" Not allowing Dart the opportunity to respond, he welcomed them into his home, with its antique furnishings and spectacular sixty-mile view of the rolling hills of western Connecticut. The ceilings were low and the floors creaked under foot. The living room smelled of woodsmoke and pine needles. "Teddy has made it over to fish a couple times. Doc Ray, too."

Dart had heard about those weekends. More drinking than fishing. "Maybe I could make the next one," Dart lied.

"What about you, Lewellan?" Templeton asked. "Do you like to fish?"

"I like fish sticks," she replied.

They all laughed. Abby put her arm around the girl and held her closely.

A people person, Tommy Templeton's real gift as a police artist had been his ability to make friends quickly and to coax images from the unwilling minds of his witnesses. His was the craft of instant friendships. Since he had been divorced and left the force, six years earlier, Templeton had lived alone, creating commercial art for the tourist shops in southern Maine. He painted seagulls and fishing trawlers, and he drank too much and got out too little. There was no escaping the rumor mill of HPD.

Despite the view, Tommy Templeton worked in a studio with the shades drawn because sunlight compromised his computer screens. The computer gear—two flatbed scanners, a color laser printer, and a pair of Macintoshes, occupied the tops of three doors supported by rough-wood sawhorses and steel file cabinets. Cables and wires ran between them in a confusing tangle. He had pinned various pieces of computer art, both color and black-and-white, on his walls. There were nudes, landscapes, wildlife, and three self-portraits. The images, some of them vaguely familiar to Dart, were impressive. Like many artists, Templeton carried an aura of eccentricity. There was a duck decoy wearing a pair of reading glasses in the far corner that immediately grabbed Abby's attention. But it was the full-frontal nude that captured Lewellan's attention.

"She's beautiful," the young woman said.

"She's titled 'Venus,'" Tommy Templeton said proudly. "I morphed her."

"What's that mean?"

"She's a composite photograph. Do you know what a composite is? It's like pasting several photographs on top of one another, except that you can see through them. 'Venus' is a combination of seven different photographs. Qualities from each."

Let's not get into details, Dart thought, examining the Vargas-like round breasts, wide hips, narrow waist, long legs, and square shoulders. "Tom's Fantasy Girl" seemed more appropriate, although the photographic quality of the image made this woman appear absolutely real. Knowing that she was not made the effect disarming.

"I'll show you," Templeton said as he sat Lewellan down into a chair in front of an oversize computer screen. Dart and Abby stepped back, allowing Templeton to take over. The man called up a file on the computer, and five vehicles appeared on-screen. Below them was an interesting-looking contraption—a cross between the

157

space shuttle and a Porsche that on examination contained some element of each. "This is exactly what we're going to do," he explained. "You and me," he said as went about scanning each of the five mug shots that Lewellan Page had identified as the man that she had seen outside of Gerald Lawrence's apartment on the night of his hanging.

With the photographs on-screen and in front of Lewellan, he asked, "Do you recognize these, Lewellan?"

She nodded.

"We're going to see if we can combine these into the man you saw. Okay?"

"Okay."

Templeton talked her through a careful examination of each of the mug shots, asking her to identify exactly which feature of which shot looked most like the man she had witnessed. He began with the shape of the head; Lewellan picked the third man. Tommy Templeton placed a series of black dots around this face, omitting the hair, and then clicked a button on the mouse and connected them all. After a few mouse-controlled instructions, this same face, hairless and without ears, appeared in the empty box at the bottom of the large screen. Dragging a small black square across the screen with the mouse, he then erased the contents of the face itself, and only the shape of the head remained. This empty head looked ghostly and odd to Dart, who stood behind the two of them.

Abby's fingers brushed against Dart's hand,

and she slipped hers into his, and they hooked together, holding hands.

"The chin's not right," Lewellan told the former police artist.

"Okay. Let's change that." He erased the chin. "Here," he said, handing her an aluminum pen with a wire attached. "Do you want to draw it?"

She tried several times and on her fourth attempt appeared satisfied. Templeton worked with the image for a moment—his artist's eye knowing how to improve it—at which point she declared, "That's good. That's real good!"

They worked together, light pen and mouse, and high-lighted two different sets of eyes, each of which Lewellan felt contained something of the man she had seen. Templeton instructed the computer to merge the two. The computer then animated the evolution from photo A to photo B, stepping through a series of frames. With each successive frame, the eyes of photo A grew more similar to those in photo B. Lewellan studied each of these individual frames, selected one, and Templeton then merged these eyes into the empty face in the bottom box. This concept of ever-changing, slightly altered frames was what made morphing so effective, Dart realized. With an Identi-Kit, the witness was only given a choice of eyes number 1, eyes number 2, etc. With morphing, the features of several different faces could be made to evolve into a single face, with no one feature of the final composition exactly as it was in any of the others.

"The department should have this," Dart let slip as the face in the bottom box slowly grew to something recognizable. Tommy Templeton's eyes flashed darkly—the argument for better technology, among other issues, had contributed to his early retirement.

An hour later the suspect's face had eyes, eyebrows, and hair. They took a break and stood on the porch, and Templeton smoked three cigarettes in a row. Lewellan and Tommy Templeton talked about the special effects in *Terminator 2* and *Jurassic Park*. Dart watched a small plane make for the horizon. Abby Lang, her coat wrapped around her as a blanket, drank in the late-afternoon sun.

They resumed their work by concentrating on noses. This time, it took three successive morphings to produce a nose that satisfied Lewellan, and then only after Tommy Templeton had touched it up with a computerized "airbrush." Dart had wandered off to study some of the artwork, and it was only as he returned to check up on their progress that he realized the eyes were familiar to him. This realization stopped him cold. The suspect still lacked a mouth and ears.

"Are you okay?" Abby asked.

It was dark out. Dart didn't know how long he had been standing there lost in thought, but it had been at least forty or fifty minutes.

Templeton and Lewellan Page took another break to rest their eyes, and Templeton found some pretzels for them to eat. When the two went back to work at the computers, Dart and Abby took Mac for a walk. Mac walked like an arthritic boxer, hobbling along, his collar jingling.

"Do you want to spend the night tonight?" she

asked. Dart had been doing more and more of that lately. They had not discussed their relationship on any serious terms, but he thought about her often, and he missed her when a couple of days passed without contact.

"I'd like that," he said.

"Good. Me too."

He told her he would need to drop Mac at his apartment and offered to pick up some dinner on the way back over. She told him that she would cook chicken if he made a salad, and with that they had dinner planned. He felt a slight pang of guilt, and he missed Ginny, and it made him wonder if she had gotten any further with her attempt to compile the list for him, and how he hadn't heard from her in a few weeks.

"You're off somewhere," Abby said.

"Just thinking, that's all."

They returned to the house in silence. She took his hand again. She wore gloves. Dart did not. "We could use more time like this," she said.

Dart wasn't sure how to reply to that, so he let it go. He led the dog back to the car. "How many kids grow up like Lewellan?" he asked sadly. "She had never seen the woods except on television. Her entire image of the outside world is from television. What kind of society are we creating?"

" 'Save one life, you save the world,' " she quoted.

"It's overwhelming," he said.

"She'll never forget this experience," Abby offered. "Maybe by losing Gerry Law we gain Lewellan Page."

161

"I doubt it," Dart admitted.

"Yeah," she agreed. "Me too. But it was a nice thought."

They reentered the house. Tommy Templeton's voice could be heard congratulating the girl. The two, still on their break, were looking at a coffee table book of wild animal photographs.

"Are you going to look?" Lewellan asked Dart.

"Is it done?" Dart asked.

"Not quite," Templeton asked.

Abby sat down with the girl and the book, and Templeton came over to Dart and motioned Dart out onto the deck, which produced an immediate anxiety in the detective.

Tommy Templeton's face, part shadow, part light, looked like a mask and offered Dart a disturbed expression. "We're getting close," he said, though it sounded more like a warning.

"What is it, Tommy?"

"Maybe nothing."

"What?"

"I'm not sure."

"The face?" Dart asked.

"Yes."

"It looks familiar," Dart stated.

Templeton nodded. "The eyes."

"Who?"

Templeton shook his head.

"Who, Tommy?" Dart repeated.

"Doesn't make any sense, and besides, the rest of the face doesn't work at all."

"Who?"

"I can't make it out," he said, "but it sure as hell seems familiar to me."

Dart nodded. "I know. The eyes."

"Yeah. Weird, isn't it?" the man asked.

Dart didn't answer. He asked, "Do we trust this?"

"I do. She's good," came the reply, "which is not exactly what you're asking, is it? Is this the face she saw, or is it someone she has seen since and has convinced herself otherwise? We both know the score with eyewitnesses, Joe, don't we? They're about as reliable as the mail. But she has a face in her head—I guarantee you that. Whether it's real or imagined, I can't tell you."

Half an hour later, Templeton called Abby and Dart into his studio.

His heart pounding strongly, Dart approached the computer screen, but Templeton directed him away. "The printer," Templeton said, pointing. "We've enlarged it. It's just coming out."

The four of them stepped up to the laser printer, where a piece of paper was being slowly ejected, upside down so that only the white of the paper showed. Dart wanted to grab it and flip it over, but he waited for it to finish printing. Templeton picked it up and turned it over.

The image was that of a face. It looked so much like a photograph that Dart briefly forgot that it was not. Lifelike and human. Dart reached out and touched the sheet of paper, feeling an incredible sense of relief.

The face was jowly, the brow strong. The high cheekbones reminded him of an Irishman. Try as he did, he could no longer make the face into that of Walter Zeller. Even the eyes looked different. He felt giddy. He felt high, as if he'd been drinking.

"There's your man," Templeton said, handing Dart the image.

"That's him," Lewellan Page confirmed.

Dart felt both confusion and happiness. It was one time he felt thrilled to be wrong about the identification of a suspect.

But his stomach rolled and his bowels loosened when, at the door, saying good-bye, Tommy Templeton leaned in close to him and whispered, "I'd like to play with this image, Joe. I'll fax you a copy if I get anything."

"But I thought—" Dart complained. His euphoria popped like a balloon, his objection interrupted by Templeton.

"Inside every face, there's another face," Templeton cautioned in a sinister tone of voice. "Call it instinct, call it a hunch . . . This isn't the face that I expected."

Abby saw the two men whispering and caught eyes with Dart, her face a knot of concern. Lewellan Page ran out to the car and opened the back door and petted the dog.

"Let me work with it," Templeton told the detective. "I'll give you a call."

Leave it alone, Dart wanted to say. But he nodded, wishing that secrets could stay hidden, and that a person's face could never change.

CHAPTER
16

There's no question in my mind that the rug in Payne's study was vacuumed sometime just before the suicide, but not being a detective," Bragg said sarcastically, "I don't see how that might bear upon the investigation." Teddy Bragg looked better today, more color to his face, less to his eyes. He smelled like cigarettes. The file for the Halloween suicide, Harold Payne, lay open on his desk. The small office was cluttered with paperwork. A Lucite microscope, a forensic science award, sat in the corner gathering dust alongside a canning jar containing a pancreas suspended in a clear fluid. Dart had never asked about the pancreas, but he'd seen it there for years. Lights glowed on a small FM clock radio, indicating it was switched on, but the volume was evidently turned down.

"Before the suicide?" Dart asked curiously.

"Definitely prior to the shooting, yes. We've lifted blood splatter from the surface of the rug."

"What's the point?" Kowalski asked irritably.

Bragg answered, "The point, detective, is who vacuumed that rug, when, and why? We checked with the wife, who explained that the house-cleaner had been there the same day; but for reasons that I'll get into, that doesn't cut it."

"She was in there—the wife," Dart reminded, "ahead of our arrival."

"Yes, so she could be lying."

Kowalski glanced over at Dart with a look that penetrated. Perhaps, Dart thought, he too understood that this might lead back to Zeller.

Bragg cautioned, "We *know* by the vacuum pattern—the width of the swath—that it wasn't any of the machines in the house. Furthermore, we've checked the bags of the two machines and IDed wool fibers with the proper dye lot to match the study rug—and that tells us two things: one, the rug *was* vacuumed, possibly that same day; two, someone else using a different machine vacuumed the rug *after* the housecleaner but *before* the suicide.

"The upstairs canister vacuum," he continued, "would appear to have resided upstairs and only worked the upstairs." To Dart he said, "You know how I hate inconsistencies like this. It's petty bullshit, I know. But it bugs the crap out of me."

Kowalski complained, "It doesn't *matter*." He added, "Not to me. Does it affect your ruling in any way?"

"Roman, great minds think alike," Bragg said. "I asked myself the same question: Does any of this matter? The kill is by his own hand, it's clean—in a manner of speaking—and convincing. So what do we care?"

"Exactly."

"But we *do* care," Bragg contradicted. "All because of one tiny piece of evidence."

Kowalski's brow knitted. "What's that?"

"You see," Bragg said to Dart, "these portable battery-charged vacuums don't get up much horsepower. These Dustbuster things. Oh, they're fine for crumbs on the counter, or spilled sugar, but you put them to work on an Oriental wool rug like we find in Payne's study, and they just don't measure up—not when measured against our industrial-strength twenty-amp variety. It's like one of those cheap television ads on cable: You vacuum an area with yours, and we'll go over the top of the same area with ours and lift a good amount of material that your vacuum missed. And that's just what happened." He met eyes with both men—in Bragg's Dart could see a contained but eager excitement. *Scientists have to get their kicks somewhere*, he thought.

Ted Bragg motioned for them to sit tight and went off in search of something. He returned a moment later with two wax paper bags. He placed them down on a light table and set a ruler between them. He then carefully opened each bag and drew the contents out onto the light table with a set of plastic chopsticks. He was careful and exact with his actions. "On the left is what we vacuumed from the study. On the right is what came from the door mat outside the kitchen door in the garage."

Seeing the evidence before him, Dart began to piece together Bragg's evidence. The pile from the study included dust, crumbs, hairs, and an abundance of fibers, mostly wool by their curled appearance. The doormat in the garage had netted some sticks, dust, and what appeared to be a small blob of oil and dirt. But both groups shared similar items: small elliptically shaped pieces of vegetation.

"Pine needles?" Dart asked.

"You see?" Bragg encouraged. "I told you it's interesting."

"You call *that* interesting?" Kowalski challenged.

"We haven't divined the species," the lab man reported, maintaining his attention on Dart. "But, as you can see, a similar vegetation was found both in the study rug and on the garage doormat."

"So *what*?" Kowalski complained irritably.

"On the very *top* of the garage doormat," Bragg clarified. "Determining a person's actions—what a person may or may not have done—is a responsibility we both share—you, from a wide variety of evidence and witnesses; me from the translation of the physical sciences. I can tell you a couple of interesting facts, Roman, and maybe you can make sense of them for me."

Kowalski looked like a kid in the schoolyard who didn't want to play; he pursed his lips and looked around nervously for somewhere to steal a smoke.

"That rug in the study had been vacuumed— it's not something I can necessarily *prove* but it's something I *know* to be a fact. Our examination of the machine used to vacuum that rug earlier in the day came up negative for any such organics. And yet our subsequent vacuuming of the same area produced this as-yet-unidentified organic matter, most likely some kind of conifer needle.

We also picked up a trace amount of phosphorus and nitrogen compounds—common potting soil, Detective. Similar organic matter *and* soil was discovered atop the garage doormat, suggesting someone had wiped his or her feet on the way into the house. I questioned the wife; it was not she. A little tough to question the victim, but there was nothing on the soles of his slippers to suggest a similar organic matter. We returned to the home and inspected eleven pairs of boots and shoes: all negative."

Kowalski said nervously, "So the wife was screwing the gardener in the old man's study and they made a mess of things. They cleaned up, but not so good. Maybe the old man found out and put a bullet through his lid."

Bragg nodded agreement as he said, "Might be, except that the gardener put the beds up for winter three weeks ago, and a search of the premises revealed no such potting soil. The beds were heavily mulched. Oat straw. We picked up *no* trace amounts in our vacuum filters." He hesitated and said, "What we *did* come up with was *this*." He produced a clear plastic container. There were small blue crystals inside. "It's a salt and fertilizer compound sold as deicer. The blue is a dye they add for marketing purposes. The compound melts ice but doesn't kill common plants, flowers, or grass." He summarized: "Three items—the conifer needles, the potting soil, and the rock salt. It's enough of a signature, Ivy, if you bring me a suspect."

The unspoken message interested Dart more than the facts: Ted Bragg had invested an inordinate amount of time in this case that otherwise would have been considered a "grounder." His poorly staffed forensic sciences division was a busy place; they put investigations to bed as quickly as possible. Bragg, or his assistant, Samantha Richardson, had returned to Payne's, possibly more than once, in search of evidence. It revealed to Dart how unsettled the man was with his discoveries.

All that Bragg could do was present the evidence in hopes of interesting the lead detective. Ultimately, it was the lead detective's call whether to pursue that evidence. He clearly saw Kowalski as the weak link.

"So what exactly are you saying?" Kowalski asked rhetorically, answering, "What you're saying is that some Joe entered the house through a locked garage and did a little house-cleaning before he left, *after which*, our friend Harry Payne blows his hat off with a nine millimeter. Am I missing something here?" He addressed Dart, "This sounds like a bunch of bullshit to me—no offense, Teddy. What do *you* think?" he asked Dart in a leading tone.

Dart hesitated.

Kowalski said, "Fuck the pine needles and the goddamned potting soil. There's always crap at any crime scene that you can't explain. Am I right, or am I right?"

"You're probably right," Dart confessed. "Where do we go with this?" he asked Bragg.

"Where you go with it is your business," Bragg

reminded, clearly upset. "I'm just telling you what I found."

"Where would *you* go with it?" Dart restated.

Kowalski rocked uncomfortably onto his heels.

Bragg pondered the question, he searched Kowalski's eyes and then Dart's. "A botanist, probably. Identify the organic matter. That may or may not tell us something. And I think I would run a crew out to the Payne house once more to do some detail work between the garage entrance to the kitchen and the door to the study."

"But the garage was *locked*," Kowalski protested.

"I can't argue that," Bragg agreed, "but Ivy asked me what I'd do, and that's what I'd do."

"Yeah, well," Kowalski complained, "I say forget about it. This is not a fly ball, boys. It's a *grounder*. The guy ate a nine-millimeter—case and casket closed. You want to beat it stupid, that's your business. Me? I got other shit to do." Kowalski flicked his thick black hair off his forehead with his meaty hand and said, "Later."

Dart saw him reaching for a smoke before he was out of the lab.

Bragg said, "Something like this comes up, you know who I wish were still around?"

"Yeah, I know," Dart acknowledged, his stomach burning. *I know*, he thought privately. *And just maybe he's closer to this that you think.*

CHAPTER
17

The small, two-acre patch of grass along the west bank of the Connecticut River was technically part of Riverside Park, though not directly connected to it. This particular section was beneath the Charter Oak Bridge, a relatively new structure linking Hartford and East Hartford. The river's brown surface reflected the gray of the sky and the delicate etching of the dormant trees that lined its banks. A pair of ducks raced down the very center of the waterway, their wings singing. A brisk November chill raised Ginny's collar and had brought out a winter wool sweater. She wore her green oil slicker, partially open, green rubber half-boots with leather laces, and a pair of small pink gloves. The winter river was quieter than that of spring or summer, void of sound, as if sleeping while awaiting its blanket of ice, which had already begun to creep in from the edges.

Dart took a deep breath. "You look worried. What's wrong?" He felt he knew her well enough to ask this, although it implied an intimacy that she was clearly not comfortable with on that day.

"Nothing."

"If it's personal—"

"It's not," she snapped.

He felt too much a part of her to separate himself from her tension; it attached to him and slowly choked a ring around his upper throat, restricting his air and increasing his heart rate.

"The name of this woman that you gave me, Danielle Payne," she said, referring to the late Harold Payne's wife, "is in the system as a victim a domestic abuse."

For Dart, this confirmed that at least one verifiable way existed for the killer to identify his victims—this could not be explained by coincidence. The second part of the victim list seemed to be associated with convicted offenders. He said, "You could have told me that over the phone."

"It's bigger than that. Bigger than we thought. More confusing."

She didn't appreciate nagging, and so he waited her out, but the anxiety swelled in his chest.

She said, "Your friends Stapleton and Lawrence had both recently purchased extensive health care policies. Two-hundred-and-fifty-dollar deductible. The kind of policies you would associate with the affluent. Both within three months prior to their suicides. These are both men with no prior coverage. What did me in was your friend Harold Payne—"

Stop calling them my friends, he wanted to complain.

"He had a policy in place, but it was one thousand deductible. Exactly three months ago, he reapplied and obtained a two-hundred-and-fifty-dollar deductible."

Dart wasn't sure what to make of this information. Thinking aloud, he muttered, "All three suicides had new or recently altered insurance policies."

"Yes."

"Which connects them all, one to the other."

"Absolutely," she agreed.

It seemed to Dart yet another way that a killer might have identified his victims, and this, in turn, worried him because Ginny had been exploring the same database. "Why?" he asked, still puzzled.

"I don't have any idea. But it would seem that someone is buying these policies for them, and if that's the case, I may be able to find out who that is by accessing billing."

"Can you do that?"

"This is computers, Dart. You can do anything."

"Safely?"

"More lectures?"

The comment infuriated him, and for a moment he felt tempted to give her a piece of his mind but restrained himself by chewing on his lower lip. "Maybe one of the companies had some kind of marketing campaign in place."

"Offering policies for wife beaters and convicted sex offenders?"

"The demographics are similar," he said, realizing immediately that Payne's affluent lifestyle distanced him from both Stapleton and Lawrence. "I don't know," Dart conceded. "That's not right."

She handed him a large manila envelope and

said, "Victims of domestic violence, as identified by the insurers—Hartford, East Hartford, West Hartford. It's a big list, Dart, and probably quite incomplete. You might want to try your Sex Crimes files."

Guilt in the form of a searing heat flashed up his spine—*does she know about Abby?* he wondered. Hartford was a small town and rumors circulated freely. *Is she trying to tell me something?*

"Right," he said, attempting to interpret her expression while at the same time avoiding contact with her eyes. She could read him far too well.

But his eyes did stray to hers, and he saw that she was looking over his shoulder, not directly at him, and her expression was one of concern, causing him to glance back quickly.

In the distance, a ramped footbridge climbed up from ground level to a landing where it turned and rose by a series of formed-concrete steps to the pedestrian way on Charter Oak Bridge. Silhouetted on the landing stood the figure of a tall man.

Dart looked quickly away, his pulse pounding with this sight, returning his attention to Ginny and saying softly, "Is he still there?"

"He's heading up the stairs."

Dart ventured another glance and asked, "How long was he there?"

"I don't know," she answered, her voice reflecting her fear.

"Did he approach from the bottom or the bridge?"

"I don't know!" she repeated harshly.

Dart's first temptation was to turn and go after the man, despite the fact that it could have been any pedestrian simply pausing to enjoy the river view. But he felt uneasy about leaving Ginny alone in an isolated location, especially given her discovery of a possible conspiracy involving the three suicides.

"Listen—" he said.

"Go," she prompted.

"Are you sure?"

"Go! I'm fine."

Dart took off at a run. The entrance to the pedestrian ramp was a hundred yards ahead, the ramp itself climbing in his direction. He crossed several islands of weeds and a pair of paved roads that saw little, if any, traffic at that time of year. Reaching the ramp, he pushed hard, climbing it quickly while glancing down at where he and Ginny had been talking. Ginny, her head tilted back, her chin raised, watched him intently.

Dart flew up the concrete steps and up onto the bridge itself, and looked in both directions: first left, up the inclined arch of the bridge; then right, toward the city, and then down at ground level. He panted, out of breath, blood pounding in both ears. A car in the midst of a right-hand turn was visible to him only briefly. He blinked his eyes closed in an act of concentration, attempting to burn the image into his memory. But like the car, the image escaped, an undefinable blur, leaving only a color imprinted on the underside of his eyelids: blue-gray.

Dart recovered his breath and turned back to the steps to rejoin Ginny, but she and her car were gone, leaving Dart with that color imprinted into his vision, lingering like the afterglow of a flash camera: blue-gray.

He blocked out all else but this color, allowing it to swim within his head, and a voice quickly filled the void. It was the voice of a twelve-year-old black girl that interrupted him, the voice of Lewellan Page, resonating within her mother's kitchen as she offered to Lieutenant Abby Lang a description of the car that she had witnessed parked behind Gerald Lawrence's Battles Street apartment on the night of his "suicide." *Blue, maybe. Gray* . . . he recalled her saying.

The killer? Dart wondered, furious that he had not seen enough of the vehicle to register a make, a model, or a year.

CHAPTER
18

Standing inside the roadside phone booth, dialing the number, Walter Zeller experienced a parent's anger. Stupidity, he thought, is an art form in the proper hands. He had never been a parent, but he understood a parent's frustration well enough.

He collected his strength, preparing himself for the confrontation, annoyed by its necessity, alarmed by the degree of emotional resolve that this required, like dredging up the black muck of the river bottom to clear the way for further passage.

Traffic blew by him on the commercialized strip that could have been Anywhere, USA. Oversized plastic signs declaring DRIVE THRU WINDOW and AMERICA'S FAVORITE; cheap marketing gimmicks like giant anchors perched out front, or a lobster claw reaching for the sky like a church steeple. He felt quite above such fanfare, sick of it, disgusted by the greed, the blatant disregard of aesthetics, and the public's seemingly insatiable appetite for neon, repetitive architecture, and Low Everyday Prices! Sick to death.

Throughout his years of public service, he believed that he had concealed well his sentimentality. Only Lucky had ever seen that side of the otherwise iron-willed sergeant. Yet dialing this number and anticipating the voice on the other end flooded him with such emotions, alarming him with a vulnerability that both relieved and ashamed him. Relieved, because it reminded him of his own humanity. Ashamed, because Walter Zeller was above sniveling about the past. His blunt fingertip hesitated alongside the final digit. An eighteen-wheeler roared past, carrying behind it a train of raised dust and the stench of diesel and burning rubber. Zeller stabbed the button. Fuck it, he thought.

"Dartelli," the voice answered.

Walter Zeller hesitated, a knot in his throat.

"Hello? I can't hear you."

Without introduction, Zeller asked, "Why do it the easy way when there's a hard way?"

"Sarge?"

Zeller registered the astonishment in Dart's voice, the fear and concern, his decades of skilled interrogation techniques not lost. "Are they suicides, Ivy?"

Silence as even the kid's breathing stopped.

"Answer me!" Maintain the upper hand at all times.

"No."

"Of course not. Good. Very good."

"I've been trying to—"

"Don't try—do!" he said, purposely interrupting to prevent the kid the completion of even a single thought, keeping him off balance and out of sorts. Maintain control. "They took their own lives, but they're not suicides, Ivy. Do you understand?"

"No."

"Don't get sidetracked with insurance records, for Christ's sake. What the hell can that accomplish?"

"It was you on the bridge?"

Disappointed that he'd allowed the man a complete sentence, Zeller strung together a series of thoughts and voiced them as a single spoken stream. "I'm your fucking guardian angel, Ivy. I'm watching over you so that you don't go astray, and believe me, it's a fucking full-time job with you. What's happened to you? Making a huge tangle out of something so simple. Overthinking," he said, raising a complaint that he had voiced dozens of times. "Making problems instead of solving them. Losing track of the basics. Didn't you retain anything? For any conviction to stick, the detective needs to be able to connect all the dots himself. That is, unless the snitch is willing to take the witness stand, and I can tell you right fucking now that that is not the direction we're going—you and me. The basics, damn it all. Didn't you retain anything? Shit! If the suicides aren't suicides, and if, on the other hand, these guys all killed themselves, then what the fuck is going on here? Make sense of it, Ivy. Don't make a mountain of confusion. What about their blood, Ivy? The basics! Sometimes the enemy is within." He slammed the phone into the cradle, his hand still shaking, though not from the cold.

Things never went as planned, and people were as unpredictable as the weather. Walter Zeller felt the need to take the kid by the shoulders and shake some sense into him—set him straight. He stood in the phone booth looking down at his trembling hands, wondering what was happening to him. How could he let the kid get to him this way? How had he become involved in the first place? Kowalski was the one he had targeted—as dumb as stone, and yet smart enough to let a sleeping dog lie. The truth would out soon enough, all by itself.

Joe Dartelli, the pride and joy of his police career, was another thing entirely. Dartelli, with his college degree and his barnyard sense of where the rat was hiding, was proving nothing but trouble.

I'll put him in the hospital if I have to, Zeller thought, just like they're trying to do to me.

He glanced down the street nervously, alert for the familiar Toyota, for the cracked and bent face behind the wheel—the hired knee-breaker he had been outrunning all this time. Out-smarting. Out-thinking.

Looking down once again, he felt relieved to see that his hands had stopped shaking. He was under control again, and for Zeller, control was everything.

CHAPTER
19

Dart was part theatre critic, part acting coach. It was his job to make this woman tell him what she didn't want to. Any interrogation amounted to the same thing: a con game of give-and-take, of tricks, the challenge of making someone say something that he or she had no intention of saying. Any investigator worth his salt knew that everyone held secrets. The skill was finding a way to pry it out.

The CAPers interrogation rooms were a pair of small unattractive cubicles, each containing a cheap table and two metal chairs. Dart dragged a third chair inside and shut the door, well aware of the effects of such an austere environment. Interrogation offered only a single door. That door lead either to jail or to freedom, depending on how the critics rated a performance.

Danielle Payne, the wife of the Halloween suicide, had an artificial look of surprise around her eyes that could be attributed only to a face lift. Her skin was flawlessly smooth, her lips a sensual red, and the rest of her could have been the model for Tommy Templeton's Venus, a pinup of epic proportions with a pair of breasts that would have made her surgeon proud, displayed in a tight turtleneck top that accentuated the lack of any visible means of support, defying all rules of gravity and age. That she had been married to a known pornographer could be easily determined by her lousy taste in clothing, her platinum hair, the gum that she chewed between her front teeth, and a heightened sense of sexual readiness, communicated by repetitively placing her hand into her crotch and withdrawing it slowly, and a tendency to shift her upper body around restlessly, jiggling her breasts and twisting her narrow waist as if she needed an itch scratched. Scratched hard, by the look of her.

The attorney to her right, Dart's left, was a silver-tongued, six-hundred-grand-a-year asshole by the name of Gambelli. His mere presence warned Dart not to expect much.

After formal introductions for the sake of a tape recorder, he asked the woman to recount her activities on the night of her husband's suicide—a suicide that Dart considered a murder but lacked the evidence to investigate as such. Throughout her narration, Dart sensed in her an underlying nervousness that he associated with lying. There were two different kinds of anxiety that surfaced in an interrogation—the person uncomfortable and unfamiliar with being in the company of a cop; and the person who had something to hide.

Danielle Payne fell firmly into the second category.

"How would you describe your relationship with your husband, Ms. Payne?"

"My relationship?" she asked, checking with the attorney, who offered a barely visible nod.

"Warm and fuzzy?" Dart offered. "Turbulent. . . . Nurturing?"

"We got on okay, I guess."

"Okay?" Dart asked. "Affectionate? Romantic? Distant? Cold?"

"We liked each other fine. Harry, you know, had his work, his stuff, and I had my stuff too. Okay, I guess."

"He was never rough with you," Dart stated, clearly making her uncomfortable.

"Rough?" she gasped, blushing.

"Physically abusive," Dart clarified.

Gambelli tugged at his French cuff and said, "Where are you going with this, Dartelli?"

Danielle Payne squirmed in her chair, all sexuality lost. Her face puckered up into a knot of worry.

"Abusive situations are difficult on the victim of that abuse." *I ought to know*, he thought, thinking of his alcoholic mother and hiding inside the dryer.

"Meaning?" Gambelli questioned.

"Ms. Payne," Dart said, doing his best to ignore the attorney, "was your husband ever physically abusive toward you?"

"Did he rough me up some? Sure he did," she admitted. "He's gone now. What's it matter if I tell you. He was not an angel. So what? Show me a man who is."

"And you put up with this behavior of his," Dart said. "You tolerated it. You endured it."

She shrugged. "We've got a nice place to live. I drive a Mercedes. Have you ever driven a Mercedes?" she asked, her eyes searching Dart, as if to say that this mattered a great deal. Dart shook his head no. She said, "It's a nice car. A real nice car, a Mercedes. So what do you know?"

"Isn't it true," Dart asked her, "that on at least six different occasions you admitted yourself to the emergency room for injuries sustained from conflicts with your late husband, that on two occasions you telephoned Nine-one-one and asked for help from the police?"

She said defensively, "It was all a mistake."

"He's dead," Dart reminded. "You don't need to fear him. You don't need to lie to me."

She looked away. Her attorney advised her that she need not answer any question that she chose not to. Her eyes pooled with tears, she waved him off.

Dart waited until she appeared more at ease. He needed to judge her reaction carefully to this, his most important question. He studied her and asked, "Were you ever approached by a man offering to help you with your husband?"

Her expression disappointed him, for she didn't appear to understand the implication that Dart was attempting, Whereas her attorney certainly did.

"I don't want you to answer that," the attorney snapped to his client.

But Danielle Payne had already formed an answer in her head, and she spoke it. "They approached *him*, not me. It was his problem, not mine. Nothing I could do about it."

For the first time in this meeting, Dart and Gambelli met eyes, neither able to contain their astonishment at her answer. Dart's eyes said sternly, *Let me pursue this*. Gambelli's were a cauldron of concern.

The attorney admonished. "Danielle, please!"

But she had to protest, "He didn't tell me any more than that—only that they could help him and he was going to try it." To Dart she said, "Harry loved me loads. He didn't want to be mean. Really. He didn't want to hurt me."

"They?" Dart asked, knowing full well that the attorney would interrupt, which he did. But Danielle Payne seemed to be venting.

"What's he care what I say? He's dead and gone. What's it matter to him?"

Seizing quickly on this, Dart asked, "Who offered to help your husband, Ms. Payne? What do you mean by that?" Dart had imagined just the opposite—that Walter Zeller had made himself available for hire to women who wanted their abusive spouses eliminated, that he had created a profession out of reversing his years of investigating homicides. An abused wife or lover, or the mother of an abused child, would have plenty of motivation to see the sex offender killed. A carefully manufactured suicide would be quickly cleared. Zeller could carry out his own passion and earn a living while convincing himself he was doing the world a favor. This fit Zeller's control-

185

ling personality and his disenchantment with the legal system that he had abandoned. But Danielle Payne was throwing him off completely: The mention of a third party, and this third party approaching Payne himself, did not fit with any of Dart's preconceived notions.

"I don't know," she answered, and he trusted the confusion in her eyes. "Harry said he couldn't tell me, but that things were going to get better, that *he* was going to be better, and that I just had to trust him and the doctors."

Gambelli released a chest full of air and said, "Enough!" attempting to silence his client. To Dart, he said, "I'd like to speak with her alone, Detective. If you intend to pursue this any further, I must speak with her first."

"Doctors?" Dart said to the woman.

"Do *not* answer that, Danielle," Gambelli warned, and this time his client obeyed. She nodded, and hung her head. She wore sky blue eye shadow on eyelids edged with pencil, her lashes gobbed with mascara.

The woman murmured, "There's nothing to tell. I don't know any more than that."

Gambelli shook his head in disgust and slapped his legs with open palms.

"Doctors," Dart repeated, in the voice of a man thinking aloud.

"I never met 'em," she said. "But Harry was better toward me, nicer and all, and so I wasn't complaining."

A thought occurred to Dart. "Did your husband ask that you leave the house that evening?"

"No way," she answered sharply.

"It was Halloween," Dart countered. "Didn't he want you home to help give out the candy?"

She hung her head again. "It isn't a friendly neighborhood," she said.

At least not toward convicted pornographers, Dart thought, realizing that the Paynes would have been shunned following his arrest.

"He didn't have a meeting planned?"

Gambelli allowed this question to pass.

"No. Not so as he told me about."

Reading from his notes, he questioned her about the housecleaner, and she confirmed that the house had been cleaned that same morning. She also confirmed that there was no Dustbuster or similar small vacuum in the house. "And who had access to your garage? It operates via a remote, is that right?"

"A clicker, yeah. Sure. Harry and me, we both had clickers in our cars."

"And you used yours upon your return?" Dart asked.

She nodded.

He said, "And the garage door was down at the time?"

"Sure it was. What's this with the garage door and all?"

Dart believed that Bragg's evidence—the pine needles, rock salt, and potting soil found in the garage and inside the study—pointed toward Payne's killer having entered through the garage. Once inside the garage, the kitchen door was unlocked and would have allowed egress, unde-tected. Access to the garage was only through the automatic door openers, one of which Danielle Payne controlled. It was this combination of facts that had lead him to consider that she had arranged for her husband's staged suicide— providing her garage door opener to a killer she had hired.

"And none of your husband's business associates would have a garage door opener for your house."

"Of course not!"

"Your housecleaner?"

"No."

"And your security system that night. It would have been on or off?"

"Harry liked to keep it on when we were home. He didn't want no surprise visits." She blushed and averted her eyes. It was the police he had hoped to avoid. "But Halloween it would have been off for sure. At least I think it would have been."

Dart dropped the biggest bombshell he had in his arsenal, hoping for a direct hit. It stemmed from a phone call he had placed earlier that day. "You weren't with your friends, the Fallowfields, that evening, Ms. Payne, as you claim to have been in your *sworn statement*." Dart glanced at Gambelli, knowing that the attorney, if not his client, would understand her vulnerability. "We checked with the Fallowfields. You saw them only for a drink that evening."

The woman glanced at her attorney.

"I don't want to file perjury charges," he said, leaning heavily on the word and presenting it as a serious possibility. "And I wouldn't want to drag you through the routine of being booked and charged with that or with more serious crimes. But I do need some answers, and so I turn it over to you—the two of you—as to where we go from here."

Her frightened eyes appealed to Gambelli. The attorney sought out and located the woman's signed statement and read it over. He then said, "I would advise you to answer the detective's questions, Danielle. Given the circumstances, I think it's in everyone's best interest." He looked over at Dart with a mixture of anger and respect and seemed to be fully involved for the first time.

"Where were you that night, Ms. Payne?"

For all her forty-odd years, she looked more like a child as she appealed again with her eyes. Gambelli simply glared back at ner. She told the detective. "With a friend."

"A friend?"

"In bed, okay? I was in bed with a friend."

"You were having an affair," he stated.

"No shit," she answered angrily. "We were fucking our brains out, okay? You want the details?"

"I want his name. I want the exact times."

She asked her attorney, "Do I have to?"

Gambelli nodded.

She provided Dart the details of her assignation, and said, "You satisfied?" It would require a phone call to verify, but he suspected she was telling the truth.

"The doctors," Dart said. "I need everything and anything that you can tell me."

"I don't know shit, I'm telling you! Only that

Harry said that some doctors were going to help him get better—about hitting me, you know, about roughing me up—and that I wasn't to tell no one."

"Did he meet with these doctors?" Dart asked.

"I don't know. He must have. Right?"

"Did he take medication?"

"Injections," she said, touching her own arm. "I know that because I saw the Band-Aid on his arm one night, and he said how that was part of making him better."

"Injections," Dart repeated, taking this down in his notepad. "Those were his words, 'making him better,'" Dart checked.

"Right."

"And you took that to mean?"

"Better . . . you know . . . less hitting . . . less rough stuff. Not that I mind it a little rough, you know—the for-fun kind of rough, but Harry had a temper on him that wouldn't quit sometimes. And it wasn't me, you know—he used to tell me that. It wasn't me. It was just me being a woman. It was like something chemical in him. Like a bad seed. Like that movie where the guy changes into the crazy doctor who kills people, you know? Like that."

"You never met these doctors."

"No."

"Never spoke to them on the phone."

"Not that I know of."

"And he received these injections . . .?"

"Every two weeks, just about. Seems to me. He'd had maybe four or five."

"Your husband changed his medical insurance," Dart stated. "Do you remember that?"

"Don't know anything about it. Swear."

"The dates of which appear to coincide with this treatment."

"He didn't tell me jack shit about anything to do with money. That was his department. My department . . ." She hesitated and then said, "My department was the bedroom." She locked eyes with Dart, hers a fire of fierce intensity and resentment. He had demeaned her, debased her with this questioning.

"If these doctors should contact you—"

"They won't."

"But if they should."

"I should call you," she stated. "Forget it. No way. Harry's dead. Let him be. They were trying to help him. So maybe they'll help someone else."

An alarm sounded in Dart's head. Zeller had made a riddle out of it—people taking their own lives but not committing suicide. *A drug gone bad,* he thought. *Guinea pigs. Test subjects.*

As Zeller had warned: The blood of the victims could be the key.

CHAPTER
20

"Joe, I've got another one," Abby announced in a forced whisper, dragging a chair over to his desk. She smelled like lilacs in bloom; her cheeks were flushed and her blond hair needed combing.

Dart's attention was elsewhere. He had just hung up from speaking first with Teddy Bragg and then with pathologist Dr. Victor Ray, requesting the results of Harold Payne's blood toxicology. The discussions had strayed into unfamiliar territory as Dart explored what could and could not be detected by such tests, finally persuading Dr. Ray to request a complete workup, since, typically, blood toxicology tested only for the more common narcotics and alcohol levels and tightwad Teddy Bragg had not wanted to release the funds necessary for such testing without "some damn good reasons," which Dart found impossible to provide.

Abby placed a computer printout on the desk in front of Dart, a single line highlighted in a bright yellow. Reading the name on the file, his body reacted as if he had taken a niacin tablet— every pore on fire. His blood pressure rose so quickly that he could hardly hear her whisper. "This is from *our* files," she said, meaning Sex Crimes. "And *this*," she emphasized, "is from CAPers." Another highlighted line that shared the same name.

He forced himself to inhale, a drowning man attempting to recover.

"A suicide, Joe—and a *suspected* sex offender. As far as I can tell, the two have never been connected," she said excitedly, "which I can explain. We do not reveal the identities of *suspected* offenders because of the libel suit lost in New Haven. Only arrests and convictions. This guy was never arrested—we didn't have enough evidence." She paused and said, "Do you recognize the name, Joe? Remember that case? Think what the papers would have done if we'd showed them this," she said, tapping the Sex Crimes folder. "Can you believe it?" She waited, knowing he would recognize the name. And although he did, he said nothing. He wasn't sure what to say, in part because he felt in a state of physical shock. She misunderstood his hesitation. "It's the Ice Man, Joe! Come on! The Ice Man! And he flew out of a window just like Stapleton did. What's that, coincidence? Stapleton *was not the first.*" A critical part of the job working a string of crimes was to identify the first in the series. Abby, believing as Dart did that they were on to a string, was ebullient with her discovery. "Get it?"

"I was second on the Ice Man," he informed her. A lump filled his throat, painfully choking him. He understood at that moment that there was no running away, only avoidance. Things believed dead and buried inevitably returned, either symbolically or literally, stepping out of the grave. He saw no way to tell her, no way to ask her to return the files and forget about it. The Ice Man had crawled back out of his grave. A part of Dart actually felt relief; the remainder of him was in a state of total panic.

"Kowalski was the lead," he explained. "I was the second."

"Talk about coincidence," she said, lowering her voice. "Teddy is going to pull the evidence for us."

"What?" Dart asked, astonished.

"Yeah, isn't that great?" she said, mistaking his reaction for enthusiasm. "He agreed to review it with Rankin and Haite after lunch—to see if we can make any physical comparisons to Stapleton and the others."

The 3-D animated software had already made just such a connection—no wonder that Bragg felt prompted to delve into possible connections.

Dart felt short of breath. He could feel his skin go alternately hot and cold. His head swam. *Damage control*, he warned himself.

"What's wrong, Joe?" she asked cautiously. "I thought you'd be thrilled. It's an obvious connection."

Dart felt paralyzed by the numbness sweeping through him—he was in the midst of an anxiety attack. *He heard her footsteps coming down the stairs and the* whoosh *of her dress.* He looked up, only to see Abby.

He weighed the options available to him.

She placed her hand tenderly on his arm, and that did it. He snapped his head toward her, startling her, and said, "How would you like to take a walk?"

Concern stealing the excitement from her face, she pushed her chair back and stood.

A bitter cold had descended on the city in anticipation of winter, still more than a month away. They walked from headquarters toward a path that led down to the river. They passed a few smokers and then found themselves alone in the woods.

He wasn't sure how or where to start.

"I was the second on the Ice Man," he repeated. "Kowalski was the primary, but he was worthless and everyone knew it. They wouldn't assign Zeller because he had lost Lucky only a few months before and there wasn't much left of him. But I consulted him nonetheless, because then, as now, there's none better."

"Yes, I remember a lot of it," she said sadly. "I was directly involved because it was the Asian Strangler, because of the Sex Crimes connection, although I was still with CAPers then."

"So," he explained, "even though I was technically the second, it actually ended up my case in many ways."

"Nothing new for a Kowalski investigation."

They stopped; she leaned against a tree stump and Dart sat onto a rock embedded in the earth. But he didn't feel connected to the earth; he felt almost as if he were floating. He continued. "The guy was found naked and frozen—as you'll recall—his head bashed in from the jump, no identification. The pressure to clear it got pretty intense. Media slump. City Hall going ballistic. They came down on Kowalski like a ton of bricks. I was left pretty much unscathed. I continued to consult Zeller. He was drinking pretty heavily at the time and was starting to lose it. I loved him like a father," Dart confessed, his throat tight. "It was hard for me to see him like that."

"I'm sure." She studied him. "Hard on anybody, Joe."

"Kowalski ended up in the hot seat, but because of his connections he was pretty well

195

protected. Spent most of his time defending an investigation that had basically gone nowhere."

"If it's any consolation, Joe," she said, still misunderstanding him, "I'm sure you did as good a job as could be done, given the circumstances."

"Me? No. It was Zeller who broke the case."

"Meaning?" She had that Abby look of concern that he had come to know—knitted brow, pursed lips, lowered chin. If she had read those files, then she knew that the case had never been "broken," but simply cleared as a jumper.

"It was Zeller who ID'd him. He had jumped from a window on the night of that terrible blizzard. Hit hard, and either landed or rolled into the street. Covered by the falling snow, he was struck by a city plow and pushed three blocks down the street, where he was deposited under a snowbank for three weeks. When it finally thawed, we had the Ice Man on our hands." He stood and she followed, and they walked deeper into the woods. Gray and brown tree trunks; leaves mushy underfoot. He wasn't sure how much to tell her, but he began to realize that it was all going to come out, that secrets were a thing of the past. *If nothing else*, he thought, *this is a dress rehearsal for my discharge.* "Zeller found the apartment first." *It should have sent up a red flag*, he thought. "He didn't want it to appear that he was working Kowalski's turf, so he funneled the information through me—pointing me without actually telling me anything." *He's doing the same thing again*, he realized.

"He was the best," she said admiringly.

"Maybe too good," Dart replied, confusing

her, judging by her expression. "He taught me—drummed into me, is more like it—to always return to the crime scene, not just once, but several times, that you always see it differently. And so that's what I did." He stopped. This was the dangerous territory, and despite his resolve to tell her everything he felt himself holding back, and he hated himself for it. This was the voice of the devil, he realized—still looking for a way out, still believing that the secret could be reburied.

"Are you going to explain that?" she asked. She pulled at her jacket, fending off the cold. She sat down on a log and Dart joined her.

He nodded and swallowed, his mouth and throat bone dry, and said, "It wasn't from my repeat visits, but Teddy Bragg's report and the accompanying inventory of the Ice Man's apartment. It listed a spool of hemp rope. It was put down as a fifty-foot spool of three-eighths-inch hemp. Your mind does funny things. Who knows where my mind was, or what it was up to, but that hemp rope leapt out at me and wrapped itself around my neck like a noose." Again he tried to swallow. Again his throat constricted. "Lucky Zeller had been found tied up with three-eighths-inch hemp."

Abby, squinting, rocked forward nervously, her hands clamped in a viselike grip between her thighs.

Dart said, "I had access to the other Asian Strangler reports—Lucky wasn't the only one. All three of the victims had been tied and bound with hemp rope. I was very proud of myself, and

197

not thinking it through. I wrote it up and put it into the file. I requested that Teddy Bragg collect the spool from the apartment."

"Oh, God," she said, seeing clearly where Dart was headed.

"Not long after that, I started thinking what you're thinking now, and it terrified me too." He hesitated and said, "I stole two pieces of the rope from the property room—one used on Lucky Zeller, the other from the spool found in the apartment. I circumvented Teddy and submitted the samples to the lab and intercepted the return report so that no one saw it but me. It came back that the two were from the same manufacturer— more than likely the same lot run."

"Oh, Christ."

"Zeller had somehow tracked down his wife's killer—the Asian Strangler—and, as far as I was concerned, had probably caved in his hat and then tossed him out a window to cover it up." He looked up at the bare limbs and the gray sky— it all seemed so dead. "I had to cover myself, because the State Police lab would itemize the work done for us in their monthly bill, and Teddy Bragg, meticulous as he is, would see it. So I properly filed the lab report in with the Ice Man file, in case he checked—put it right where it belonged."

"Oh, shit!" she said.

Good little Boy Scout, he was chiding himself as he held up a finger to stop her briefly. "I had some thinking to do. The Asian Strangler was dead. A man who tortured and mutilated women. No cost to society. No more concerns about the threat he posed. And I had to think: *What's so wrong here?* If I was right, Zeller had evened the scales, had done us all a favor, and maybe had found a way to live with the loss of his wife. He was no longer drinking. He was looking better, even talking about teaching down at the university." He continued, "But I had left quite a trail of evidence. I had to bring it to Kowalski's attention—to Haite and Rankin—or let it slide. Leave it where it was—divided between the property room and the file room."

She paled noticeably.

He said strongly, "It was entirely circumstantial. I knew damn well that this was no *grounder*. We wouldn't get a conviction—not if Walter Zeller was in fact the killer; he wouldn't leave that kind of trail—"

"Oh, shit," she said, realizing what she had done by alerting Haite to the Ice Man files.

Dart felt resolved now to tell it all. In a way it felt good to him. "But I did bring Zeller the evidence that I had. I told him what I knew, and what I thought he had done. He must have gone ten minutes without saying anything. Then he looked over at me and told me that it was time to retire. He showed no remorse, no guilt. But he had hate in his eyes—he had wanted to stay on in the department, and he knew that I had ended that."

She scooted over to him and held him, and he felt the warmth of her through his jacket. "I've opened it up again."

"It's better, I think. This thing had damned

near killed me. And now Stapleton and Lawrence and Payne—all far too close to the Ice Man."

"Oh, shit," she gasped.

"It's him, Abby. I may never prove it—I don't know how he's doing it—but I know it in my heart, and that means that I'm responsible for those deaths. You want to talk about motivation to solve a case?"

She leaned back and caught eyes with him. "They're slime, Joe. Every one of them is pure slime. Trust me on this. There's no great loss here."

"Look the other way?" he said, disgusted. "You don't think I've considered that? A jury of one? Uniform justice? Shoot the guy in the alley and it's easier on everyone? You try that out. It's not something you can live with and keep coming to work."

"Bullshit," she said. "You don't *know* that you're right. You can't prove it—you said so yourself. You need to find Zeller, to collect more evidence."

To take control, Dart felt like adding.

"Haite will tear you apart. You'll be suspended, investigated—and you never will find out the truth." She added, "Do you think Kowalski will?" She checked her watch. "There's still time."

"For what? Me to get out of the country?" he mocked.

"To get the Ice Man files and the evidence and make them disappear."

"You're not serious," Dart said.

"I got you into this."

"Abby—"

"I *am* serious," she said. "And damn it, I'm going to need your help."

CHAPTER
21

The meeting took take place at a dirt cul-de-sac called "the swing," a dirt track that led to an old tree overhanging the river, used in the summer to swing and splash. In November the place was certain to be deserted.

Dart remembered the location from his rookie year when the swing had been one of his patrol responsibilities. He had come upon a coed group of skinny-dipping teens and had scared them half to death.

To reach the swing, he drove to the East Hartford side, crossing Charter Oak Bridge, and headed north until the treacherous dirt track that led steeply down toward the river, and executed a hairpin turn before descending into the bulb-shaped parking area littered with beer cans. He locked the Volvo and took Mac for a short walk, going slowly so that the old dog didn't push his arthritic bones. When Dart stopped, drinking in the view of the peaceful river and a gaggle of Canada geese skimming its surface, Mac came alongside and leaned his weight into Dart, catching his chin on Dart's knee—for Mac, the ultimate sign of affection. He reached down and petted his head. Mac was old, having lived two more years than the vet had given him, and yet it was true: He was Dart's best friend. The idea of losing him was too much to bear, and for this shared moment of quietude, Dart felt grateful.

He continued on and reached the edge of the river, where a thin shelf of bone white ice stretched twenty yards toward the main current. Rocks had been tossed through the ice, puncturing it with small dark holes that had bubbled river water and then scabbed over.

As darkness settled in, from across the river came the lights of the water treatment facility and the power generating station.

Dart couldn't escape the feeling of being watched, paranoia tickling at the edges of his rational mind. And yet the area appeared to be clear.

As he climbed back up to the parking area, Mac at his side, he heard the sound of Gorman's arriving car.

Bud Gorman, Dart's friend whose job involved tracking a person's credit history and spending patterns, was dressed for the cold, his big ears protruding from beneath a knit cap. Dart didn't think of the man as possessing a nervous disposition, but this spying did make him jumpy—his nose twitched like a rabbit's. "That's an old dog," he said.

"What did you find out?" Dart asked, knowing to keep this business. Gorman was a talker.

"Walter Zeller drew unemployment for two months, March to early June, three years ago."

"After he retired," Dart said.

"I suppose so. July through December the same year, he worked for something called Proctor Securities."

"Yes, I remember," Dart said.

"He pulled in six hundred forty-three a week, after withholdings. We have record of the usual phone and utility bill payments, some credit card activity for this same three-month period. Lived at—"

"Four-twenty-four Winchester Court."

"Yeah."

"Come the first of January last year, his credit records move to Seattle, as you indicated. He leaves his account here open to cover some automatic withdrawals. But here's the strange part about the Seattle side," he added ominously. "I show virtually no financial activity, except for some electronic fund transfers—automatic deposits—his pension. Each month, a single withdrawal is made against this account—my guess is a certified check or bank payment that is probably then mailed to whatever location Zeller has specified."

"The amount?"

"Twenty-three hundred. The same every month. The only other withdrawals appear tax related and, again, are not drawn on account checks but paid into the bank funds instead and drawn from there."

"And that's all you show?"

"The man is out of the system, Joe. He's existing in a strictly cash environment is my guess. If he's spending cash, then I can't trace him."

No one can, Dart thought, wondering if that was the point.

To show Dart that he had done a thorough job, Gorman added, "Credit card activity up to January was retail mostly. Department store records show jeans, boots, shirts, socks, and underwear—strictly basic stuff."

"Weapons? Airline tickets? Train tickets? Hotel rooms?"

"Nothing like that."

"Gasoline?"

"No. Nothing. That's what I'm saying—he's strictly cash."

"You mentioned taxes?"

"He filed all taxes as a resident of Washington State, but no financial trail indicating that he spends any time there."

"Or anywhere else," Dart reminded.

"True. That's right. It's almost as if he's disappeared."

He has, Dart thought.

"And if he had a bank account in some other state?"

"I'd know. Same with credit cards, department store accounts—I can track anything that requires his social security number."

The night swallowed them in an envelope of darkness. The air was wet and accompanied by a bone-chilling cold that cut through Dart's jacket and sweater. Mac, sitting alongside Dart, leaned his weight warmly against Dart's right leg. The detective reached down and petted the dog and pulled on his ears, which Mac loved.

"And if he could get around the social security number? Obtain a false number?" Dart asked.

"That's a hell of a lot more difficult than it used to be."

"But if he could?" Dart asked, thinking, *New social security number, driver's license, bank accounts, credit cards . . .*

"We'd never find him," Gorman replied, his disappointment obvious. "Right?"

"Yeah," answered Dart. "I think that's just the point."

CHAPTER
22

Bragg said, "You're as nervous as a fox in a chicken coop."

"It's the chickens that should be nervous," Dart said.

"Whatever." Bragg was often trying to sell himself as the country farmer that a boy from Brooklyn could never be. There was a new leak in the small closet that Bragg used for a lab. The area smelled strongly of photo chemicals from the huge developer in the next room.

"You look sick, Teddy. You feel all right?"

"Fine."

"Pale. You smoke too much."

"Shut up."

"I'm *worried* about you," Dart objected. "Or doesn't that count?"

"No. It doesn't count." He said, "You worried about that crippled dog of yours, too. He turned out fine."

"He's not crippled."

"See what I mean?" Bragg bumped Dart's shoulder with his own. "Look closer," he encouraged.

Dart leaned over the lab counter and pressed his eye closer to the loupe.

"It's the organic matter from the Payne suicide. It's called a bald cypress. It grows here, but it's not considered common by any means."

Samantha Richardson joined in, "The Paynes do *not* have a bald cypress on their property." Dart had forgotten all about her, she had remained so quiet. She was dressed in blue jeans, a white shirt, and a forest green sweater vest. She was wearing wire-rim glasses. It was the first time that Dart had seen her in glasses.

"Sam followed up on this at my request," Bragg informed him.

"Why?"

"We both know why, goddamn it," Bragg answered angrily. "Lang made all that stink about the Ice Man—Nesbit—and although that got nowhere, Haite sees the unusual number of suicides, and he's looking for a possible connection. It's Lang's fault, not mine. Don't blame me."

"Or me," Samantha chimed in.

"I got bigger fish to fry than this," Bragg complained. "But he wants each and every piece of evidence on *every* one of these suicides followed up on. If there *is* a connection, he wants it. Don't blame me! Christ, he's got Kowalski running around like . . . like . . ."

"A fox in a henhouse." Dart completed.

"Fuck off."

"Thank you."

"So we're reworking the Lawrence evidence, the Nesbit stuff, Stapleton, Payne—it's a shitload of work."

Mention of the Ice Man—Nesbit—caused Dart a flash of panic, but he concealed it. Bragg's explanation was filling in some gaps. Haite had sent Dart a memo inquiring about a complete blood workup on Payne. So far, Dart had avoided an answer.

"And this is about the only unexplained trace evidence at the Payne suicide," Richardson completed.

Bragg added, "And Haite—like me, like you—sees the possibility that these bald cypress might have been left by a visitor, and he—like me, like you—wants to know who that visitor might have been and what the fuck he was doing there."

"I see," said Dart, thinking, *I know who it was. I know what he was doing there. But Haite, of all people, is not going to believe it without a hell of a lot more evidence.*

"No bald cypress there," Dart said to Richardson.

"Not at the Paynes', no."

"Which is where you come in," said Bragg. "'Cause there's only the two of us here, and I got other fish to cook."

"To *fry*," Dart corrected.

"Fuck off." To Richardson, Bragg said, "Tell him."

"HHS has a listing of all bald cypresses in Hartford, East Hartford, and West Hartford."

"HHS?"

"The Hartford Horticultural Society. They keep track of rare species." She reached back to the counter and handed Dart a fax. "Only eleven in the area."

"Which is where you come in," Bragg repeated.

"You want me to go hunting down *trees*?" Dart asked, perplexed.

"Trees, rock salt, and potting soil," Bragg reminded. "We lifted all three, in combination. It's a definite signature. And it's not *me*," Bragg objected, "but your wonderful Sergeant Haite who wants this. You want to take issue, take it upstairs."

"No, thanks."

"I didn't think so."

"I could help after work," Richardson offered Dart.

"No, you couldn't," Bragg countered.

There was something in the woman's eyes that said this had nothing to do with bald cypress leaves, and Dart felt it clear to his toes. "I'd like that," he said, not knowing where his words came from.

"Good," she said.

"Not good," Bragg complained.

"Fuck off," Dart said, though in good humor, and Bragg cracked a smile.

The detective folded the fax neatly and slipped

it into his pocket. He could feel Richardson's eyes still boring into him as he left the lab.

It felt good.

CHAPTER
23

At seven-thirty on a cold November night, an hour and a half after the day shift ended, Dart and Samantha Richardson were out hunting down the registered locations of bald cypresses. Sam took East Hartford, and the greatest concentration—seven—of the trees. Dart took the city.

Residents at the first two of Dart's four locations politely explained that they had never heard of the species and offered for Dart to look around, which he did. As it turned out, there were no bald cypresses at either location. He reached Sam by cell phone and was told, with reluctance on her part, that the horticultural list had been complied some seven years earlier. Many of the trees could now be dead, and worse, others might have been planted within the last few years and not be included on the list.

The door of the third location was answered by a matronly woman with bluish hair and substantial girth. Closer to East Hartford, this was a decidedly nicer house than Dart's first two attempts. There was a small backyard with a bird-bath, but the bald cypress was to be found *inside* the house, making Dart skeptical about the possibility of this leading him to Payne's visitor. The futility of this search began to wear on him. He felt depressed and stretched thin—nothing about these cases ever seemed to connect; he worked on hunches, but with so little evidence. Here he was, chasing a *tree*! He felt like an idiot.

At 9:00 P.M., Dart once again connected by phone with Richardson, who was having equally bad luck, and she informed him that she intended to head home and try again tomorrow. Dart had promised himself one last try, but he too gave it up.

After work the next night, at a few minutes past 7:00 P.M. Dart drove over toward Pope Park South to search the last of his four locations. Although a scant few blocks from the Trinity College enclave, the Hamilton Court address was unfamiliar to him and not the kind of place that Dart felt easy visiting alone at night. It was a tough neighborhood, and the proximity to Pope Park made for some tension as it doubled as a needle park after dark. On the park's northern boundary, Park Street ran east-west and was the most dangerous of any street in the city at night. Anything and everything was available there, from crack cocaine to teenage boys—the weapons count was astronomical. If a patrol car cruised Park Street, it did so with a team, heavily armed and ever alert.

Hamilton Court turned out to be a filthy, narrow alley less than fifty yards long that bisected a steep hill and connected Hamilton Street with Park Terrace. Dart turned onto the street and kept on driving, reluctant to park or even to slow down. Four decrepit clapboard buildings lined the alley, two on each side, surrounded by broken and decaying chain-link fences.

Driving past, Dart hoped the entrance to these houses might be on Zion, at the top of the hill, but he made a pass through the alley twice and determined that their only access was off Hamilton Court. Number 11 was pale yellow, the windows of the ground floor alit. The rotting wood trim had once been white.

Dart parked and locked the car with the engine running, thankful that he kept two car keys for just this purpose. He removed his police identification card and slung it's chain around his neck, hopeful that a shooter would think twice before dropping a cop. Cop killers had short lives once inside Hartford jails. He walked over to the sagging stairs and climbed them quickly with sharp, quick movements as he kept an eye on everything around him. *Stupid time of night to be here*, he thought to himself, heart pounding, his hand ready to draw his weapon. This was a shoot-first-ask-questions-later-neighborhood—a concept that didn't sit well with Dart, but one he understood.

He knocked sharply and waited. No one answered. *Fine with me*, he thought as he turned to return to his waiting car.

As he stepped down onto the second step, he heard and felt something crunch beneath his shoe, and the alarm inside his policeman's brain sounded. He wanted to label it glass, but it didn't fit. *Almost like glass*, his senses told him. *Don't stop!* the same internal voice warned. But he did. The steps proved too dark and he withdrew his small penlight, condemning himself for being such a Boy Scout, and shined the light onto the step. The cone of light caught tiny white stones, like stars in the night sky. But stones did not pulverize as these had, and so Dart looked closer, still checking over his shoulder for a mugger or a kid with a semiautomatic. Cautiously, he knelt, reached out and carefully pinched some of the material between his fingers. The same alarm sounded with this tactile contact: *rock salt!*

Bragg had connected rock salt to the Payne suicide—to Payne's possible visitor—and although Dart might have been elated with such a discovery, in this neighborhood, on this street at this time of night, he half wished that his foot had missed that step.

Mac tried to bark from the back of the Volvo, sounding like a vacuum cleaner with its belt out of adjustment. Dart glanced up to see if it was a warning, but decided it was only old Mac longing for company, wanting to go home. *Me too, boy.*

Dart placed the dust into his palm and shined the light on it. A watery-blue hue—*just as Teddy had described it.*

In theory, because 11 Hamilton Court was listed as a location of a bald cypress tree, with this discovery Dart had two of the three elements identified by Bragg. The detective in Dart could not ignore this. Like it or not the wretched old house seemed inexorably linked to Harold Payne. He deposited the pinch of rock salt in his top

212

pocket, gathered his courage, and decided to look around back.

A narrow dirt driveway ran alongside the building and accessed a rickety wooden slat fence that had once been painted green. Having no legal right to enter, and keeping in mind that 11 Hamilton Court might prove valuable, Dart elected to stay out, but he found a space in the rundown fence to peer through. Inside this back area, it was dark, and his eyes took a nervous moment to adjust. Along with his anxiety, he felt excitement.

Unable to see, he lifted the penlight and shined it inside, and what he saw caused him to gasp. Once an enclosed garden it was now a place of ruin and neglect. Lying on the ground, the printing wet and faded, the paper burst open like a rotting corpse, a bag of potting soil had spilled its contents across the path to the back stoop. *The third element that Bragg had described!* To the left of the area stood a scraggly tree, its limbs barren for winter, at the base of which—and, in fact, littered across the entire area including where Dart stood—was a carpet of small needles, some a dull green, others brown and amber. *A bald cypress tree,* Dart knew, without knowing. He collected some of the fallen needles into his pocket.

He quickly turned off his penlight and glanced up the sheer wall of the worn house, his heart racing, his skin prickling. It seemed so gloomy and desolate, like a haunted house from a film or a nightmare. But this place was real, and the effect on Dart, palpable.

Whoever lived here had been inside Harold Payne's on the night of the killing—not suicide, but *killing*. And the cop's instinct welling up inside of him said that this person had been more than just a visitor.

Dart made for the car, unlocked it, and climbed inside. Mac greeted him with a slobbery kiss. "We're not going home, boy," he informed the dog, intending to keep 11 Hamilton Court under surveillance.

Abby reached Dart on his cell phone at eight-fifteen, reminding him that he was forty-five minutes late for dinner. He told her briefly about his find and that he and Mac were keeping an eye on 11 Hamilton Court from up on Zion. Without a bit of annoyance, she announced that two dinners to go were on their way.

Twenty minutes later Abby Lang, in blue jeans and a deerskin jacket, was sitting in the front seat of the Volvo, working on a chicken salad. For Dart, the most difficult part of police work was sitting around waiting for something to happen, which was one reason he had eschewed Narcotics.

"Lewellan's mother has given her consent for the girl to participate in a lineup," Abby announced proudly. "If we ever get a suspect."

"And how did you pull that off?" Dart asked, thrilled that they might have a viable witness but still confused by the face that the girl and Tommy Templeton had created—not Zeller, not Kowalski. He was toying with the idea that Zeller had hired these hits—but kept his own distance in case something went wrong, which, when attempting to stage suicides, seemed inevitable.

"Magic."

"I'd say so," Dart replied.

"A while later, with two paper coffee cups riding the dashboard, Dart said, "I have a confession to make."

She rocked her head on the car seat and looked at him. "Okay," she said.

"It's *not* okay." He hoped that she might pick up on what he meant, but she waited him out. "I'm getting used to this. Comfortable with it. You and me, I'm talking about."

"I know what you're talking about."

"And yet, at the same time, I still think about Ginny."

"I still think about my marriage."

"I know you do," he said.

She took a deep breath and said, "There are times when I'm madly in love with you, Joe. Others, when I'm not so sure."

"I feel that."

"I'm sorry," she apologized. "I wish it were different. I really do."

"I'd like to see more of the kids. They're always going off somewhere just as I arrive."

"I don't want to hurt them," she said. "They're too young to understand all this."

The seat cushion crackled as she adjusted herself. He could hear the drone of city life— traffic, mostly. A disturbing silence hung over them.

She added, "Charles and I have planned all along to get together for a week and see if we can't put it back together. I told you about that," she said defensively. "I . . . we . . . it's for the kids' sake."

"I thought maybe that had changed, given the last month."

"No," she said, crushing him, "that hasn't changed."

"That's not fair," he complained.

She popped open her door and scrambled out of the car. She jumped across an icy puddle and up onto the sidewalk and started away from him at a brisk pace. She was risking both the surveillance and her own safety. He, too, broke the rules. He left the car and chased after her. She heard him coming and increased her stride.

"Abby," he called after her.

"Don't!" she objected.

"Come back to the car. It's my mistake."

She stopped and turned, and he bumped into her. She pushed him away forcibly and hollered loudly, "You're damn right it's *your* mistake. And a *big* one. These are my *children* we're talking about."

"I'm sorry," Dart apologized. He approached her tentatively. She eyed him skeptically, and then the two of them wound together, arm in arm, and she whispered into his ear, "Asshole."

"Jerk. Let's drop it, okay?" he asked. "Whatever happens, happens."

She nodded. Halfway back to the car, she took his hand. Joe Dart laced his fingers with hers and squeezed.

★　★　★

At eleven-thirty the downstairs light at 11 Hamilton Court went dark, followed several minutes later by an upstairs light going on. Dart explained, "An automatic timer."

"Agreed. Either that or someone has been walking around in the dark for the last five minutes."

Together, they watched the building until one in the morning, when the upstairs light went off. Dart repositioned the car on Park Terrace, where Abby could keep an eye on him as he crossed and once again knocked on the front door. No answer. He returned to the back of his car, moved a sleeping Mac out of the way, and got into his first-aid kit. Using a piece of white athletic tape, he bridged the hinged side of the house's front door, placing it at ankle height. If the door were opened, the tape would tear loose from the hinge.

Around back, again with Abby watching, Dart wedged a thin stick into the crack of the only gate in the dilapidated green fence. If the gate door were opened, the stick would fall to the ground. Simple tricks—he and Zeller had used them dozens of times.

He dropped off Abby, hoping she might invite him up, but she did not. On the way home, he worried about this, and again when he took Mac for a short walk.

He slept poorly until 3:00 A.M., having no idea what had awakened him—a nightmare? a sound? something out on the street? And then the thoughts cluttered his head like bats trapped in an attic.

He lay awake for hours, spinning, churning—

driven by the possibilities that 11 Hamilton Court offered. Confused by Abby's mixture of hot and cold.

If he was to get a look inside that house, he was going to have to convince Haite to involve the State Police. Haite, in turn, would need to involve Captain Rankin. A real mess.

In the morning, he returned to 11 Hamilton Court. Again, he knocked on the front door, and again no one answered. The piece of white tape remained in place. Disappointed not to find a sign of anyone, he moved around back, his heart busy in his chest, his palms damp and cold. He hated this neighborhood.

He found the stick that he had jammed into the gate's crack lying in the dirt on the ground. Dart picked it up and held it. In the oozing mud outside the gate, he saw shoe prints coming and going. Shoe prints not his own.

Sometime during the night someone had been inside.

The rock salt and leaves that he had collected the night before were now in separate envelopes on the front seat of his car, marked and labeled. *Evidence*, he thought.

Perhaps just enough to convince Haite to authorize the raid.

CHAPTER
24

It had been a busy few hours.

Dart loosened his tie and unbuttoned his collar. "I need an ERT for an evidence collection raid on a house in the south end," Dart explained to Sergeant John Haite. The skin around the man's eyes was an ink blue, reminding Dart of a raccoon mask. CAPers was run by two sergeants, John Haite or Dave Almedi, each with his own group of detectives and his own desk in a glassed room off the division's floor. The two were rarely in at the same time because their units rotated in and out of twelve-hour tours. Dart took a metal chair across from Haite's cluttered desk. The fluorescent lights made their skin glow an ugly yellow-green.

"A what?" Haite asked rhetorically.

The idea of using an Emergency Response Team to do a raid for the sole purpose of collecting evidence was an idea all Dart's. It would require writs and warrants and probable cause. Dart explained, "I can place an unknown person inside Harold Payne's study on the night he . . . committed suicide. Bragg will support me in that whoever this was may have attempted to conceal his or her presence by vacuuming the rug."

Haite appeared skeptical.

Dart handed over Bragg's report, completed only an hour earlier, that showed an identical chemical composition between the rock salt recovered at Payne's and the salt Dart had collected at 11 Hamilton Court. "This links this suspect to both Payne's and the house at Eleven Hamilton Court. I contacted the owner, who put me in touch with a property management firm—"

"Peter Sharpe," Haite said. All the slum property was handled by Sharpe. He was hated by the police.

"Yeah. The place is rented to one Wallace Sparco, white male, fifty-two." Dart passed Haite the photocopy of Sparco's driver's license. He went in for the kill by handling him next the computerized rendering Lewellan Page had witnessed at Gerald Lawrence's. Although imperfect, the similarity was undeniable. "Wallace Sparco has been busy making suicides," Dart said.

"Shit," came Haite's reply, comparing the two photographs. He looked over at Dart with basset hound eyes of irritation. He didn't want things more complicated. "They are *not* suicides?"

"That's what I need to prove or disprove."

"These are not your investigations. Where the hell is Kowalski on this?"

"It's an end run, Sergeant," Dart went ahead reluctantly. "I don't feel good about it, but that's the way it is."

"An end run on Kowalski?"

"Each one of these suicides is his," Dart pointed out.

"Oh, shit." Haite tilted back in his chair. "Oh, *shit*."

"I know," said Dart. "I don't like it either."

"Fuck this," Haite said, exasperated. "I don't need this kind of trouble."

Dart waited him out. He knew better than to push Haite.

"Someone tapped both Payne and Lawrence and set them up to look like suicides?" Haite muttered. "Why?"

"To keep us from catching on. To keep going. To clean house: They're both sex offenders, Sergeant. Pornography. Wife beating. Stapleton too."

"Stapleton is who?"

"The jumper at the Granada Inn. August."

"Oh, shit." He scratched his head. "Oh, fuck."

"I know," Dart repeated.

"And what the hell are you asking for?"

"An evidence raid with an Emergency Response Team in case it gets ugly. That's a lousy area, Pope Park."

"I know."

"A way to get in and out without Sparco any the wiser."

"Fuck that," Haite said. "We just get the paper right and we kick it and search it. So what?"

"Sparco is one careful son of a bitch, Sergeant. We have less than zero to go on. If we don't find some kind of evidence connecting him to these crime scenes, we don't want to tip our hand that we've been there."

"It's illegal. Have you considered that? No matter what, we have to post the place that it was searched."

"Those search notices have a habit of blowing off the door, Sergeant."

"Oh, fuck. What's happened to you, Dartelli? Blow off the door? You're suggesting we *purposely* avoid posting notice? *That is illegal, Detective!*" He had raised his voice to shouting. Dart knew that by now the other guys would be looking this way, but with his back to the floor he couldn't see.

"We post it, and if it blows off, it blows off."

"This is not like you," the sergeant condemned. He added, "This sounds much more like Kowalski or Drummond than you. What's gotten into you?"

"Three murders made to look like suicides," Dart answered. "We've got a jury of one running wild, Sergeant. If we don't do *something*, the numbers are going to increase."

Haite and Zeller had come up through the ranks at the same time. There was mutual respect between the men, but a healthy competition as well. If anyone felt as strongly about Zeller as Dart, it was this man sitting across from him. Were Dart to share the possibility of Zeller's involvement with Haite, the detective risked being reassigned. Without ironclad proof, John Haite was not about to bring down Walter Zeller. So Dart avoided mentioning his former sergeant or the Ice Man investigation. But Haite had just reviewed the case a few days earlier.

"What about the Ice Man?" he asked. "He took a dive just like Stapleton."

Dart met eyes strongly with his sergeant. "Yes, he did." He offered nothing more. Telephones rang out on the floor. Haite and Dart maintained an unblinking eye contact.

"You're saying the Ice Man was a sex offender? Do we *know* this? Can we *prove* this?"

Dart replied, "I didn't say anything about the Ice Man, Sergeant. Do you have a specific question that you want to ask?"

Haite, still maintaining eye contact, bored a hole through Dart. He understood the meaning of Dart's reserved tone of voice—he was trying to warn the sergeant off. Perhaps the only coincidence that Haite could pick upon—without Dart's cooperation—was the date of Zeller's retirement, which followed quickly after the Ice Man investigation.

"No questions," Haite whispered dryly, fingering the photocopy of Wallace Sparco's driver's license, and Dart had to wonder what the man saw in the face. Did he, too, see the resemblance to Zeller?

Dart nodded. "Fine with me." He hesitated and asked again, "And the ERT raid?"

"I'll see what I can do." Haite now looked as pale as Teddy Bragg.

Two vans pulled onto Park Terrace at 1:00 A.M. One was painted gray and carried a red diagonal stripe that read: MANNY'S STEAM AND CLEAN. It had been confiscated by the State Police in a drug bust two years earlier and was now outfitted with a personal computer and printer, communications hardware, and an elaborate video setup. The second van was a customized beige Dodge with what appeared to be darkly tinted windows but were in fact one-way glass. Behind the glass, six men and one woman sat on opposing steel mesh benches. Clad all in black, wearing combat boots that laced over the ankle, four were members of the State Police ERT unit. One of the outsiders was Joe Dartelli, who had suffered through an egregiously boring ninety-minute briefing that had been lectured by the commander of the State Police unit, Tom Schultz. The remaining two, a woman named Gritch and a man named Yates, were a team that someone at HPD had coined "Ted Bragg on amphetamines": evidence technicians whose specialty was speed and efficiency.

They all wore communications devices in their ears, night-vision goggles perched on their foreheads, bullet-resistant vests, black handcuffs, black nine-millimeter semiautomatic handguns in their belt holster, and maglights Velcroed to their belts. Gritch and Yates carried bulging black canvas bags at their sides, the straps slung over their shoulders and necks. They all wore black farm hats that carried the single word POLICE in bright yellow stitching. The veterans called these "target caps" for obvious reasons. The ERT members wore the hats backward like black and Hispanic kids. The protective vests carried bold yellow print across the back: STATE POLICE. All but Dart also carried a stun grenade and a smoke grenade—both of which Dart had argued to leave behind. But ERT, the most militarylike unit of the State Police, did not, would not, vary from procedure.

One of the ERT members sitting directly across from Dart said, "A military unit could put a scope on those windows and tell us if we were facing any life-forms."

"Life-forms, Brandon?" one of the others teased. "What are you expecting, Klingons?"

"Attack dogs, asshole. Animals *and* humans. The scopes work off infrared. You can scope right through *walls* with the newer ones." Brandon held a bunch of electronic gear in his arms. Dart easily identified him as the techie.

"Hey, commander," a third said to Schultz. "We ever gonna get anything like that?"

"On our budget? Who the fuck you kidding?" Schultz was the marine drill-sergeant type who had given the briefing. Every other word was a swearword or a denigrating, obscene comment involving some aspect of female anatomy. "Tit-sucker." "Fist-fucker." "Cunt breath." A real charmer.

Gritch apparently tolerated Schultz, storing away enough harassment ammunition to retire comfortably if she ever chose to press a suit.

After the ninety-minute soliloquy, Schultz and Dart had entered into a brief but vehement discussion of chain of command, Dart emphasizing that it was his raid, Schultz insisting it was his team. They compromised whereby Schultz would handle the team logistics while Dart directed the actual reconnaissance—in this case, the physical inspection and the collection of evidence.

The search warrant had to specify what it was that Dart was looking for, if that item was to be removed for lab work. The trick—one of the oldest tricks—was for him to list everything and anything that he could think might be found in the search. It took a cooperating judge to go along with such practice, but there were plenty. On Dart's list was everything from a portable vacuum cleaner to lamp cord, wool rugs, to latex gloves.

"Scope on," Schultz directed Brandon, who carried what looked like a black metallic snake clipped at the calf and thigh to the outside of his right leg. He reached up to his head and flipped a small device into place that looked like a dentist's mirror and came to rest two inches off his eye. His right hand worked a small box attached to his belt that Dart could not fully see. He reported, "Scope fully functional." ERT members, Dart thought, apparently saw little use for verbs.

Schultz checked his watch. It had a black face and was on a black plastic band. *Probably wearing black shorts*, Dart thought. Schultz looked up at the van's ceiling, which Dart now understood was this man's reaction to radio communication, because as lead detective Dart was also able to hear the voice traffic from the operations van. "Two minutes," Schultz told his troops.

Dart felt the prickle of heat in his scalp.

Exactly two minutes later, following a brief communication check between members of the unit, the van started up and turned into Hamilton Court.

Schultz rattled off orders. "Single file, people. We stay in shadow where possible. Brandon will scope the back gate; we move on my signals—we speak as little as possible. Any resistance, we withdraw to the park and our support transportation. Questions?"

"If we encounter weapons fire?" one of Schultz's men asked.

"Dartelli leads the retreat to Park. You, Brandon, and I take up defensive positions and follow ASAP. Anyone else?"

Dart felt his heartbeat strongly. He wanted to think of this as a drill, but his adrenaline told him differently. The van stopped and the doors flew open. The team moved quickly, quietly into the shadows. Dart, a part of them, could barely see the others.

"Okay," Schultz said.

He followed at the back behind Gritch. The unit was well trained and moved as an entity. The van, having hesitated only long enough to disgorge the team, purred down the alley. Schultz held them in shadow for exactly one minute and then moved himself and his gadget man, Brandon, across to the green wooden gate. The two knelt and Brandon uncoupled the black snake from his leg and inserted it under the fence. The snake was, in fact, a fiber-optic camera, the small dentist mirror at his eye a viewing scope. Brandon inspected the back garden area and, with a hand signal, pronounced it clear. Schultz, using a speed key, unlocked the gate and then signaled the unit forward, his ERT man leading the way, followed by the evidence technicians and then Dart.

Within seconds, the unit was lined up in shadow alongside the house. Dart's heart pounded heavily and he felt sweat trickling down his ribs. Brandon slipped the fiber-optic camera under the weather seal of the back door and used the video gear to inspect the inside. A moment later, Schultz had opened this door as well. Again, he waved them forward.

They were inside.

Dart had only used night-vision equipment once, in a seminar hosted by the New England Law Enforcement Association. The goggles were bulky, and the view from within them an eerie combination of green, black, and white. The unit moved ahead fluidly, but Dart felt awkward and disoriented, as if he had stepped into a video game. With his world reduced to glowing colors, he moved forward one unsure foot at a time.

Inside, the house was as it was outside—old and worn. In this first room there was a shoddy couch, a tilting standing lamp, a frayed recliner, and an old television set. Gritch and Yates fixed their attention onto Dart, who immediately pointed to the recliner; the two evidence techni-cians attacked the piece, working silently, efficiently, pulling cushions, sweeping, dusting for latent prints, digging at the crevices. Glassine and white paper bags, premarked with room loca-tions, were used to capture the finds. In seconds the recliner was itself again. "No prints," Gritch whispered into her microphone, playing in Dart's right ear.

Dart scanned the room, experiencing tunnel vision, annoyed by the goggles.

Schultz and his commandos were gone, presumably conducting a preliminary search. Gritch tried dusting the television remote. She shook her head at Dart. Yates took a special solvent and cleaned the dust away, leaving no trace of their having been here.

Dart looked across at an upright piano missing several keys. There were a half dozen photographs in acrylic frames on top. He pointed these out to Gritch and Yates as well, and again they descended on their targets with an uncanny quickness and efficiency. Bags were opened—somehow silently—and Gritch produced a special camera. Yates removed what looked like a flashlight from his pouch, switched it on, and directed it at the photographs. Without the goggles, the special light would have appeared an extremely dull violet. Inside the night vision it appeared as if he had shined a halogen flashlight onto the subjects. Gritch fired off a series of shots, and to Dart's surprise the camera worked in absolute silence. It would be explained later that the camera was digital, recording the images onto a computer disk. These images could be enlarged and manipulated electronically.

Room by room, the team moved through the house. The kitchen was tiny. Gritch and Yates spent most of their three minutes there dusting objects and pulling tape in hopes of lifting latent prints. Dart checked the refrigerator and made mental notes: male food. Bacon, eggs, hot dogs, beer, Diet Coke, turkey sausage, English muffins, ice cream, orange juice, and a dozen frozen dinners. Yates swiped the toilet rim and bagged the tissue from the downstairs half bath. Gritch seemed to inventory the cleaning products, paying special attention to those that retained price labels.

All the while, a steady stream of communication flowed in to Dart and Schultz from the operations van. Mostly, this came in the form of a running time count: "one minute," "two minutes thirty seconds . . ." These were punctuated by announcements of "traffic approaching" and "traffic clear." This barrage instilled in Dart a sense of protection, of security; knowing that three plainclothes street officers were working the immediate neighborhood and were in constant touch with the operations van.

They had been inside the building just over five minutes before Dart began to understand Schultz's actions more clearly. Saddled with a team of six—concerned for the unit's safety—the team leader was deftly deploying his manpower to avoid having more than three people occupy any one of the small rooms. Dart, Gritch, and Yates were orchestrated as a team, while Schultz and his three armed ERT men swept the next area and kept on constant alert.

Dart and the evidence team next found themselves headed down a narrow wooden staircase into an unfinished basement area that housed a washer/dryer, a clothesline, several cardboard boxes of storage, and, just to the side of the staircase, a workbench cluttered with fly-tying materials and hardware. Gritch signaled Dart, pointing to the side of the clothes washer, and to the shelves above. She shook her head no. Dart returned the gesture. Her message was unclear to him. She touched her communication pack and whispered, "No detergent, no bleach." Dart saw then what wasn't there, realizing, as Zeller might have once schooled him, that what was missing was as important as what was present, and that Gritch and Yates had been carefully schooled in such matters. Dart nodded, making a mental note.

Dart pointed out the fly-tying work area, and the team descended on it, furiously photographing, sampling, and collecting. Again, Dart found himself impressed, all their combined movements measured, coordinated, and productive. They left the basement within two minutes.

Schultz directed Dart and the evidence team to the second floor, where a narrow hall accessed two bedrooms and two baths. The main bedroom was larger than the guest room and had its bath adjoining. There was enough ambient light here that Dart could remove the annoying goggles, but Gritch and Yates kept wearing theirs.

"Seven minutes," came the steady voice in Dart's earpiece. The evidence pair went about photographing and sampling areas of the room while the detective stood back, studying the layout. The bed's headboard was centered between two windows that faced the alley. Across from the bed, a chest of drawers awkwardly spanned the corner, just clear of the door to the bath, to the right of which was a door to a closet. Something about the room troubled Dart, though he couldn't put his finger on it—the neatness? the cleanliness? the lack of personality? He wasn't sure.

It clearly had been lived in. He could make out a small pile of coins on top of the dresser, a Bic pen, and what might be a roll of antacids. Yates was already busy working these for latent prints. Dart edged over to the closet and carefully opened it, his hand sweating inside the latex glove. There were a dozen shirts on hangers, and a white wire rack that held folded jeans, socks, underwear, T-shirt, a sweatsuit and other clothing.

Gritch tapped Dart on the shoulder, moved him, and began shooting photographs of the closeted clothing, Yates training the special low-level flashlight on the contents.

"We have an unidentified male approaching on foot on Zion," the voice in Dart's ear announced.

"Heads up, people," Schultz's voice said into Dart's earpiece. "Let's rendezvous at the base of stairs immediately." He paused. "Right *now*, people."

Yates returned to the clothes dresser and wiped down the pen and several of the coins. Gritch prepared and then bagged the digital camera and said to Dart, "This was *closed*, correct?"

"Yes."

She shut the closet door. "Fully closed?"

"Fully closed," Dart acknowledged.

"Suspect is turning down Hamilton," came the spotter in Dart's right ear.

"Team leader," inquired the male voice from the van, "do you copy that please?"

"Copy," replied Schultz.

"Prepare to evacuate all personnel," the operations van announced calmly.

"Roger."

Over the communications device Schultz ordered, "Down here *now*, people. Get the lead out!"

As Dart headed out of the bedroom, he glanced over his shoulder to see both Gritch and Yates dash into the bathroom and then *back* out through the bedroom, their heads and the ungainly goggles sweeping left to right. During the briefing, Schultz had informed Dart that he wanted these two particular technicians because of their incredible photographic memories. He had told a story about Gritch returning from a raid and reciting forty-five titles of books contained on the study's shelves—he estimated that Gritch had been inside there less than a minute. A later SID report had confirmed all forty-five titles.

"Report?" the operations van requested.

"Subject is entering Hamilton Court," the male voice replied. "You'll need to abort via the back route. Copy?"

How could the dispatcher sound so calm? Dart wondered. His chest felt on the verge of exploding.

"Copy," said the van.

"Back route. Copy," replied Schultz.

Schultz and his two men were waiting at the bottom of the stairs.

"We have an abort situation," Schultz announced over the unit intercom. "Unidentified subject approaching." He tripped a button on his belt pack and said to the operations van, "Status?"

"The back is still clear," Dart heard in his earpiece.

Schultz repeated this.

Schultz now addressed Dart directly, the night-vision goggles making him look like some kind of bug. "Your call, Detective. Do we apprehend or not?" This was first time Dart heard emotion override the man's military manner—Schultz *wanted* to stay and apprehend the suspect.

Dart asked Gritch, "How did we do in here?"

"Well below what we might have hoped for." Yates nodded his agreement. She was saying that they had *nothing*. No evidence of consequence.

In a flurry of activity, Dart then heard the operations van direct the field surveillance operatives.

OPERATIONS VAN: This is Control. Shepherd, can we get a video of the subject with a drive-by?

DETECTIVE SHEPHERD: Negative. He's already in the alley. If you get a pickup you'll be lucky. I'd advise the team to enter Pope Park. We'll pick up at York Street.

OPERATIONS VAN: Negative on Pope Park. We're rolling. Team leader, acknowledge abort.

Schultz, off mike, said, "Well?"

Dart did not want to apprehend, given the lack of evidence. He *wanted* this suspect, but not yet. "Negative." Then he immediately voiced a consideration to Brandon. "Can we get a look at him?"

Brandon, aware of the order of rank, looked to Schultz for the answer.

"We can get *anything*, Detective." Schultz said. "It's your call."

PERSONNEL VAN: What's the call?

OPERATIONS VAN: Team leader?

FIELD AGENT: Suspect has passed target. He's turning down the drive.

Schultz yanked the gooseneck microphone to in front of his mouth and said for everyone to hear, "He's going for the back door. We'll take the front." He threw the switch on his communications device and spoke.

SCHULTZ: We'll need ten seconds.

OPERATIONS VAN: You won't get it.

Schultz placed his gloved hand on the doorknob.

Pointing at Brandon, Dart asked, "Can we leave the camera set up in here?"

"If we leave Brandon, we can," came Schultz's answer. "We don't have the necessary warrants for wire surveillance, but we are allowed in here. If you want to record this guy, it's going to have to be in person. Your decision."

"But we'll pick it up in the van?" Dart asked.

"In the *operations* van, yes," Schultz answered.

"Brandon and I stay," Dart said.

OPERATIONS VAN: Suspect is inside the back gate. You better get out.

Dart heard a rattle at the back door as a key turned.

Schultz faced his crew and said, "We're going to take him, people. Positions!"

"No!" Dart objected with a harsh whisper, his body in full sweat, the sound of the key in the lock somehow louder.

"We can't make it." Schultz countered, "We're too late."

Dart argued, "We hide. Ride him out. Maybe we get a shot to leave."

Schultz and Dart faced each other, and despite the goggles, Dart felt as if he were looking directly into the man's eyes and that they were locked in a battle of wills.

Schultz acquiesced. "Observation *only* until further notice. Go!"

The door came unlocked and cracked open tentatively.

The ERT crew scattered and disappeared instantly. Brandon and Dart raced up the stairs. Dart didn't see where the others went, only Schultz, who stashed himself into the front coat closet. As he reached the landing, following closely on Brandon's heels, Dart heard something like static in his right ear and realized it was Schultz, barely whispering over the intercom:

SCHULTZ: I want location reports. Check in ASAP. Give me suspect's position, people.

ERT AGENT PHILGIM: I'm in the kitchen.

ERT AGENT DONALDSON: Donaldson. Basement stairs.

ERT AGENT BRANDON: Brandon. Upstairs bedroom.

DART: Dartelli. Upstairs bedroom.

SCHULTZ: Split it up, up there.

ERT AGENT YATES: Yates. Basement with Donaldson.

ERT AGENT PHILGIM: He's inside.

Silence over the intercom. Dart heard a floorboard creak downstairs, and he prayed it was the suspect, not one of Schultz's commandos. He didn't want a dead suspect, and these ERT types were weapons-sharp. Brandon, following orders, motioned for Dart to enter the closet and that he, Brandon, would take up a position in the bathroom.

To Dart, it felt as if several minutes passed before another voice came over the intercom.

ERT AGENT GRITCH: Gritch. Living room. He's heading for the stairs. He's using a *flashlight*," she emphasized.

The idea of a flashlight didn't sit well with Dart. The resident would certainly use the lights—*unless*, Dart thought, *he wanted to disguise his coming and going.*

Perhaps hiding in the closet affected Dart, so much of his youth having been spent hiding in places like this. Perhaps it was that even all these years later by imitating his actions as a child, he was suddenly a part of those emotions. A surge of frustration, anxiety, and anger swept through him, stealing control of the rhythm of his heart. He realized that he was not standing inside this darkened closet by choice but because someone else had directed him here. Brandon. Schultz. It

237

didn't matter who. He had done this not by choice, but necessity. Adrenaline filled him with panic. He felt claustrophobic, as if this tiny space were shrinking in on him. He heard footsteps coming up—and he could actually smell his mother's cheap perfume, could hear the *woosh* of her dress. He knew where he was, a cop standing in a darkened closet, that it was their suspect coming up the stairs, not his mother. But nonetheless, he smelled her. No mistaking that perfume. He yanked the goggles down over his eyes and wondered if the beating of his heart could be heard through the closet door.

SCHULTZ: Suspect is at top of stairs. Donaldson, Philgim, provide backup.

Schultz was seeing to it that Dart and Brandon—an HPD cop and a techie; the lowest of the low in his opinion, no doubt—had some ERT support, something Dart could do without. He mustn't lose this suspect or find himself in a firefight.

He heard breathing on the other side of the closet door, and it was everything he could do not to imagine his mother. *I'm a grown man!* he told himself. And yet the past remained. He held his breath—he could hide better than the best of them. He reached down and fingered his weapon. If that door came open, there was going to be hell to pay.

He could picture the two ERT men ascending the stairs delicately, not emitting a sound despite the old planks. Trained to be weightless. Trained killers. He wondered what their nightmares were. What demons possessed *them*?

The sound of the suspect's heavy breathing passed by the door, grew faint, and then disappeared.

ERT AGENT PHILGIM: Suspect is inside the bathroom.

Dart heard a sweep of fingers on the outside face of the door, like a faint scratching, and realized that the ERT men were signaling him, warning they were in the room. They didn't want Dart firing on them.

SCHULTZ: I don't want Brandon at risk. Apprehend suspect. Repeat: Apprehend.
ERT AGENT PHILGIM: Apprehend. Copy.

Dart gently eased the closet door open. Philgim's goggles swung to face him. The agent nodded, pointed toward the bathroom and then to the weapon in his hand. Dart slipped his sidearm out. Philgim pointed to Donaldson, who was also facing Dart. Donaldson held a phosphorous grenade up for Dart to see and indicated for Dart to remove his goggles—the bright light would be blinding. Dart nodded, lowered his head, pulled the goggles up onto his head, and covered his eyes.

ERT AGENT PHILGIM: Brandon. Phos. grenade.

Dart heard the click of a tongue. Brandon, being in the same room as the suspect, could not speak, not even in a whisper, and yet had communicated his acknowledgment.

These people aren't human, Dart told himself.

He heard a loud *pop*, and even with his eyes shielded, a flash of blinding white light flooded him. There was a series of harsh shouts and commands as the ERT agents announced themselves. "Police! Stay where you are! No movement! Hold it!" They moved in careful orchestration, one protecting the other.

Dart, screening himself with the doorjamb, saw the suspect kneeling on the floor, both hands over his eyes. The grenade had blinded him. The effect would last several minutes. There was a smell of bitter smoke and a gray haze floating on the ceiling.

The porcelain lid that belonged on the top of the toilet tank was off, and a wet brick and a plastic bag containing small glass vials sat on the closed seat. The brick, ostensibly inside the toilet to conserve water, turned out to be a hollow plastic imitation—a hiding place designed and sold as such. In their quick assessment of the bathroom Yate and Gritch had missed this.

Philgim yanked the man's arms behind his back, announcing, "You are under arrest on suspicion of tampering with crime scene evidence." This was the way the search warrant read. Dart was amazed at the team's efficiency, and the way that they stuck to procedure. The handcuffs snapped into place.

"Fuck off!" said the husky voice of the suspect, his head still bent toward the ground.

Dart knew that voice. It belonged to Roman Kowalski.

CHAPTER
25

John Haite looked exhausted, rubbing his eyes to get the sleep out. He, Dart, and Kowalski sat in the second of the two CAPers interrogation rooms, Dart still dressed in black. On the room's only table was the plastic bag containing the glass vials that Dart had seen on the toilet. Brandon's fiber-optic video had recorded all of Kowalski's movements once inside the bathroom. Ironically, by their efficiency, the ERT team had invalidated this evidence by showing that Kowalski had collected it, and Kowalski's name was not listed on the warrant. It was a bugaboo that had both Haite and Dart in a lather.

"I want to hear that again," Haite said angrily. Dart had to let Haite conduct the first round of questioning. Rank had its privileges.

Kowalski said, "A phone call. A tip. A snitch. I got the call. I responded. I was told if the key was outside, the place would be empty, but I wasn't about to go inside calling hellos. What the fuck? Guy told me there was some shit hidden inside a fake brick in the toilet. I headed straight there. He was talking like I wouldn't have much time—"

"All without a warrant," Haite interrupted.

"I understand the problem here," Kowalski answered.

"And we're supposed to buy this?" Haite questioned.

"What the fuck do I care, Sergeant? That's the way it is."

"Watch it!" Haite warned.

"The key to the back door?" Dart asked.

"Hanging on the nail, right where the snitch told me I'd find it."

"Jesus, what a pile of shit," Haite said. "And what about this?" he said, pointing to the bag on the table.

"He told me where to find that too," Kowalski said reluctantly. "I know it sounds bad—"

"It sounds god-awful," Haite corrected. "*Impossible* is more like it."

"It's the way it went down," the man said sheepishly.

"Bullshit," Haite counted. "It's fucking bullshit, Kowalski, and we all three know it. You had better shit or get off the pot, pal, because otherwise a load of trouble is coming your way."

Dart, trying to calm things down, asked, "What did the snitch say about this stuff?" He pointed to the table.

"He said there was shit pertaining to the suicides that I'd be interested in. He said there was some kind of cover-up, some kind of cleanup man involved. He said there was evidence there that could bust the thing wide open, and that if I was interested I had better get my butt over to Hamilton Court. Shit, it sounded good to me," he complained. To Haite he whined, "It sounded *good*, Sergeant. What the fuck do I know?"

"You know about warrants, for Chrissakes! Procedure. Jesus, you're a fuck-up." He hesitated, his voice rising as he went. "And that is if we believe any of this crap, because I, for one, don't believe a goddamn bit of it, Detective. Not one goddamn bit. You're a fucking embarrassment to this division, a fuck-up of a cop, and you'll be waving traffic or doing time when I'm through with you! Now tell us what the fuck you're up to, who the hell this Wallace Sparco is, and how the hell you fit in, or I'm sending your ass to booking and you're getting a number, pal."

Kowalski paled. In all his years of service, Dart had never seen the man lose his color. Despite that, he placed his spread hands onto the table and said calmly, "I got a call from a snitch."

"A snitch you'd never heard of before," Haite pressed.

"True. But he knew about the suicides. He seemed to know what he was talking about. He told me I'd be interested. Told me where the key was. Told me what I'd find. I followed up on it. Then you guys," he said to Dart. "Honest-to-fucking God, it's all I know."

"Without a warrant!" Haite protested.

"I know, I know."

"This stuff is useless to us!" Haite shouted, pointing at the table. "It's probably key evidence to this fucking investigation, and it's absolutely *useless*!"

It wasn't until Haite put it so succinctly that

243

Dart understood. He couldn't mention it to the others—they would never believe it. It was Zeller. He had found a way to invalidate the evidence. Knowing Kowalski would sucker into anything easy, he had made a pawn out of the man and used him to cancel out this evidence.

Dart stood up.

"Where the fuck are *you* going?" Haite thundered.

"There's something I've got to do."

Tommy Templeton did not appreciate being awakened at four in the morning. He had lit a cigarette coming out of bed and opened the door with it dangling from his mouth. He was wearing a pair of blue boxer shorts. "Exactly what the fuck are you doing?" he asked Dart.

The detective handed him an envelope. "I need five, maybe ten minutes of your time."

"You look like a fucking Ninja."

"It's been a long night. We've got Kowalski in lockup. It's a mess."

"Come in. Let me put some coffee on. I can't think without coffee."

"I'll get the coffee. You take care of that."

Templeton undid the clasp and opened the manila envelope. He slipped out a five-by-seven black-and-white photograph and turned it around. "Walter Zeller? What the hey?"

"You can do what you do in reverse, right?"

Templeton appeared puzzled. "I'm telling you, I need coffee. You got the advantage here."

"This morphing stuff."

Glancing at the photograph again, Templeton's brow knitted. "Sure."

"I have a driver's license photo. I have the composite that you made with the girl."

"Yeah, so?"

"I think they're both Zeller," Dart said. "And this is not for public consumption."

"Jesus fucking Christ," Templeton swore. "Skip the coffee. I'm awake now."

Ten minutes later the two sat before Templeton's monitor. The artist had carefully enlarged Sparco's drivers license photo and superimposed this into the scanned image of Zeller's police ID. Zeller's face fit perfectly inside Sparco's. "It's the distance between the eyes and temples," the artist explained. "Those are two givens that can't be changed." He worked with a small pen on a digitized pad and gently erased Sparco's jowls, thinned the man's swollen lips, and reduced the discolored bags under his eyes. A moment later, there was only Zeller's face on the screen.

"Looks like you get a gold star, Dartelli."

"What if I don't want it?" Joe Dart asked.

CHAPTER
26

With Bud Gorman having retraced Zeller's former employment to Proctor Security, Dart started with Terry Proctor.

The security firm occupied the top two floors of a four-story cement and steel structure on Asylum Street. The receptionist, in her late twenties, wore a gray wool Italian suit with black buttons and a white blouse buttoned at the collar. At Dart's office, the receptionist was an Irish sergeant with a wart on his chin and a scowl on his face. After waiting a few minutes, Dart was led down a hallway lined with corporate citations and black-and-white photographs of international cities. Terry Proctor imagined himself a big player in corporate security, when in fact he was small potatoes. The big boys, like Kroll Associates, had never heard of him and never would. His office overlooked a section of the Connecticut River, brown and lazy, and a view east of barren trees interrupted by buildings. It had been decorated like a cheap tearoom. Muzak played from hidden speakers, making Dart slightly nauseated. He half expected a cocktail waitress.

Proctor was ruggedly handsome, six two, with piercing blue eyes and wide shoulders, but he dressed like a used-car salesman. He wore gold-plated cuff links and black glasses etched with a bi-focal line. His hairpiece matched his glasses; his smile, the cufflinks—gold fillings. Dart sank into a brown vinyl couch that hissed at him like a snake. Proctor worked a remote control device, aimed it at the wall, and the music stopped. *Thank God!*

"I had hoped you might be looking for employment," Proctor said. To Dart he came across as a male madam trying to lure Dart into homosexual prostitution.

"Walter Zeller worked for you after he left the department," Dart said.

"It was quite the coup when we got Walter," Proctor said, though he looked a little nervous, Dart thought. "A huge disappointment when he left. But then again, with all he'd been through—personally—not too big a surprise. I'm not sure he'll ever be happy in the private sector." He advised, "Some people aren't made for this work. And I'm not saying it's easier or more difficult than what you're doing, where you are now—different is all." He toyed with his wristwatch—also goldplated, some of the finish worn off.

"Can I ask what he was working on when he was with you?"

"Of course you can ask." He smiled a tooth-paste smile and offered Dart a patronizing look. "If only I could answer," he said, the smile not leaving his face. "The strongest selling point for any private security firm is confidentiality, Detective—the *cornerstone* of our business. I'm sure you understand."

"It goes no further than me," Dart promised. "I'm not here to lift your skirt."

"Joe," the man said earnestly, leaning forward and speaking softly. Dart wondered if the office had a hidden tape recorder. He basically confirmed this when Proctor reached out and triggered the remote, returning the music and covering his voice. Guys like Proctor thought of themselves as big shots; the real big shots never let on. "You wouldn't believe the NDAs I have to sign. Nondisclosure agreements. The boilerplate runs twenty pages. Many go over fifty." This length seemed to be a source of pride for Proctor. "You wouldn't believe the penalties—seven figures in some cases. I'm bound legally and morally to keep my lips zipped—that's all there is to it." He didn't have a moral ounce in his body. "So are my employees. It's one reason we pull such large paychecks. People come to us to keep things quiet. Okay? Sorry."

"So even if you *wanted* to help me, you couldn't," Dart tested.

"Of course I'd like to help."

"Bullshit. Let me tell you something, Proctor. I'll come here with subpoenas if I have to."

"You'll have to," the man said, offering another staged smile, seemingly unaffected.

"Corporate? Private? *Anything* you can give me."

"Sorry."

Dart saw resistance in the man's eyes. He didn't want Dart to have this information. *Out of stubbornness, or guilt?*

"I'm in a position where I have to have no comment, Joe. I wish I could help you. Okay? Sorry."

"What makes a man leave a cushy security job after only a couple months?" Dart asked. "That's not privileged."

"I told you: As far as I could tell he just wasn't ready for this. We operate differently than you guys. Sure, we pay well; and for that we expect loyalty, dedication, attention to detail. My take is that Walter needed more time. He needed more time to grieve over his wife's death—that's my opinion."

"You're saying it was for personal reasons."

"Absolutely."

"Nothing to do with his work," Dart pressed. The man looked uncomfortable.

"You can answer that," Dart reminded.

Proctor flashed his plastic smile. "You want to tell me what it is that *you* are working on, Joe? What's your interest in Zeller?"

"Are we *both* interested in Zeller?" Dart asked.

"We serve a necessary function. I help ease your workload whether you acknowledge that or not."

"You break laws to accomplish your clients' needs. We uphold those laws."

"We break the little laws—the ones you *wish* you could break. Chain of custody? Warrants for search and seizure? We're rarely after a court settlement. We do what we're hired to do."

"To break the law."

"Not at all. You *know* that, Joe. We play within the accepted boundaries. If we didn't, we would be out of business. You *know* that."

"You won't help me with Zeller?" Dart asked.

"I can't. It's not that I don't want to—"

"And if I subpoena you, and it happens to leak to the media—"

"Are you *threatening* me, Joe?"

"I'm warning you, Terry," he said, having never met the man before. "I'd rather keep the gloves on, but if they come off . . . I want you to know that I'm serious about this. We're not talking about taking bedroom pictures of some CEO's unfaithful wife." This somehow caught Proctor where he lived. The man squared his shoulders and sat back in his chair, his face red, his fists and jaw clenched.

In an angry voice he said, "Don't be an asshole, Dartelli. It doesn't suit you."

"I need answers."

"You won't get them here."

"I'll get them."

"We'll see."

On his way back, Dart found a pay phone and called Gorman. "I need a client list for a security firm in town. Can you get it for me?"

"Proctor Securities?"

"Can you do it?"

"I can identify all deposits, and I can trace those deposits to bank accounts. Will that do?"

Dart gave him the dates of Zeller's employment at Proctor.

"Are we getting somewhere?" Gorman asked hopefully. Part of the reason for the man's participation over the years, Dart had come to understand, was the excitement. The speeding tickets were just an excuse.

"We're getting somewhere," Dart answered. *But the closer we get, the worse it looks.*

CHAPTER
27

"I tell ya," Teddy Bragg said to Dart, sitting in the cramped forensic sciences office. "This *is* rocket science, or might as well be, so if I lose you, speak up because I don't want to have to explain *everything* all over again."

Dart felt uneasy. Bragg had excitement in his bloodshot eyes, and he offered a wide smile of his capped teeth. Recently, Bragg had not been smiling about anything. His skin had a little more color to it. He had come to Dart in person, something unheard of for Bragg. He had ranted on about how Dart should thank him for doing all the necessary research because without it he wouldn't know what he knew, and now that he knew what he knew, he knew it was important. "Critically important," he had said.

Dart had followed him down the hall with his heart in his throat. He'd never seen Bragg like this.

"You look better," Dart said.

"Feel better." He pointed to a canister in the corner of the office that, amid all the other debris, Dart had failed to notice. "O-two," he said, "good old oxygen—or *new* oxygen, actually." He smiled again, showing off his dental work.

"Let me get this straight," Dart offered, seeing the open pack of cigarettes on the man's desk. "You're still smoking, but now you're taking oxygen as well."

"Physician, heal thyself."

"But you're no MD, Buzz."

"Mind your own business. It works. Don't knock it. Are you paying attention? Are you?"

"Yes."

He handed Dart a photocopy of a page containing too many boxes, all filled with numbers. "Full blood workup that you requested. Harold Payne."

"What's it tell us?" Dark asked.

"It tells *me. I* tell *you*," he replied arrogantly. "What it tells *me*, is that your boy was a quart low on androgens. Everything else checks out fine."

"Androgens?"

"Male hormones. Testosterone and company. The 'hard' in hard-on."

"Slow down, Buzz."

"We aren't even started yet. I tell ya—this is a wolf in sheep's clothing. This is the kind of thing that a guy like me *lives* for. You been there. You know."

"Androgens," Dart repeated. He took out his notepad.

Seeing this, Bragg said, "Good boy. Now you're getting the point."

"What *is* the point? Or do you have to take me through two years of pre-med first?"

"Don't get cute," Bragg warned. "Most hormones can be categorized as either peptides or lipids. Peptides are chains of amino acids; lipids are fats and oils. Steroids are an example of a lipid. Did you hear me? Steroids. Do I have your interest yet? Both males and females possess endocrine systems that deliver estrogens, what we think of as female hormones, and androgens, the male hormones, in varying quantities. Those quantities control development and maturity of the genitals, body hair, breasts, voice range— human sexuality." He craned forward, "Pay attention! Some say the *psychology* of sex as well, because many peptides have association with psychological activity. It is a delicate and precious balance responsible for the propagation of all species. A peptide is a chain of amino acids—you make it longer and it becomes a protein. In its shorter version it acts as a hormone. On an atomic level, there are some fascinating things that take place—but I'll save you that, unless you're interested."

"Give me the Cliff Notes version."

Bragg warned, "You're going to need to study this if you're ever going to understand it. This won't come easy, Ivy. This isn't ballistics or even DNA fingerprinting. This is heady stuff. We would have missed this if you hadn't pushed for that workup, but you did, and I gotta tell ya, I love this shit!"

"But worth *what*?" Dart repeated.

"We're talking about *vastly* diminished levels of androgens, Ivy. *Radically* diminished levels, if you follow me."

"I *want* to follow you. I'm trying," Dart said.

"I'll tell ya something—based on this blood work, I would have bet the farm that Payne was a neuter. No testicles. But I checked." Answering Dart's puzzled expression he said, "Damn right. I checked with Doc Ray—jewels intact. Which means that there is *no medical explanation* for these deficiencies. And let me just say that hormone deficiency has been a major focus of the medical community for decades, and I'm quite aware of the science as a whole and certain treatments in specific."

"Does this have to do with—"

"His being a wife beater? It certainly *could*. You bet. And if you ask *me*, it *does*. Opinions might vary. But there's the rub: lower levels should make this guy passive; abnormally *higher* levels of androgens would be anticipated in a sex offender. And that's where the research I was talking about comes in." He pointed to a stack of books. He was speaking so excitedly that Dart could barely understand him. "I got some of this online last night. Some of it from standard reference. I've posted a couple of e-mails; I should know more by tomorrow or Friday. Fascinating stuff," he said.

"Let me get this straight: Payne's levels were *lower* than normal. And given his abhorrent behavior with his wife, we would expect *higher* levels."

"I would," Bragg corrected. "Yes. And here's the bigger problem: The blood workup did not reveal any medication—the synthetic or animal hormones we would expect to encounter with chemical castration."

"Castration?"

"Let me give you some background." He pointed to the stack of books and newspaper articles on the countertop. "First off, keep in mind that we're talking about sex offenders, Ivy. Very important! We're talking about men who take ten-year-old girls behind toolsheds and force them to have sex. Full penetration. Oral sex. Anal sex. You name it. It ain't pretty. If it's assault, then they break a few limbs in the process. Beat her up. Or if it's a Harold Payne, then it's the beating her up that counts. Bruises. Contusions. Lacerations. Fractures. These guys are beasts."

"If you're asking if we care about these guys dying, all I can say is—"

"I'm not! I tell ya, I'm not crying over losing Harold Payne—not if he took his own life. But we're both questioning that, aren't we? Of course we are, or you wouldn't be here. Listen to me— several years back, late eighties, Finland instituted a program of voluntary castration for its sex offenders. They traded these men freedom for castration. The group was monitored and studied over a four-year period. The results were impressive: two to four percent recidivism versus eighty in the control group—a ninety-eight percent reduction in sexual assault; and even these figures are skewed. The two to four percent repeat offenders were picked up for offenses like voyeurism and flashing. In fact, none of the castrated offenders went on to commit a violent sexual act. Not *one*.

"The castrations were *voluntary*, don't forget," Bragg continued. "I tell ya, it's a relatively simple procedure: the testicles are removed and replaced by prosthesis. And don't feel too sorry: A percentage of the group reported having intercourse about once a month. But the abhorrent behavior, caused by either 'defective' hormone production—if you will—or the body's overproduction, was eliminated entirely. Simple English: Castration works."

"But Payne's equipment was intact," Dart reminded.

"Scientists and researchers in this country

bowed to the religious right and deemed castration barbaric. This, despite the obvious success. But it led to other attempts: The U.S. decided that a less barbaric solution would be to administer high doses of estrogen, in theory to counterbalance the ill effects of the over-production of testosterone. That's known as chemical castration. It was tried on a voluntary basis in some of our prisons. It failed on two counts. One, because of the inherent social problems with this approach: breast development, loss of facial hair, a change of voice. Two, it just plain didn't work. The funding was scrapped and the program dropped. We reverted to locking away sex offenders, but for far too brief a time."

"Teddy—"

"Where am I going with this?" he asked rhetorically. "Let me tell ya." He spun his chair around and produced one of several gray cardboard boxes, the size and shape of a shoe box. He removed the lid and pulled out a plastic bag, inside of which was a smaller plastic bag, inside of which were the glass vials recovered from 11 Hamilton Court. "Don't jump all over me about the inadmissibility of this evidence, because I've heard all about it. And besides, that's your problem. I don't give a shit. My job is to make sense of evidence. And boy, can I make sense of this."

"Talk to me."

"Dead viruses," he said, pointing to the vials. "Mean anything?"

"Vaccine?"

"Good boy," Bragg said, clearly impressed.

"Only in this case you're wrong. Close, but no cigar."

Mention of a cigar reminded Dart of Zeller, and he studied Bragg closely to see if maybe the man knew more than he was letting on. He decided that he wasn't. "So?"

"There are three systems currently in wide use for the delivery of gene therapy."

"Gene therapy," Dart echoed.

"DNA. The building block of life."

"I got that," Dart said anxiously.

"My guess is that our Mr. Payne was in a gene therapy program."

Dart finally saw what Bragg was getting at. He nearly shouted, "A program involving sex offenders, wife beaters?"

Bragg nodded. "It's called anti-sense technology. What it amounts to is divining which gene produces ill effects and then attaching DNA material to that gene to resequence its behavior. It's been effective with Huntington's disease, high cholesterol. It's a wide-open field. The government has been actively mapping human DNA since the eighties in something called the Human Genome Project. Everyone's involved—even Bill Gates."

"We found injection marks," Dart stuttered. "We thought maybe giving blood or selling plasma."

Bragg acted out giving himself a shot in the arm. "Shooting up dead viruses mixed with fresh genes. It's the ultimate solution," he said. "Nothing barbaric about it. Fix the gene, correct the hormonal imbalance, improve the behavior.

257

Like cutting the nuts off without a knife. Break the chain. I'm not saying that's what's going on here. But it's possible."

"How possible?"

"*Quite* possible." Bragg pointed to the vials. "If this shit is what I think it is, it's the cutting edge."

CHAPTER
28

"And what do *you* think?" Abby asked.

"I think Zeller knows about these gene therapy tests. I think he doesn't want anybody offering a 'cure' to sex offenders—another excuse to parole them. Nesbit was on parole at the time he killed Lucky and the three others."

"It's difficult, isn't it?"

"How's that?" Dart asked.

"No tears for guys like Gerald Lawrence. There's a part of me—a big part—that wishes them dead. I work with their victims—but week in and week out—and what's been done to them makes me sick. Oh yes," she reassured him, "me too. Don't think I get used to this. You *never* get used to it."

This came as a relief to Dart, who had worried that she had become hardened—that something had been stolen from her as well. He explained, "That was a major part of my reasoning for not going forward with the Ice Man: Who cares? Making them dead is somehow more satisfying than locking them up. But what if there is treatment?"

"And what about so many sex offenders expressing remorse and genuinely wanting to stop?" she asked. "I know. It's not an easy issue."

"I know what has to be done," Dart said, dreading this thought.

"Well, I know what has to be done too," she said seductively. She wore a pair of tight blue jeans and a loose-fitting gray sweater that Dart found provocative, because when she leaned over it fell open at the neck. Drinking a beer from the bottle, she was sitting in Dart's one remaining captain's chair, her left leg kicked up over the arm.

He was prepping a radicchio and shrimp risotto and trying to concentrate on the recipe. Mac was snoring at Abby's feet.

"Before you start that," she said, "take a break. Once you get going on a risotto, you can't stop." She motioned him into a chair. "Tell me about Kowalski."

Dart opened a beer. "It's possible that he's telling the truth. He told us the same story three times in a row. And he remembered details well. The trouble with interviewing a cop—he knows what you're looking for. He could be full of shit. It's hard to say."

"But you believe him," she stated.

"I do. Haite doesn't. And I can't tell Haite because it involves Zeller, and I'm not ready to lay all that on him."

"Personally, I've never believed anything Kowalski says. He's a bullshitter from way back." She asked, "What's his status?"

"It'll be reviewed. Meanwhile, he's still active."

"I don't imagine he's too keen on you."

"He never has been."

She took a pull on the beer and set down the bottle. There was something brewing in her.

"What about these tests?" he asked.

"You mean, have I heard anything? Have they discovered some abnormal gene in sex offenders? To my knowledge: no. But listen, there have been rumors for years about a crime gene. You've heard that stuff. The *Times* reported last February that the gene—a combination of genes—had been identified. Nothing's impossible." She asked rhetorically, "Is there a Prozac for sex offense? Not that I've heard of. Not yet. But as Teddy Bragg says, 'Stay tuned.'"

"Would you have heard if there is such a thing being tested?"

"Doubtful. No. Something that controversial would be cloaked in secrecy. I wouldn't know about it until it hit the mainstream. And there's nothing close to mainstream. I do keep up."

It felt right to have her here. Comfortable. Easy. She drew down the beer, got up, and found her way through the kitchen drawers until she had what she needed to set the table. Dart enjoyed his moment off his feet.

"What are you thinking about?" she asked him, placing down a fork for his place.

"Kowalski," he lied. He coughed.

"That cough sounds bad," she said. "You live with that thing, don't you?"

He didn't feel like telling her about it. He had never told anyone and didn't see why he should start now. He said, "It's not the best story" and wondered how it was that his mouth had so purposely disobeyed his brain. "It's a bad story, actually," he added, wondering where that too had come from.

"You don't have to tell me, you know."

No, I don't want to, his brain answered. "I had what you might call a reckless mother. A drinker. She was a drinker. And my father was nobody. I never knew him. At least I don't think I did. But my mother was . . . her brother was a dealer. Big time. Lots of money. She was, I don't know, confused. He took care of her. She was eighty miles of bad road is what she was. And I was on that road, at least at the beginning I was. The beginning for me. As a kid, you know. I ran errands. Cooked. Booze mostly, the errands. Bought her booze for her. I think about it now— this kid buying brown bags in the back alley. Jesus, what a time in my life that was."

"Bad road?" she asked.

"An angry drunk," he answered. He tried the beer. He didn't want to talk about this, and he thought if he kept his mouth busy then maybe she would get the hint. Change the subject. It didn't seem to work: She stared at him, waiting.

"She got confused about things. Money. The booze. Sometimes she would drink an entire bottle while I was at school, and by the time I got home she would think that I had never bought

261

the bottle, that I had spent her money—as if it were hers anyway, the money. She got a check once a month. From the brother. Drug money, I later found out. Bad money."

He felt a little more relaxed. It wasn't as hard to talk about as he had imagined. She seemed interested, but not terribly upset. He had always thought that if he talked about it, the person would get upset—the way he felt about it. Mad. Real mad.

"So you got sick?" she asked. "The cough," she reminded.

"No, no," he said. "Not sick. I . . . she . . . when she got mad, when she mixed things up, she . . . she took it out on me. I was handy, I guess."

"Hit you?" she asked, but in a way that sought to clarify, not accuse.

"Yeah," he answered. "I guess so." He thought about starting to eat the risotto. He was feeling nervous, not comfortable at all. "Yeah, she hit me," he admitted. How many times had he lied to the school nurse about this? How many years had he covered for her? And on this particular night he suddenly unloads. *What the hell is going on?* he wondered. "Hit me all the time. And you can only take so much of that—I could only take so much of that—before you learn to run. It kind of trains you to be a coward," he said. This came the hardest for him—that he had run. All these years later, and it still felt cheap to run from her. As if he didn't measure up. He had always wanted to hit her back. He had never lifted a hand. Her face all bloated, her eyes unfocused. Who could hit *that*? he wondered.

"You don't have to talk about this," she repeated. A few minutes had passed. He realized he hadn't touched his food. "But I want to hear, if you do want to talk about it."

"I ran," he said. He felt the stinging in his eyes, and he wondered if he should leave the table. "I ran," he said again. He swallowed. It felt as if a chicken bone were stuck in there. "And I learned to hide until she settled down. Passed out is more like it. Used to find her on the floor. Like a beached whale. Lying there. I couldn't move her. Thought she was dead. Wishful thinking, I suppose." He felt tears running, and powerless to do anything about it. Abby didn't seem fazed. She was still staring at him intensely, but he felt no judgment coming from her. *She's trained for this shit*, he thought, suddenly understanding why he had picked this particular woman to unload on. *She's the one who could handle it.*

He continued, "So I hid. The broom closet. The basement. There was a piece of furniture in the dining room that I could fit into. But she found me. Almost always. Until I discovered the dryer. The clothes dryer."

Her face remained impassive, revealing no opinion, no sympathy, no pity, and yet he knew that she had heard him. He wondered if she could be so objective, so internally calm, or was this some kind of act that she had learned as a professional?

"She never thought to look in the clothes

263

dryer," he explained. "It became my first choice. And more than once I had been doing a load of laundry, and I would yank that laundry out of there as fast as I could and climb inside and pull the door closed."

"The heat," she said. "Your lungs."

He nodded. His throat felt scratchy, but he didn't want to cough in front of her, for it suddenly felt as if it would seem he had forced it. So he swallowed it away and said roughly, "Yeah. I figure I fried them hiding in there."

He drank. Something to do. Keep his hands busy. Stop them from shaking. Somewhere to avert his eyes. He thought that maybe five minutes passed in complete silence. It felt more like an hour.

"Thank you," she said.

He felt embarrassed all of a sudden. He had lowered his mask, and felt incredibly vulnerable.

"Is she still alive?"

"No, but she lasted a long time. I was eighteen. And I was still living with her. Don't ask me why." He hesitated. "She had control. I suppose that's why."

Abby came out of her chair and approached him. She bumped his chair and slipped a leg over him and sat down in his lap, facing him. She stroked his hair back at his temples and repeated, "Thank you." She rubbed away the snail tracks left by his tears.

He experienced a kind of giddy high, flooded by the relief of having told someone. She seemed to float over him; he barely felt her sitting there, though he was aroused by the contact. Her warmth there. She leaned forward to kiss him, wiggling herself closer, sparing no contact, to where her legs swallowed his waist and gripped him. The kiss was gentle but by no means innocent. He kissed his way across her chin and down her neck, and as he did she whispered, "Harder," and he sucked the soft skin of her neck into his lips, and she shuddered and purred, "Umm," and he felt himself grow harder.

She pressed her chest gently against his, rubbing her breasts lightly against him, her hips following the same motion. He leaned her back and kissed down into the loose neck of the sweater, his tongue painting her, as her hands slipped behind him and pulled his shirt free, and warm fingers scrambled over his back, sending flashes up his spine and gooseflesh head to toe.

Abby knew his secret, and knew his pleasure as well. Her back was hot to touch, and the more he kissed her neck the more excited she grew until she muffled a knowing laugh of pleasure signaling that they had crossed a line. He kissed her breasts through the sweater, and as he did, she pulled it up and off in a sweeping, liberating motion, and his lips found her nipples hard beneath the bra. She placed her hand on the back of his head and pulled his mouth firmly against her, and again she cooed in that same provocative, pleasurable sound. She slipped her hands down and unzipped her jeans. And then in an explosion of energy, the game was briefly hers. She got out of the chair and led him down the hall and into the bedroom, undressing herself as she went.

When they reached the bed, she was naked above the waist and her pants were down around her calves. Her underwear was athletic gray with a wide band of elastic. She turned to him, undressed him quickly, and pulled him down to her. They pressed together and he could feel the fast, rhythmic pounding in her chest. Her skin was incredibly soft—not a hard body at all. She was not heavy, but neither was she taut and firm. Her skin was creamy, spongy—it felt as if he were experiencing her for the first time. She moved herself against his erection, her fingernails skating down his back.

Her hands found his buttocks and held him against her as she gently rocked her hips, and all at once he felt her wetness. Dart kissed her on the shoulder and worked his way up her neck, and as he did she leaned her head back and he could feel her smiling. "You know something?" she asked, without wanting his answer. "That day we talked about the Lawrence file? I wanted to jump you right there and then." She groaned as he drew a warm circle around her nipple with his tongue, and she shuddered as he gently pinched her between his teeth.

She pushed his head back and kissed him wetly on his lips. Her fingers were everywhere at once. He felt lightheaded and dizzy.

He kissed her other breast and drew the nipple into his mouth and felt her harden. "I like that," she whispered, brushing his nipples lightly with her fingers. Her hips continued to rock and then she took hold of him and rubbed the very tip of him against her, slick and hot with her juices. "I like this too," she said. She ran him up and down herself, her eyes pinched tightly shut, her chest a florid red. He wanted inside of her, but she held him at bay, enjoying the contact.

He closed his eyes. She rolled him over, and suddenly he was inside her mouth and a surge of intense pleasure overcame him. Her tongue worked magic on him, and just as he feared there might be no turning back she kissed her way back up his belly and straddled him, opening herself to him, sliding against him, but still not allowing him inside.

He rolled her back over, and she pulled him on top of her, and she allowed just the head of him to enter. Dreamy and lost, she struggled to keep her eyes open, blinking furiously. "Wait," she whispered, still working him against herself. She squinted tightly. "Um," she said. "Yes." She worked him faster. She was slippery, and the air was rich with her scent. As she came, she choked out a growling noise that coincided with the ripple of spasms that ran through her body in hot waves. "God, yes," she said, her back arched, her breasts thrust out. Dart kissed her breast and she shrieked. "Yes . . . Yes!"

Her eyes held within them a crazed, frantic expression—like someone awakened quickly from a dream. She looked both puzzled and thrilled, her cheeks aglow, her smile bright. Clutching his buttocks, she continued to drive him into her, establishing a rhythm, hooking his ankles with hers and linked together, rocking her hips off the bed and further swallowing him inside her warmth.

"We better be careful," Dart warned, feeling himself losing control.

She grinned, her eyes squinting pleasurably. "Tell me when you're close," she said.

He chuckled nervously.

Holding her gaze on him, she drew him into her with a heavy thrust of her hands, increasing the pace. "Hmm?" she teased, clearly feeling him swell within her. "Tell me when you're going to come," she said.

He kissed her on the neck and up toward her jawline. She cooed. "I want you to pull out and come on my breasts," she whispered. "I want you to come all over me."

The words pushed Dart over his limit. He felt himself about to explode, and he said, "You're going to get your wish."

As he slipped from within her, he was met there by her warm hand. "Come for me," she hissed at him hotly. "Come big." She snuggled lower beneath him, so that he straddled her, and she worked him until, in a surge of building heat, he erupted, spraying onto her chest. "Yes!" she said, still working him as with her left hand she spread his lather across her skin. Then she released him and, with both hands, rubbed his seed, like lotion, into her skin, over her breasts, her chest a ruby red, her eyes shut, her thin lips grinning and quivering as if she were speaking. The scent of him potent, her nipples firm and erect, she hummed in pleasure, continuing to massage herself, warmly satisfied, nodding lightly, as if agreeing with something being said, something that she might be thinking. Her hands flowed over her chest, his spent fluid quickly dry. "So smooth," she said, "so soft," opening her eyes again. They smiled together. "Feel," she said, directing his hand to her breast and dragging it across skin that held a mysterious texture, like a fine dry oil. The white skin of her breasts glowed warmly in the light, painted with him. The air smelled of them, thick and intoxicating. He felt lightheaded.

"Amazing, isn't it?" she said, still holding his wrist, using his hand to work her breasts. "Nice," she whispered. "That was very nice."

Dart rolled off and collapsed beside her, winded and dizzy with delight. He lay this way. Her fingers laced across her white belly, eyes shut, she grinned but said nothing. Dart stroked her arm, and her smile enlarged, and again she nodded privately. It was this secrecy, this privacy of pleasure, that he found so intriguing. He stared at her through the room's dusty twilight.

A few minutes later, her eyes still shut, she asked, "Do you have a silk shirt I could borrow?"

"I have plenty of shirts."

"Silk?"

"I have one that's silk," he answered. Ginny had given it to him for a birthday. "It's black."

"You don't mind?" she asked, rocking her head now to face him, their noses only inches apart.

"Not at all."

"My skin feels *so good*," she said in a way that stimulated him.

She jumped up unexpectedly, turned on the bedside light, and, naked except for her socks, approached and searched his closet. Finding the shirt, she turned to face him then, her chest still flushed with pink, her face and eyes sparkling, her breasts shining dully, and she slipped her right arm into the sleeve.

Feeling he had been rude not to offer, Dart said, "Would you like a shower? Share a shower?"

"Oh, no," she said definitely, grinning that sly grin of hers yet again. "I don't want to lose this."

At that moment, the building's hallway fire alarm sounded loudly, and Dart jumped. He smelled smoke. A curling fear ran down his spine. He had a great fear of fire, stemming from his drunken mother being a smoker.

Perhaps it was the clothes dryer as a child, or the memory of a range fire he had witnessed out west as a teenager—great sheets of bright orange sweeping the plains and spewing a thick charcoal gray into the blue, boundless sky—or perhaps, he thought, it was simply an intuitive response to something that could kill so quickly, but Dart felt a surge of panic, and though he saw Abby's horrified expression and her mouth moving, he heard no words. They had both pulled on their clothes—he didn't remember that happening—and were standing in his hallway. With her hands, she searched the apartment door for heat; she dropped to her knees and sniffed between the carpet and door.

"It's okay," he heard her say, as if someone had finally turned up the volume.

"Ready?" he asked.

"We're going," she announced over the abrasive fire alarm. Far in the distance, the first wail of a siren was heard. "Ready?"

He nodded, his attention riveted on all that he was leaving behind, on memories and artifacts of his time here with Ginny. She took hold of the doorknob.

"Slowly," he cautioned, stepping aside.

She nodded and eased the door open. There was no flash of flame, no billow of smoke, only the increased volume of the alarm and the sounds of harried shouting and racing footsteps. Mac took off down the stairs. A general sense of chaos surrounded them as they hurried to the central stairs and began their descent. The smell of oil smoke was overpowering. It smelled of fear and old paint and dust, of all those years Dart had used these stairs, forsaking the tired elevator. It smelled final.

The smoke grew thicker as they descended, enveloping them like a fog. They checked for each other at each turn of the metal handrail. Her wide eyes glanced over at him. From below came sounds of panic. Two floors down, Dart caught sight of several familiar faces and wondered how he could live in the same place for so many years and know so few of his neighbors. They knew him, most knew he was a policeman, and though he knew some by name, not nearly enough.

"Mrs. Amory," he said to Abby as he stopped at the fire door to the ground floor. Eleanor Amory went about in a motorized wheelchair and had picked this apartment building because of its location on a city bus route. She was in her late seventies and fiercely independent. Abby apparently understood just by the way he spoke, and she stopped and helped him check the door for heat before they passed through and into the downstairs hallway. The smoke was heavier here, and Dart believed that it was coming from the parking garage, that a car was on fire, and this lessened his panic because fire could be contained well in the concrete garage. They ran down the long hallway, and only then was Dart aware that the only light came from the emergency lights, a fact that had escaped him. *All the training*, he thought, wondering how panic had so easily engulfed him, feeling it behind him now, and glad to have it gone.

"Which apartment?" he heard Abby call from behind him.

He kicked the door in, signaled her inside, and motioned for Abby to take the rooms to the left. Dart took those to the right.

Eleanor Amory was not in the kitchen, or the small sitting room or in any of the three closets that Dart searched quickly.

"Joe!" Abby called out.

Eleanor Amory was in her bedroom coiled into a ball in the far corner, a nightgown bunched at her knees, a collapsible wheelchair propped against the wall alongside her. She was in shock, her dull blue eyes glassy and open wide in a fixed stare.

Abby stooped, tried to communicate with the woman, but it was of no use. She tentatively eased her arms into the fold of the woman's bent knees, and behind her head, and together with Dart, they hoisted her, and Dart took her fully into his arms as Abby helped the woman to take hold around his neck.

A moment later they were outside, in the alley behind the building, and Eleanor Amory was in the care of emergency personnel. Abby stood holding the woman's hand. The alley was dark, awash in the scattering, fractured light of emergency vehicles, and from the building's garage a thick coiling plume of black smoke rushed into the night sky. The area was crowded with onlookers as well as with residents of the building, in pajamas, raincoats, and whatever else they had grabbed. Several held pets tightly in their arms. One woman was crying as she stared up at her windows. Mac was sitting away from the chaos like an old person watching a parade.

Dart felt the cold. He felt awkward and out of place, accustomed to being the one responding to an emergency rather than experiencing it first-hand. There were so many things he wished he'd taken. Photographs. Gifts. Letters. His first uniform as a patrolman. He ran down an inventory as he watched four fully clad firemen become swallowed by the smoke as they charged the garage. He hoped for a quick resolution. The night air was filled with the sound of communication radios spitting static, of children crying and adults sobbing, and an endless roar of orders being shouted about. To the lay person, the bystander, the efforts of the emergency crews seemed chaotic and disorganized. But Dart knew better.

He crossed his arms tightly to fend off the cold. A harsh and unforgiving voice whispered,

"Don't turn around, Ivy. Nod if you can hear me." Dart nodded. He smelled the stale aroma of cigar smoke despite the petroleum in the air, and he recognized the deep slow voice and the way that voice spoke his nickname. "I can't afford the attention," Walter Zeller said. Dart, stunned, could feel the man's presence as he stepped closer and continued in a hushed whisper. "Your Volvo has had a slight problem, is all—an electrical short under the dash; if there had been less plastic in it, it might have never burned at all."

Dart had so many things to say that nothing came out, his thoughts bottle-necked somewhere near his tongue. What with the fire and the chaos, and the surprise that Zeller had orchestrated all of this to make contact with him.

"You'll figure this out. At least if you have any sense left in you, you will." He added, "I can't do your fucking work for you, kid. I told you that. Wish I could. But then you wouldn't hold up on the stand, would you? You gotta do this yourself. You gotta get your mind off your pecker and back onto your desk.

"What I want you to think about, Ivy, is—and I want you to remember this: You're looking at what you know, what you're familiar with, rather than digging in and finding what's really the cause here." He added, "That they're all connected."

"The gene therapy," Dart said.

"Maybe you *are* listening." He added, "Maybe I should have just called you again. You know how I like to do things *in person*."

"So you torched my car?" Dart said, exasper-

274

ated. He made a move to turn around, but Zeller stopped him with a stern "Don't!" He added, "It's not safe for me."

"For *you?*"

"They're murders, Ivy, but it's not what you think. I *know* what you think. Do your fucking homework. Do us both a favor."

An old beat-up car pulled into the far end of the alley. Not a police car, not fire. In the flashing lights Dart couldn't make out the color or the face of the man who opened the car door and peered out quickly before climbing back in and driving off as a patrolman approached him to tell him to move.

"You see that?" Zeller asked. "They're after *me*, Ivy. Why? Because I know the truth— because I *found out the truth*! Find it, damn it all. Do your fucking homework."

Dart said softly, "The hormones." He waited a second and turned his head slightly and said: "A treatment of some sort."

Zeller didn't answer.

Dart attempted to turn around for a second time, expecting his effort to be blocked, but instead faced the dark shadows immediately behind him broken only by the rhythmic, hypnotic pulse of vehicle emergency lights.

Zeller was gone—vanished, though Dart could still hear the man's whispers over his shoulder.

His teacher. His mentor.

Gone.

His killer?

For a fraction of a second Dart wondered if he had imagined this conversation. He scanned the area again, carefully probing every possible hiding place.

Gone.

They're murders, Ivy, but it's not what you think.

Lies! Dart thought. *Tricks! He's toying with me. Find it, damn it all. Do your fucking homework.*

Dart felt sick to his stomach. The smoke curled into the night sky, and then it too was gone.

CHAPTER
29

Over the course of the transition between day and night tours, detectives worked poorly, sometimes falling asleep at their desks, in the middle of interrogations, or even during phone calls. Moods went sour, and tempers flared. Haite's unit, including Dart and Kowalski, had just switched to the graveyard shift, and walking through CAPers was like entering an area laden with land mines. To make matters worse, the building was going to shit; a leak that no one seemed able to stop ran a slow but constant drip into a five-gallon white plastic container in the far corner by the coffee machine. The uninterrupted sound of it was a source of constant irritation, covered only by the drone of activity to which Dart and his colleagues had long since become accustomed.

Dart cleared a domestic stabbing in the north end—a black woman had killed her drunken lover. He felt lucky because it was an early call, eight-thirty at night, and that took his name off the phone list. The rest of the night would be spent writing up an easy report, speaking with the on-call prosecuting attorney, and waiting for sunrise to free him.

He was midway into his report when the familiar banter inside CAPers slowly trickled down to nothing and the room was silent. This took a moment to register, at which point Dart looked up and spun around to see Ginny Rice standing in the CAPers' doorway. Everyone in the division had closely followed the drama of their split, and her unexpected appearance had quieted his colleagues.

She wore a pair of Gap khakis and a white shirt under a green sweater. She had two earrings in her left ear and a small gold chain worn as a necklace.

Dart stood and walked over to greet here, doing so in as quiet a voice as possible. "Hey there," he said.

"Hey, Dart. Somewhere where we can talk?"

He lead Ginny to the crib and sat down with her at the scarred table, where a copy of *Guns and Ammo* lay open.

"I may be in some trouble," she said. Up close, she appeared dazed, or overtired. Worn at the edges.

"What kind of trouble?"

"It may be nothing."

He reached over and took her hand, a mass of confusion. He wondered how, after the pain she had caused him, he could feel so instantly comfortable with her.

She said, "The new policies. Remember? I accessed billing—" Twice Dart had covered for her, had helped her out of a legal knothole, only to have her caught hacking a third time. That had brought a federal conviction, something that Dart could not help with. Now he found himself feeling guilty about having asked her to do this.

"It turns out, there are *dozens* of new accounts, all paid for by fund transfers from the *same* account. It's a Union Bank corporate account."

"Dozens?"

She nodded. "All males, and though I haven't confirmed all of them, I know that at least three have wives who were kicked by the system as victims of abuse."

The tests, Dart thought. He said nothing.

"I think what happened was that I tripped a security gate going into Union Trust."

"You broke into a bank."

"Electronically," she said, adding defensively. "How else could I identify who paid for all this insurance?"

"It was a perk," he said, guessing that the insurance coverage had been used as an incentive to gain test subjects.

"What?"

"Never mind," he said.

"I thought I had a hole in the firewall," she explained. "I thought I had a clean entry. But maybe I stepped on something getting out. I'm not sure. All I know is that *my* software detected surveillance—"

"They *watched* you?" he exclaimed.

She nodded. "Chances are, they know what I went after."

"And did you come straight here?"

Her face tightened. "I shouldn't have done that, should I?"

"You never know," Dart said. "It's doubtful they would have put you under physical surveillance. If it was federal—"

"They would have busted me," she answered. "You see?" She craned forward, "That's one reason I came straight here. I'm hoping—hell, I'm praying—that maybe you, HPD, has some kind of white-collar crime thing in place. Because otherwise—"

"It's private," he answered.

"Yeah, private. And shit, they could sue the pants off me. I'd rather face you guys than a corporation any day."

"They can sue you either way." He added, "They won't, though." Corporations rarely sued. That brought the case public, and exposed their system as vulnerable to electronic attack. They preferred keeping things as quiet as possible, often dropping all charges in exchange for a gag order against the hacker. On occasion the hacker got a job offer from that very same company. He reminded, "And you *wouldn't* rather face us. You're on probation. A second conviction—"

"And I do time. I know." She crossed her arms and shuddered. "I'm scared to death, Dartelli." She said, "But hey, I got the name of the company for you. At least I didn't come out empty-handed."

"The people buying these policies?"

"Paid out of a corporate account under the name Roxin Incorporated."

Bud Gorman would be able to answer questions about Roxin. Dart wrote the name down.

She said, "I thought you'd like that."

Dart looked up from his notebook, still angry with her. "Why, Gin? Why take the chance?"

"What, you're going to get mad at me for helping you?"

"I appreciate the help. It's not that—"

She interrupted. "I want us back together."

The building was heated by forced air, and it was the only sound in the room as Dart averted his eyes back to his notebook, and Ginny scratched at some epoxy stuck to the table.

"I miss you," she said.

"I miss you too," he answered honestly. "You're involved with someone," he reminded her.

"From what I hear, we both are."

"Yes, I am too. Sort of."

"Sort of?"

"I am."

"Abby Lang," she said.

He had nothing to say. Ginny had left him. What he did now was his business, and his alone.

He said, "Companies have their own computer security systems, isn't that right? They monitor their own systems for breaches. This bank, for instance."

"It's subcontracted usually. Yeah."

"So if anyone knows about you, it's them—this private firm or the bank itself."

"I did it from home," she said, as always, two steps ahead of him. "All my stuff is on my home machine."

"Can they trace it back to you?"

"Depends how good they are," she replied. "How long they were on to me. I had the call switched through New Haven and routed through a Yale web site. Normally they wouldn't be able to break that, but I was on there pretty long. They might have. Depends."

"And if they did?"

"They could act, or they could sit on me and go for a second hit. Two or three hits are more convincing . . . easier to use against me."

"But you will *not* go back there."

"No." She chuckled nervously. "Not likely."

"So we wait and see," he offered. She nodded. "Are you okay?"

"Worried."

"Yeah," he agreed.

"If they're private, they might watch me, something like that. I think that's what's bugging me the most—the idea of that. You know, surveillance."

"They might," he admitted. "But if they misstep," he reminded her, "then you can turn right around and sue them—and that just might get the charges dropped."

She nodded, but her fear was palpable.

"It's a thought," he said. "If you suspect something like that—electronic surveillance, anything like that—you should let me know. Maybe we can turn the cards on them." He asked, "Are you okay?" She looked like hell.

Again she nodded, but it was all show. "What about it?" she asked. "What about us?"

"Zeller used to say to me. 'You come to a fork in the road, take it,'" Dart answered.

It elicited a smile from her. A soft laugh. Dart coughed.

"I guess that's where I am," he said, "at that fork in the road."

She pursed her lips. "I understand."

"I'm not saying no."

"I understand."

"Abby may try to reconcile with her ex. If she does, and it works . . . Who knows?"

"And you're all right with that?" she asked incredulously.

"It's a unique relationship," he answered. "We're very much in the here-and-now."

"Well, I can't say that I'm not jealous."

"Tomorrow is a long way off, where Abby and I are concerned."

She looked up at him with tears in her eyes. He let go of her hand. "I'm sorry," she said.

"Yeah," answered Joe Dart. "Me too."

Dart called Bud Gorman at home and caught him before he went to bed.

"I need yet another favor," Dart said cautiously, testing if he had asked for too much lately. Referring to the speeding tickets, he added, "I'm going to owe you a hell of a lot of fixes."

"Screw fixing the speeding tickets. I'm getting a Jeep. I hit a piece of metal yesterday—one little piece of shit on the center line. I was only doing about seventy . . ." *Probably in a thirty-five zone,*

Dart thought. "Thing had such low clearance, it jumped up and punctured my gas tank. Lucky I didn't flame out. Shopped Jeeps this afternoon. It's not safe out there."

"It's a company called Roxin Incorporated."

"It's called Roxin Laboratories, Inc.," Gorman corrected. "It's a biotech, genetics firm. I take it you got the e-mail I sent you."

Genetics? Dart thought. "But how do you know—?"

"Did you get the e-mail or not?" Gorman interrupted.

"I haven't checked today. It's swing shift. I'm brain dead." *Genetics,* he thought again. Roxin Laboratories, Inc., had purchased medical insurance policies for known sex offenders—protecting themselves in case the test program went badly. *And it's gone badly,* Dart thought.

"Brain dead, huh? Well, come alive for a minute, 'cause what I'm talking about is the Proctor Securities client list you asked for. I turned up every check written to the company for the last twenty-four months. Posted the list onto CompuServe for you."

"But Roxin?" Dart again began but was immediately interrupted.

"Is *on the list,* Joe. Proctor Securities is on retainer to them. They're a big client. I placed them in the top ten of my Proctor list."

"Oh, my God," Dart blurted out. Zeller would have discovered Roxin while working for Proctor. It fit.

"You want a credit run on Roxin?" Gorman offered. "No problem."

Dart couldn't get a word out. His mind cluttered with a dozen thoughts.

"Joe? You there?" Gorman added, "Know anybody who can get me a good deal on a Jeep?"

CHAPTER
30

The space-age facility was surrounded by a nine-foot wrought iron fence enclosing what appeared to be three or four acres of park. The fence carried evenly spaced signs warning against unlawful trespass. In the crotch of an elm tree, Dart spotted one of what he suspected were dozens of hidden security cameras. Roxin Laboratories was a small fortress. Nine miles west of downtown and a few miles south of the town of Avon, nestled away in a thickly wooded hillside and overlooking the Farmington River, the physical plant consisted of a large five-story geodesic dome of steel and mirrored glass, and a similarly constructed multistory laboratory attached like a box to the dome's south. There were two vehicular entrances—the main one with a manned booth and an automated entrance to the employees' parking lot alongside the box. Dart showed his ID to the guard and parked in a visitor's spot close to the main doors.

All security guards wore dark blue uniforms, pressed and starched, with emblems stitched onto the right sleeve and name panels above the right breast pocket. Dart surrendered his weapon and his cellular phone and passed through a cleverly disguised metal detector, met there by a man in his early twenties who owned a severe haircut and piercing green eyes and who introduced himself as Richard. Richard wore a light blue suit and expensive shoes shined to a mirror finish. He instructed Dart on how to use his visitor's pass in order to log in to the computerized security system.

To Dart, this felt a little bit like entering a prison.

The elevator panel operated only after Richard swiped his credit-card-sized security pass through the reader. He and Dart changed elevator cars on the third level, after passing through another security station and entering the lab building. A series of air locks gained them access to the second set of elevators and offices and labs beyond.

The need for an escort became quickly apparent—hallways and doors lacked identification, except for a cryptic band of bricked colors, reminding Dart of nautical flags. On foot, they crossed a skybridge connecting the elevator bank to the third floor of the lab building, high above what Richard called the "terrarium"—a small enclosed courtyard complete with a running fountain and a living lily pond. Offices looked out onto the courtyard. "The security is somewhat ominous, I know," Richard apologized, "but recombinant genetics is not to be taken lightly. The security has much less to do with the integrity of our ideas than it does with the preservation of environmental continuity."

"That's certainly reassuring," Dart said.

Richard attempted what passed for a smile. "Yes, well, we wouldn't want anything getting away from us," Richard explained.

"No," Dart agreed, "we wouldn't." After another ten yards, Dart said, "Expensive facility," exploring with a compliment.

"When we started up, biotechs were the darlings of Wall Street. The board wanted to make a statement with the facility—and I think they have."

"Definitely," Dart agreed.

"We've had enormous success with our arthritis drug—Artharest, is its commercial name," he announced. "And big things are expected of our prostate drug—an anticancer gene therapy drug."

They arrived at a door marked with a red flag, two blues and another red. Richard used his ID card to gain them access and showed Dart inside a generous conference room. The table, a series of thick slabs of black granite on a chrome frame, had down its center three flat conferencing microphones that looked more like ashtrays. The chairs were black leather slung between polished steel and braided wire. A large abstract mural of polished pink stone and blue glass occupied most of the far wall. A set of floor-to-ceiling white laminate cabinets occupied the far end of the room, presumably housing audiovisual equipment.

Richard seated him, asked if he could bring

him something to drink, and when Dart declined, retreated through a door that made a sound as if locking behind him. Four excruciatingly long minutes later, the door opened and a tall, slightly heavy, middle-aged woman with dull blond hair wearing a conservative gray suit and cream blouse entered, graceful and poised. She carried a large black leather briefcase with her that she parked in the chair next to the one into which she lowered herself. She wore cream tights and black shoes with low heels.

She had never been pretty, though always smart, Dart decided, before she spoke a word. "Welcome to Roxin," she said, like a tour guide, allowing the heel of her shoe to flap off her foot.

"It's quite the place," Dart said. "You don't see it from the road."

"No. Only from the river, and only then if you're looking. It's remarkable for its privacy."

"I'm told that your time is extremely valuable, so I'll get right to it," he said.

"That's kind of you, Detective."

"I need to confirm some names with you . . . men involved in a test you're conducting . . ."

"A clinical trial?" she corrected. "Which one?"

Dart felt out of his element. Dr. Arielle Martinson was Roxin's director of research and development and CEO. It surprised him that he had gained access to the top on his first try—not at all what he had expected. Typically he had to stair-step his way up the corporate ladder.

"I have the names here," he said, passing her a sheet from his notebook. The small, wrinkled piece of notepaper suddenly seemed unprofessional to him. He felt half-tempted to apologize for it.

Martinson was a woman with a formidable presence, commanding a great deal of space around her, the kind of person in whom he immediately sensed both leadership and integrity. The two articles he had gleaned from the *Wall Street Journal* and the *New York Times* cast her as a woman pioneer in a predominantly male field, the recipient of dozens of prestigious awards including a three-hundred-thousand-dollar Mac-Arthur while at Michigan, where she had worked as part of the Human Genome Project. Her specialty was hormonal gene therapy. The *Journal* had speculated that Roxin was on the verge of a gene therapy treatment for menopausal side effects, with a market projection of eight hundred million dollars annually.

She had a nervous habit of tugging her short-cropped dark hair down past her right ear and fiddling with it. She kept herself nearly in profile to him, shielding the practice as best as possible, as if she was aware of it but could not control herself. This, from a woman who seemed, by all measurable appearances, in total control.

She accepted the notepaper, read the names from it, and made a phone call, reciting the names into the receiver for the benefit of someone named Angelica. "I see," she said, thanking the woman before hanging up. She half turned to not quite face Dart and, looking at him out of the side of her eyes, said, "Yes, they are listed with us, though I'm afraid that's all I can share with you at this time."

Dart was amazed by her frankness. He had expected the runaround. "They are," he repeated, not quite knowing where to go, having prepared for a battle.

"Yes."

He thought, considering alternatives. He felt certain from her preemptive statement that she would not discuss the nature of the trial. "Are you aware that all three men are deceased?" He paused, "Suicides?"

The news clearly had an effect, though she contained her surprise well. "Clinical trials are conducted in the blind, Detective. Are you aware of that? As the creator of the drug, we can either hire an independent or remain with an in-house team for our stage-two efficacy trials. Either way, these trials are conducted in the blind; that is, though we're made aware of the names of the participants, and occasionally have a role in selecting those individuals, we are not informed as to who is receiving the actual drug and, in stage three, to whom the placebo is administered, if, in fact, placebo testing is involved."

"I see," Dart said, again feeling out of his element. "Would you be willing to discuss the *nature* of this particular trial?" he inquired.

"Your mention of suicide troubles me, obviously," she said. "And all that I can tell you is that were the suicides in *any way* linked to the trial, we most certainly would have been notified. I can assure you of that. Guidelines are quite rigid in that regard."

"So you're saying these three suicides are *unrelated*?" he asked incredulously.

"Can you prove otherwise?" she asked, voicing concern, not anger.

He decided to drop the bomb. "We're not entirely sure they *were* suicides, Dr. Martinson."

She turned as gray as her suit, and her hand became busy with the lock of hair. "Sabotage?" she asked. "Are you saying that someone is attempting to sabotage my clinical trials?"

"If the suicides *were* connected to the trials?" he asked, "what then?"

She smirked, not liking that thought one bit. She shook her head, offering him a better view of her neck, her hair whipping out of the way and briefly revealing what looked like a wide scar just below her ear. Her hand returned there quickly, and turning her head away, she said, "If our drug is made to appear to cause severe depression or other psychological side effects, I can assure you that the trials would be immediately halted and we would take a serious look at the casual relationship. But let me say, too, that one of the *benefits* of gene therapy is the specific targeting of the medication, and therefore the lessening of many side effects associated with other groups of medications. As to how it would affect us—well, it would devastate us, of course. We don't think highly of killing our test subjects, Detective. And let me just say that these drugs see *rigorous* testing prior to human trials, and I certainly would not expect severe psychological disorders to go unnoticed and therefore untreated."

"You'd catch it first," he said.

"You bet we would," she answered.

"So someone could hurt your company if they

were to imply an association between your trial and these suicides?"

"This kind of sabotage could ruin us." She appeared nervous then, irritable and anxious to be done with Dart. She said, "To be perfectly honest, Detective, the idea of this is frightening, and I'd like to get right on it. Again," she said strongly, "I think if there were any such connection to be made, I most certainly would have heard about it, but if you'd excuse me—"

"I need to know what's going on," he said bluntly.

"I understand," she said.

"I may be able to help you," he offered.

"Yes." She attempted a smile, but it failed. She was too shaken.

"One last question," Dart said. He felt invasive with these questions. Here was Martinson, having been told that someone was trying to sabotage her company, and he, Dart, continued to pry into every dirty corner. "Is Proctor Securities— your security firm—ever involved in these trials in any way? Do they ever have access to these trials or to the trial results?"

"I should say not!" She flushed a bright crimson. "They police our parking lots for God's sake. They help us with corporate espionage from at home *and* abroad." Her eyes went wide and she snapped, "Where the hell are *they* when we need them?" He could see her making a mental note about this. She pulled herself together and said, "This is a highly competitive field, Detective, with tens—*hundreds*—of millions of dollars at stake. If one product fails, another may be in position to take its place. Terry Proctor is supposed to stay on top of that kind of thing. Protect our interests." She tried another smile, this one more effective. "Can we continue this another time?"

Dart nodded. She spun her head around as she stood and Dart stole a look at her neck.

Definitely a scar. A knife wound. And by the look of it, a nasty one.

CHAPTER
31

Dart didn't want to return to 11 Hamilton Court because the house was being kept under surveillance on the hope that Wallace Sparco—*Walter Zeller*—might be apprehended. But it was Zeller's own teachings that leaned Dart toward going back and reexamining its contents. That house remained the only physical link to the visitor at the Payne suicide. *Always return to the crime scene*, Zeller had taught him.

"Usually I hate being on call," Samantha Richardson said, flirting with Dart as she unlocked the door to the photo lab. Bragg's assistant and photographer wore blue jeans and a red flannel top that looked suspiciously like pajamas. At eleven-thirty at night, anything was possible—people showed up in the strangest clothes. Dart was hardly sleeping, between the night tour and day calls, like the one at Roxin Laboratories. He felt a wreck, and looked it too.

At night, the tiny basement forensics lab smelled no better than during the daytime, thanks to the photographic processor in the adjacent room. Richardson pulled a pair of chairs in front of the computer monitor, and Dart joined her.

"For initial viewing, we downsize the images for higher resolution," she explained. The ERT team had shot digitized images, not photographs. Richardson prepared Dart for what he would see. "Shooting in relative darkness, as they did, the lighting, as you can imagine, is off. The camera sees things much as your night-vision goggles. One of the nice things, however, is that we can ask the computer to compensate and correct the lighting deficiencies. Fill in color. Enhance. And often the images get surprisingly close to a well-lighted, even daylight, look. That's what we'll do," she told him. "We'll start with the degraded image and enhance. We can always get back to the original."

The first image, a shot of the sitting room with the recliner and television, appeared on the screen. At first, a difficult green and white, a black bar moved slowly down the screen, and as if lifting a shade, the room was suddenly in full color. The technology amazed Dart. "You'll like this," she said, typing furiously and then grabbing the computer's mouse. The floor of the room suddenly tilted, and the image became fully three-dimensional, as if Dart were on a ladder looking down.

"What the hell?" Dart asked.

293

"The digital cameras are stereo-optic—another advantage. The computer uses algorithms to create the three-D effect." She rotated the room, so that Dart was looking from a different direction, but the left of the screen was blank. She explained, "The computer cannot fill that which the camera never saw." She pointed to the blank side of the frame and said, "This is where the photographer was standing while taking the shot."

Dart gushed with enthusiasm over the technology, which Richardson clearly appreciated. She complained, "Only the Staties can afford the cameras, but maybe one of these days . . ."

Frame by frame, Richardson walked Dart through the house and through the evidence. The ability to manipulate the point of view afforded Dart the opportunity to see the rooms from many angles. He studied each carefully, occasionally requesting an enlargement of a particular area, something the computer could render in seconds. Room by room, he sought out any physical evidence that might provide insight into where to look for Walter Zeller, aka Wallace Sparco.

"The killer is inside them." Zeller's words continued to haunt him. As much as Dart believed Zeller was the killer, the only convincing physical evidence that he possessed connected the resident of 11 Hamilton Court to Payne's suicide. Everything else remained circumstantial. And though he now believed that Zeller was Sparco, it didn't necessarily mean that Sparco/Zeller had actually killed Payne. Perhaps, as Zeller wanted Dart to believe, it was the Roxin

drug that connected all the suicides, and Martinson and her company were in fact the ones to blame. No matter, 11 Hamilton Court seemed to offer Dart the main hope of finding answers and its resident. If he could only locate Zeller. . . .

For several days now he had cursed himself for not attempting to bring in Zeller at the fire. He wasn't sure how he might have accomplished that. He had ended up outside, unarmed and in shock. But he blamed himself for falling under Zeller's controlling spell, ever the student, the listener.

"Are you with me?" Richardson asked.

"Sure."

She led him through a series of enhanced images that took them down the basement stairs and into the laundry room. Even under the effects of the computer's improved colors, the room appeared dingy and dank. Dart recalled the moldy, suffocating smells.

"There," he said, leaning forward and pointing out the workbench. "Can you enlarge that?"

Richardson rendered the image into 3-D, rotated it to face the workbench, and then stepped the computer through a series of enlargements, drawing the workbench progressively closer. "Fly-tying gear," he said.

"Fly fishing," she said.

"Yes."

There was a small fly-tying vise that sat beneath an adjustable light, both mounted to the workbench and with a magnifying glass attached above the vise. The shelves were littered with feathers and plastic containers too grainy in enlargement to see well. If Dart had not known that Wallace Sparco was in fact Walter Zeller, he might have passed right by this as he had on the night of the raid. But suspecting this might be Zeller's lair, the fly-tying kit stuck out. Walter Zeller hated fishing. The kit made sense only as an effort to create a fictional identity for Sparco. As such, its existence could be explained. But Dart the student, the man who knew Walter Zeller nearly as well as Zeller himself, read more into it. The ruse was too elaborate to be explained as an effort to mislead investigators. He could have left a tennis racket or a bag of golf clubs. *It's more important than that*, Dart thought.

"That's as good as we're going to get it," Samantha Richardson said.

Dart checked his watch. "No," he said, "we can do better."

Dart knocked on the car door and then slipped inside. The man behind the wheel had blond hair and a dark mustache. He looked younger than his thirty-eight years. Dart knew him as Jack. He had forgotten his last name.

"Anything?" Dart asked, glancing down the street at 11 Hamilton Court.

"Nothing."

"Lights?"

"I said nothing, didn't I?"

"I'm going inside," Dart informed him.

"If you're going inside, I'm going to take a leak."

"If I'm going inside, I want you as a backup."

He indicated his cellular phone. "If someone shows up, I want a warning."

"Well," the man protested, "I want to take a leak. You wait for me, I'll be your backup."

Dart wrote down his cellular number. "Don't be long," he requested.

"You want a doughnut or coffee?" Jack asked.

"No, thanks."

Dart returned to his department-issue Taurus. With the Volvo out of commission, getting to work had meant hitching a ride with a friend or taking a city bus. He was tired of both, neither of which worked well for the night tour.

He sat behind the wheel for ten minutes. Then, pissed off, decided to wait no longer.

He slipped on a pair of latex gloves and entered through the back door, using the key that hung on the nail that Kowalski had claimed had been described to him in the "anonymous" phone call. The nail was there all right, and the key that hung on it. And the nail was rusted, not a recent addition. All of this would be part of Kowalski's scheduled IA review.

The second time into a building always felt more familiar, though entering alone, and without backup, made Dart queasy. He was not afraid, but apprehensive. He moved quickly through the sitting room, where the room's only lamp, on a security timer, was dark. At one o'clock, the bedroom light upstairs would be switched off automatically, also on a timer. Dart headed immediately to the basement, pulled the door shut behind him, and switched on the lights.

Step by step, he cautiously descended, feeling

an increasing sensation of dread. He passed the washer/dryer; ducked under a clothesline, and approached the workbench and the fly-tying kit. As seen on the lab's computer, the surface was littered with Baggies and small plastic vials. Dart studied these more closely. Some were filled with feathers, others animal fur, others contained bare metal fishhooks in varying sizes. Lead shot, metal filings, pipe cleaners, rolls of thin wire, thread. He leafed through the contents. And then again. It did not escape him that Kowalski liked to fly-fish, nor that Kowalski had been caught here. Nor that Kowalski, for his bungling of Lucky Zeller's murder investigation, was a known enemy of Zeller's.

Again, struck by the significance of the fly-tying kit, Dart inspected the contents of the workbench more carefully: elk hair, pheasant feathers, partridge, bobwhite, peacock. Synthetics of every color . . . A small plastic vial of thin aluminum shavings. Another, half-filled with copper shavings . . .

Dart paused, his hand on the prescription-size plastic vial containing the copper shavings. He experienced a flash of heat like a nausea that began in his stomach and rose into his throat like a bubble. He recalled Teddy Bragg's review of the Gerald Lawrence evidence—the man's hanging himself with a lamp cord. Dart fished out his notebook and flipped backward until he found Lawrence's name written in caps at the top of a page. He skimmed down through his notes: *copper filings on clothing and skin consistent with the lamp wire.*

Copper filings . . . Dart shook the small vial. It contained a few coiled pieces of different-gauge copper wire. He held it up to the light. A small crescent of fine copper shavings filled the bottom.

His hand shaking, he set down the vial and drew up the stool beneath himself, his legs suddenly watery. He studied each of the vials more carefully, separating out the Baggies of swatches of brightly colored fabrics—pieces of carpeting and clothing—as he remembered Teddy Bragg detailing "the usual hairs and fibers" discovered at each of the crime scenes. The last small film canister that he opened offered all the convincing he needed. He tapped out its contents onto the table: human hairs. But it was the color that both intrigued and excited him: *They were red!*

And he understood.

CHAPTER
32

"What the hell?" Ted Bragg's shirt was buttoned lopsidedly and there was sleep dust stuck to the lid of his left eye. "Richardson is on call tonight. This *morning*," he corrected, checking his watch. It was 3:00 A.M. Dart had been at 11 Hamilton Court only a few hours earlier. It seemed like a lifetime to him now.

"I needed the best, Teddy. I needed you."

"That's bullshit, and we both know it. Rich-ardson is good." He sized up Dart. "You look like shit."

"I feel like shit," Dart said.

He checked his watch again.

"So what's so fucking important?" He added, "I tell ya, this had better be good."

"Do you have your stuff?"

"It's in the car."

"I'll help you," Dart offered.

Bragg shook his head in disgust. "May I remind you: *I* am *not* on call tonight."

They removed two heavy bags from Bragg's trunk. Dart was trying hard to reveal none of the turmoil and excitement he felt. Convinced that he finally understood each of the suicides, only Bragg was capable of confirming this, for him and for Bragg himself. But to be truly effective, he would have to trick the man.

"Where is everybody?" Bragg questioned.

"I haven't called it in," Dart answered, leading him up the flight of stairs.

"Smells like smoke in here," Bragg said, moving up the stairs slowly. "Are you trying to tell me that you've called me to a crime scene that you haven't called in?"

"That's right."

Bragg stepped inside the apartment door and set down the bags. "That's not like you, Ivy."

"No."

"I tell ya, if you're yanking my chain—"

"I'm not. I need an over-the-top is all," Dart told him.

"Yeah, right—an over-the-top," Bragg

repeated caustically. "Since when do I do a half-ass job, Ivy? Answer me that."

"You're the best, Teddy."

"Fuck you." Bragg stooped toward the bags. "You're playing assistant, I'll tell you that much. This just became a two-man team." He snapped on his gloves and went to work.

Dart heaved a sigh of relief.

Forty minutes later, Bragg sat down, clearly exhausted.

He had scrutinized every detail of the crime scene, collecting and bagging evidence at each step. He had been particularly intrigued with his discovery that the carpet below the broken window appeared to have been vacuumed. He had given Dart an all-knowing look that the detective had relished clear to his core.

Bragg packed up his gear, keeping the dozen or so evidence bags separate. He sat on a wicker chair. Dart leaned against the wall. "Well?" Dart asked.

"I tell ya, I see what it is about it that gave you the hard-on. I've got glass from the broken window—inside, on the carpet—that says the perpetrator most likely entered from the fire escape. Mud and some familiar organic matter—it looks like those same cypress needles to me—those from his shoe soles—good supporting evidence. All this in an area that appears to have been vacuumed—again, familiar. Maybe we find rock salt and potting soil when all is said and done—my guess is that we will. But I've got synthetics and what looks like cotton fibers *on top* of that area, meaning we've got timing problems—just like at Harold Payne's suicide."

Dart answered him with a nod, attempting to keep any emotion off his face.

Bragg said, "It looks like some guy comes in and taps someone. You have a body, I'm assuming?" Dart didn't answer. Annoyed, Bragg said, "The blood splatter is telling me small weapons fire at close range. Drags the body, from yea to yea," he said, pointing to the carpet marks that ran from the television to the window, "and, judging by the blood smear out there, tosses the stiff over the rail toward that Dumpster. The Dumpster is next, Ivy. I gotta get a look down there." He smiled proudly. "You found the body in the Dumpster, am I right?"

Dart said, "You've never been to my place, have you, Teddy?" He rounded the corner into the kitchen and retrieved a beer from the refrigerator. He handed it to the forensics man.

"Your place?" No. Why do you ask?" Bragg drank generously from the can.

"Did I tell you that Ginny took most of the furniture when she split?" Dart looked out into the empty living room. Bragg's eyes followed his closely.

"Is that right?" Bragg asked uneasily. He shifted in the chair restlessly.

Dart drank a long gulp of beer. "Yup."

"Left you three chairs, did she?" Bragg asked, counting the chair he was sitting in and two others by the breakfast table across the room.

"Three. That's right."

Bragg's eyes filled with concern. "What the

hell's going on?" Agitated, he glanced at Dart sharply. "This is *your* place, huh?"

"Yup."

"Oh, shit. Listen, we all lose our cool eventually, Ivy. It happens. If you called me because you want help getting rid of the evidence . . . I can't do that for you. I can walk away from here. I can never mention this. But I can't help you."

Dart smiled. "It's that convincing, isn't it?" he asked.

"What?"

"The evidence."

Bragg looked around. "What are you saying?"

"I had to make sure it was convincing."

Bragg said, "You called me because we're friends. I understand that—"

Interrupting, Dart said, "I called you because you're the last line of defense. You're the final arbiter. You're the one who signs off on this stuff. You're the guy, Teddy." Dart reached down and sorted through Bragg's evidence bags, all neatly marked and labeled. He found three of those he was after and dropped them into Bragg's lap.

Bragg studied them. His forehead was shiny with perspiration. "I won't destroy evidence for you, Ivy."

Dart laughed. He met eyes with the man and said, "Those fibers are from the basement of 11 Hamilton Court. A fly-tying setup in the basement. Everything in little containers."

"Fishing?"

"It has nothing to do with fishing."

Bragg lifted one of the bags then and inspected its contents closely, confused and nervous.

"Animal hairs, metal shavings, synthetics, feathers—all there on that fly-tying table." Dart explained, "The crime scenes—the suicides—were works of fiction. The hairs and fibers were *props*, Teddy. Planted by a very clever individual. They told a story that we were comfortable reading." He pointed to the living room. "It took me a little over two hours to set this up—but then I'm new at this."

Bragg's eyes went wide as he began to comprehend. "You *staged* this?"

"I had to see if it could be done. I had to see if I could fool the best. You *are* the best, Teddy. It couldn't be Richardson. I scripted this crime scene, and I used the necessary props to be convincing."

"You woke me up for a staged crime scene?" Bragg checked his watch.

"We're predictable, Teddy. You, me—all of us." He added, "if you know us well enough."

Bragg put down the beer and got out of the chair and walked a few feet to the edge of the living room and looked it over. "Staged?" he asked incredulously.

Dart gave the man time to think it over, to see the various ramifications of someone planting trace evidence at a crime scene. He finally announced, "They were all homicides, Teddy. Every last one of them."

Bragg considered this for a long time. "Yeah? Think so? I tell ya—to be this good," he declared strongly, "you gotta be better than smart. You gotta be one of us."

"That's right."

Bragg paled. "You *know* who it is?"

Dart nodded. "Yeah," he answered. "I know."

CHAPTER
33

Wallace Sparco was feeling out of form. He should have been feeling good; another worthless piece of shit was about to stop using up air. But Dart was getting too close; he was making a real pain in the ass out of himself.

Beneath Sparco's forest green safari jacket, Zeller wore a hooded sweatshirt and a tan fishing vest, its pouches and pockets loaded with goodies. The bulk of it added the look of weight to him, which made him feel better. He thought of himself as a big man; it was difficult for him to feel this thin, this slight, this *insignificant*.

Zeller's hands sweated lightly inside the black golf gloves that gripped the steering wheel. Dennis Greenwood lived just north of Colt Park, on Norwich Street in the south end, dictating that Zeller conduct himself with extreme self-confidence and work quickly. Norwich Street was immediately west of Dutch Point, an area so dangerous that city cabs stayed out. A white man—no matter how big—walking the streets in this area offered himself as a potential victim. To enter this area at night was so risky that Zeller— looking and behaving like Wallace Sparco—felt forced to make his move during dusk. He turned left onto Wyllys and parked, checked his sidearm, pulled the hood over his head, grabbed the small duffel bag, and made for the two-story tenement less than half a block away. Dennis Greenwood rented the upper floor, accessible only from the back. Sparco threaded his way over soggy litter, dog shit, and foul-smelling trash and found his way to the rickety wooden stairs, which he climbed in a hurry.

One thing nice about this neighborhood was that the cops would get nothing from any witness. No cooperation whatsoever. Zeller could have killed the man out in the street, and Dart and company would not get so much as a description.

Surveillance here had been difficult. Zeller had patrolled the area only three times and decided it was too tough a neighborhood to park his car and effect a stakeout. He did know that Greenwood had no phone, no credit cards, no current girlfriend. The black man had held a variety of jobs over the last six months, including a position at the Murphy Road Post Office. He had either quit or been fired, always because of drugs and alcohol. Four months earlier, his driver's license had been reinstated after a six-week stint with a city-provided twelve-step rehabilitation program. There was no car registered in his name, although as of a week ago, he drove an eight-hour shift for Yellow Cab. The shift ended at four in the afternoon.

It was five-fifteen.

Sparco reached the scarred wooden door and knocked sharply. The drawn shade parted slightly and Sparco saw an eyeball peering back out at him.

"I'm working with the clinical trial," Zeller said in his best Wallace Sparco voice—a little lower than his own. "We have a change in your medication. Open the door please, Mr. Greenwood."

He waited through the metallic sound of four locks being disengaged, and the abrasive rubbing of the door on the jamb as it came open. His hands felt damp and uncomfortable inside the leather gloves, but he accepted their necessity.

"How are you doing?" Zeller asked, stepping inside, tapping the toe of his right shoe in an absent-minded nervous gesture. It all had to go perfectly to pull off Greenwood the way Zeller wanted it.

"Okay, I guess."

The black man was in his early thirties, his skin more cream than charcoal. He had a wide, flat nose and thick lips that parted slightly to reveal a chipped front tooth. Mildly handsome, his face knew no smile, and the hard, distrustful eyes knew no friends.

The studio apartment was dingy, dark, and smelled of cigarette smoke and bitter coffee. A worse-for-wear color television glowed blue from the corner—a cop show rerun. The countertop of the pullman kitchen held empty bags from fast-food chains. The furniture consisted of a ratty twin bed, a single straight-back chair, and a milk crate used as a footrest in front of a red vinyl overstuffed chair that had seen better days. Sparco saw no reading material whatsoever. A pelt of dirty clothes hung from a hook by the bathroom. The apartment's only two windows had been boarded over with irregular sheets of dirty plywood recovered from construction sites, pieced together poorly with screws, nails, and duct tape. It was worse than any prison cell Zeller had ever seen. For Dennis Greenwood, this was home.

Sparco, his shoulders slouching, set down the duffel bag, which occupied Greenwood's attention and drove a look of suspicion into the man's hard eyes. His brow furrowed and his jaw muscles flexed tight as chestnuts.

"I need to ask you some questions about how things are going," Sparco said. "Maybe take some blood."

"I just had my tests," he complained.

Sparco stepped closer to his victim and said in a warm, friendly voice, "Hey, I'm just following orders, you got to understand." He met eyes with the man and then delivered the blow as a sharpened spear—a single devastating thrust of his right fist into the exact center of the man's chest.

Greenwood's body seized. His knees gave out. He tried to breathe, but the blow to the solar plexus had been perfectly delivered and the effect was immediate—his nervous system stunned numb and useless.

Sparco spun him around in an instant, sagged along with him, supporting him as they sank down to a kneeling position and then slapped a pair of handcuffs on him, locking his arms behind his back. He then forced the man's flapping chin up, sealing his mouth closed, both covering the man's lips and pinching his nose. With his right hand Sparco awkwardly fished out a small plastic bag filled with cocaine—annoyed by the need for the glove—and bringing the bag to his teeth, tore a corner off it.

Greenwood's breathing would return before the use of his limbs—the body's first reaction was for survival. Wallace Sparco waited, his left hand muzzling the man's air supply. The chest began to heave, straining for air; Sparco reinforced his grip. Greenwood blinked repeatedly, reminding Zeller of a bird. He choked him down hard, pinching his nose and denying him air. Greenwood's body recovered quickly, and he began to struggle, rocking his head, pushing back with his legs, desperate to breathe.

Sparco, still cupping the man's mouth, raised the bag of coke to the man's nose and inverted it at the same time that he released his finger pinch. In one enormous breath, Greenwood sucked in the contents—a gram of cocaine. As the white powder spilled over his upper lip he looked as if he had dipped his face in baking flour. His eyes went wild and wide as the coke froze his lungs and rushed to his head. He tried to scream but, still muzzled, managed only a whimper.

Sparco hooked his elbow around his victim's windpipe in a practiced choke hold, took his own right wrist in his left, and applied a constant steady pressure like a vise, being careful not to bruise. Three years earlier the Hartford police had been taught this defensive move, and then, a few months later, refused to use it after three suspects had died of crushed windpipes.

"This is for Melanie," Zeller, not Sparco, whispered hotly into the man's ear. Melanie, eleven years old, fondled, raped, and sodomized over a seven-month period by this bastard. At Greenwood's trial he had testified that he had gotten her high on coke before "doing" her. Melanie, for whom Greenwood had wept while on the stand, a performance that bought him thirty days in jail and a two-year probation from a judge with a known drinking problem. *The system.*

Dennis Greenwood passed into the semiconscious state that Zeller intended—an oxygen-deprived narcosis, neither awake nor fully unconscious.

Sparco moved smoothly; his actions had been choreographed and the routine rehearsed. He dragged the body over to and into the red, overstuffed chair facing the television, went over to the sink and poured a glass of water, and returned to the body. He opened his safari jacket and, without looking, removed the unlabeled brown prescription bottle with the tamper-proof cap. He primed the pump first, tilting the man's head back and pouring a tiny amount of water down his throat. Greenwood coughed violently, spraying the water. Sparco tried again, this time massaging the man's throat, and the water went down. He then emptied all twenty-seven of the ten-milligram Valiums into Greenwood's mouth, and chased them with a mouthful of water. Greenwood swallowed repeatedly, the visible pulse beneath the skin of his neck revealing the effects of the cocaine on his heart.

Zeller cleaned up the man's chin with Wallace Sparco's light blue handkerchief, as attentive as a mother with her newborn, and then studied the room carefully.

He found a small plate by the sink. He set it down by the unconscious victim and tapped the coke bag until a dusting fell there. Then, in what he considered a brilliant touch, holding it by the edge, he used Greenwood's laminated driver's license to move this dusting of cocaine around on the plate and then left the license in plain sight sitting there.

From his fishing vest he removed the short length of a plastic drinking straw that he had prepared in advance—it already had traces of cocaine up inside it. He pushed the body around, accessing the man's handcuffed hands, and pinched the straw with Greenwood's fingers so that it retained his latent prints, and then placed the straw on the plate.

He put the man's prints onto the prescription vial as well and dropped it into the chair alongside the victim's leg, its plastic lid left by the plate.

Walter Zeller had attended dozens of similar crime scenes. Wallace Sparco studied it carefully to make sure it added up. He liked it—it looked good.

The duffel bag housed the cordless Dustbuster. Sparco ran the device over the floor where the cocaine had fallen as a snowy dust, lifting every last grain. He then vacuumed the entire area between the apartment's door and the kitchen sink—the area in which he had walked. Putting the vacuum away he turned once again to his fishing vest, this time carefully examining its contents. He selected three vials, popping one lid at a time, and carefully sprinkling a tiny amount of household dust, then a pinch of cotton and synthetic fibers, and finally a trace of cigarette ash—a recipe for Teddy Bragg's aardvark to find.

Greenwood twitched awkwardly and unexpectedly, and Zeller wondered if the blood vessels in his head had exploded and killed him before the Valium was given a chance. He hoped not. Wallace Sparco paid it no mind. His work was completed: If he wasn't dead already, Greenwood would suffer an irreversible coma within the hour, death within three.

Sparco removed the handcuffs and checked to make sure there was no bruising from them. He walked gingerly to the door. The locks were the variety that offered a spring-loaded tongue meeting a steel housing screwed into the jamb. A knob could be twisted and a toggle thrown to set the lock open or allow it to close. Sparco threw the toggle on all three, releasing their metal tongues. The fourth lock was a deadbolt mounted inside the door. There was little Sparco could do about that. He pulled the door shut firmly, setting in place three of the four locks. When, in twenty to forty hours, the body's decomposition announced itself to neighbors, the police would have to kick the door, splintering and destroying the jamb, perhaps covering up that the dead bolt had not been used.

It was dark out, and bitterly cold, and Wallace

Sparco felt the heart of Walter Zeller beating strongly in his chest, as if it were he who had been drugged. He felt none of the remorse that he understood any sane man would feel but stopped short of judging himself insane. Conversely, he took no vain pride in his work—it was something that had to be done, that was all; someone had to dispose of the trash. *With no Davids in this world*, he thought, *the Goliaths would rule unchecked.*

Zeller pulled the sweatshirt hood up over Sparco's baseball cap and gray hair, looking once again like an executioner or a Franciscan priest. He forced himself to walk slowly down the stairs, not wanting to attract attention or to appear a man in a hurry.

Image was everything. An act: one man playing another; one man living, one man dying. A murder turned into suicide.

And Walter Zeller—*the Creator*—nowhere to be seen.

CHAPTER
34

Ted Bragg was kneeling by the door to the second-story apartment at 21 Norwich Street. The suicide had been called in at four in the afternoon, and Dart alerted shortly thereafter.

Bragg informed the detective, "A woman in the

apartment downstairs smelled him. I'm guessing he's two days old."

"Who's primary?"

"I am," answered Greg Thompson from behind. "Just interviewed the neighbor. Didn't see or hear a thing. Just smelled the Jordon is all. Shit like this guy, stinks bad," he added.

Looking around the room, Bragg said to Thompson. "What we're going to see, what we're going to find, is a suicide—a drug overdose. What we're looking at," he corrected, "is a homicide."

Thompson appeared bothered. "Says who?"

"Says the evidence," Bragg answered. "I think I can show you, but it's going to require several hours, and everyone coming and going wears shoe covers, hair nets, and gloves."

"It'll never happen," Thompson said.

"That's the way it's going to be," Bragg insisted.

Dart pulled out the piece of paper from his coat pocket and unfolded it. Greenwood's name was a third of the way down Ginny's list of men whose medical insurance had been paid for by Roxin. He had written the letters NP alongside Greenwood's name—No Phone.

For Dart, the room felt dark and cold, the burden of this man's death weighing on him. For the past two days he had been using this list to try to anticipate Zeller's next kill. He had interviewed or spoken to six of the list of twenty-four. Dennis Greenwood had no phone, and Dart, not liking the neighborhood, had not traveled out here—not during the night shift. Now Greenwood was dead—though exactly how Zeller might have accomplished this still mystified him.

"The guy had a sheet," Thompson said to Dart.

"Sex crimes," Dart said back, glancing over at the dead man's gray face with its swollen eyes.

Greg Thompson's jaw dropped. "Now just how in the hell did you know that?"

CHAPTER
35

Dart needed the support of the department if he was to convince Dr. Martinson to suspend her clinical trial, turn over all the names, and then for either Proctor or HPD to provide protection for these men until Zeller was apprehended. Greenwood's murder confirmed for Dart that this was the only course of action.

Worse, he now needed to break the news of Zeller's involvement to Haite, convincingly and yet carefully, without mentioning Zeller's name, never putting Haite in the position of being required to report Zeller to Internal Affairs and thereby losing control. Until Zeller's actual arrest, it would be better if he were thought of as Wallace Sparco. That would keep both Internal Affairs and the upper brass out of the investigation. If the pursuit took on task force proportions, Zeller would never be caught. He was far too savvy.

Dart waited outside Christ Church Cathedral, not properly dressed for the cold weather, shifting back and forth on painful feet, nervous, cold, and tense. One of the first Gothic Revival churches built in the New World, the cathedral, with its tall spire shaped of brown stone, was said to have been created to bring the congregation to "heavenly thoughts." Dart's thoughts were on a baser level, though he looked skyward and asked for some help.

John Haite winced as he spotted Dart from afar. A man who liked to leave the office at Jennings Road and not bring it home with him, Haite motioned his wife and son inside the church. Coming over to Dart with a determined look, he said, "What's the meaning of this?"

"I need to talk to you."

"My son is in his first Thanksgiving pageant. I'm not on duty tonight. I traded with—"

"I know," Dart interrupted, "but it has to be you. And it can't wait until tomorrow's shift. I'm sorry, Sergeant."

"This is bullshit," Haite said. "Impossible."

"There's been another suicide," Dart informed him. "Another *homicide*," he corrected. "Tomorrow's Friday; we're the night shift; that leaves the entire weekend; it's never going to be the right time."

Haite glanced around. He waved to a few of the other parents just arriving with their preschoolers. He seemed embarrassed. He whispered angrily, "Nice fucking timing."

Vespers had just concluded in the chapel, and Dart spotted a priest at a side door. He approached the man, showed him his shield, and asked for a room in private for a few minutes. The priest quickly agreed. Dart waved Haite toward the door, and the sergeant approached reluctantly, apologizing and gesticulating deferentially to the priest, who showed them into a small choir room with rich, dark wood paneling and a lush red carpet. Dart found it interesting to see Haite's more humble side; he was a more religious man than Dart would have guessed.

Haite was clearly uncomfortable here. A large dark table occupied the center, surrounded by four straight-back chairs. In the main hall, a pianist and guitarist could be heard practicing the program's children's songs, including "Old MacDonald's Farm." The setting felt surreal.

Dart placed an impatient Haite in one of the chairs and then leaned a shoulder against the paneling, alongside some choir robes on hangers. "We have a difficult situation," he began.

"We have a psycho who's killing sex offenders, is what we have," Haite interjected.

"If it were only so simple," Dart said, winning the man's surprise and full attention.

"Go on."

"I have to be careful how I put this."

"You have seven minutes," he said, checking his watch. "Otherwise, we do this little dance tomorrow night."

"I have a list of names. . . . You don't want to know how I came by it. Stapleton, Lawrence, Payne, and tonight's victim, Greenwood, are all on this list. So are twenty others. I have reason to believe that a similar if not identical list is in the possession of a drug research company located out in Avon. All men. All test subjects for some kind of hormonal therapy—genetic therapy—that I believe is aimed at changing or eliminating their violent behavior toward women. Kind of a Prozac for sex offenders."

Haite looked as if someone had slapped him across the face, except that both cheeks were bright red. He mumbled, "You need some time off."

Dart continued, "It is also my belief—some of which I can prove—that a lone individual is staging murders to look like suicides to keep this drug company from bringing the product to market. To see that the drug fails in the clinical trials. To keep sex offenders behind bars, not wandering the streets under treatment."

"I can support that attitude," Haite said bluntly.

"They're all homicides, Sergeant: Lawrence. Stapleton. Payne. Staged brilliantly. Teddy Braggs can prove it—or at least make a strong case. The technique is ingenious, the methodology impeccable."

"Why suicide? Why not just kill the bastards?"

"To invalidate the clinical trials. To keep us off the investigation. To kill as many as possible before anyone catches on."

Haite nodded. "Okay," he said, "let's say you're right."

"The individual in question is known to us as Wallace Sparco."

"Of Eleven Hamilton Court. An ERT raid that

blew up in our faces and had us arresting one of our own. Don't lead with your failures, Dartelli."

Dart tried hard to ignore him. "What's of particular interest to us, Sergeant, is that this individual perpetrating these crimes"—and Dart paused here to collect himself—"is . . ."—he searched for a way to say this—"*confidently familiar* with police investigative procedure. Especially as regards the collection of hairs-and-fiber evidence, chain of custody, et cetera."

"He's a cop?" Haite was no dummy, he knew where Dart was going with this. He said, "You're thinking *Kowalski*?"

Dart shook his head no and spoke extra slowly, "Someone with a personal grudge against sex offenders; someone, lets say, whose wife may have been violently raped and murdered." He paused, watching the color drain from Haite's complexion. "Someone with a firm understanding of hairs-and-fibers evidence collection techniques, and a sharp enough mind to use that understanding against us."

"God," the sergeant said, his eyes wide.

Dart glanced at an oil painting of Jesus that hung above the handbells.

Haite said, "You think it's—"

Dart quickly interrupted. "Better if this is kept speculative until such a time as the individual is apprehended, I think."

Haite thought for two of his remaining five minutes in total silence, glancing intermittently at Dart with something like hatred in his eyes. He seemed to blame Dart for all this trouble, like a parent blaming a child.

Dart, letting the blame roll off him, felt that he had made his point well, and so far, Haite had kept a cool head. It was going better than he had hoped. Dart said, "I need the weight of this department behind me—the support that these were murders—if I'm to convince this company, Roxin Laboratories, to suspend their trials."

"Forget it," Haite said, shattering Dart's brief flirtation with success.

"But, Sergeant—"

"One thing at a time, Detective! The investigation *first*. The suspect *first*. You are *not* putting this department into the position of defending a *theory*—one in which we've brought no charges against anyone and have nothing but some hairs-and-fibers evidence to go on. We have to involve the prosecutor's office, we have to do this all aboveboard. You want to shut down this trial, you had better have a suspect in custody—"

"But, Sergeant—"

"For now, they are suicides," Haite roared, his voice no doubt carrying into the main hall. "They've been *cleared* as suicides. You're talking about reopening *cleared* cases."

"He'll go on killing," Dart reminded in a hoarse whisper. He felt devastated, as if he'd had the wind knocked out of him.

"Some perverts? Some child molesters? You think that's going to shake up a lot of people, do you? Get a clue, Dartelli."

"He'll kill them," Dart repeated.

"That's *your* problem, Detective. You are *my* problem. This is your theory, not mine. You prove it, or you lose it, but do *not* go making *any* accusations until you damn well know what you're talking about—until you can *prove* it to me and the prosecuting attorney's office. What you're talking about here . . ." He rolled his eyes. They were filled with tears, his friendship with Zeller getting the better of him. "I, for one, hope to God you're wrong." He checked his watch, looked at Dart, and snapped, "Not *one word* of this to anyone. *Anyone.* Not until you hand me the smoking gun—with an arm attached to it. Do you understand?"

"Do you know what you're saying?" Dart asked. "What you're condoning?" He looked around the room. *And in a church, no less,* he felt like adding.

"Not *one word*," the sergeant repeated.

"Please," Dartelli said, speaking the *one word* he hoped might get through.

Haite kicked back the chair as he stood, and it nearly went over. "You really are a Boy Scout," he said viciously, storming out of the room but stopping and turning to face Dart from the open doorway. "You didn't learn anything from him, did you?"

Dart straightened the chair and followed Haite out into the cold.

CHAPTER
36

The house was a large Victorian on a one-acre fenced estate in West Hartford, just down the street from the governor's mansion. Towering elms and oaks lined the street. The smell of woodsmoke tinged the air. One neighbor had already put up Christmas lights—a team of seven perfectly sculpted reindeer made of tiny white lights, arcing up toward the sky, drawing a sleigh parked on the grass. Hoping for snow. This was a Mercedes-Benz neighborhood. Dart felt conspicuous in his Taurus.

He checked himself twice in the rearview mirror, attempting to improve on the disheveled and unkempt appearance that seemed stuck on him. He jerked the mirror back into place, slipped a breath mint into his mouth, and climbed out of the car.

Dr. Arielle Martinson answered her own front door carrying a yellow legal pad and half-glasses. She wore stone-washed designer jeans, a man-tailored flannel shirt. Without makeup, she looked a few years older. He noticed a shock of gray on the right side of her head that he had missed during their first encounter. She had pulled back her hair just prior to answering the door, for she held a hair elastic wrapped around two fingers, and her hair still held that shape of someone standing in a strong wind. But it was down by the time she greeted Dart and she shook her head again, freeing her hair more, making sure to cover that scar.

She admitted him with hardly any small talk. He, the cop, taking note of the exquisite furnishings—oriental rugs, flowing drapes, and antiques; the security system—the motion detector winking high in the ceiling's corner; and the hand-carved door to the library as she directed him through.

She had been working at one of two computers, one on a mahogany partner's desk with a burgundy leather top. A reproduction Tiffany lamp. An original oil painting over the fireplace. A brown Lab lying between the leather couch and the leaded window. She offered him coffee, tea, or "something stronger." He declined, mentioning that he was on duty. She found herself a glass of white wine in the kitchen and quickly returned.

"It's a beautiful house," he said.

Taking a chair with needlepoint upholstery, she said, "It's late. Let's get down to business, shall we? What brings you back so soon, Detective?"

"A man named Greenwood. A drug overdose suicide. Discovered late this afternoon. We think he's part of your trial."

She pursed her lips. "I have no comment."

"I only wondered—"

"No comment is no comment," she said curtly. Her heaving chest showed him that she was agitated. Her darting eyes provoked a sense of concern in him, as if she were attempting to conceal someone hiding in the room.

"We're on the same team here," he reminded.

"Following our last meeting, I attempted some inquiries. But a blind trial is just that, I'm afraid. Again, I assure you that if the suicides were found to be related *in any way* to our trial, I would be well aware of it, and the trial would be halted. But I have *not* been made aware of such a relationship, in spite of my inquiries. I understand that you have a job to do. I have no quarrel with that. I would suggest to you that—"

"They are murders. We've confirmed that," Dart interrupted, silencing her. "Related directly to your trial. I need to stop the trials."

"You can *prove* to me that they are related?" The fingers of her right hand ran up and down the stem of the wineglass nervously.

Dart said, "We need to offer these men protection—"

"Impossible."

"They're targets!"

She stared at him for a moment and then said, "Detective Dartelli, I can't divulge to you the nature of any of our trials, but what you are suggesting would most certainly compromise the trial, most likely nullify any results, and thereby cost this company *millions* of dollars. I can promise you, Detective—*promise*—that we'll fight any such attempt on your part. You and your department will bear huge legal costs if we have anything to say about it. I don't think either of us wants that."

"We need your cooperation," he almost pleaded. *I need to bring proof to my superiors*, he thought. *I need to shut you down.*

"No. That's not going to happen," she said sternly.

"You have Proctor working on this, is that it? You think you can handle this without—"

Dart caught himself midsentence, recalling Zeller at the fire and the man's intimation that Zeller was himself a target. He met eyes with Martinson. Hers were stone cold and her breathing had calmed to where her chest was not moving at all. Frighteningly confident. Proctor had been told to rid her of this problem called Walter Zeller. *She knows about Zeller!* Dart realized.

"You need me," he told her.

Her gaze remained unflinching. She sipped the wine and rested the glass cradled in her hands in her lap, and her fingers toyed with the stem again.

"The suicides will eventually be linked to your clinical trial," Dart warned, "to your drug—this Prozac for sex offenders." She stiffened noticeably, a look of hate filling her face. Unless a person is held responsible *by the police*, tried, and convicted, your drug will be blamed." He didn't want a gang of rent-a-cops hunting down Zeller and performing roadside justice. No matter what his crimes, the sergeant deserved better. Suddenly he felt his sentiments shifting toward Zeller, found himself believing that he owed it to Zeller to find him first. "Do you understand me?" Dart asked angrily. Her impassive front was getting to him. She had still not recovered from his calling her drug Prozac for sex offenders. He sensed that he knew something that she didn't want him to know, and that in desperation, he might have played that card wrongly.

"I think we both understand each other," she returned, her voice dry despite the wine.

"Unless these suicides become reclassified as homicides, your drug will be blamed. You said yourself that such a ruling would be devastating to your company. That reclassification is up to *me*, doctor."

"No comment." She lifted her chin and literally looked down her nose at him.

What was her game? he wondered. "You need me," he repeated. If murder, it would appear that someone had attempted to sabotage her research; if suicide, that the drug had fatal side effects.

"I *need* to get back to my work," she said stubbornly.

"You need me to do this," he said again.

"Need you?" She smirked, and said, "Let's assume, hypothetically, that you're right—that someone may be testing what you've called a Prozac for sex offenders. Do you see the importance of such a thing? Can you begin to understand the social and economic implications of such a treatment? The benefits to society? Even were this company to be *partly effective* in its goal—let's say that we could reduce physical and sexual abuse by ten, or fifteen, or twenty percent with no adverse side effects—can you argue effectively against such a treatment? But there are those who would stop such a thing if they could. Oh, yes. Believe me, there are. They would say a crime committed is a crime to be paid for. They would do *anything* to see such a treatment fail— *anything*—this hypothetical company's competitors, certain rights organizations—it's a long list. You say you *may be able* to reclassify these suicides as homicides, Detective. Let's say, hypothetically of course, that this company had over *ten years* in such an effort—where would you put your faith?" She drank some of the wine and caught eyes with Dart. "What I'm telling you, Detective, if you're *listening*, is that I'm not convinced that these men, these suicides of yours, were ever part of *any* Roxin trial." Dart felt the words like a blow to his chest. "You seem like a perfectly nice man; I wouldn't want to embarrass you." She spun the wineglass in her fingers. "You may be made to look foolish if you pursue this any further," she cautioned.

Can she get the names off the list? he suddenly wondered. He had no documentation from Martinson concerning the participation of Stapleton, Lawrence, and Payne in the trial, only a verbal comment made to him several days earlier. *She could deny it all.* If she could destroy the record of their participation then her only concern for their killer would be that he be taken care of—quickly and quietly, the less publicity the better. And that he, Dart, not make trouble.

"If someone has convinced you to go outside the law on this, Dr. Martinson, I strongly advise you to seek a second opinion—preferably a *legal* opinion. There's no reason to further—"

"My impression," she said sharply, interrupting him and coming to her feet, her chest heaving once again, "is that we are both wasting our time, Detective, and that we both have better things to do than to sit around speculating. I have, in fact, solicited just the legal opinion for which you seem to be strongly lobbying, and that has come back an unqualified 'No comment.' *Unqualified*," she repeated. "I'll show you to the door now."

"This is not the way to handle this," Dart warned. "You're making a big mistake."

"And you, Detective, had better be careful, or you may need your own attorney, your own second opinion." She paused by the front door. The threat came not from her words, but from her eyes. "Don't meddle, Detective." She turned the handle and opened the door. The cold air rushed in and stung Dart's face.

"We can work together on this," Dart offered one last time.

"I don't think so. No thank you." She opened the door. Dart stepped outside, suddenly chilled to the bone.

He was out on Farmington Avenue when his cellular rang, and the phone got hung up in his pocket trying to come out. He thought he had missed the call because it stopped ringing just before he answered. The line was in fact dead, but a moment later it rang again.

"Dartelli," he answered.

"You're finally thinking like a cop," said Zeller's voice. Dart immediately checked the rearview mirror and the cars in front of him, but it was a pitch black night, *and besides,* he thought, *Zeller would never make it that easy.*

"I can help you, Sarge. But you—"

"Save it, Ivy. Just do your fucking job. That's help enough. There's a science editor at the *New York Times* might be interested in what you know. His name is Rosenburg. Good writer."

The line went dead.

Dart jerked the wheel, skidded off the shoulder, and came to an abrupt stop at the top of a hill. He jumped out of the car and searched for a vehicle executing a U-turn or parked conspicuously. Below him was an intersection with a gas station and a bookstore on opposing corners. He looked for someone standing at a pay phone, or an idle car.

Nothing.

Besides, he thought for a second time, *he would never make it that easy.*

CHAPTER
37

With the surveillance of 11 Hamilton Court failing to produce any sign of Wallace Sparco, and with a Be On Lookout alert having failed to raise his vehicle, Dart felt his only chance of finding the man—of *saving* him, perhaps—lay within that building. But when during the Friday night shift he approached Haite to discuss the technical merits of the search-and-seizure warrant issued on the house, Haite forbade him to enter "or get anywhere near" 11 Hamilton Court. What began as a civilized discussion ended in a shouting match with all of CAPers staring at the two through the glass wall of Haite's shared office. Dart stormed out and, feeling the brunt of everyone's attention, continued into the hall looking for somewhere to calm down. He hurried down the hall and seeing Abby's light on, knocked and entered. They hadn't seen each other in nearly a week, a fact that had escaped Dart until he found himself standing there looking at her.

"What are you doing here?" he asked her.

"This is my office."

"At night."

"I make my own schedule. I'm a one-person division." She hesitated and then explained, "I'm trying to get onto your schedule so we might see more of each other." Another hesitation. "I've missed you."

"The kids?"

"It's actually better this way. They sleep at night. I'm with them in the mornings and after-noons. I should have tried this sooner."

"When do you sleep?"

"I don't," she answered. "You look like you're ready to break something. Not something I've done, I hope."

"Haite. He's bullheaded. I misjudged him. Brought him into my confidence when I probably shouldn't have. Sent him off the deep end. He suddenly wants nothing to do with these suicides. He keeps assigning me domestics."

"The night shift," she reminded him. Domestic quarrels and assaults were almost entirely the domain of the night shift.

"Yeah, I know. But I've got bigger fish to fry and he knows it. It scares him, is the thing."

"Which fish?"

"I told him—not directly, but I told him—about Zeller."

"Oh, shit," she gasped.

"Seems his loyalty outweighs his concern over—and these are his words—'a bunch of perverts' getting killed."

She nodded, as if she understood, or had encountered such resistance herself. She said, "I had a case involving a gym teacher. Junior high. Molesting his girl athletes, a peephole in the shower, stealing underwear from their lockers—the whole nine yards. He raped three of them. Got one pregnant, or maybe we'd have never known. The school board tried to pressure me not to press charges. Said it would hurt enrollment. Said that they'd fire him, and that that was enough. They got to someone upstairs—I don't know how. And they fired him, and ran him out of town. And I pressed charges before he got out of town. But no press. No publicity."

"I never heard about that."

"No one did," she said. "It damn near cost me my badge." Looking at him coyly, she added, "But I kept my badge. In fact I got my own division." She grinned. "I found out who they got to."

Dart and others had wondered how she had managed to pull a Sex Crimes division out of CAPers, and now, years later, it was explained. He was struck with an idea.

"What is it?" she asked, seeing his change of expression.

"A thought," he said, feeling more calm than when he'd entered. He placed a knee onto the room's only other chair. "You are your own division," he said, thinking aloud.

"True story."

"You don't go through Haite for warrants."

"Thank God."

"What?" he asked. "Directly to the PA?"

"Do not pass GO."

"Do you operate under special probable cause requirements, or the same as the rest of us?" He clarified, "Does the prosecuting attorney hold you to a Sex Crimes—"

"Angle?" she filled in for him. "No," she answered. She added sarcastically, "Surprisingly enough, they treat me like I'm a lieutenant."

"I didn't mean—"

"I know you didn't, but it sounded a little that way."

"I need to extend the search warrant for Hamilton Court," he stated. "I need inside."

"*I* can get inside," she said. "You can accompany me." Checking her watch, she said, "It'll be a phoner this time of night. Who's the on-call judge?"

"Cryst."

"Cynthia Cryst?" she said. "A *woman*, Joe. Piece of cake. Trust me on this." She pushed her paperwork out of the way and pulled a blank pad in front of her. "This is a grounder."

They entered 11 Hamilton Court an hour later, Abby carrying the signed warrant in her pocket. The automatic timer had the sitting room light switched on—it was 9:55 P.M.

Abby, via Dart, had listed three items on the warrant that had been left off of earlier warrants: grocery store shopping bags, the framed photographs on the piano, and "articles of clothing."

With both of them wearing latex gloves, he collected the framed photographs into a white paper sack.

"The photos I can understand," she said. "Even though you assume it's Zeller who put them there to create this Wallace Sparco identity, you think there may be some significance to them, something he might tell you without intending to. But the shopping bags?" she asked.

"He thought to put food here," Dart explained, having led her into the kitchen. "Again, as you said, to build the perception that Sparco lived here. Sparco didn't live here. Neither did Zeller. He used this as a staging area—at least up until we discovered it; he must have used someplace else after that . . . He knew it was virtually impossible not to carry something of yourself into every crime scene, and to take something of the crime scene back to your house with you—it's the nature of hairs-and-fibers—it's what he drummed into me all those years. I was the one with the degree, but he was the one who understood fiber evidence handshakes and piggybacking."

"So he came here, changed clothes—changed *identities*," she corrected, "did the crime, came back, changed back. . . ." She understood it then. "The chain of evidence would always lead back to here."

"If we ever found anything at a crime scene— and he took extra precautions to see that we wouldn't, like vacuuming and laying false evidence—we would only find his safe house, not the man himself."

"But grocery bags?" she inquired skeptically.

"Maybe he was too smart for his own good," Dart said, searching drawers. "He buys groceries to convince us Sparco lived here. Even eats some of it, to give the place a lived-in effect. But if he saved the grocery bags—" Dart thought aloud, sorting through the contents of another drawer.

Abby yanked open the cabinet below the sink, pulled out the trash can, and hoisted the trash bag—a plastic grocery bag. She completed for him, "Then he would use them as trash bags."

"You're brilliant," he crowed.

"I know. It's true, isn't it? But not brilliant enough to know why you care about this," she added.

He took it from her and turned it around for her to see the green writing on the side. "Shopway," he said, reading the name.

"That's up on Park," she said, naming the worst street in town.

"How many groceries between here and Shopway?" he quizzed.

"Two. Three, maybe. Catering to the college kids."

"Catering to the whites," he said. Shopway was an inner-city store.

"You're trying to narrow down his neighborhood," she said, impressed. "To identify someplace we might find him." She added, "We put the Shopway under surveillance, assuming it's closer to home."

Dart grinned at her, dumping what little trash the bag held and collecting the grocery sack as evidence.

Then he opened the downstairs coat closet and searched through the three jackets hanging there.

Abby said, "He would have bought these at a secondhand store—a Salvation Army, something like that. You're looking for tags, something to further narrow the neighborhood."

"Nothing," Dart mumbled, shutting the closet door and leading her upstairs.

Following closely, Abby said, "My guess is that he's going to wish he hadn't trained you so well."

"Compliments," Dart said, "will get you everywhere." He entered the bedroom and headed for the closet.

Abby switched on the light. Dart turned quickly, shook his head, and said, "No!"

"This," he said, checking through the clothes, "may have started out secondhand . . . and he would have bought it big, so that it fit him, but wasn't his size . . . and some of it would have gotten thrown out: the Payne stuff for instance—too much blood. But he has a thing about clean clothes. Did you ever notice? Freshly ironed shirts, pressed pants. He and Lucky got in an argument once because she wanted to save money, but the Sarge insisted on sending out his shirts. It was almost a—"

"Fetish," she completed for him, holding up the shirttail of one of the hanging shirts. "Is this what you're looking for?" Next to her gloved right thumb was a blue commercial laundry tag, neatly pinned with a thread of plastic to the shirttail.

Excitement stole into Dart: A grocery store was unlikely to have an address for a customer; *but a commercial laundry just might.*

As they climbed back into the Taurus, their body language expressing their urgency, Dart told her, "I would have found the laundry tag." He started the car. "But I might have missed that grocery bag," he confessed.

"You see?" she crowd. "You need me."

The map on Abby's office wall consisted of enlarged photocopies of a one-square-mile area surrounding the Park Street Shopway supermarket. Dart had made a pot of coffee, having worked through his shift, but stayed at Jennings Road. Abby had gone home for a few hours sleep, having returned a few minutes earlier, just before nine. Using the yellow pages, Dart had spent the wee hours narrowing down the location of the city's nineteen commercial laundries. Six pushpins were now stuck into the improvised map.

At 9:02 Dart, yellow pages at his side, hung up the phone, stepped over to the map, and withdrew one of the pushpins. "White tags pinned to the collar using safety pins," he said.

At 9:30, Abby complained, "White tags, green tags, pink tags—but no *blue* tags."

"We'll find it," Dart said.

"Not near the Shopway," she said, removing the last of the pins.

Dart stared at the map, thoughts buzzing in his head. "Maybe I'm wrong," he said, feeling depressed. This was his sleep time, and a Saturday morning to boot. His body was experiencing jet lag. His head hurt. His back was sore from having fallen asleep in a chair. He envied her the few hours sleep.

Abby excused herself and left the room. Dart, who had been trying since Thursday to return a call left by Ginny, dialed her number. Her machine picked up. He cradled the phone, jealousy consuming him. Ginny was *always* home on a Saturday morning. This meant that she hadn't slept there the night before. He'd wondered why he hadn't heard from her. Typically they played phone tag until one reached the other.

Abby returned and said brightly, "So I guess we try every friggin' laundry in the city until we find one that uses blue tags." She plopped down into a chair by a phone and said, "Do you want to start with the *A*'s or the *N*'s?"

An hour later Abby hung up and reported, "Well, you'll be happy to know that I finally found a company using blue tags,"—at which point Dart hung up in the middle of a call. "You shouldn't have done that," she said. "They use blue tags, but their numbers aren't close to this five-digit one that we have."

His moment of elation past, Dart sank down

in his chair and rubbed his eyes. "Did they say anything about blue tags?"

"He gave me the name of the company that wholesales the tags," she replied, and Dart realized that this was where he should have started all along. "Nutmeg Supplies out of Bridgeport. But it's Saturday, and they won't reopen until Monday. So if we can wait—"

"We can't," he reminded.

"No. I didn't think so."

"But we may not have to," Dart said, recalling that Bud Gorman often worked weekends.

Gorman was an avid NASCAR fan, and liked to travel to NASCAR races all over the country. He managed this without chewing up too much vacation time by working six-day weeks and then trading in this extra time for a Friday or Saturday of his choice, buying himself three-day weekends whenever a race required an extra travel day. Dart reached him and was put on hold.

Gorman returned to the phone angrily. "You never return my calls."

"I've hardly been home."

"I have the Roxin information for you—who they are; what they're about."

"I have more urgent, local needs."

"Dr. Arielle Martinson," Gorman said, ignoring him. "Three venture capital firms and an industrialist from Sweden own seventy-three percent. Martinson's been at the helm since the inception. She came out of the University of Michigan, where she chaired the genetics research program, which saw a hell of a lot of

338

federal funding and where this industrialist, Cederberg, first met her. A real slow start to earnings, as with most biotechs—six years until it made a nickel. Has done very well with an arthritis treatment—"

"Artharest," Dart interjected, forcibly interrupting the man. "Another time, Bud. Thanks. I've got an—"

"What you might be interested to know," the man continued, undaunted, "is that Martinson—who pulls in eight hundred a year, plus stock options, incidentally—has nearly an entire year of her life missing. I mean, I've got basically *nothing* on her. I show some medical expenses, some attorney expenses, and that's about it. 'That's all, folks.' My guess is, she went off to what amounts to the funny farm in Switzerland. But it wasn't no vacation—I don't show that kind of spending pattern at all."

Dart recalled the thick scar behind her ear and her nervous habit—her compulsion—of attempting to keep it hidden.

"My guess is, if I could get into her insurance records . . .," Gorman said wishfully. Dart made a note to call Ginny and see what she could do. He felt himself sweating. Gorman had agitated him.

Dart charged in before Gorman could start again. "I need the name—and the phone number for that matter, if you've got it—for the owner of something called Nutmeg Supplies in Bridgeport."

"Wait a second," Gorman said, disgruntled. "Let me write this down."

Dart repeated his request, and gave his extension in the conference room.

"Gimme a couple minutes."

When the phone rang and Dart answered it, Gorman read off the information without saying hello. He ended with "No charge" and hung up.

Dart reached the owner of Nutmeg Supplies at home and heard football in the background on television. The television made him think of home, and that made him think of Mac, and even with the neighbor kid walking and feeding the dog during the days, he felt awful having to lock the dog up so much on night shift. The owner of Nutmeg Supplies, a man named Corwin, grew angry with Dart at first, believing the call was a phone solicitation. "I'm with the Hartford police," Dart repeated for a third time.

"I thought it was a gimmick," the man said apologetically. "That you was selling home security or one of them steering wheel locks or something."

"I'm not selling anything," Dart said.

"I understand that." He apologized again.

Dart stressed the urgency of his case, building up Corwin's importance and underscoring that the information was vital to an active homicide investigation. The man rallied to the call, an unusual but welcome response. "I'll need to go down to the office. Blue tags, you said? Only blues?"

"Blue. Five digits, starting with nine-eight."

"If we sold them," Corwin said confidently, "I'll know who to." He paused. "You did say *murder*, right?"

"That's right."

"That's what I thought you said."

Forty-five minutes later, Corwin called back. "I got two retail and one commercial with blue tags. The ninety-eight thousand series went to Abe's over on Seymour."

"Seymour?" Dart shouted into the phone without meaning to.

"Yeah, Seymour Street. Abe's Commercial Laundry."

Dart checked the open yellow pages for an address. "Abe's is not listed in the Yellow Pages," he complained.

"They're *commercial*, not retail. They do institutional work—nursing homes, that sort of thing. I doubt they would advertise."

"No retail?" Dart asked.

"Some, probably. There's a storefront of sorts, as I recall—mind you, I haven't done a delivery in ten years. It's not a big part of their business—retail. That's a bad part of town."

"Yes, it is."

"Even ten years ago."

"Yes."

"Commercial work, mostly. They're a good customer for us. Big volume."

Dart thanked the man and was already turning through the white pages, his finger running down columns. A manicured nail entered his vision—Abby had found the listing. Corwin clarified, "You said a murder investigation, right?"

"Yes I did."

"And I helped?"

"Very much."

"That's okay . . . I like that. . . . Hey, Detective?" he said, holding an impatient Dart on the phone. "Nail the bastard."

Dart thanked him again and hung up. He told Abby, "He said to nail the bastard."

"What did you say?" she asked.

"I thanked him."

She was over checking the map, pinned to the wall. "It's Seymour Street, just south of Park Street." "We can't go in there alone, Joe," she chided. "Not without a cruiser. Not without backup."

He didn't want to get into this with her. Haite would resist giving him any help, would never grant him backup. What made this worse, much worse, for Dart was that just the sound of the words *Seymour Street* was familiar to him, but he couldn't remember why, could not place the voice speaking those words, Corwin's voice too fresh, too present, in his mind.

But then that voice came to him. After seven years of hearing a voice daily it did not stay blurred for long. Walter Zeller had been raised in his parents' house on Seymour Street, back when Park Street had been a good neighborhood, not a demilitarized zone. He had spoken of that house, that time, often, affectionately, nostalgically, referring to it simply as Seymour Street.

Dart could not remember what had happened to the house. Zeller had inherited it upon his mother's death four years ago. That much he remembered well, because Zeller had paid some inheritance tax rather than sell the place, despite its almost worthless value. He wasn't sure what had become of the place after that.

Perhaps, Dart thought, *Wallace Sparco lives there now.*

CHAPTER
38

This was it—Dart knew before he set foot out the door.

He stole four hours sleep at home after walking Mac around the block and fixing himself a tuna sandwich. By five-thirty it was dark outside, and it occurred to him that the earlier the better because the worst gang violence came after ten at night, by the time the drugs and the alcohol and the restless anger had taken hold. He dressed in black jeans and a navy blue sweatshirt so that he could walk with hood up and buy himself some disguise.

He made the trip alone, believing that he would find Zeller at the house on Seymour Street, that the man had chosen the perfect safe house—no one from outside, not even a cop, would enter the heart of Park Street at this time of night without good reason and plenty of backup. Maybe Zeller had cut himself a protection deal with one of the gangs—establishing himself on an inner-city warning system consisting of cellular phones and CB radios. The cops always arrived five minutes too late.

As he drove past the courthouse and a string of gentrified houses used as law offices, he was struck by the irony of their closeness to Park Street only a few short blocks to the south. Law and lawlessness, coexisting side by side. Two blocks from these law offices fourteen-year-old girls hustled themselves on street corners and crack dealers sold their goods from the sidewalk. Dart drove with his sweatshirt's hood pulled up, and he drove fast, running stop signs and disobeying traffic lights.

On the seat beside him lay a loaded shotgun. Under the sweatshirt, he wore a flak jacket, in the pocket a speed key. His sidearm had a round loaded into the chamber. In his left pocket he carried two ammunition magazines taped together into a "speed clip." The car doors were locked. The closer he drew to Park Street, the slower the traffic and the busier the activities. This was the south end's Sin Street—the night was alive with possibility.

Despite the November cold, the dark street corners were crowded with Puerto Ricans and a sprinkling of Spanish, Italians, and Portuguese, all under twenty-five. Le Soledos and the Latin Kings ruled this turf. The wrong color socks could cost a kid his life. To show a weapon was to start a fight. They had teethed on Stallone and Lee and Schwarzenegger and Snipes and considered themselves equal to the task. It felt to Dart as if anyone older than thirty had been exiled. The place was ruled by restless youth.

Forty-thousand-dollar BMWs and Mercedes Benzes cruised Park Street at ten miles an hour, driven by teenage kids doing business over cellular phones—and proud of it. To honk at a car for driving too slowly was to invite a stream of bullets.

If it could be snorted, mainlined, or smoked, it was available. If it could be fucked, it was pimped. If it had been stolen, it was for sale. If it was living, it could be made dead.

He felt the glare of suspicious eyes but did not exchange glances. In a moving car a white person would briefly be tolerated—business was business, and a good deal of Park Street's business came in from the white enclaves to the west.

But for a white person to make more than two passes down this street would quickly spread the word. He knew that he was being watched, monitored. And if Zeller had bought protection, then to leave the car was to face an army of hungry street rats looking to make trouble.

He parked the Taurus on Walcott, three short blocks from Seymour. He grabbed the shotgun and hurried from the car, carrying the weapon in plain view, moving at a slow jog, moving deeper and deeper into darkness and hoping to reach Funk Street without incident.

Streetlights around here were knocked out as quickly as they were replaced. To view this area from overhead in a passing plane, it would appear as a square black box, lit only by the brilliance of Park Street, a block to the north.

Dart cut left, crossed the street, and jogged down Funk toward Seymour, his heart somewhere up around his ears, his body feeling as if he had stepped inside an oven.

Then, across the street, appeared a group of youths like a pack of hungry dogs. Where they had come from, he did not know. But there they were.

He had spent much of the last four years interrogating cold-blooded killers no older than these kids—killers who showed absolutely no remorse, proud to kill for a pair of basketball shoes or a leather jacket or the imagined love of a sweetheart. Blank eyes. Dialogue borrowed from movies. Human shells, void of love, filled with unspeakable hate.

They spotted him and they catcalled. They liked the shotgun, they yelled and taunted. Dart cut across the street at a run, not looking back. *Appear in control*, the frightened voice inside of him encouraged. When he heard their footsteps at a run, he knew that he had problems. He turned up the steam, broke into an all-out sprint. *A cop running from a bunch of punks. . . .* He couldn't let go of this thought, and yet he couldn't run fast enough.

Halfway down Funk, he violated his own rule and glanced over his shoulder. They were coming for him. They too were running.

He felt the desperate fear of the hunted. Never mind that he was armed equally, he was outnumbered. He faced armed children who would kill out of boredom, who would kill because of the color of a man's skin. He faced the very real possibility of firing his weapon at a minor. Could he bring himself to do such a thing? He had no idea if and when self-defense could or would overcome reason.

They were fast runners. They were gaining on him.

He often had dreams in which his legs grew impossibly heavy. He would run as hard as he could and yet be caught in a slow-motion crawl. And now the bad dreams came face-to-face with reality as he felt a huge weight bear down on him, drain him, drive him into the pavement as if his limbs were suddenly cement and the pavement beneath his feet a thick gripping mud.

"Yo, dude!" a high, winded voice called out from behind.

Dart reached Seymour and cut right, running smack into a group of four Hispanics in their twenties. Dart fell to the sidewalk and quickly scrambled to his knees. One of the kids drew a weapon and aimed it at Dart.

"Police!" Dart announced, more from instinct than consideration. He tugged back the shotgun's recoil and engaged a shell.

"Bullshit," the kid with the weapon said. "Gimme your gun."

Dart, winded and out of breath, heard the fast slap of shoes as the other gang quickly approached. The Hispanic holding the gun had only a fraction of a second to make his decision. He seemed to take in Dart's shotgun. Perhaps he recognized it as a police issue. He looked to his friends, shrugged, and gently returned his weapon to inside his jacket. He nodded. "Be cool, man." Perhaps he had simply thought Dart out of his mind.

Dart ran on, his muscles aching as he tensed, expecting he might be shot in the back.

But instead he heard angry shouts from behind him as the kids from Funk Street collided with the Hispanics on Seymour. He heard the words, "He's heat, man! He's *heat*."

Dart slowed to a fast walk, barely able to catch his breath. Up ahead, the facades on the buildings looked vaguely familiar, and he thought he remembered the look from the old photos on Zeller's hallway wall. Seymour Street. For just that second he lost his focus, neglected to take in his surroundings. He leapt up into the air as a pair of alley dogs barked from only inches away, and he landed poorly, twisting his right ankle. He went down hard, dropping the weapon, and rose painfully to his knees. The dogs bellowed, edging toward him, heads down, teeth glaring. He picked up the fallen shotgun. One of the dogs lunged at him. Dart jumped back and fell onto the ankle and went down for a second time.

He growled back ferociously. The dogs whined and took off.

Regaining his feet, he glanced across the street and this time recognized the building without question. A faded photograph: Zeller with his aging parents, all grouped on the steps that served as a porch. The photo was daytime.

Now it was night.

The building's upper-story windows were lit.

The back door was locked. Dart tried it a second time, gently twisting the knob, leaning his weight against the frame, but it wouldn't budge. The only accessible window was locked and seemed to be nailed shut from the inside. Dart leaned his shotgun against the wall and slipped out the speed key. He shoved it into the upper lock, squeezed its trigger, and twisted, hearing a slight *click*. With the dead bolt free, Dart turned the doorknob and pushed, and the door came open, scraping against the sill. He took hold of the shotgun and stepped inside. He grabbed the doorknob, lifted the door on its hinges, and shut it silently.

The first thing that caught his attention was the smell of cigar smoke. It was both familiar and frightening. He stood absolutely still, caught up in memories, a surge of emotion flooding him. With all his determination, he had not given much thought as to how he might handle an actual confrontation with his mentor. He couldn't help but still love this man, respect him, trust him even. He had formed his professional identity within this man's formidable shadow, had been protected by him, and had, in turn, guarded him as both patron and teacher. He stood at that moment, shotgun in hand, intending to confront him—to accuse him of plotting and carrying out a string of homicides. Charges that would result in Zeller being brought downtown, to where he had earned his reputation as the best of the best.

The kitchen was small and dated back to the fifties: chipped linoleum, a stained sink, and pitted fixtures. The countertop carried crumbs and detritus of past meals. A string of small black ants paraded along the seam of the splash, disappearing behind an old toaster. The cigar smoke hung in the air. He felt it as a warning: Zeller was not far.

Dart set down the shotgun, having intended it for street defense, not necessary with Zeller. Then, having second thoughts, he picked it back up. He moved stealthily into a small sitting room and turned up a narrow flight of stairs. Zeller had been raised here; he had told so many stories about his youth and this place that Dart found himself imagining he knew the floor plan, disappointed now that the real item did not live up to his memory. It was far less grand than Zeller had painted it. Embellished by memory, the home's size had been exaggerated by its former resident. Dart felt a growing sense of dread as he climbed the stairs: Zeller, a murderer, waiting somewhere in a house he knew well. Dart, the reluctant inquisitor, a stranger here. Zeller did not surprise well; he tended to lash out and ask questions later. Dart neared the top of the stairs, an equally narrow hallway leading to an open door immediately to the right and two opposing doors directly ahead. All the doors were open, all dark. It felt to Dart like a shell game—he expected to find Zeller in one of the three. But he worried too about the noise he'd made with the kitchen door—Zeller could well be expecting him.

Dart searched his memory for a clue left by one of Zeller's family stories. He could *hear* the man's voice inside his head, could see him sitting there. . . . *Something about as a kid having witnessed a mugging down on the street*, he recalled, leading him to favor Zeller's room as being either of the two directly ahead of him. He would duck into the nearest room first, establishing a defensive position behind the doorjamb, then wait for some sure indication of Zeller's position. His heart seemed stuck up in his throat, his chest was tight, and his mouth dry.

He was drunk on fear; his knees felt like water. Circulating his head were the crime scenes of the so-called suicides, the deaths so neatly orchestrated. Would this be how someone found Joe Dartelli? Were these to be his last few minutes— sneaking around an unfamiliar house in pursuit of a man he felt as close to as a father? He wondered what thoughts had been inside his mother's numbed mind when she had pursued him. Had she, in her own way, been as terrified of finding Dart as he was of finding Zeller?

He lifted the stock of the shotgun, training the barrel at the floor in front of him; it would require only a slight lift and a squeeze of the trigger. At close range, a shotgun made everyone an expert marksman.

He counted down slowly from five, an old habit meant to settle the nerves. As far as he could tell, the technique failed miserably: *three . . . two . . .* He took one quick step up the last stair and turned quickly to his right.

The back of a wooden chair hit him squarely in the chest, as if the person on the other end of it were swinging for a home run. As the wind exploded from him, Dart raised the shotgun and pulled the trigger, and then pulled it again, but nothing happened—jammed from the tumble out on the street. The concussion of the chair lifted him off his feet; he skidded across the hall and banged into the far wall, expelling what little air remained. Dart gasped for breath, his chest feeling paralyzed, his ribs bruised. The shotgun flew from his hands as a boot connected with it. That same brown boot then came for Dart's face, swinging straight up toward his chin, but Dart managed to lean away to one side, sagging, and the blow missed.

Walter Zeller lost his balance and caught himself on the banister, nearly going down the stairs instead. The brief look that Dart caught of the man's face showed a person different from the one Dart remembered: haggard and worn, destroyed by grief and guilt and exhaustion. *He's an old man*, Dart thought, knowing that Zeller was only in his early fifties. He wore a dark green plaid flannel shirt and blue jeans, but they fit him loosely, like a man diseased. He had a weathered round face, sparse graying hair, and an Irish nose broken too many times to count. He looked hard and mean, but to Dart the man's soft blue eyes gave away his true personality.

Dart tried to reach for his weapon, but his arms weighed tons and his chest had been set afire by the crushing blow of the chair. His one feeble effort was to rear back and slide his right foot along the floor, connecting with the one boot that held all of Zeller's unsteady weight. For Zeller, it happened too quickly—first he lost his balance, and then Dart kicked away his only solid platform, sending him down the stairway headfirst. He went down hard, turning a full somersault. Dart, whose arms still would not function, rolled himself face down on the dusty floor and drove himself forward with his feet. His hurt ankle cried out. Splinters tore from the floor and embedded into his chest and arms. He heard Zeller groan, curse, and then start back up the stairs. "You're dead, Ivy," the sergeant barked, clawing his way up the stairs. Dart had lived ten years believing in that voice and everything it said.

Dart propelled himself to the end of the hallway and into the dark room to the right. His arms began to tingle; they were coming back to life. He rolled across the rug, about to lodge himself beneath the bed but grasped the absurdity of trying to hide. As a child he had developed himself into a professional hider, and as he reached again for those talents he glanced around, assessing that he had to get out of the room. Now!

He heard the recoil of the shotgun and a shell bang and roll on the hardwood floor. Zeller was in the hallway; had cleared the weapon.

Dart could move both shoulders; he had feeling in both hands though he still found it hard to walk. He struggled to breathe—his chest felt caved in; his head pounded from a lack of oxygen. Of the room's two windows, one faced the street, the other, nearest to Dart, faced a flat rooftop.

Footsteps . . .

He tried for his sidearm, but both hands proved useless. He was a sitting duck.

No time to break the glass first; this registered immediately. He came to his feet, tucked his head into his chest, and ran backward, ducking and propelling himself through the pane of glass. His head smacked the top frame, dizzying him. Glass flew everywhere in a deafening explosion. Dart felt the cold of the outside air. He felt a warm trickle down his back. He rolled across the hard tar until the crunching sound stopped and he was out of the shards of glass. He came to his feet and headed across the roof to the unforgiving brick wall that faced him.

"Forget it, Ivy!" Zeller yelled across the expanse. "We should talk."

This flat rooftop was wedged between two taller buildings. The brick building Dart now faced also looked flat-roofed, but a full story higher. A steel ladder fixed to the brick wall led up to the other roof. That meant that there had to be roof access between the two buildings.

"Ivy, don't run! Don't force me. We can talk!"

Dart paused and glanced over his shoulder. Zeller was through the window and coming toward him, the shotgun cradled in his arms. *Talk?* Dart wondered, eyeing the weapon. He could barely catch his breath. The trickle down his back was definitely blood; the top of his shirt was warm and damp with it. He hobbled along the wall, away from his pursuer, working the injured ankle. For the first time in his life he didn't trust Walter Zeller. *He's out to kill me.*

"Don't!" Zeller warned loudly as Dart rounded the corner. "I know what you know," he cautioned, in a voice that indicated he was running now. "Talk to me!"

Dart found the steel fire door that he had anticipated. The silver duct tape was not anticipated. It had been placed at the level of the handle— blocking the latch open—and told him immediately that Zeller had intended this door as part of a well-planned escape route. *Anticipate the unexpected*: a Zeller credo. The shouting at him had been for the specific purpose of distracting and stopping Dart before he discovered a way off the roof. *Confine the suspect to a specific area*— Dart knew the tricks. He hoisted his sluggish arm, forced his unwilling fingers around the handle, and tugged hard on the door. It swung open.

Tearing the tape from the doorjamb, he ducked inside. The door thumped shut and locked behind him.

The enormous room spread out twenty feet below him like something from a science fiction film, and smelled immediately familiar: huge gray machines lying like sleeping beasts, cheek by jowl, their metallic skins glistening in the dull light of half a dozen exit signs, the unmistakable odor of cleaning solvents. Dart was inside Abe's Commercial Cleaners.

A few steps down was a wooden balcony with offices to the left. Dart stumbled down the stairs, dragging his bad ankle as if it belonged to someone else. Zeller had chosen his route wisely: The heavy machinery would offer good cover. With this idea foremost in mind, Dart hurried to the far staircase, his vision limited by the darkness, and made for the ground floor.

Two successive shotgun blasts ruptured the door he had come through and flung it open as if it were made of paper.

"I-vy . . .," the familiar voice called out threateningly. Zeller sounded furious. Dart had witnessed the consequences of this temper enough times to know that the possibility of negotiation had passed. Zeller made statements; he would make one now. The shotgun would do that.

Dart hobbled down the final step and onto the shop floor.

Giant commercial laundering machines made up the first row. Dart cut through this to the next—a long line of dry cleaning machines—dodging fifty-five-gallon drums of cleaning solvents and reminding Dart that this was no place for small weapons fire. He heard Zeller come down the metal staircase to the shop floor. The thought of entering into a firefight with the man seemed absurd, and yet the deeper he moved into this maze of behemoth equipment the more vulnerable he felt—and the more it seemed inevitable. Zeller obviously knew his way around here. Dart did not.

Dart headed for the nearest illuminated exit sign, cutting through a row of enormous dryers. He threw his hip into the panic bar and smacked his head against the unwilling door. Chained shut.

"They chain 'em shut at night, Ivy," came the casual voice of Zeller from somewhere out on the floor. "You're shit out of luck."

Dart checked the padlock—number coded. The speed key wouldn't do him any good. But there had to be at least one exit out of here—Zeller's planned escape route. But where? He instinctively moved toward the back, away from Seymour Street. *Where?* he kept thinking as he moved along the row of dryers installed cheek by jowl. *If all the exits are chained* . . . He tried to make sense of this, knowing that Zeller had more than just the rooftop exit at his disposal.

Not the roof . . . not the doors . . . He spotted it then—a black shape in the farthest corner of the vast room: a drain.

The faster he ran, the larger the building seemed to him. The back wall was not drawing any closer. Impossibly, the far wall seemed to move away from him.

"Bad choice," Zeller hollered, his voice echoing in the cavernous structure. "Bad thinking, Ivy."

Dart glanced around, realizing he had entered a box canyon of sorts, the brick wall to his left, the line of interconnected dryers to his right. The dryers were too sheer, too high to attempt to climb. His only other way was to reach the drain and hope it was Zeller's exit—or turn around and get back out into the center of the building where he would be less confined. He limped badly the harder he ran—he wasn't going to reach the drain in time.

Running at a sprint, he looked right: the machines; he looked left, the wall. He looked right again . . .

And then the obvious hit him.

Out of breath, Dart stopped. He was facing a clothes dryer.

CHAPTER
39

Dart pulled himself up into the clothes dryer, drew his legs in, and curled into the all-too-familiar position. Thrown into a storm of memory, he all but lost track of where one life left off and the other began: suddenly ten years old again, the footsteps avidly pursuing him. He was a driver who had lost hold of the wheel, a pilot who had lost track of the horizon. Bitter fear seared his throat.

The latch mechanism on the commercial machine was far more serious than what he had faced as a child. His fingers studied it quickly, attempting to decipher its secrets. Whereas his family machine had had a friction catch, this behemoth, used for carrying a hundred pounds of wet laundry, closed via a locking tongue operated solely from the outside. To get out, Dart needed to block the tongue from catching. Removing his wallet from his back pocket required an act of gymnastics. A credit card was too thick; a photo, too thin. His fingers located his laminated driver's license, held it firmly against the metal jamb, and drew the door slowly closed so that the springed latch was held out of its hole by the card. Dart snugged the door into place, firmly shut.

He was swallowed in a darkness and smell

whose familiarity overpowered him. Rationally he knew where he was—who he was. But somehow the past won out. In the darkness of the dryer, a film played before his eyes and he saw his drunken mother stumbling toward him. For Dart, there suddenly was no Walter Zeller, only memories of terror. It felt as if his lungs were burning. His throat tickled. He was hiding from the Beast. Nothing, but nothing, would make him give himself away.

Her footsteps grew louder. His heart swelled painfully, choking him, beating as fast as the clanging wheels of a runaway train. His body steamed with sweat. *She'll kill you!* a voice inside him warned. *This time she'll kill you.*

He'll kill you! a deeper voice echoed. *He has nothing to lose.*

White sparks filled his vision like fireflies. The smell of his own fear overpowered the tangy lint-flavored metal that had meant sanctuary. The back of his shirt was damp with his blood and his ankle throbbed. The sound of shoes approaching—dragging on the cement floor—grew closer.

The Beast was upon him.

The person out there was so close Dart could hear the breathing. He felt a fool for sitting awaiting his fate—a passive acceptance, a relinquishing of control. He wanted to *do* something, not just sit by and await the hell that might come.

"Bad choice, Ivy," Zeller shouted, bringing him back.

A nearby dryer kicked into action. Then another switched on, closer this time.

"Round and round we go," Zeller said. One by one, he was turning on all the machines. He intended to bake Dart out.

Yet another dryer roared into action.

Incredibly close! he realized, imagining the horror of being trapped inside a machine capable of that kind of severe heat. He began a slow but even count: *one thousand one, one thousand two* . . . The heat generated was enough to turn water to steam—he would burn in minutes.

But if he timed it right . . .

One thousand five, one thousand six . . .

He racked his brain trying to dredge up an image of the front of the machine. Were the controls to the right or left of the door? First he thought left; then he saw a totally different image that had the controls to the right. Which to trust?

"You won't like it," Zeller warned, shouting above the din. He was exceptionally close.

One thousand nine . . .

The wall behind Dart shook and rumbled as this, the next machine over, was switched on. *Nine seconds between machines.*

He began the count all over again: *One thousand one* . . .

The ensuing noise was deafening, too loud to overhear Zeller's footsteps. Nearly too loud to maintain the rhythmic count in his head. It would come down to timing.

One thousand six . . .

He cocked his leg back, tucking it up into his chest. With his right hand he needed to make a choice: his weapon, or a firm grip on the rim of the drum so that he could get out quickly? He wanted out.

Above all, he wanted out.

One thousand eight . . .

He kicked the door open with all his strength and knew immediately that he had connected with Zeller. He heard the big man cough out "Umph" as he went down hard and lost his grip on the shotgun. It slid a few feet away.

Dart leapt out forgetting about his bad ankle, and collapsed to the cement floor as his ankle gave out.

Zeller's head was bleeding. It left a smeared trail as he wiggled and stretched for the shotgun.

Dart, still down himself, reached for his weapon.

Zeller managed to snag the stock of the shotgun with his right hand. He sucked it toward him. The barrel moved like a huge rotating gun turret until Dart was looking directly into the sole dark eye of the end of the barrel. Dart's sidearm was aimed at Zeller's face. No more than a yard apart, both men motionless, lying on the cold cement floor.

"Long time, no see," Zeller said loudly, above the roar of the dryers. The side of his face was bleeding badly, though all head wounds were bleeders. Dart intended to say something, but the words caught in his throat. "Let me explain something," the man continued, "because you always needed to hear things straight. You never could get things right the first time around."

"Bullshit," Dart managed to cough out. He

felt on the verge of tears. Zeller was going to pull the trigger—he felt certain of it. His life had come down to this one fragile moment—the one man he had come to respect in life intended to kill him. He felt his own finger grip more firmly on the trigger. Another fractional pressure and the back of Zeller's head would explode against the brick wall.

"You ain't bringing me in," Zeller announced proudly. "Fuck that look, Ivy. Save it for the Jordons out on Seymour Street. What I'm telling you is that you ain't gonna do it. Not because you can't, but because I'm not going to let you. You *failed*, you see—"

Dart felt his heart jump. Zeller knew all the right buttons to push . . .

"You are *not* gonna bring me in for this. That ain't gonna happen. So you have to do it, big fella. No aiming that thing as some kind of threat, because it ain't no threat to me, it's the *solution*. You got it?" He waited for Dart to respond, but his patience ran out. "You got it?" he repeated, shouting. "Pull the fucking trigger, Ivy." He said more loudly, "Pull the fucking trigger before I dust you, asshole." The end of the shotgun rotated an inch, trained on Dart's throat. "From here I can take your head clean off your body. You thought about that?"

"It crossed my mind," Dart hollered.

"So pull the fucking trigger." Again he waited. "I've been inside the system, Ivy. I'm not going through that." He added, "Not even for something I believe in."

Dart's eyes stung. He felt so *angry* at the man.

Zeller bellowed, "There was a time I wanted to *recruit* you. Can you imagine that? I convinced myself that you could—that you *would*—help. But then I feared that Boy Scout attitude of yours. You live in a fucking bubble, Ivy: righteous ignorance. You're your own morality play. You want to know why Ginny left you? Because you're too *good*. You protect this image of yourself. Fuck the image, Ivy."

Dart felt absolutely still all of a sudden. He could hear the traffic through the wall and, far in the distance, something dripping. The air felt hot and incredibly thin. His finger begged him to squeeze the trigger. It was as if, for a moment, he had connected with God. He had never been in this place before.

"Nice try," Dart said, realizing that Zeller was attempting to trick him into firing.

"You don't get it, do you? You still don't fucking get it! You think you're so fucking smart, Mr. Detective? Let me tell you something: I avoided your shift because I didn't want you becoming lead—not on *any* of them. Give me a Kowalski or a Thompson, but keep me away from Joe Dartelli. Not because you're such hot shit—but because you're so well *trained*," said the man who had trained him. Zeller smirked, pleased with himself.

Dart glanced toward the wall, wondering if he could roll fast enough. . . .

"You so much as twitch," Zeller declared, "and Doc Ray is going to need a sponge mop to bring you home."

"They're trying to help," Dart said. If he was

363

going to be accused of being overly righteous, then he was going to speak his mind.

"Martinson?" Zeller asked. He smiled. Dart knew that smile—it was Zeller's unforgiving smile, the one that gave way to the anger and fury. "You're going to tell *me* about Arielle Martinson? You were always so fucking naive. I thought we broke you of that." He blinked rapidly. Maybe he had lost enough blood to pass out. "Righteous and naive. You shoulda been a fucking minister, you know that?" Moving the weapon back toward Dart's eyes, he said dryly, "And no fucking sense of humor either."

"The suicides were meant to make them scrub the testing," Dart said, trying to buy himself some time, to find some way out of this. He was not going to shoot Zeller; he was determined to bring him up on charges.

"Gold fucking star, Ivy." He blinked rapidly again. "And why the fuck would I want to do that?"

If Zeller blinked repeatedly like that again, Dart thought he might manage to knock the shotgun barrel toward the wall. But far enough? he wondered. The spray pattern of a shotgun was far wider than its small barrel opening.

"I know what you're thinking, because I *know you*, Ivy. You're so fucking predictable. That's *your* problem. You're thinking I flipped out; you're thinking it's for Lucky—God rest her sweet soul." This last bit was said in the true voice of Walter Zeller—the Zeller who Dart knew and respected. "But you don't know shit." He offered Dart a look of disappointment and said,

"Martinson was raped while at the university. Cut up bad."

Dart recalled the ugly scar behind her ear. *Victims everywhere*—and he knew by the man's tone of voice where Zeller was going with it. Dart didn't want to hear this.

"It took her over a year to recover. After that, she made it her life's work to *do* something about sex offense. It became a passion, and from there, an obsession. She became *consumed* by it. She made mistakes—bad business decisions—based on the conviction that gene therapy was the answer. An *unproven* technology, mind you! She devoted funds that she shouldn't have—got herself into trouble. She *had* to make it work— that's the hole she dug for herself." He blinked repeatedly like a man about to lose consciousness. "They've conducted three different trials in five years—all to shitty results. Nesbit—the Ice Man—was in the first group. They paroled him early to be part of that trial. That was the only reason he was out and able to kill Lucky—"

The fire door at the top of the stairs cried out over the top of the roar—the door by which they had entered. Dart felt paralyzed by what Zeller had told him—his mind swimming. The cop in both of them knew from the distinct, prolonged sound that it was not a squeak caused by wind. It was not the door settling all of its own.

Someone had come through that door, had entered.

They both lifted their heads at once to listen more clearly, the threats of only seconds before gone.

Footsteps coming down the first set of stairs that lead to the balcony.

Dart wanted the rest of Zeller's explanation.

Staring up into the darkness, Zeller hissed, "You stupid shit, Dartelli. You led him here." He whispered incredulously, "You let yourself be *followed*? Jesus Christ!"

Dart felt himself shrink. He had not checked for someone following him, too preoccupied with the dangers of Park Street.

Zeller's hand came off the weapon, drew a zipper across his lips, and signaled first to Dart and then to himself—he wanted Dart to follow him. Adversaries, they were suddenly partners.

Again.

The transition felt natural. Dart didn't question it. Zeller rocked up onto his knees, grabbed the shotgun, checked over his shoulder for Dart, and stood in a crouch, moving along the line of groaning dryers, keeping close to the machines. He lifted his hand and stopped Dart short of the very end. He pointed to a depression in the corner of the floor where a large mesh grate covered a manhole. He signaled that Dart should cover with his weapon as he would go first and lift the grate for Dart who was to follow and enter the hole ahead of Zeller. Dart signaled back that he would hold the grate for Zeller instead, but the Sergeant flashed his middle finger at his former protégé. Then he raised his index finger as if to say, Ready?

Dart nodded. He pushed past Zeller, for the first time offering him his back. He edged slowly toward the corner of this last dryer and sneaked his face out just far enough to see around the corner so that he could defend their position.

Zeller's breath was hot on Dart's neck. The detective jumped, not expecting it. Zeller placed a hand firmly on Dart's shoulder and spoke into his ear. "His name is Alverez. You met him at the fire. He was the one in the car. The reason we don't kill the bastard is that they'll only replace him. And we don't want that. Got it?"

Dart nodded.

Zeller glanced around the corner of the roaring machine and gently eased himself away. He went back to hand signals—he had seen someone— and then hurried into the corner with the grate.

His heart aching, Dart edged his left eye around the dryer. The man pursuing them was looking lost, standing motionless in the center of the aisle. He was carrying what looked like an Uzi.

Zeller managed to open the grate without being heard over the rumbling of the dryers. He signaled Dart, and Dart limped over to him, pocketed his sidearm, and slipped quietly down the steel tube, using hand and foot grips welded into its wall, his ankle screaming. Zeller passed him the shotgun and followed, easing the grate down into place above him. Flashing sparks indicated that Alverez had seen them. A spray of bullets skimmed off the grate throwing fireworks overhead.

Zeller winced and buckled on his way down the ladder, and though Dart did not see the man's blood spilling from his shoulder, when Zeller reached out and accepted the shotgun,

367

Dart knew that he'd been hit. Zeller switched on a small penlight as he came off the last rung and pointed down the storm sewer—a cement pipe perhaps four feet high. He signaled for Dart to defend their backside, then crouched and lead the way into the claustrophobic tunnel. The bottom of the pipe was dry. After only a few feet, when a spray of bullets echoed back at the base of entrance tube, Zeller switched off the light. Alverez had fired a volley down through the grate in defense.

The grate banged on the cement floor, above and far behind them.

Alverez was inside.

Zeller allowed Dart to run fully into him, stopping him. He grabbed for the detective's hand and pulled it down to a cold metal grip. Dart tested his toe forward and felt it slip out into nothingness. This pipe ended here. He crouched and began to descend, using the ladder of grips that Zeller had indicated. At the last rung, he stepped off into water so cold that it caught his breath. The sergeant flashed his penlight only once, aiming it down a large, arching stone ceiling that was dripping water and coated in a green slime. The water in which they stood was pitch black. Dart heard the distinct sound of scurrying rats but ignored it—he didn't want to think about being in a storm sewer with a few hundred irritated rats at his feet. Zeller pulled on Dart, and led the way.

From behind them came the unmistakable sound of shoes scraping on cement.

* * *

With his left hand held out against the tunnel's wall as a guide, Dart followed the sound of Zeller's splashing. The sergeant had clearly practiced this escape, for he moved knowingly in the darkness. Dart's ankle, chilled by the water, felt a little better.

When they were a good twenty yards down this tunnel, Dart heard Alverez spit out the single word "Shit!" followed by the sound of a falling man landing hard—he had gone off the end of the pipe into the larger tunnel. The man fired off a stream of semiautomatic weapon fire in anger, made apparent to Dart only by a terrifying whistling in the air around him.

Alverez was coming after them with a vengeance. Dart's hope that he might be too injured to follow were dashed.

Dart's left hand went into space as the wall ran out.

"Sssst!" Zeller said, to his immediate left.

Dart blindly negotiated the turn into a similar tunnel, and they started off again. He realized that the intersection was yet another of Zeller's ploys. Alverez would be forced to make a choice—hopefully the wrong one.

He and Zeller stayed in this connecting tunnel for several minutes before taking a right; they were following the layout of the city blocks overhead. By all indications, they had lost Alverez—ten minutes later, Zeller stopped them, and they listened intently. There were no sounds from behind. Only rats. Dart's feet were numb, and he could feel the chill spreading up his legs and into his bones. Zeller led on.

They took one more right and walked through shallower water for another fifteen minutes, at which point Dart heard a small waterfall ahead of them. Zeller allowed the detective to bump into him once again. As he stopped, he heard a deeper sound beyond the small waterfall, and for the first time his eyes sensed a distant circle of gray at the center of the black in which he had lived for the past eternal forty minutes.

They then reached the source of this gray. The water that held them spilled from the end of the storm sewer falling to a mass of ice below. The river spread out before them, etched with the bare branches of dormant trees, reaching into a canopy of low clouds that reflected back the dull amber glare of the sleeping city.

CHAPTER
40

"We can't take a taxi. They might think of that, they might even be listening in on a scanner. It wouldn't take a genius to guess that a pickup down by the river, at this time of night, would be us." Zeller led Dart along the river's edge. Dart's ankle felt almost normal.

"It was you up on Charter Oak Bridge," he said to the man in front of him.

Speaking back as they walked, Zeller said, "Yeah. I had to know what you were up to. And then Ginny was involved, and that other woman—Lang—and I realized we had problems."

"Alverez?"

"An out-of-towner. A guy hired to break my knees—yours too by now. Convince us to shut up." He led through some shrubs that tore at Dart's clothing, and then along the river's edge again. "I've been avoiding him for *months*. But with you in the picture, I imagine they'll bring in more help." He said in a troubled voice, "I heard a rumor a shooter's been hired."

"That's hardly breaking knees."

"The difference between a spot fire and a range fire is getting an early jump."

"Hired by whom? Proctor?" Dart asked.

"One thing I'll say about you, Ivy—you do your homework."

They walked in silence past the glaring lights of the power plant until they reached Charter Oak Bridge. They climbed the same steps where Dart had seen Zeller standing, and in minutes were up on the bridge.

"My car's back in the south end," Dart reminded wistfully.

"He'll watch it after he realizes we lost him. Stay away. Same with your apartment. Same with Jennings Road. He'll look for you there. In his eyes you've hooked up with me, Ivy. You're fucked. They have a hell of a lot to protect. They've been trying for me for months. Even if you hadn't stirred the nest by going to Roxin, you'd be on their list now anyway."

"You know about my visit?" Dart asked, astonished.

"Ivy, I know fucking everything. How quickly we forget."

"But they *need* me," Dart protested. "They need me to bring you in for the murders. They should be *helping* me."

"Don't you get it, Ivy? Are you that fucking ignorant?"

"Maybe I am."

Zeller stopped and turned around. Dart could barely make out the man's face in the ambient light. As a car passed and Zeller was caught in the headlights, his eye sockets filled with black shadow. He said, "The Laterin *doesn't work.*"

"Laterin?"

"The drug they're testing," he said condescendingly. *"It doesn't work."*

Dart ruminated on this. Zeller seemed to be making one last bid for innocence.

"Listen. How do you monitor whether or not a drug aimed at sex offenders works? This isn't cancer—you don't take an X ray," he said condescendingly. "You keep the guy under surveillance—you monitor his every move." Zeller spoke slowly. "Proctor Security had the contract to keep these creeps under surveillance. I was working for them. And what did I find out? A full *half* of these assholes repeatedly reoffend. They're no better than they were." His jaw seemed to move mechanically, inhumanly. Dart couldn't catch his breath. "And Martinson, or someone over there, skewed the findings, and I, without meaning to, caught on. I got pissed off

372

at Proctor one day and he made a boo-boo and hinted at something he shouldn't have. I got a look at some files and turned up altered reports—Proctor was giving them the results they wanted. So what was my next step?" the teacher asked.

"Roxin's files."

"Exactly. Harder to break into at the time, but not impossible. Since then they've made the place into Fort Knox. I *saw* the fucking test results, Ivy—the *real* ones. The shit they're testing—the Laterin—did nothing.

"Oh, Christ," Dart said.

"They caught me at it—*nearly* caught me, nearly physically had me—and I've been on the run ever since. Once I got started . . . you know . . . Alverez was brought in. The paperwork that I saw was shredded. Deleted. Whatever. Bet on it. I couldn't produce a shard of evidence to support what I knew. So only the one choice," he said, leaving it for Dart to draw his own conclusion. "What fucking choice was there?"

Dart felt in turmoil. He had deciphered the suicides as murders, concluded that the murders were the work of someone attempting to discredit Roxin—Walter Zeller. But what Zeller now told him turned all that on its head. Dart mumbled, thinking aloud. "If I had left them as suicides, if I had connected them to the clinical trial—"

"What the fuck do you think I've been trying to tell you with these phone calls—and risking seeing you in person! You were doing *too good* a job. You were pissing me off. All you had to do was connect the deaths to Roxin's clinical trial." He led Dart off Charter Oak, electing to leave a main thoroughfare. "The rest would have fallen into place."

Zeller said, "She's running out of money—Martinson. This Laterin thing has consumed her for ten years. She's moved her resources around, thrown too much money at Laterin. She has probably cooked the books, but eventually that catches up to you. They've been in various stages of clinical trials on Laterin for years. She *needs* this to work. If it doesn't, she's shit-out-of-luck. This fails, she's out of business. Everyone goes home—some of us happy." Zeller checked over his shoulder. "Don't look now," he said.

Dart glanced back and saw a police patrol car approaching at a crawl.

Zeller told him, "The woods behind my old place. Two hours. Be there." He cut down a side alley, leaving Dart alone, disappearing in a heartbeat. He had perfected the art of vanishing.

The patrol car pulled alongside, rolling at a walker's speed. Dart, displaying his shield, walked over to the car. "What's the problem here?"

"Your piece," the uniformed driver said, adding, "sir," and making a head motion in Dart's direction. "Didn't know who you was."

Dart's sweatshirt had ridden up over his holstered weapon, which was now in plain view.

"How about the other guy?"

"He's with me," Dart replied. *He was*, he thought.

"Couple of guys in clothes wet from the knees down, walking these particular streets on a cold night carrying hardware . . .," the cop explained.

374

"I understand," Dart said.

"You on duty, sir?" the cop asked, trying to impress now. "You want, I could give you a ride back to Jennings Road."

"I could use a ride," Dart said. "But not to Jennings Road."

CHAPTER
41

They met in the dark alongside the droning hum of the electrical substation not far from Zeller's former home; its mechanics were silhouetted against the sky like a giant schematic. It had snowed an inch, the first of the year, and the temperature had dropped into the twenties. Dart arrived first and was shivering by the time Zeller approached telegraphing the pain he was in without meaning to. Alverez had clearly wounded him back in the sewers.

Dart was for moving out from under the loud hum of the overhead wires. He strained toward the wooded darkness. "This shit makes too much noise," Dart complained, glancing overhead. Stepping closer to Zeller, he pointed into the dark.

"You're jumpy. Take it easy." Zeller's voice was tight. Dart worried for him.

"Are you all right?"

"Fucking peachy. Thanks."

"What now?"

Zeller said, "It's my job to sell you on leaving these as suicides. Let Martinson take the fall she deserves." He paused. "I'd like to tell you that I'll turn myself in, but I won't. I'm not going to be locked up."

"It's too late," Dart explained. "I've already convinced Teddy Bragg and Haite that they were *staged* suicides. The good news is that Haite wants nothing to do with it."

"Well, there you go," Zeller said. "Go along with him. Let them stand."

"It won't bring down Roxin. Martinson has dropped the names of the suicides from their list of participants—covered her bases."

It was difficult to see in the dark, but Dart thought that he saw Zeller nod, as if he had expected something like this. His voice colored by pain and discouragement, Zeller said, "She pulls that off, and it's all been for nothing." He added, "Bitch."

"I think you're wrong about the files—the records of the clinical trials," Dart said, taking control of where they should head. He couldn't remember contradicting Zeller so directly. "Being deleted," he continued. "Shredded. Does that sound like Martinson? You say they've been in clinical trial for years. A person like her—a devoted scientist—is *not* going to destroy test data. Not for any reason."

"Bullshit. It's gone."

"Hidden, maybe, but not gone." He explained, "She needs that data. She created that data. It's important to her. She won't destroy it."

376

"I disagree."

"If I'm her, I destroy all physical evidence of those files, but only *after* I've hidden a copy away for my own use."

"And what? You're going to subpoena it?"

"We've got Ginny," Dart reminded him.

"The computer? You think Martinson has it in a computer?" Zeller asked, amused by the absurdity.

"Where else? Password protected. Safe. Easy to get at—but impossible for anyone else to access."

"Doubtful, Ivy. It's gone. She shredded it." He reminded, "I was *told* that those files were shredded."

"Shredded, maybe, but not destroyed."

"You're not making sense," Zeller said angrily. "She's not going to give you those files, Ivy, believe me. You make noise about them and she'll destroy them, sure as shit."

"Maybe that's what we want," Dart said obliquely. "For her to erase them."

"Make some fucking sense, would you?" Zeller reached into his shirt pocket and pulled out a mashed cigar. He tore open the crinkled cellophane and broke the cigar in half where it was torn, stuffed it into his mouth, and bit a piece off the end, spitting it out. Zeller located a match, cupped it, lit the cigar. "I fucked this up, Ivy. What I'm trying to tell you"—he puffed on the cigar and blew out the flame—"is that it's over."

Dart saw a small red dot blink against the fence's galvanized pipe. It seemed like nothing more than the lingering aftermath of Zeller's lighting the match, but Dart's sight remained fixed and the dot moved.

It moved quickly toward Zeller's head, and Dart identified it for what it was: an electronic sighting device used by marksmen. The red dot touched the fence behind Zeller's shoulder and then quickly found his neck.

Dart slapped out with his open hand, catching a stunned Zeller on the side of the face and knocking him to the side. Zeller stumbled, dropped the cigar, and fell.

To Dart, the bullet sounded like a thin, fast wind at ear height. Zeller didn't hear it. He misunderstood, shoving the detective away and prepared to fight. When the red dot found Dart's cheek, Zeller lurched forward and returned a life-saving shove. Dart went down into the wet snow as the second bullet splintered off a piece of a tree trunk behind them. The two immediately crawled toward the cover of the trees, their attention fixed on the other man, alert for the glowing red dot of the assassin. As the dot found Zeller's back, Dart hissed, "Right!" and the sergeant rolled to his right. The ground, where he'd been crawling a fraction of a second before, exploded into mud and dirt. "Right," Dart instructed again, and again the earth erupted under the power of the bullet. Zeller came to his knees and crawled fast, aware that the marksman was locked onto him, that all it required of the killer was to sweep the sight back and forth and await the signal. Dart moved left, intentionally widening the space between them, to give the marksman a larger dead space where the technology would fail to send a signal.

But it was Zeller the red dot hunted, and Dart experienced an increasing sense of dread. "Left . . . right . . ." He called out commands, attempting to steer him clear, knowing well that the laser at the end of a weapon was faster, far more agile than its human target.

A piece of Zeller's leg exploded as a bullet hit from behind. Zeller splashed facedown in the muck.

"Roll!" Dart coughed out, emotion choking him. The dot wandered onto Zeller's ribs and then froze there.

The sergeant rolled, but not before Dart heard the distinctive sound of another bullet taking a piece of him. Zeller groaned, came to his knees, and scrambled to his right in a zigzag pattern. The ground around him came alive with a series of small explosions. Dart raced ahead toward the trees, feeling helpless, looking on as Zeller's efforts slowed.

Dart spun around, withdrew his weapon, and stretched into a prone position. He fired blindly into the dark. The shot echoed loudly. The red dot weaved across the open space toward him. Dart searched for the source of that light but saw nothing. He fired again. A wounded Zeller hurried on hands and knees into the woods, like a crippled dog.

Dart's attention divided between the red dot as it raced across the snow toward him, and the seething darkness that hid the shooter. If he rolled to his left, he would meet the laser. To roll to his right would only disorient him. He held his ground, his heart pounding, his finger begging to squeeze off another round.

Zeller fired two consecutive shots, intentionally drawing the red dot away from Dart and back toward himself.

The shooter was good. He knew that his targets had turned to face him, that his next shot, although silenced, would produce a muzzle flash identifying his location. The flash would give either Dart or Zeller—or both—a target to aim at. By challenging him, Dart and Zeller forced him to reconsider spraying bullets at them. The laser wandered across the snow, the full attention of both cops fixed to it. It moved toward Zeller, stopped, and headed back toward Dart. Zeller scrambled backward, still facing in the direction of the shooter, but moving toward, and finally reaching, the woods. He pulled himself to a position partially blocked by a tree.

Dart lay prone, his weapon aimed in front of him, but his eyes on the lethal red dot sweeping the snow. It edged steadily closer: *ten feet . . . five feet . . . three feet . . .*

Zeller, also tracking its progress, fired yet another round and then quickly rolled away, attempting to escape having made himself a target with his own muzzle flash.

The dull red dot jerked wildly in Zeller's direction. The sergeant fired again, buying time for Dart as he scrambled farther back into the woods. He lost sight of the small red dot, causing panic— his world had been reduced to this one small orb of red light; to misplace it could mean death.

Red light flashed in his left eye. Dart jerked his head away as if from a burning match. The tree trunk that he was pressed against exploded, and wooden shrapnel splintered his face, clouding his vision and temporarily blinding him. He knew then that he was a dead man—couldn't see, couldn't flee the all-seeing laser. He would be targeted and killed. He pressed himself flat to the ground, reducing his profile while frantically trying to clear his eyes of the debris.

Zeller, his eyesight adjusted to the darkness, saw Dart take a face full of bark and splinters. Zeller knew that the next sound he'd hear would be Dart's last moment on earth.

No time for him to find a better position. It had to be now.

Like shooting fish in a barrel, using a scope like that. For himself, Zeller realized, it was over: He had tried to bring down Roxin and he had failed. The Davids didn't always win out over the Goliaths—justice was something strived for, but not always won; as a cop, he had lived this truth for over twenty years. He pushed his back against the tree, pulled his knees into his chest, braced his arm, raised his weapon, and he fired. *I will not be locked up*, he thought. The report echoed through the woods, and the shot drew the respect of the shooter, who abandoned the electronic search in Dart's direction, and he turned the laser onto Zeller.

Zeller fired again, thinking, *Show me that muzzle flash . . .*

The red dot crept across the snow, up a tree,

and found Zeller's knee. The sergeant braced himself. *Give me a target*, he mentally challenged.

A yellow-white flash came from within the woods straight ahead.

The woods echoed with a volley of reports as Zeller squeezed off a succession of shots, intentionally creating a wide pattern. His knee blew apart. His shoulder exploded. He managed one final shot. *Run like hell, Dartelli*, he thought to himself. *Go with God.*

Dart, pressed into the snow, cleared his eyes. Zeller had clearly emptied his magazine and had to be in the process of reloading, for the woods were absolutely silent. As his eyes cleared, he could discern the rigid symmetry of the black tree trunks rising from the white snow, and the surreal geometry of the power substation to his left. He lay perfectly still, waiting—expecting the red dot to find him.

He came to his knees and scrambled wildly through the snow, stealing his way more deeply into the trees. He awaited a signal from Zeller but knew that with the shooter still out there, the sergeant too would lie low. He relived the events of the past few minutes once again—the sound of Zeller unloading, the ensuing silence.

Zeller might have hit him, Dart realized.

He crept forward, his eyes better now. He could make out the smooth white bark of the trees, the glowing ceiling of low clouds bouncing back the city light, the unbroken clarity of the snow, as sheer and smooth as a silk scarf.

Minutes passed, and still nothing. Dart

wormed through the trees, making his way back toward the small clearing by the substation where he had last seen Zeller. He moved carefully, stopping every few feet, his body protected by a tree, eyes alert for the laser's searching red dot. He waited and listened, and then he moved on, cautiously. He couldn't be sure of time, but it seemed that five or ten minutes passed. And still *nothing*. No human sounds. No movement. Fear gripped him.

The hum of the power station grew louder. Again he paused, assessing the area, ever alert for the sharpshooter's laser. The closer he came to the clearing, the more of a target he presented. At the start, Zeller had been in this approximate area. He looked for him left, and then right. He scanned the snow for tracks. The silence was frightening. It occurred to him that Zeller, believing he had hit the shooter, might have gone after him to confirm the kill. He realized that his best move might have been to remain relatively close to where he had been injured in case Zeller was himself now seeking out Dart, the two of them going around in circles. He moved forward, stopped, and waited. *Nothing*. Systematically, he moved forward again.

When he looked left, he saw him: Zeller was about ten yards away, sitting up, still facing the area from which the shots had come. Dart hissed at him, but not loud enough to gain his attention—or else Zeller was simply refusing to acknowledge, his attention all on the shooter.

It was bad form for Dart to approach the sergeant and increase the size of their target, so he hunkered down behind a pair of trees and waited. After another five minutes of absolute silence, of bone-numbing cold, he began resenting the man's behavior. At a stakeout that had gone bad, Zeller had once kept him waiting like this for over forty-five minutes. When Zeller lit up a cigar, Dart would know the sergeant considered the area clear. Dart waited another three minutes and ran out of patience. He had seen Zeller take at least two shots—he might have passed out.

Dart weaved his way through the standing tree trunks and hissed once more, this time close enough, loudly enough, to be heard. Again, Zeller refused to acknowledge him in any way. So typically arrogant. Dart felt angry at the man—he would go to any length to remind Dart of the hierarchy of their relationship. He would sit by a phone and allow it to ring until Dart answered it. It infuriated Dart. He finally reached the man— Zeller was leaning against a small evergreen that bent away from him with his weight, a pair of white-bark birches in front of him as a screen. He held his gun in both hands, resting on the ground between his legs. His knee looked badly hit.

It was the position of Zeller's gun that sent alarm shivering through Dart—the arm was slack, the barrel of the weapon planted into the wet snow and mud. Zeller revered his weapons, preached the code of proper care and handling. Treating the weapon like this was unthinkable.

Dart took another few cautious steps, coming to within an arm's reach. He smelled blood. He leaned forward in the dim light. "Sarge," he whispered anxiously, glancing over his shoulder, all the while expecting the laser's searching dot. "Sarge," he repeated.

The man didn't move.

Dart looked into Zeller's face. The hole was quite small, immediately below the left eye. He gasped. "Sarge!" he blurted out, the knot tightening in his throat, his chest burning, his eyes filling with tears. He didn't reach out to touch him, to disturb him, only to check for a pulse. He gripped the man's warm wrist, realizing in a flood of memory that the two had rarely touched, even to shake hands, realizing that, had Zeller had even a single heartbeat of life left within him, he would have broken Dart's grip instantly and told him to keep his hands to himself.

Walter Zeller was dead.

Forgetting himself, forgetting all training, placing himself at serious jeopardy, Joe Dartelli raised his face to the sullen sky and shrieked, "No!" so loudly and for so long that to hear it from a suburban home one would have imagined a wounded animal. He stood then, weapon in hand, not thinking of lasers or semiautomatic weapons, but only of revenge. He ducked and moved deftly and quickly through the trees, as smoothly as water over rock. He ran across the clearing, his feet slipping on the wet snow, and entered the opposing woods. Tree by tree, he worked his way across the front of this copse, knowing the shooter could not have been too far into the trees during the attack.

At his feet, brass casings lay scattered about.

Warm when first ejected, they had melted small tunnels into the snow. The ground was scuffed and muddy from the shooter's frantic movements.

The path of mud indicated that the shooter may have dragged himself off into the woods, back toward Zeller's former home. Whether he had followed one of them here, or had been keeping the place under surveillance and had overheard them, Dart couldn't know.

The prints were not clean, and the snow was discolored with either blood or mud or both.

Neglecting concern for his own safety, Dart quickly cut his way through the trees and shrubs, leaving the hum of electricity behind him. The track left by the shooter grew heavier and more labored until it became apparent to Dart that the man had been wounded, had crawled his way through the trees. He pressed ahead, knowing that he must be gaining on the man.

Through the woods came the plaintive cry of sirens—at least two, perhaps three or more. The shots had been heard and reported. Dart suddenly had to contend with the pressure of time—he could not afford to be brought downtown for an officer-involved shooting investigation. The key to dealing with Martinson would be speed, timing.

He heard groaning before he saw the man. He passed the black shape of the man's discarded weapon and kicked it aside. The shooter lay on his side, curled in a fetal position, clutching his bleeding stomach with both hands, ignoring his wounded shoulder. It was too dark to see much of his face, but his fingers were spread open, his hands clearly empty. He was a tall, lanky man—*not* the same build as the man in the laundry.

Zeller had hit him twice—a serious gut shot and a minor bleeder in the shoulder. The gut shot was final. Even with an ambulance, he didn't look as if he'd survive.

The sirens quickly drew closer. Dart heard one of the cars come to a stop up on the highway rest area where Dart had parked.

Dart leveled his handgun, sighting down the short barrel at the man's head. The shooter cowered, curling up tighter. Dart's arm began to shake. A voice from inside him demanded he pull the trigger. *Do it!* this voice pleaded. Dart's finger found the trigger guard and then the trigger itself. His thumb tripped the safety, allowing the gun to be fired. He stared down the dark tube at the man's head.

The man shook with fear.

He couldn't do it. Dart lowered the weapon, securing the safety, and walked silently off into the woods.

He knew well what hell Zeller's murder would create—three, perhaps as many as five, investigators would be assigned. The forensics work would be exhaustive, the meetings endless. When the second dead man proved to be a hired killer from out of state, the governor and the FBI would be brought in. The press would get wind of it and the story would take off like wildfire, stealing headlines and news radio leads from Greenwich to Putnam, perhaps as far as Boston and Providence. And in the process, Dart knew, the opportunity to sink Roxin would disappear quickly. The cover-ups would begin, the fictitious stories welded in place, the connections quickly distanced. Within a few short hours following the first news leak of Zeller's death, any and all hope of exposing Roxin could be lost, all Zeller's efforts defeated.

Zeller's methods had ultimately killed him— Dart could not escape this thought. Despite his good intentions, the man had chosen the wrong solution. By violating the very laws he had once upheld, he had dug himself into isolation and desperation, convincing himself, no doubt, that he was engaged in noble self-sacrifice. The truth, it seemed to Dart, was more that Lucky's death had pushed him over the edge. And it felt sad to Dart that such a man could become so lost. *So maybe I am a Boy Scout*, Dart thought.

Dart went off, first at a walk, then at a run, in the opposite direction from the arriving police who were already crowding into the woods. As shouts raised behind him, he felt filled with an overwhelming wish that Zeller's death would not be in vain.

Martinson had not destroyed the files. Dart felt certain of it.

CHAPTER
42

Haite glanced up from his desk at the detective standing in his office doorway and said, "Jesus H. Christ." Dart was all mud, blood, and wet clothes. "Shut the door," were Haite's next words, closely followed by, "You were *there*!" Dart nodded. "What the hell happened?"

"I won't be dragged into the investigation," Dart said.

"The hell you won't." Haite glanced over at the wall clock—it was one in the morning. "I've got a dozen patrol and four detectives out there." The CAPers office area was empty. "What the hell happened?"

"The shooter?"

"Died in transit. DOA at HH," he said, referring to Hartford Hospital.

Dart looked Haite directly in the eyes and said, "I was wrong about the suicides. They weren't murders."

"Is that right?" Haite asked, not believing Dart for a moment but not questioning him either. This was what Haite wanted to hear.

"I misread the evidence, Sergeant. It's my fault," Dart said.

"Did you?"

"Yes. I may be able to prove that Roxin Laboratories is involved in a cover-up concerning a gene therapy treatment they are testing. The drug apparently has severe psychological side effects, resulting, I assume, in some of these suicides. It's a terrible thing."

"Where does Zeller fit in?" Haite asked bluntly.

"I don't believe I have ever mentioned Zeller's name to you, sir. I'm not sure what you're referring to." The use of "sir" was certain to catch Haite's attention. "His death," Dart choked out, "is certainly a tragedy to us all."

"I want him to die a hero, not a criminal," Haite hissed, openly honest. "How much of this is going to surface?"

"How much of *what*?" Dart asked in his best innocent Boy Scout voice.

"You can keep it that way?" Haite asked, sounding both surprised and impressed.

"We're under some time pressure, sir," Dart said, making sure to repeat the formal address. He coughed and picked some mud out of his teeth. "If we're going to prove Roxin's involvement, we have to move quickly. We'll need a variety of warrants, a full ERT, the surveillance van. . . . If we fail," he said, maintaining his eye contact with Haite, "I fear that accusations may be made against Sergeant Zeller in an effort to discredit him and divert blame from where it belongs."

"You can really keep him out of this?" Haite asked again.

"I wasn't aware that he was ever implicated in anything," Dart answered calmly, playing his part. "Has his name ever come up in regards to any of these investigations?"

Haite dragged a hand across his mouth, contemplating Dart's offer.

Do this for Zeller! Dart's eyes told the man.

"Can you actually pull this off, Dartelli?" Haite understood that to commit the resources Dart was requesting would necessitate his own involvement, putting his ass on the line should Dart's plan fail and the truth of Zeller's criminal activity be revealed. They would both be risking their careers to save Zeller's reputation. "Can you?" Haite repeated, wanting an answer that they both knew Dart could not give.

"I had a good teacher," said Joe Dart.

CHAPTER
43

They needed Martinson's password.

Driving a department-confiscated Lexus, Dart approached the employee parking lot entrance to Roxin at 2:30 A.M. He wore jeans, a sweater, and a windbreaker.

The lineman at the top of the phone pole, armed with a high-powered monocular, worked Narcotics but had done a good deal of undercover surveillance work. Across town, the worker down the manhole not far from the governor's mansion was with SNET, and was awaiting court permission to tap into a high-speed data transmission line that serviced a remote computer terminal located in the study of Dr. Arielle Martinson's home. Ginny had determined the existence of this remote terminal after questioning Dart thoroughly about the computers he had seen there. Bud Gorman's check of SNET billing had confirmed it.

The unmarked black ERT step van was parked half a mile down the hill from Roxin, the team ready with black ladders to assault the facility's west wall if necessary.

Haite was in the command van with two techies. Parked near Roxin's main entrance, it had the rear left wheel jacked off the ground, and a number of tools lying nearby, as if abandoned with a flat tire. In fact, the all-wheel-drive vehicle could be driven right off the jack, if required.

In Dart's left ear, a small earpiece kept him in touch with the command van, and thereby, Ginny and the spotter atop the phone pole. He wore taped to his chest a fiber-optic camera no thicker than a fountain pen and curved on a piece of flex so as to capture Dart's point of view—an interesting twist demanded by the judge issuing the warrants. There were few guidelines for a hostile raid on a computer network. They were improvising.

As Dart pulled up to the unmanned security gate, he switched on the video recorder—no bigger than a Walkman—and spoke to the microphone clipped under the collar of his jacket. "Position one. I'm all yours, Gin."

The techies inside the van were recording his every word.

Dart heard Ginny's voice answer. Wearing a telephone headset at her kitchen table with two laptops in front of her, both connected to high-speed data lines, Ginny echoed "Position one" and said, "Here goes nothing."

Dart wondered what this validation must feel like to her. She had hacked into Roxin's mainframe with the *permission* of the court and *at Dart's request*. In return for her cooperation, the court had agreed to expunge her criminal record, including taking her off probation. And now, with the law behind her, she was attempting to take control of the security area of Roxin's computer and open the arm of the gate from a remote location miles away.

The security gate resembled the ones at car rental lots—a red and white horizontal bar prevented entry and a long row of sharp spikes, designed to puncture tires, inhibited exit.

Dart waited nervously for Ginny's magic.

"Anything?" he heard her ask.

"No."

"One second," she said. "How 'bout this?"

The gate opened.

"Bingo!" Dart said as he drove through. "You're a genius."

"Let's just hope I can get you back out," she said, only half teasing.

At this hour, his was the only car in the lot. He drove toward the several-story block of glass and metal that attached at the north end to the giant dome. The place looked like an enormous glowing spaceship.

Dart switched off the headlights. "I'm facing the second door from the south end," he informed Ginny. "There's no number on it."

"The stairways are to your right?" she asked.

The glassed-in stairways were clearly visible to him. "That's right."

"Correct," confirmed the spotter, also listening in.

"I've got it," she informed him. "I've logged you into the system under the employee name of Nealy. George Nealy. He's listed as a biochemical engineer assigned to B-block—whatever that is. Did you get that?"

"George Nealy. B-block," Dart answered. To get him in, Ginny had needed to choose an existing employee's identity. If stopped by security, he would claim to have lost his ID card somewhere between the parking lot and wherever they caught up to him.

"Can you get me in?" he asked.

"Tell me when you're at the door," she answered.

Dart climbed out of the car, reckoning that by now the night security had been notified of Nealy's use of the parking lot. Outside the door was a stainless steel device used to read ID cards. Dart had none.

Standing at the door, he said, "I'm here."

"Stand by," Ginny said in his ear.

Dart's nerves were already shot. He had no idea how he would make it through the next half hour. He checked in both directions repeatedly.

"How 'bout that?" Ginny asked.

The security device's blue-green LCD read:

INCORRECT SIGN-ON INFORMATION—PLEASE TRY AGAIN.

Dart tried to open the door. "No," he informed her. He worried that she was in over her head. Completely unfamiliar with Roxin's security system, she had to come to understand it all on the fly. *Real time,* as she called it.

"Stand by," she repeated. "How 'bout that?" she inquired.

INCORRECT SIGN-ON INFORMATION—*PLEASE TRY AGAIN.*

"Negative," Dart announced, sweat streaming from his armpits with the temperature one degree below freezing.

"This is lookout," reported the man atop the phone pole. "I have an unidentified individual, on foot, heading south along the east side."

Dart looked up. He could just make out a tiny black dot a hundred yards away. A security guard—and heading toward him.

"We have one more try," Ginny explained. "If we fail, then Nealy will not be permitted inside, and if we're to continue, I'll have to check you into the parking lot under a different name and try again."

INCORRECT SIGN-ON INFORMATION—ACCESS DENIED—PLEASE CONTACT THE SECURITY DESK—THANK YOU.

"We're toast," Dart announced.

"Unidentified individual is seventy yards and closing," reported the lookout.

"The gate?" Ginny asked, panicked.

Dart looked over his shoulder. The entrance gate rose and fell.

"You got it."

"Hold the phone," she said.

The guard approached, now less than fifty yards away. The man waved, still too far for his face to be seen, and conversely, Dart's could not be seen by him.

"We're running out of headroom," Dart warned.

Another few yards, and Dart's face would be identifiable. How many Roxin employees would a security guard recognize?

"Joe?" she asked.

Dart read:

WELCOME: DR. JANET JORGENSON

The door clicked. Dart pulled on the handle. It opened.

The guard was twenty yards away. They could clearly see each other. *You've got to think on your feet*, Zeller had once schooled him. *He's an outside guard*, Dart thought. *Disarm his suspicion.* Dart raised his voice and offered, "You want me to hold the door for you?"

The guard shook his head. "No, thanks," he answered.

Dart stepped inside, his armpits soaked, his throat dry. The elevator was straight ahead; a door marked the stairs to his right. Not wanting to wait for an elevator car, and recalling from his earlier trip to Roxin that elevators also required security access, Dart chose to use the stairs. The door thumped shut behind him.

"Janet Jorgenson?" he complained into the

microphone, climbing the stairs. His new identity had given him a sex change.

In his left ear he heard, "The name was immediately above Nealy's on the list. What can I tell you?"

"Who am I?" Dart asked, although it didn't matter—he couldn't very well pose as Jorgenson.

"The thing is," she explained, "the way the system works—the reason Nealy would *not* work back there—you have to be a certain security clearance to have access to all doors. Otherwise you're supposed to take a particular door at a certain time of day. Nealy wasn't being allowed in. Jorgenson's got the run of the place—clearance five," she told him.

"Who am I?" Dart repeated, feeling uneasy about this.

"Vice president and deputy director of R and D," she said.

"You made me Martinson's assistant?" Dart queried angrily. Security might notify Proctor of an unexpected late-night visit—if Proctor had any sense, he had his team on alert. Proctor was likely to know Martinson's next-in-command, and it seemed to Dart he might question a visit by her at this wee hour of the morning, might see Dart's ruse for what it was. It pushed him to hurry.

"This is seat-of-the-pants, Dartelli." she sounded bitter.

He wondered what Haite was thinking as he heard two ex-lovers argue during a sting. He charged up the stairs as quickly as his bad ankle would carry him.

The lookout atop the phone pole reported, "The unidentified individual is inspecting the Lexus. He appears to be using a handheld communications device."

"Scanning," returned the voice of the dispatcher.

Dart continued up at a run, passing the door marked with a large "2."

"We've intercepted the radio transmission," the calm voice of the dispatcher said. "The individual called in the vehicle registration number and is awaiting callback. The sergeant is recommending that you abort operations at once. Repeat: Recommending you abort. Do you copy?" After a brief hesitation the dispatcher said, "Evacuation plan A as in Alpha. Do you copy?"

Plan A called for Dart to head on foot toward the ERT's position, where the elite team would help him over the perimeter fence and to safety. All this was said not for Dart's benefit but for that of whoever might be listening in to the unsecured frequency they were using. If Proctor's people were in fact monitoring police radio transmissions—something Haite and Dart *hoped* was happening—then perhaps Dart's arrival at Roxin would act as an invitation.

"I'm on the third floor," Dart announced. *Are you listening?* he wondered. "A blue rectangle, a yellow triangle, and green circle," he announced to Ginny.

"Blue, yellow, green," she repeated. "Box, triangle, circle. Stand by."

This office door, like every other, housed an ID reader to the right of the jamb. The cryptic code on the doors was playing to Roxin's advantage. Ginny had to locate the specific door in the database. He waited impatiently. Finally he heard her say, "Try it."

Dart pushed down on the door lever, and the locked door came open. "Got it!" he said brightly. "I'm in."

Access to the office was certain to show on the security screens in the lobby. Ginny had been schooled *not* to attempt to shield Dart's activities from these screens. Although it risked Dart's getting caught, it also allowed security to inform Proctor, or other superiors, of Dart's movements—something critical to the sting working.

The clock was now running and the trap set: the cheese was there for the taking. Dart slipped into a chair in front of a computer monitor, where a screen saver drew geometric patterns on the screen. He tapped the SHIFT key, and the screen saver vanished, replaced by dozens of computer software icons.

"I'm at a terminal," Dart announced softly.

"Well done, people," Haite said for the benefit of anyone eavesdropping.

Joe Dart was on-line.

If Dart was right about Martinson's scientific ego, then she had stored copies of the earlier clinical trial reports somewhere in the mainframe's memory, and only Martinson herself could retrieve them. Ginny could not gain entrance to the password-protected file without the cooperation of Martinson herself.

By 2:00 AM, under the authority of a wire

surveillance warrant, Martinson's two unpublished home phone lines were being monitored. Under separate warrant, Terry Proctor's residential lines were under tap-and-trace surveillance, forbidding recording but allowing the identification of phone numbers coming and going over the lines.

Since the inception of the surveillance, no traffic had been reported at Martinson's. Records would later show that Proctor's lines had been incredibly active that night.

"I'm logged on," Dart announced for Ginny's benefit. His hope was that, if not immediately, within minutes this radio traffic would be overheard by Proctor's people and passed up to both Proctor and Martinson.

Dart therefore had to slip up, making believable mistakes as he went. The Lexus—a car not registered to any Roxin employee—was part of that fiction; use of the police radio frequencies—impossible to scramble with so many participants involved—was also part of the ruse. Proctor had to be led to believe that Dart was close to uncovering Martinson's files.

But so what? Dart doubted that Terry Proctor was aware of the existence of any such evidence. It seemed likely that once Zeller had blown open Martinston's scam, Proctor would have advised her to destroy all evidence—he would have accepted Martinson's word that she had done so. Only Martinson—and intuitively, Dart—knew the truth: No way would she destroy eleven years of research. Dart would have to enlighten Proctor, without it seeming intentional, and to sting him into panicking Martinson to finally destroy the evidence she held so dearly.

By necessity, Ginny was also part of the ruse, manipulating and monitoring and preparing to trap Martinson.

Most important was that Dart not allow himself to be discovered or abducted before completing the sting. To be caught was to fail.

"Logged on and awaiting instructions," Dart repeated.

"Okay, Dart," Ginny said, "here's what I want you to do."

Keystroke by keystroke, Ginny navigated Dart flawlessly through a hole in the upper-level security firewall that she herself had run only an hour earlier.

The Roxin Laboratories ROX NET logo, in gold and silver, sparkled on the screen, followed by a greeting and a cautionary non-disclosure statement warning of FBI investigation.

"I'm in," Dart acknowledged.

"Enter the following," Ginny instructed, rambling off a series of entries for Dart to duplicate.

He began typing furiously. Nervous, he made several mistakes and had to start again.

"Hold it," Ginny said anxiously, now not having to play-act. "I'm seeing some movement within the facility."

The lookout said, "I copy that. Lights have come on in the box."

"I think they're on to you, Joe," Ginny said, her voice gripped in fear.

Dart took the news two different ways: If they

were coming after him, then they knew he had broken into their computer and they knew where to find him—all of which was good, because Terry Proctor was certain to be notified; but he could not allow himself to be caught.

"I'm moving," Dart announced. Dart left the room in a hurry, his sole mission for the next five to ten minutes to distance himself from security while maintaining the possibility of computer access. Roxin's security computers were capable of tracking access on an office-by-office basis. The moment Dart had entered the office, the computer had registered that access and alerted the guards. Similarly, every time a security guard used his pass to enter a hallway, or an elevator, Ginny knew about it. The result was a kind of electronic cat-and-mouse—each side able to monitor the other's movement.

Had Ginny been given days or weeks to override the security systems, she might have been capable of misleading security by creating false electronic clues for Dart's whereabouts, thus giving him the advantage. But as it was, she was lucky to be able to monitor movements at all, and Dart was forced to keep on the move. Working against the security team was the facility's all-glass design, for each time a hallway or office light went on, the lookout saw this and warned Dart of his pursuers' location.

As he ran into the hall, Dart heard the lookout warn, "E-S ascending. Repeat: Eagle-Sam ascending. Copy?"

"Eagle-Sam. Copy," Dart replied, already running down the hall in a northerly direction.

For communications purposes, they had designated the structure's four imposing elevator hubs east and west, south and north. East-south was the elevator bank nearest the parked car. Dart turned around and ran to the stairs adjacent to elevators E-N and descended to the second floor.

The complexity of the layout worked against Dart and in the favor of those who pursued him: He was a rat in a maze, and the keepers knew the way. Armed keepers, at that. Dart bounded down, pausing occasionally for the telltale sounds of anyone approaching, with a running dialogue in his ear as the lookout and Ginny both advised him of security's location.

At 2:53 A.M. Eastern Standard Time, November 19, Dr. Arielle Martinson was recorded as logging onto Rox Net from a remote terminal in West Hartford. Ginny was right there with her.

Using a land-link telephone line that connected her to the command van via the only scrambled radio frequency available to HPD, she announced cryptically, "The fish is on the line," just as she had been told to. "Access password," she spelled, "is *L-E-A-N-M-O-N-T*."

Ginny studied Martinson's on-line movement, as her second laptop computer, patched into the high-speed data line by the SNET worker down the manhole outside the governor's mansion, recorded Martinson's every keystroke. Ginny divided her attention between the one laptop, monitoring security, and the other, monitoring Martinson. Rox Net's central interface utilized

403

both graphics and menus, allowing the user to click through desired addresses and functions. Martinson was clearly no stranger to the network. She moved quickly and flawlessly, often clicking her choice so fast that Ginny had no time to read or make note of it, though her laptop did record it.

Martinson's first choice, selected from the welcoming menu, was, for OTHER SERVICES. Ginny missed the names of the next two selections because of Martinson's speed, but she caught the heading DAILY DIARY because it required a password. Martinson typed in: 1E2Q3T4Z, and Ginny wrote this down, despite the fact that the laptop continued to capture it all.

The CEO chose OPTIONS next, followed by SET DATE FUNCTION, and Ginny took note of it all because Martinson had to slow down to enter a date: June 14, 2000.

Ginny followed her with a computer hacker's admiration. She had expected her to have used the network's personal file area, a section devoted to an individual user's personal storage. It was the logical location to upload information into the server. As a rule, network software restricted user storage to such limited areas, and only such areas, allowing the system operator to predict, control, secure, and maintain a specified amount of storage. Martinson had cleverly found another location that would allow the uploading of files, one that, through a series of passwords and now a date function, installed several secure gates in place, effectively locking the information away so that she, and only she, could access it.

A colorful calendar filled Ginny's screen with the date, June 14, 2000, highlighted in a small box. There was a To-Do list, complete with Preferences. A time-of-day work space for appointments and calls. A small spreadsheet to track cash and credit card expenses.

The calendar work space was left blank—a particularly clever move. Even if a hacker sleuthed the several passwords needed to reach this location, even if the hacker then arbitrarily landed ahead on June 14, in the year 2000, there was nothing to see, nothing that announced the prized information hidden within. Nothing but a single asterisk at the very bottom of the screen in a box marked MEMO.

Martinson clicked on MEMO.

An information box presented itself in the middle of the screen.

RESTRICTED BY PASSWORD
PLEASE ENTER 8-DIGIT
ALPHANUMERIC STRING

Ginny looked on as Martinson typed: L-A-T-E-R-I-N-5. The letters meant nothing to her.

The screen filled with the first page of a technical report. Ginny was momentarily distracted by the contents of this page. It had something to do with drug testing. . . .

"I've got it!" she spoke into the phone. But Martinson caught her off-guard by suddenly selecting EDIT . . . DELETE. The screen responded.

MEMO IS 76 PAGES.
DELETE CONTENTS?
(Y)es (N)o

Martinson moved too quickly. Before Ginny could notify the SNET workman to interrupt the transmission, Martinson sent the necessary "Y" down the high-speed transmission line.

Into the phone, Ginny shouted, "Disconnect!"

But the screen suddenly read:

DELETING CONTENTS IS
UNRECOVERABLE.
ARE YOU SURE?
(Y)es (N)o

This final protection device saved them.

"Disconnect!" Ginny shouted again.

But the blinking cursor, frozen in its position on the screen, told her that the SNET man had done his job. Martinson was disconnected.

"Ready," Ginny informed Dart.

Although able to access the system's security functions by modem—a necessity to allow people like Proctor to monitor functions from the field—Ginny had no modem access to this user-area side of the Roxin network. Access was restricted to actual terminal nodes, to prevent the kind of hacking that Ginny had in mind. Where the SNET man had managed to hard-wire Ginny the ability to *monitor* Martinson's line, she lacked the necessary software cryptography to manipulate data.

That job was up to Dartelli.

* * *

Dart reached the second floor at the same time that the security guards pursuing him charged into the third floor office where he had been working.

He told Ginny the color code on the door that he was facing, and a moment later, when the small indicator light turned from red to green, he opened this door and entered a glassed-in area. Behind the wall of glass and a stainless steel entrance purification chamber, he saw a clean-room lab, with no computer terminal. The idea of breaking into a genetics lab did not thrill Dart; he turned around and hurried out, seeking another office.

The next door down was marked with a blue box, a yellow box, and two red circles. Ginny, believing she was getting the hang of things said, "You're in." Dart tried the door. It was locked. The blue-green characters marched across the reader:

ACCESS DENIED—PLEASE CONTACT SECURITY. THANK YOU.

"No good," he announced.

"Try again," she advised.

"Same thing."

"Shit," she said, "they've locked me out. We're screwed!"

The computer's security program had identified Ginny's raid and blocked her access.

Dart stood there in the darkened corridor, his heart pounding in his chest, wondering what to do.

He couldn't think clearly. It was as if, all at once, his mind went blank.

"E-S, descending by stairs. E-N, descending by stairs," warned the lookout suddenly. "Eagle-Nova, descending. Eagle-Sam, descending. Do you copy?" The security team pursuing him had split up, coming toward him from both directions, leaving Dart sandwiched. Trapped. By Ginny's attempting to gain him access, the computer had once again identified his location.

How many guards on the night watch? Dart wondered. One at the front security desk; one at the third-floor security desk; two, possibly four roamers. *Four to six, total,* he decided. If that number held, he guessed that the team sent to bring him in would be no larger than a pair—leave one man by the car, one to roam the west side of the building, and send two after him.

Dart glanced back at the reader.

ACCESS DENIED—PLEASE CONTACT SECURITY.

"Approaching the second floor," the lookout reported.

In an attempt to divide and conquer, the pair had split, each taking one of the stairways. No doubt the computers had been used to shut down the elevators, in an attempt to bracket Dart into being caught.

"Lookout, how many in each stairway?" His feet began to carry him toward the south stairs, the closest to him. The plan formulated quickly in his mind: *A security guard will carry a master "key,"* a card allowing him access to the various rooms.

"One each," returned the steady voice.

Perfect, Dart thought.

"Arriving second floor," the lookout warned. Dart was on the second floor.

The door to the fire stairs was ten feet away. Five . . .

His only hope was surprise. A rent-a-cop in pursuit would be excited and probably poorly trained. He would be thinking that his target was attempting to run away and hide; he would be in a hurry.

A wedge of yellow light arced across the hallway floor as the guard opened the door to the stairs. This wedge spread open like a fan unfolding, illuminating the far wall.

A boot and a dark pant leg stepped through. The guard had gotten ahead of Dart by a fraction of a second. The other guard, at the far end of the hall, could not be far off.

Dart threw himself to the floor, diving for that leg as if it were home plate. He hooked his left arm out and snagged the leg as he slid past, pulling the stunned guard with him. The man went down, looking as if he'd hit a banana peel, all limbs in the air at once. A *whoosh* of air was expelled from his lungs.

Dart scrambled atop him, grabbed him by the hair, and snapped the man's head down firmly against the hard floor. The sound of the contact instantly made Dart nauseated. The guard groaned sickeningly.

He's alive. Thank god, Dart thought as he reached down and ripped the man's credit-card-size pass from where it was clipped to his pocket. Dart flipped it over, establishing that it did, in fact, carry a magnetic stripe.

He had one shot, he realized. After that, they would block use of this card as well.

"Hold it! Stay where you are!" roared a voice from the far end of the hall.

Dart came to his feet and charged through the door and into the stairway. *Down or up?* he debated. His legs carried him up.

Behind him, in the hallway, he heard the fast-paced running of the guard coming in hot pursuit.

In his left ear he heard Ginny. "We gotta get this happening, Dart. We're running out of time. And I mean *fast.*"

Dart ran all the way up to the top of the stairs and through to the hall, attempting to slow down his thoughts and concentrate. His adrenaline was his biggest enemy.

Using the guard's card to enter a room would alert security to his location, and would, in turn, limit his chance to do what had to be done. It gave him an idea.

He slid the stolen card into the first security box he encountered. The light turned green. Dart spun the doorknob, threw the door open, and then quickly pulled it shut. He ran to the next security box, the next door, and followed the same procedure. And the next. One eye trained nervously on the fire stairs through which he had just come, he crossed the hall and used the card on two more offices, blocking the first with a pen to keep it from closing. The security computer would now show six offices accessed.

Backtracking, Dart entered through the door that he had blocked by the pen. He could hear the security man's footfalls charging up the fire stairs. He had only a few seconds . . .

With the door open, he shoved his stolen card into the reader and began violently rocking the card back and forth. The sound of the feet stopped, Dart guessing the guard was standing immediately on the other side but was being more cautious than his partner below. Dart continued to wiggle the security card. It cracked along the left edge. With one tremendous effort, Dart tore the card straight across, leaving a significant piece of it down inside the reader, to prevent another card from being inserted.

He pushed the door firmly shut just as he heard the fire stairs door whine open. The guard was on the sixth floor with him.

Dart slipped into the first chair that fronted a terminal. He touched the space bar, and the screen saver cleared.

"Go," he said to Ginny.

A voice interrupted and instructed, "The tiger's in the garden." Terry Proctor had arrived. Dart felt a chill run through him, right into his bowels. It was a huge risk for Proctor to come here in person, illustrating to Dart just how desperate the man was.

Dart pulled out the cellular, hoping for privacy—getting off the police frequency—pushed RECALL and SEND and a moment later, Ginny answered. "We've got less than two minutes. Now listen carefully . . ."

Level by level, Ginny steered Dart through the proper key combinations and necessary passwords. To ensure that Dart was on track, Ginny kept repeating anxiously, "What's the title line? What's the title line?" Dart would read the upper-most title and await the next instruction.

Out in the hallway, Dart heard the security guard open a door and then silence. *He'll have to search every office*, Dart thought, realizing he had bought himself some time.

He could picture the operation continuing outside. Proctor's arrival had triggered a third phase, independent of Dart: The lookout confirmed that Proctor had entered; the ERT team, dressed all in black, was presently scaling the walls of the compound, on their way to sealing the building's exits. Proctor would be trapped.

This changed the dynamics—there was no predicting the behavior of a cornered animal.

"Are you listening?" an almost hysterical Ginny asked. She said, "*L-A-T-E-R-I-N*-5. Did you get that?"

Dart typed it in and hit the ENTER key.

The cover page of the clinical trial appeared on his screen. Dart felt a huge wash of relief. It was dated fourteen months earlier.

"The file is seventy-six pages long," Ginny told him.

He heard a banging behind—the security guard was at his door.

"I'm not going to get out of here with this disk," Dart informed her, realizing his situation. He had a disk in his pocket on which he was supposed to record the information; that seemed impossible now. After a long beat of silence, he asked, "Are you there?"

In his left ear he heard the dispatcher in the

command van announce, "The garden is surrounded." The ERT team was in place.

The security guard's deep voice attempted to whisper a radioed request, but Dart overheard it through the door: "I need a master key, ASAP. Third floor."

"Okay," Ginny said into the cellular, "here's what we're going to do." A fraction of a second later she snapped, "Oh shit, hang on. You've got visitors."

Glancing toward the door, and knowing that the security guard was coming through it any second, Dart said, "I *can't* hang on. There's no time."

"Mark the complete text. I'll get back to you."

"Ginny?" Dart shouted into the phone.

There was no answer.

Ginny's second laptop alerted him the moment Martinson's password was used to log on to the system. Many of the commonly used security softwares prevented the duplication of a password if one person was presently on the system. Ginny had hoped that was the case—that by Dart already being on the network, Martinson, or whomever Martinson had called, would be denied access. To her horror, the system allowed this other person access onto the network.

Dart guessed that this person was Terry Proctor and that he might even be in the lobby now, following Martinson's instructions to erase the files.

Ginny felt helpless. The screen followed the intruder's every move. He traveled past the main menu and along the route Ginny now knew only too well. In a matter of thirty to sixty seconds, the intruder would be on top of Dart; how the system would perform was anybody's guess. Ginny's guess was that it would freeze, locking up, and that only the system operator would be able to correct it. And the SYSOP worked for Martinson, which meant the files would never be seen again.

Dart couldn't copy the text to a disk because the disk might be confiscated by the security guards and destroyed.

It left Ginny only one choice. Using a modem line, she was going to have to attempt to raid the system's security firewall a second time, attempting to avoid her earlier mistake.

She picked up the phone and said to Dart, "Is the text marked?"

"I'm ready," Dart said into the phone. He heard the sound of someone running. The master key—a *real* key, not some security card—was seconds away from being delivered.

Ginny said, "Go to the Edit menu. Select *Cut*."

"*Cut?*" Dart barked. "You mean *copy*!"

"I said *cut*, Detective. Do it now."

"But I'll lose the file!" Dart protested.

"Edit. *Cut*!" Ginny ordered. "Do it *now*!"

Ginny's eyes widened as she followed the activity on the second laptop. She watched as Proctor typed *L-A-T* . . .

"This is not up for discussion. Do it fucking *now*!"

* * *

414

Dart's index finger hesitated above the button on the computer's mouse. He felt a bead of sweat trickle down his jaw. He heard the key in the door. And then he heard that same key turn.

Cut would make the blocked text disappear. *Does she know what she's doing?*

"Now!" he heard repeated in his ear.

His index finger punched the button automatically and the seventy-six pages of clinical trial reports disappeared from the screen.

"Thank God," Ginny said through the phone. "Now," she added, "if you want to see those files again, there's something you've got to do—"

"Not right now," Dart interrupted, dropping the cellular phone and springing out of the office chair and dragging it to the door just as the doorknob turned.

Dart blocked the door with his foot, flipped the chair upside down, wheels in the air, and wedged it inside the handle to prevent the door from opening.

He glanced up at the ceiling: large rectangular panes suspended by an angle-iron aluminum frame. It offered one possibility of escape.

The door came partially open, encountering the chair. The guards on the other side leaned their weight into it. The sound was deafening.

A bead of sweat slipped into Dart's eyes, stinging him.

Dart considered going out the window. The golf-ball-like architecture crowned at the top of each module. Being on the top floor, this office's windowpanes were more parallel to the ground than those of the floors below and would be easier to climb. Dart was not one for heights, but it seemed to offer him the fastest exit.

He took two steps toward the window and reached it before identifying the hollow *thump* underfoot. He stooped to inspect the source of that sound.

Behind him the office chair slipped. The door popped open two or three inches and several fingers appeared in the crack, groping to remove the chair.

Dart flung himself across the room, drove his shoulder into the door, and broke all four of the man's fingers. An animal cry erupted from the far side of the door. Dart hiked the chair back into position and leaped over to the windows.

Along the office's perimeter, a series of floor panels covered spaces created to house phone lines, transmission lines, computer cables, and electrical conduit. To allow easy access, the office carpet had not been glued here, and Dart pulled it back. He yanked up the first-floor panel and found himself staring down into a darkened dead space through a tangle of wires. Three feet below him was the suspended acoustical tile of a fifth-floor-office ceiling. Steel I-beams supported the floor of the office Dart was currently inside.

He didn't hesitate. He sat down, forced his toes through the mesh of wires, and lowered himself down.

The door banged and the chair slipped again.

Dart kicked at the pressboard panel beneath him, broke it in pieces, and could see through to a desktop in the office below. He let go his purchase and fell through the dead space and down into the office below, landing awkwardly on the desk, driving a sharp pain into his injured ankle.

He heard the chair explode above him. They were inside.

Dart jumped off the desk, ignoring his pain, and ran for the door. A moment later he was running quickly toward the fire stairs, hoping he had enough of a lead.

"That sounded ugly," the voice said in his left ear.

"Patch me through to Ginny," Dart said. "I've lost the phone." Like it or not, Proctor's people would now hear every word.

On Ginny's instructions, Dart headed for the bottom of the stairs. As Dart ran, she talked nonstop.

Ginny's detected raid on the Roxin server had triggered the mainframe to adopt a defensive position, eliminating an outsider's ability to access the machine through modem and pulling the system temporarily off-line. The situation could be reversed, but only from the SYSOP terminal inside Roxin's data processing center, which Ginny guessed was likely to be located on the facility's basement level.

"How can you possibly be sure about this?" Dart questioned on the run.

"There are three different systems they could be using, and I know every one of them. They all share the ability to take modem communications off-line. By definition, they cannot be put back on-line using software; they require someone to throw a physical switch—a button. It's what keeps them secure. The front panels are all basically the same: some system indicators and either one or two buttons. I know the way this works, Joe. This is my area of expertise," Ginny reminded.

"You're going to have to trust me. And listen, Joe, once we're back on-line, I need a couple minutes, minimum."

"What am I looking for?" He asked.

"It will be a plain vanilla box—maybe a stack of them, depending how many incoming lines there are. If there's more than one, you'll have to trip each master. The front panel will show a series of seven small lights across it, red probably; in all likelihood, only the farthest right-hand light will be lit. On the far right-hand side of the box itself will be a vertical stack of red lights—one for each incoming line—these are actually buttons, not lights. *Below* these lights," she emphasized, "there is another button off by itself." Then, editing herself, she said, "On two of the machines it is below. On the Black Box model it is above. But it will either read 'Master,' or 'Group On-line,' or 'All.'"

"Master, Group On-line, or All," he repeated.

"Yes. And that is the one you want. One or more of those masters is going to be red. When you push it, it will change to green or amber. At that point we're back on-line." She asked, "Is that enough of a description?"

"Sounds good."

"You can describe things to me and ask, once you're there."

"I missed that last bit," Dart said, finally

arriving at the bottom of the stairs. Ginny repeated herself. "Okay," Dart said, cowering from the time pressure. "I'm on the basement level. What room am I looking for?"

"Data Processing," Ginny replied.

Dart reevaluated his situation. There were, at the very minimum, three guards after him. Proctor, and anyone accompanying him, had to be thrown into the mix. That made four or more after him. They had lost track of him. With Proctor running things, Dart felt certain they would do the smart thing: conduct a floor-by-floor search. At the same time, at least one guard would watch the computer, monitoring the system to see if Dart attempted to use a security card to gain access anywhere. This person would guide the search team.

The voice of the lookout scratched into Dart's ear like fingernails down a blackboard. "They're taking their time, but they're working their way down. I'm showing them at the second floor."

By going to the basement level he had, in all likelihood, trapped himself.

He ran down the hall where, instead of the cryptic color system, the doors actually carried titles. Several were marked SERVICE PERSONNEL ONLY. Another read FOOD SERVICES. He passed two bathrooms. Something marked HIGH VOLTAGE DO NOT ENTER.

Dart turned right down a long corridor. The basement was a rabbit warren. He passed a door marked TECHNICAL SERVICES.

"Ginny?" he said into the air.

"Right here." She spoke into his ear.

"I'm looking at Technical Services. Haven't seen anything like Data Processing."

"Basement level?"

"Right."

"Security?"

"You bet," Dart confirmed, wondering how he could get inside.

"Check the crack below the door," Ginny advised. "The gap at the bottom of the door. Cold air sinks," she said. "The computer room will be real cold."

Dart dropped to his knees and poked his fingers through. "You got it. Real cold."

"Let's give it a try," she said.

Dart stood back up, his knees killing him. He stared at the door in confusion. It was a heavy steel door, and it was locked. He pulled his gun out of his holster. It was all he could think of.

"Whatever you do," Ginny said, as if standing there, "don't break that door down."

"I *have* to," Dart replied.

"You can't. Same reason we can't have your bad boys breaking in," she said, referring to the ERT team. "That kind of illegal access will cause the mainframe to suspend. The *only* person able to undo that is the SYSOP himself."

"Shit," Dart replied. He glanced up: acoustic panels. "Hold on," Dart said.

"You need a security card," Ginny advised. "It's the only way. Trust me."

"Maybe not," Dart corrected, heading back down the hallway toward the bathrooms that he had passed.

The lookout interrupted and said, "They're

descending fire stairs, north and south, approaching level one."

Dart pushed into the mens room and flicked on the light. He glanced up: acoustical panels hung in a suspended frame. He ran back into the hallway, down to the intersection of the other corridor and made a mental note of distance and angle. He returned to the bathroom, pulled himself up onto the sink's countertop, and pushed up on the panel. It moved out of his way.

"I'm going for it," Dart announced.

"Going for *what*?"

"We'll see."

Securing a hand-hold on a pipe within the area above the suspended ceiling, Dart hooked a foot over the stall partition and pulled himself up and through. The dead space occupied an area about four feet high—above Dart was the support structure for the first floor; below, the suspended ceiling through which he had just entered. The area was claustrophobic and vast; hallway ceiling fixtures threw enough light around for Dart to see a series of black plastic plumbing pipes and heavy steel sprinkler pipes that were suspended from the overhead I-beams. He took the time to replace the acoustic panel he had come through to hide the way he had come. He hoped the security team would pass up the mens room and continue their search elsewhere on another level.

The flimsy false ceiling, supported by strands of twisted wire, was not strong enough to hold him. Dart, flat on his stomach, distributed his weight between a plumbing pipe, where he hooked his left leg, and a fire sprinkler holding his right, his fingers groping for purchase on the overhead I-beams. If he slipped and fell, he would crash down into whatever room and unseen hazards lay below.

The parallel pipes were his only support, and he had to stay with them despite the fact that they appeared to follow the direction of the hallway—east, west—rather than the angle that Dart had projected to reach the computer room. He crawled carefully, all the while attempting to maintain his bearings. The pipes and conduit were suspended by metal plumber's "tape" and lengths of wire, requiring Dart to pause and navigate around them, reaching around each obstruction, taking hold of one pipe and shifting his weight onto the opposing one.

Dart suddenly realized he heard only static in his left ear. Either the radio had gone dead or the combination of the sublevel basement and the abundance of metal was causing interference. If he wasn't hearing them, then they weren't hearing him. He had to hurry. If the command van lost track of him for too long they would order the ERT team to hit the building, and according to Ginny such unauthorized entry would shut down the mainframe, rendering it inaccessible, the files lost.

A series of lights came on, immediately to Dart's left, blinding him. At the same time, he heard the frantic footfalls of people running immediately below him—close enough to touch. Dart remained still as two men stopped directly beneath him, and he recognized the tension-filled voice of Terry Proctor.

"Doesn't make sense," Proctor said, out of breath.

"Maybe he can get inside the rooms without the system knowing it," the man with him suggested.

There was a long pause. Dart could feel Proctor thinking, putting himself in Dart's position. Proctor said, "We stay with the plan: All rooms that aren't secure get a thorough search."

Dart heard the men separate. The guard said to Proctor, "Where are you going? There's nothing down that way."

"I need to do something," Proctor said. "Just do your fucking job," he chastised.

Rent-a-cops, Dart thought, with equal disdain.

As far as Joe could tell, the guard headed back down toward the bathrooms while Proctor hurried up the corridor. The noise level in the tight space was amazing; despite their name, the acoustic panels did little to muffle any of the sounds. When the guard entered the mens room, twenty feet behind Dart, every sound could be heard. The man stopped to urinate, and Dart could hear him work his zipper fly. He banged the stall door open. A moment later he was inspecting the womens room. Not long after, Dart heard the clatter of brooms and mops and knew the guard was in a custodial closet. The detective used the cover of this noise to continue. With the hallway lights ablaze, he could see throughout the tight crawl space, and he plotted which pairs of pipes might support him en route to the computer room.

". . . just guard it," he heard Proctor say somewhere off ahead of him.

"I'm good at *finding* people," a deep voice replied. "This is a waste of my talents."

"Listen, Alverez, if you had any talent, we wouldn't be here," Proctor objected.

"You gonna insult me," the man objected, "and I won't do the business for you."

"Do *not* fuck with me. Get in there and stay there. If and when we need your *talents*, I'll send someone for you."

"He won't talk, and he won't walk," the other man said. "I owe this fucker."

Dart felt a chill pass through him. Alverez, the man Zeller had wanted to avoid, was guarding the computer room.

Alverez continued. "Make it look like he took a tumble down some stairs. No problem."

"Down, Rambo," Proctor said disparagingly. "Just guard the fucking room."

"Ain't no problem."

"And you don't leave for *any* reason," Proctor added.

Dart heard a door open and thump shut. It seemed twenty to thirty feet to his right. *The computer room.* He studied the pipes to see how to make it over there, then he plotted a course straight ahead ten feet that connected with a single sprinkler pipe he would use to take him over the room. Minutes later, he crossed over to that single pipe. He put his butt on it, his feet out in front of him, hands overhead on an I-beam and, lying back, scooted himself forward a few inches at a time.

Alverez, he was thinking, hearing Zeller's voice: A guy hired to break my knees.

Without thought, Dart automatically reached down to pat the weapon that Haite had issued him, to make sure it was still there. In the process, he lost his balance, his left hand slipping off the I-beam. He reached out instinctively to block his fall and punched his right hand through an acoustical panel as his left hand saved him. He froze, dangling.

"Billy?" he heard a voice call out. "Hey, Billy? That you?"

Footsteps coming toward him.

Dart was looking down onto a set of plastic recycling bins, just on the other side of the wall from the corridor. He gently fingered the broken piece of panel that hung like a flap and drew it back up silently, partially patching his error.

The footsteps went past him. "Billy?" the voice called out again, growing more distant. He heard a walkie-talkie belch as this man complained, "Whoever's up on one is making too much fucking noise. Keep it down up there." A second later a heavy door thumped shut and Dart imagined that this man had left the basement. *For good?* Dart wondered. *Or to get some backup?*

He pulled himself back up and continued down the pipe, his butt sore, his fingers cramping. Each of the iron clamps and supports that hung the sprinkler system from the I-beams presented Dart with an obstacle around which he had to maneuver. Five minutes later, he was directly over the computer room, the only sounds the scraping shoes of Alverez as he paced, a bulldog confined to his pen.

All at once, the space went dark again—the basement hallway lights had timed out and had turned themselves off. The only light came in cones and shafts as it escaped the computer room below from holes created to carry conduit and computer and telephone cables. Dart allowed time for his eyes to adjust and then edged forward toward the nearest peephole.

The pipe shifted in a way that Dart had not experienced, a subtle movement that he didn't understand until he heard a regular ticking sound. He sourced that sound and discovered a leak directly beneath him—a pipe joint had failed under his weight. The sprinkler water dripped like the ticking of a clock. In a moment it would seep through the panel and begin dripping into the room where Alverez paced. Dart reached down and ran his hand along the underside of the pipe, smearing the leaking water, and briefly stopping the drip.

With his hand still on the pipe, he craned himself down to get a look through the peephole, the escaping light flooding his face.

It was no use: He couldn't control the leak.

Drip . . . drip . . . drip . . . It started up again.

Through the hole in the ceiling panel, he could make out a pair of large boxes the size of small refrigerators, and the corner edge of a desk. Directly below him was vinyl tile flooring. As he was peering down through the hole, he saw the first drop of water, like a small jewel, cascade from the ceiling to the floor, where it exploded.

Another. And another.

Dart worked his hand on the pipe furiously, to try to stop it, but the break was worse, the flow greater. The cold water seeped through his fingers and down to the room below.

Ironically, Alverez came over to inspect the leak. It was as if Dart had issued the man an invitation. And in a heartbeat, Dart understood what had to happen. There was no time to plan, to organize, to waste. Zeller would have called this a *hot spot*—an instant in time that demands reaction, not thought or consideration, one of those opportunities that comes around only once, and to think about it is to lose it.

Alverez stepped beneath the leak.

Joe Dart let go his grip, and jumped.

CHAPTER
44

Alverez looked up toward the ceiling.

Dart understood intuitively that this moment of surprise was, and would be, his only advantage over an ape like this. He anticipated his landing, the gun coming out of the holster, and firing into the man's legs if necessary.

He landed on his bad ankle.

The room swirled in a thick blue haze as nausea

erupted inside him. He lost his balance and went down onto his back.

Alverez stood there, fighting to get pieces of acoustical tile out of his eyes.

Dart glanced over and saw a bank of computer equipment. He searched for the gear that Ginny had described. Plain vanillia box . . . He didn't see what she had described to him. A good deal of the equipment was down an aisle behind the bank of keyboards.

Between Dart and that aisle stood Alverez.

Dart dared not use his gun, for that would alert Proctor—if his fall through the ceiling had not already done so—and, more important, bring the ERT team through the door, locking up the computer.

Alverez was big and stocky, and yet lightning quick. He attacked Dart as a boxer would, cagey and shifting side to side, light on his feet, ready to tangle. Enjoying this.

Dart came to his feet, woozy. Despite his reasoning, he reached for his gun and brought it out aimed at the man's huge thighs.

"Better make it count," the man said, grinning, " 'cause I'm going to take it away from you."

He faked to his right—Dart pivoting to follow—and then cut left so quickly that Dart never saw him coming. One second Dart was holding the gun, not wanting to fire it; the next, the weapon was skidding across the vinyl floor and Dart's wrist felt extremely hot and limp.

Alverez body-punched Dart low and on the side, below the ribs, stinging a kidney and buckling the detective over in agony.

Dart swung his bad foot wildly and connected the instep with the side of Alverez's knee, as if pushing a door shut. He heard something snap, and the thug's eyes went wide, and Dart kicked the same spot again, and Alverez leaned away like a tree from the wind. And then he grimaced, showing off his brown, ugly teeth like a mean dog.

His arms were apelike, unexpectedly long for such a compact body. He punched out at Dart, ramming a ball of hard knuckles into the center of his chest, stunning his diaphragm and stealing his breath.

Dart staggered back and smacked into a desk, knowing instantly that to allow himself to be pinned by a gorilla like Alverez was the end— the man would pick him to pieces, breaking bones and taking him apart like a turkey carcass after the feast. Dart's right hand wouldn't respond— it flapped at the end of his arm like a rag; he couldn't feel it at all. His left landed painfully on something cool and hard, and Dart seized it and lashed out at Alverez who, preparing to step closer and finish Dart, mistakenly anticipated Dart's attempt to come from his right. The detective smashed the stapler into the man's jaw like a set of brass knuckles, breaking the joint and leaving the man looking like a Halloween mask, his jaw grotesquely distorted.

Buying himself a moment, Dart flung himself off the desk and hobbled awkwardly around the bank of keyboards and monitors, and down the aisle. There, not ten feet away, its red lights flashing, was the exact box that Ginny had described.

A couple of minutes, he remembered Ginny saying.

Fat chance, Dart thought, wondering if he could even buy himself thirty seconds.

He placed his weight onto his bad ankle, fell down, and reached out with his broken wrist, crying out loudly with the impact.

They heard that, he thought.

Alverez spun around, his broken jaw preventing any perverse grin, his nose bleeding profusely, his eyes damp and seething with fury.

Dart had never seen that look, but it had been described dozens of times, and it registered into his core that Alverez would either kill him or change him forever. This was a hot spot, a defining moment.

Alverez charged like a wrecking ball—but the wrecking ball owned a switchblade.

The knife sank into Dart's left shoulder. Alverez removed it just as quickly with a sickening sucking sound and lowered it again, but Dart rolled hard. The switchblade punched the floor, broke the springed hinge, and folded up on the man's fingers, slicing all four to the bone. Alverez roared, released the knife, and had to shake his hand to break the blade from its grip. Blood flew like water from a hose.

Dart lunged for the communications box. *A vertical row of red lights* . . . The button marked MASTER was at the bottom of the device. Alverez growled. Dart punched the red button, and it immediately changed to green.

The system was on-line.

Alverez crawled across the floor.

The gun! Dart realized as Alverez reached for it.

Dart kicked out and caught the man's jaw with the toe of his shoe. A loud *crack* filled the room, like a gunshot, and Alverez slumped to the floor, his wounded hand bleeding badly. He was down, but not finished.

Dart rolled painfully to his left; the button remained green. Perhaps twenty seconds had passed; it felt to Dart like half an hour. He fished for his handcuffs and got one end around the wrist of Alverez's bleeding hand and, dragging the man across the floor, the other to the foot of a giant piece of computer machinery.

Dart heard the chaos out in the hall, reacting to it before he gave it any thought. He dove for the bloody gun and took hold of it just as the door swung open.

"Freeze!" one of the three uniformed guards shouted excitedly, training a weapon on Dart.

Dart, lying on his back, held his weapon with his left hand, aiming toward the man but knowing he couldn't hit the broad side of a barn. "Police," Dart said, attempting authority.

The look of surprise that swept over the man's face convinced Dart that they had no idea who he was; his only hope now was to separate Proctor from his own employees.

"Bullshit," the guard snapped, checking furtively over his shoulder. "Drop the fucking piece!"

Rent-a-cops were notorious for shooting widows, and dogs, and children. They had no excuse to carry loaded weapons with so little training. Dart didn't like that barrel being aimed at him.

One minute, he estimated. He needed to stall for several more. He felt only a swelling pain in his right hand.

"You shoot a cop and you're dead. The building is surrounded."

"What a fucking windbag," the blond man said. He looked about twenty-one. He, too, held a weapon on Dart. "I say we tap him right here."

"No," came a recognizable voice from behind. "You're in a bad situation here, Officer Dartelli," Proctor said, confirming to his subordinates that Dart was in fact a cop. It struck Dart as a curious move. "Don't do anything stupid. Anything we'll all regret."

Proctor showed himself then, stepping past his uniformed guards, his hands in the air. "I'm unarmed and defenseless." He took another tentative step forward. "Are you going to shoot me?" His eyes wandered over Dart's shoulder, and he gave away that he had spotted the green button. He knew more about the computer system than Dart would have given him credit for.

"Back!" Dart challenged, waving the barrel of the weapon slightly.

Two minutes, he thought.

"Are you really going to shoot me?" Proctor asked, hands still out away from his body. His forehead was beaded with sweat, his suit pitted below the arms.

Dart felt a dizzying drain to his system as he paled and felt cold. His shoulder was losing blood badly.

"I'm not armed," the man reminded. He smiled, as if to calm Dart. He kept walking, sliding one foot tentatively ahead of the other. He wasn't interested in reaching Dart, he wanted the mainframe.

Dart's dulled mind could barely think. The man took another step forward and Dart said overly loudly, "Yes, I copy," into the room.

The words startled Proctor, who stopped in his tracks. His eyes swept over Dart, looking but not finding the microphone.

"Video *and* audio," Dart lied, unsure if either was working any longer. He watched as the color drained from the man's face. "Anything that you'd like to say to the command van?"

"If that were true," Proctor said, taking another step forward, "they would have long since come to your help. Nice try."

Dart couldn't tell him why they *couldn't* come, so instead he said, "I haven't given them the signal."

"I don't think so," Proctor said, taking yet another step.

"Don't," Dart warned.

"Put the gun down," the unsteady guard cautioned. His arms were tiring from holding the weapon, Dart noted. His aim would be off because of this.

Three minutes . . . How much longer?

All the lights failed at once, leaving only the computer's tiny lights ablaze.

Dart saw a white flash as the guard fired and missed. Through ringing ears he heard the unmistakable sound of glass breaking and metal ripping as the ERT team set off explosive charges at five entrances.

They've ruined it! he thought, angry that Haite had authorized the raid, knowing as he did that this would jeopardize their evidence.

Not knowing where the strength or reserve came from, Dart lunged in the dark to block Proctor from reaching the computer, every muscle, every tendon screaming. He collided with the man and went down hard just as the first glow of the emergency lighting seeped into the room from the wall sconces. Proctor pushed away hard and struggled to his feet.

Dart raised the weapon and slipped his finger inside the trigger guard.

The blond security man trained his weapon on Dart.

There was a loud pop that occurred just before Dart went blind with pain. His face seemed to explode at the same time as his ears failed him, and he wailed into the room along with the others. He screamed for Zeller, and lost friends; for his mother, and lost souls. Consumed by an overpowering white light, and deprived of his hearing, he folded into a ball and fell away from the world, as would a man thrown from a cliff. Weightless, and sublime.

CHAPTER
45

A dusty image of Haite loomed above Dart wearing a look of concern, and Dart wondered why his first experience of death should be an image of his former sergeant, a man with whom he had never been particularly close. He would have preferred an image of Abby. A conversation with Zeller. A bronzed and naked body, perhaps. Anything but Haite.

He felt as if he were at sea, rocking in a light chop. He found the sensation comforting and pleasant.

"Can you hear me yet?" the sergeant asked loudly.

He remained cloudy, a vaporous apparition.

"Go away," Dart said, wanting a dream, not a nightmare. "Leave me alone."

"Stun bombs and phosphorus grenades," the sergeant explained in an apologetic voice. "ERT toys," he said.

The rocking, Dart realized, was the stretcher being carried up the stairs by a couple of paramedics with buzz cuts. He still couldn't see very well.

"Your hearing will come back," Haite said loudly.

And then the pain hit, a headache like a ton of bricks.

"Your head may hurt," he heard a voice suggest from behind him.

"No shit," said Joe Dart. He blinked away some of the pain and tried to identify which orb was the sergeant. He picked the one leaning over him. "Why? Why after all that did you abort? Jesus. . . ." His thoughts trailed off with his voice. Rage surged through him, but without any physical energy to support it, it dried up, defeated. He felt on the verge of tears. Exhaustion. Self-pity.

"No, no," Haite said.

"For me? You did it to save me? You've *wrecked* me," Dart said. He wanted Haite to hurt for this; he wanted someone to pay. He wanted to be left alone to cry.

"Ginny solved it," Haite said.

"She couldn't download the file as long as it was in the buffer," a techie's young voice explained from behind him. It took Dart a moment to identify it as the voice of the command van technician. "When you cut the text, it was captured in RAM. You *had* to do this to keep the other person attempting access from deleting the files. There it was, this chunk of text, floating in the computer's memory—but in a buffer, not on disk, not somewhere that Ginny could grab it."

Haite said, "He should rest."

The techie added excitedly, "The mainframe was set up to save all buffers to disk in the event of a power failure. Ginny realized this—realized the only thing to do at that point was to cut the power."

They cleared the stairs, and Dart felt the legs of the stretcher released, and suddenly found himself being wheeled. The bumps hurt every inch of him.

"Later," one of the paramedics complained to Haite. "Let him rest."

Ignoring him, the technician continued. "The machine itself is protected by a backup power supply, so once we cut the juice, it dumped its buffers to disk, and Ginny, waiting for it, grabbed the file. It took her a couple of seconds is all."

Seconds? Dart thought.

"After that," Haite said, "it was all ERT. We'd lost you on the radio. We weren't happy campers."

"We *got* the file?"

"We got everything," Haite confirmed. "Ginny's a fucking genius."

CHAPTER
46

Arielle Martinson looked much smaller, much older in the CAPers interrogation room, even with her high-priced attorney sitting next to her. Dart was familiar with Bernie Wormser's reputation, but had never faced him. Wormser had worked hard to arrange the interview elsewhere, but there they were, in a cramped, windowless room with a linoleum floor. Just the way Dart had wanted it.

Dart carried a tape recorder with him. His left arm was in a sling. He plugged the machine into a wall outlet, turned it on, and recorded the names of those present, the location, the date and time. Martinson appeared restless, Wormser, dead calm.

"As you know," Dart addressed Martinson, "we've charged you with interfering in a criminal investigation, in so much as Terrance Proctor, and therefore Proctor Securities, acted as your agent. In this regard, there is also the charge of first-degree murder, for the shooting death of Walter Zeller, and attempted murder for the actions taken against myself. There are federal charges concerning the rigging of certain clinical trial results—"

"You don't know anything," Martinson said venomously. Wormser touched her arm lightly. She glared at her attorney, and as he attempted to speak, cut him off. "No, Bernie. I'll dig my own grave, thank you just the same."

"I really don't think—" Wormser attempted.

"Quiet," she said, silencing him, and burning his face scarlet. To Dart she said, "Have you ever dealt with a victim of sexual assault, Detective? Physical abuse? Do you have any clue what you're dealing with here? Do you understand the trauma—the permanent damage done to a woman, and to boys as well—by such violation? Do you? Someone else's body inside yours . . . the sense of helplessness . . . the pain . . . disease . . . Someone striking you . . . drooling onto you, slobbering onto you—"

"Arielle!" Wormser chastised.

"Oh, shut up!" she roared back at him.

Dart's voice cracked as he explained, "He was shot five times, the last of which penetrated his skull just below the left eye and killed him."

Ignoring him, she said, "What if you possessed the knowledge, the ability, to reduce sexual assault—rape—by ten percent? Spousal and child abuse by twenty percent? Sixty percent? What if you knew you had that within your grasp? And what if the government, in all its banality, had structured a set of rules so confining, so slow, so difficult to maneuver through that you came to understand it might be *decades* before you could bring this technology to market? What then? Do you sit back and wait? In this country, a woman is beaten every twelve *seconds*." She glanced at her Rolex. "Since we've been sitting here, over ten women have had a fist raised to them. Would you wait decades, if you were in my shoes?"

Dart was flooded with a dozen images of Zeller. "Walter Zeller discovered your treatment of the documentation for the clinical trials. He uncovered Proctor's tampering with the facts. Subsequent to that discovery he was pursued, his life was threatened, day and night, for over twelve months—"

Interrupting him, she said, "Who *are* you? Are you listening to what I'm telling you? Do you hear what I'm saying? So what if I altered some of the paperwork? That's all it was—paperwork!"

"Arielle, I *have* to interrupt!" objected Wormser.

"Shut up, Bernie. You're being paid either way." Addressing Dart she continued, "Would

439

I have put Laterin on the market despite less-than-perfect results? You bet I would." Meeting eyes with him, she said, "I *will* if I get the chance. I'd rather stop fifteen, twenty, thirty percent of such beasts, than stand by and do nothing. Every *twelve* seconds, don't forget. And would I have resorted to such means for the sake of greed? No. For the sake of *science*, Detective. For the sake of the victim. Every new generation of Laterin that we developed showed a five- to seventeen-percent improvement. But there's no way to test it, given the *rules*. You can't test Laterin on rats or monkeys! Who are you kidding? This is a human aberration—and in large part, a genetic *defect*. You know who should be in this room, should be here instead of me? The FDA." She nodded. "You bet. That's who should be in this chair. Not me. Am I guilty of trying to *do* something? You bet I am. And damn proud of it."

"You'll go to jail for your actions," Dart told her. "But by cooperating now—as Mr. Wormser will tell you—special consideration will be given your case."

"I don't want your special consideration. How many dead women—beaten wives, raped children—equal one Walter Zeller? You tell me how to fit that into an equation. Zeller broke the law repeatedly. In the end, he committed acts of murder—"

"*You* are the murderer," Dart shouted, regretting immediately the outburst. He collected himself, met eyes with her, and said, "You rigged the data, the results of the trials, and then tried to, and eventually did, kill the man who uncovered your deceit. *You*, not Proctor, not his shooter, *you*."

Her mouth moved, but no words came out. Finally she whined, "This is important work."

A silence settled over them. Martinson's chest heaved from the stress. Dart knew he'd broken out in a sweat.

Dart said, "You can't balance one against the other. It doesn't work that way." He felt himself softening. Twenty-percent fewer sex offenders? Was it possible?

She said, "You do what you have to, Detective. We all do what we feel we have to. I'll take my chances." She paused, glanced at the annoyed Wormser and then back to Dart. "You want to know something? Don't forget that juries are made up of men *and* women. There's not a jury in this country that would convict me for what I've done. It was Zeller that committed murder, not me. A desperate man driven by the loss of his wife. I was trying to *help* the men he killed. They *wanted* that help—that much is *documented*—which is why they participated in the trials." She looked over at Wormser again. Martinson had spent her life in control. She edged to the front of her seat.

Dart informed the attorney, "Terry Proctor is going to testify against your client. You might want to keep that in mind."

"Stay where you are, Arielle," Wormser advised.

She stood up, though feebly. She ran a hand down her smooth navy blue suit and, meeting eyes with Dart, said weakly, "I was trying to help

441

solve a serious social problem. Condemn me if you will." She walked past him and continued out the door.

Dart did nothing to stop her.

CHAPTER
47

They called you a genius," Dart told her. Ginny's favorite walk was a section of the Appalachian Trail.

"Well, it shows that at least sometimes cops are right," she teased.

It was awkward for Dart walking with his arm in a sling—he hadn't realized how much walking depended on swinging his arms. His ankle was good enough for this hike, though it occasionally glowed with a twinge of pain. She had asked to see him, and he was in no mood to deny her.

Once on the trail, she found an overlook where an out-cropping of rock faced north, and they perched there, wrapped in their winter coats, their breath fogging, Dart's heart pounding. The afternoon sun was muted by clouds.

She said, "That was fun, what we did." He thought that she was referring to the raid at Roxin, but he wasn't sure.

"Yeah."

He could tell when she was nervous by the way she chewed her lip. "Where do you stand with

Abby?" she asked, not surprising him one bit. He had known what this talk would be about.

"Why?"

"I need to know."

He wanted to ask why for a second time but thought better of it. He said, "Where do *I* stand, or where do *we* stand?"

"Is there a *we*?"

"Very much so."

"That's part of what I need to know," she said.

"She's not going back with her husband, if that's what you're asking. Ultimately, it was for the kids that she ever considered it—and I think she's pretty clear that if she sacrifices herself for her kids and ends up unhappy, then that's maybe harder on the kids than the way it is now."

"And you?"

"This isn't easy, you know."

"I can make it easier," she told him. "Michael—I'm sure you've heard about Michael—has asked me to move to New Hampshire with him. I'm tempted, because it offers a chance to start over. You know. . . . And I can do my computer work from just about anywhere—I don't need to be in an office. It works for me. But there's this part of me that is still holding on to us—is still thinking that we might try again—and I need to put that part away if I'm going to do this. I owe that to Michael. I can't be leading one life and hoping for another."

"No, that's no good," he said.

The wind blew across them, whistling in Dart's ears and singing in the shrubs and treetops. The view was a vast sea of gray. Dart felt gray.

"So?" she asked.

"I don't want to lose touch," he answered. It was difficult for him to say, and his body ached with it.

"No." She looked into the wind, and when she looked back at him her eyes were shiny with tears and she gave him a smile that made his heart tight and a lump form in his throat. "It's okay," she said, one tear escaping down her cheek.

"So much has happened," he said.

"Yes, it has," she agreed, looking away again.

She was a strong person, and he admired her. He wanted to reach over and touch her, to show her the compassion he felt, but he did not. He would not confuse things. It was difficult enough as it was.

"I'm sorry," she said into the wind.

"Me too."

They walked a little while longer, and somewhere high above a town that he didn't recognize, she took his gloved hand in hers and did not let go. She held hands with him for the remainder of the walk, right until they reached their cars, at which point they finally released each other's grip. She looked into his eyes and said, "We were good together."

He nodded. He could feel the tears coming from deep within him, and he fought to hold them off.

"A good fit," she said.

He nodded again.

She kissed him once lightly on the lips, climbed into her car, and was gone.

CHAPTER
48

It seemed strange to Dart that he should know so many people in a graveyard. Patrolman Bernie Denton was buried on the west side in a family site, the victim of a gang shooting and recipient of a funeral covered on national news a few years earlier.

There were two plaques among hundreds on a long cement wall erected for those choosing cremation rather than burial. Walter Zeller's name was there, alongside Lucky's, though Lucky's avoided the nickname. He wasn't sure what he believed about an afterlife—but if there were such a thing, Zeller was in a tough place.

The sun had risen and set several dozen times since he'd walked out of the hospital a decorated cop, and yet he was still Joe Dart, confused, lonely, restless. No charges had been filed against Kowalski, and although Dart had expected him to return to the department the same man, there were subtle but discernable differences in his acerbic behavior—something had changed.

News stories had filled the screen for a while: the collapse of Roxin Laboratories, and the endless ethical debate that the news of a drug like Laterin had caused. Some were calling Dr. Arielle Martinson a saint, among them a senator from Michigan. Some others were saying her case would never reach trial—that only Proctor and Alverez would serve any time. For her part, Martinson had disappeared, fueling a bevy of rumors—one being that she had signed on with a French company that had bought several of the genetic patents through the bankruptcy court; another that she had committed suicide, following in the steps of her test subjects.

It was all too sensational for Dart. The world was changing so fast—there was no predicting anything. Today's fear was tomorrow's promise.

He had no flowers to leave her. He had brought her nothing. He owed her nothing—that was how he felt about it. But he stopped at the foot of her grave anyway, because he couldn't pass it up. He needed her. He needed that connection to the woman who had birthed him, to the person, however god-awful it had been. She was down there, under the snow and grass and earth, and Dart felt grateful for that. *We are all where we belong*, he thought.

He felt his throat constrict, and he cursed her for maintaining any hold over him, any power. *How dare she!* His eyes brimmed with tears and he wanted to hate her, but he could not.

He reached down and placed his cast in the snow, leaving an unexplained print behind. He closed his eyes and he hated her briefly, but it passed.

"I forgive you," he whispered, the tears beginning to fall. Met with an unsettling silence, and the distant sound of the Interstate's overpass.

He stood and walked away, dragging his face against the shoulder of his coat, cursing his weakness.

He followed his own prints back through the deep snow, painfully aware that there were no other prints to follow. *It's okay*, he thought, glancing over at the wall that bore Zeller's name.

Abby had kept the engine running. Kept things warm. Mac slept in the backseat.

She was driving. Dart was no good with the cast.

"You all right?" she asked, reaching over and touching his face lightly, wiping away one of his tears.

"Better," answered Joe Dartelli. All right was still a little ways off.

IF YOU HAVE ENJOYED READING THIS LARGE PRINT BOOK AND YOU WOULD LIKE MORE INFORMATION ON HOW TO ORDER A WHEELER LARGE PRINT BOOK, PLEASE WRITE TO:

WHEELER PUBLISHING, INC.
P.O. BOX 531
ACCORD, MA 02018-0531